✔ KT-153-092

Terry Pratchett is one of the most popular authors writing today. He lives behind a keyboard in Wiltshire and says he 'doesn't want to get a life, because it feels as though he's trying to lead three already'. He was appointed OBE in 1998. *Moving Pictures* is the tenth novel in his phenomenally successful Discworld series.

MOVING PICTURES

Terry Pratchett

CORGI BOOKS

MOVING PICTURES
A CORGI BOOK : 0 552 13463 5

Originally published in Great Britain
by Victor Gollancz Ltd

PRINTING HISTORY
Gollancz edition published 1990
Corgi edition published 1991

13 15 17 19 20 18 16 14

Set in 10/11pt Plantin by
Chippendale Type Ltd, Otley, West Yorkshire.

Corgi Books are published by Transworld Publishers,
61–63 Uxbridge Road, London W5 5SA,
a division of The Random House Group Ltd,
in Australia by Random House Australia (Pty) Ltd,
20 Alfred Street, Milsons Point, Sydney, NSW 2061, Australia,
in New Zealand by Random House New Zealand Ltd,
18 Poland Road, Glenfield, Auckland 10, New Zealand
and in South Africa by Random House (Pty) Ltd,
Endulini, 5a Jubilee Road, Parktown 2193, South Africa.

Printed and bound in Great Britain by
Cox & Wyman Ltd, Reading, Berkshire.

I would like to thank all the
wonderful people who made this
book possible. Thank you.
Thank you. Thank you . . .

MOVING PICTURES

A Discworld Novel

Watch . . .

This is space. It's sometimes called the final frontier.

(Except that of course you can't have a *final* frontier, because there'd be nothing for it to be a frontier *to*, but as frontiers go, it's pretty penultimate . . .)

And against the wash of stars a nebula hangs, vast and black, one red giant gleaming like the madness of gods . . .

And then the gleam is seen as the glint in a giant eye and it is eclipsed by the blink of an eyelid and the darkness moves a flipper and Great A'Tuin, star turtle, swims onward through the void.

On its back, four giant elephants. On their shoulders, rimmed with water, glittering under its tiny orbiting sunlet, spinning majestically around the mountains at its frozen Hub, lies the Discworld, world and mirror of worlds.

Nearly unreal.

Reality is not digital, an on-off state, but analog. Something *gradual*. In other words, reality is a quality that things possess in the same way that they possess, say, weight. Some people are more real than others, for example. It has been estimated that there are only about five hundred *real* people on any given planet, which is why they keep unexpectedly running into one another all the time.

The Discworld is as unreal as it is possible to be while still being just real enough to exist.

And just real enough to be in real trouble.

About thirty miles Turnwise of Ankh-Morpork the surf

boomed on the wind-blown, seagrass-waving, sand-dune-covered spit of land where the Circle Sea met the Rim Ocean.

The hill itself was visible for miles. It wasn't very high, but lay amongst the dunes like an upturned boat or a very unlucky whale, and was covered in scrub trees. No rain fell here, if it could possibly avoid it. Although the wind sculpted the dunes around it, the low summit of the hill remained in an everlasting, ringing calm.

Nothing but the sand had changed here in hundreds of years.

Until now.

A crude hut of driftwood had been built on the long curve of the beach, although describing it as 'built' was a slander on skilled crude hut builders throughout the ages; if the sea had simply been left to pile the wood up it might have done a better job.

And, inside, an old man had just died.

'Oh,' he said. He opened his eyes and looked around the interior of the hut. He hadn't seen it very clearly for the past ten years.

Then he swung, if not his legs, then at least the *memory* of his legs off the pallet of sea-heather and stood up. Then he went outside, into the diamond-bright morning. He was interested to see that he was still wearing a ghostly image of his ceremonial robe – stained and frayed, but still recognizable as having originally been a dark red plush with gold frogging – even though he was dead. Either your clothes died when you did, he thought, or maybe you just mentally dressed yourself from force of habit.

Habit also led him to the pile of driftwood beside the hut. When he tried to gather a few sticks, though, his hands passed through them.

He swore.

It was then that he noticed a figure standing by the water's edge, looking out to sea. It was leaning on a scythe. The wind whipped at its black robes.

He started to hobble towards it, remembered he was

10

dead, and began to stride. He hadn't stridden for decades, but it was amazing how it all came back to you.

Before he was halfway to the dark figure, it spoke to him.

DECCAN RIBOBE, it said.

'That's me.'

LAST KEEPER OF THE DOOR.

'Well, I suppose so.'

Death hesitated.

YOU ARE OR YOU AREN'T, he said.

Deccan scratched his nose. Of course, he thought, you have to be able to touch *yourself*. Otherwise you'd fall to bits.

'*Technic'ly*, a Keeper has to be invested by the High Priestess,' he said. 'And there ain't been a High Priestess for thousands o' years. See, I just learned it all from old Tento, who lived here before me. He jus' said to me one day, "Deccan, it looks as though I'm dyin', so it's up to you now, 'cos if there's no-one left that remembers properly it'll all start happening again and you know what that means." Well, fair enough. But that's not what you'd call a proper investmenting, I'd say.'

He looked up at the sandy hill.

'There was jus' me and him,' he said. 'And then jus' me, remembering Holy Wood. And now . . . ' He raised his hand to his mouth.

'Oo-er,' he said.

YES, said Death.

It would be wrong to say a look of panic passed across Deccan Ribobe's face, because at that moment it was several yards away and wearing a sort of fixed grin, as if it had seen the joke at last. But his spirit was definitely worried.

'See, the thing is,' it said hastily, 'no-one ever comes here, see, apart from the fishermen from the next bay, and they just leaves the fish and runs off on account of superstition and I couldn't sort of go off to find an apprentice or somethin' because of keepin' the fires alight and doin' the chantin' . . . '

11

YES.

' . . . It's a terrible responsibility, bein' the only one able to do your job . . . '

YES, said Death.

'Well, of course, I'm not telling *you* anything . . . '

NO.

' . . . I mean, I was hopin' someone'd get shipwrecked or somethin', or come treasure huntin', and I could explain it like old Tento explained it to me, teach 'em the chants, get it all sorted out before I died . . . '

YES?

'I s'pose there's no chance that I could sort of . . . '

NO.

'Thought not,' said Deccan despondently.

He looked at the waves crashing down on the shore.

'Used to be a big city down there, thousands of years ago,' he said. 'I mean, where the sea is. When it's stormy you can hear the ole temple bells ringin' under the sea.'

I KNOW.

'I used to sit out here on windy nights, listenin'. Used to imagine all them dead people down there, ringin' the bells.'

AND NOW WE MUST GO.

'Ole Tento said there was somethin' under the hill there that could make people do things. Put strange fancies in their 'eads,' said Deccan, reluctantly following the stalking figure. 'I never had any strange fancies.'

BUT *YOU* WERE CHANTING, said Death. He snapped his fingers.

A horse ceased trying to graze the sparse dune grass and trotted up to Death. Deccan was surprised to see that it left hoofprints in the sand. He'd have expected sparks, or at least fused rock.

'Er,' he said, 'can you tell me, er . . . what happens now?'

Death told him.

'Thought so,' said Deccan glumly.

Up on the low hill the fire that had been burning all

night collapsed in a shower of ash. A few embers still glowed, though.

Soon they would go out.

. . . .

. . .

. .

.

They went out.

.

. .

. . .

. . . .

Nothing happened for a whole day. Then, in a little hollow on the edge of the brooding hill, a few grains of sand shifted and left a tiny hole.

Something emerged. Something invisible. Something joyful and selfish and marvellous. Something as intangible as an idea, which is exactly what it was. A wild idea.

It was old in a way not measurable by any calendar known to Man and what it had, right now, was memories and needs. It remembered life, in other times and other universes. It needed people.

It rose against the stars, changing shape, coiling like smoke.

There were lights on the horizon.

It *liked* lights.

It regarded them for a few seconds and then, like an invisible arrow, extended itself towards the city and sped away.

It liked *action*, too . . .

And several weeks went past.

There's a saying that all roads lead to Ankh-Morpork, greatest of Discworld cities.

At least, there's a *saying* that there's a saying that all roads lead to Ankh-Morpork.

And it's wrong. All roads lead *away* from Ankh-Morpork, but sometimes people just walk along them the wrong way.

Poets long ago gave up trying to describe the city. Now

the more cunning ones try to excuse it. They say, well, maybe it *is* smelly, maybe it *is* overcrowded, maybe it *is* a bit like Hell would be if they shut the fires off and stabled a herd of incontinent cows there for a year, but you must admit that it is full of sheer, vibrant, dynamic *life*. And this is true, even though it is poets that are saying it. But people who aren't poets say, so what? Mattresses tend to be full of life too, and no-one writes odes to them. Citizens hate living there and, if they have to move away on business or adventure or, more usually, until some statute of limitations runs out, can't wait to get back so they can enjoy hating living there some more. They put stickers on the backs of their carts saying 'Ankh-Morpork – Loathe It or Leave It'. They call it The Big Wahooni, after the fruit.[1]

Every so often a ruler of the city builds a wall around Ankh-Morpork, ostensibly to keep enemies out. But Ankh-Morpork doesn't fear enemies. In fact it welcomes enemies, provided they are enemies with money to spend.[2] It has survived flood, fire, hordes, revolutions and dragons. Sometimes by accident, admittedly, but it has survived them. The cheerful and irrecoverably venal spirit of the city has been proof against anything . . .

Until now.

*   *   *

---

[1] This is the one that grows only in certain parts of heathen Howondaland. It's twenty feet long, covered in spikes the colour of ear wax, and smells like an anteater that's eaten a very bad ant.

[2] In fact the Guild of Merchants' famous publication *Wellcome to Ankh-Morporke, Citie of One Thousand Surprises* now has an entire section entitled 'Soe you're a Barbaerieian Invader?' which has notes on night life, folklorique bargains in the bazaar and, under the heading 'Steppe-ing Out', a list of restaurants that do a dependable mares' milk and yak pudding. And many a pointed-helmeted vandal has trotted back to his freezing yurt wondering why he seems to be a great deal poorer and the apparent owner of a badly-woven rug, a litre of undrinkable wine and a stuffed purple donkey in a straw hat.

Boom.

The explosion removed the windows, the door and most of the chimney.

It was the sort of thing you expected in the Street of Alchemists. The neighbours *preferred* explosions, which were at least identifiable and soon over. They were better than the smells, which crept up on you.

Explosions were part of the scenery, such as was left.

And this one was pretty good, even by the standards of local connoisseurs. There was a deep red heart to the billowing black smoke which you didn't often see. The bits of semi-molten brickwork were more molten than usual. It was, they considered, quite impressive.

Boom.

A minute or two after the explosion a figure lurched out of the ragged hole where the door had been. It had no hair, and what clothes it still had were on fire.

It staggered up to the small crowd that was admiring the devastation and by chance laid a sooty hand on a hot-meat-pie-and-sausage-in-a-bun salesman called Cut-me-own-Throat Dibbler, who had an almost magical ability to turn up wherever a sale might be made.

'Looking,' it said, in a dreamy, stunned voice, 'f'r a word. Tip of my tongue.'

'Blister?' volunteered Throat.

He recovered his commercial senses. 'After an experience like that,' he added, proffering a pastry case full of so much reclaimed organic debris that it was very nearly sapient, 'what you need is to get a hot meat pie inside you—'

'Nonono. 'S not blister. 'S what you say when you've discovered something. You goes running out into the street shoutin',' said the smouldering figure urgently. ''S'pecial word,' it added, its brow creasing under the soot.

The crowd, reluctantly satisfied that there were going to be no more explosions, gathered around. This might be nearly as good.

'Yeah, that's right,' said an elderly man, filling his

pipe. 'You runs out shouting "Fire! Fire!" ' He looked triumphant.

' 'S not that . . . '

'Or "Help!" or—'

'No, he's right,' said a woman with a basket of fish on her head. 'There's a special word. It's foreign.'

'Right, right,' said her neighbour. 'Special foreign word for people who've discovered something. It was invented by some foreign bugger in his bath—'

'Well,' said the pipe man, lighting it off the alchemist's smouldering hat, '*I* for one don't see why people in this city need to go round shouting heathen lingo just 'cos they've had a bath. Anyway, look at him. He ain't had a bath. He *needs* a bath, yes, but he ain't had one. What's he want to go round shouting foreign lingo for? We've got perfectly satisfactory words for shoutin'.'

'Like what?' said Cut-me-own-Throat.

The pipe-smoker hesitated. 'Well,' he said, 'like . . . "I've discovered something" . . . or . . . "Hooray" . . . '

'No, I'm thinking about the bugger over Tsort way, or somewhere. He was in his bath and he had this idea for something, and he ran out down the street yelling.'

'Yelling what?'

'Dunno. P'raps "Give me a towel!" '

'Bet he'd be yellin' all right if he tried that sort of thing round here,' said Throat cheerfully. 'Now, ladies and gents, I have here some sausage in a bun that'd make your—'

'Eureka,' said the soot-coloured one, swaying back and forth.

'What about it?' said Throat.

'No, that's the word. Eureka.' A worried grin spread across the black features. 'It means "I have it".'

'Have what?' said Throat.

'*It.* At least, I *had* it. Octo-cellulose. Amazing stuff. Had it in my hand. But I held it too close to the fire,' said the figure, in the perplexed tones of the nearly concussed. 'V'ry important fact. Mus' make a note of it. *Don't let it get hot.*

16

V'ry important. Mus' write down v'ry important fact.'

He tottered back into the smoking ruins.

Dibbler watched him go.

'Wonder what that was all about?' he said. Then he shrugged and raised his voice to a shout. 'Meat pies! Hot sausages! Inna bun! So fresh the pig h'an't noticed they're gone!'

The glittering, swirling idea from the hill had watched all this. The alchemist didn't even know it was there. All he knew was that he was being unusually inventive today.

Now it had spotted the pie merchant's mind.

It knew that kind of mind. It loved minds like that. A mind that could sell nightmare pies could sell dreams.

It leaped.

On a hill far away the breeze stirred the cold, grey ash.

Further down the hill, in a crack in a hollow between two rocks where a dwarf juniper bush struggled for a living, a little trickle of sand began to move.

Boom.

A fine film of plaster dust drifted down on to the desk of Mustrum Ridcully, the new Archchancellor of Unseen University, just as he was trying to tie a particularly difficult fly.

He glanced out of the stained-glass window. A smoke cloud was rising over uptown Morpork.

'Bur*saar*!'

The Bursar arrived within a few seconds, out of breath. Loud noises always upset him.

'It's the alchemists, Master,' he panted.

'That's the third time this week. Blasted firework merchants,' muttered the Archchancellor.

'I'm afraid so, Master,' said the Bursar.

'What do they think they're doing?'

'I really couldn't say, Master,' said the Bursar, getting his breath back. 'Alchemy has never interested me. It's altogether too . . . too . . . '

'Dangerous,' said the Archchancellor firmly. 'Lot of damn mixin' things up and saying, hey, what'll happen if we add a drop of the yellow stuff, and then goin' around without yer eyebrows for a fortnight.'

'I was going to say impractical,' said the Bursar. 'Trying to do things the hard way when we have perfectly simple everyday magic available.'

'I thought they were trying to cure the philosopher's stones, or somethin',' said the Archchancellor. 'Lot of damn nonsense, if you ask me. Anyway, I'm off.'

As the Archchancellor began to sidle out of the room the Bursar hastily waved a handful of papers at him.

'Before you go, Archchancellor,' he said desperately, 'I wonder if you would just care to sign a few—'

'Not now, man,' snapped the Archchancellor. 'Got to see a man about a horse, what?'

'What?'

'Right.' The door closed.

The Bursar stared at it, and sighed.

Unseen University had had many different kinds of Archchancellor over the years. Big ones, small ones, cunning ones, slightly insane ones, extremely insane ones – they'd come, they'd served, in some cases not long enough for anyone to be able to complete the official painting to be hung in the Great Hall, and they'd died. The senior wizard in a world of magic had the same prospects of long-term employment as a pogo stick tester in a minefield.

However, from the Bursar's point of view this didn't really have to matter. The name might change occasionally, but what *did* matter was that there always was *an* Archchancellor and the Archchancellor's most important job, as the Bursar saw it, was to sign things, preferably, from the Bursar's point of view, without reading them first.

This one was different. For one thing, he was hardly ever in, except to change out of his muddy clothes. And he shouted at people. Usually at the Bursar

And yet, at the time, it had seemed a really good idea

to elect an Archchancellor who hadn't set foot in the University in forty years.

There had been so much in-fighting between the various orders of wizardry in recent years that, just for once, the senior wizards had agreed that what the University needed was a period of stability, so that they could get on with their scheming and intriguing in peace and quiet for a few months. A search of the records turned up Ridcully the Brown who, after becoming a Seventh Level mage at the incredibly young age of twenty-seven, had quit the University in order to look after his family's estates deep in the country.

He looked ideal.

'Just the chap,' they all said. 'Clean sweep. New broom. A country wizard. Back to the thingumajigs, the *roots* of wizardry. Jolly old boy with a pipe and twinkly eyes. Sort of chap who can tell one herb from another, roams-the-high-forest-with-every-beast-his-brother kind of thing. Sleeps under the stars, like as not. Knows what the wind is saying, we shouldn't wonder. Got a name for all the trees, you can bank on it. Speaks to the birds, too.'

A messenger had been sent. Ridcully the Brown had sighed, cursed a bit, found his staff in the kitchen garden where it had been supporting a scarecrow, and had set out.

'And if he's any problem,' the wizards had added, in the privacy of their own heads, 'anyone who talks to trees should be *no* trouble to get rid of.'

And then he'd arrived, and it turned out that Ridcully the Brown *did* speak to the birds. In fact he shouted at birds, and what he normally shouted was, 'Winged you, yer bastard!'

The beasts of the field and fowls of the air *did* know Ridcully the Brown. They'd got so good at pattern-recognition that, for a radius of about twenty miles around the Ridcully estates, they'd run, hide or in desperate cases attack violently at the mere sight of a pointy hat.

Within twelve hours of arriving, Ridcully had installed

a pack of hunting dragons in the butler's pantry, fired his dreadful crossbow at the ravens on the ancient Tower of Art, drunk a dozen bottles of red wine, and rolled off to bed at two in the morning singing a song with words in it that some of the older and more forgetful wizards had to look up.

And then he got up at five o'clock to go duck hunting down in the marshes on the estuary.

And came back complaining that there wasn't a good trout fishin' river for miles. (You couldn't fish in the river Ankh; you had to jump up and down on the hooks even to make them sink.)

And he ordered beer with his breakfast.

And told *jokes*.

On the other hand, thought the Bursar, at least he didn't interfere with the actual running of the University. Ridcully the Brown wasn't the least interested in running anything except maybe a string of hounds. If you couldn't shoot arrows at it, hunt it or hook it, he couldn't see much point in it.

Beer at breakfast! The Bursar shuddered. Wizards weren't at their best before noon, and breakfast in the Great Hall was a quiet, fragile occasion, broken only by coughs, the quiet shuffling of the servants, and the occasional groan. People shouting for kidneys and black pudding and beer were a new phenomenon.

The only person not terrified of the ghastly man was old Windle Poons, who was one hundred and thirty years old and deaf and, while an expert on ancient magical writings, needed adequate notice and a good run-up to deal with the present day. He'd managed to absorb the fact that the new Archchancellor was going to be one of those hedgerow-and-dickie-bird chappies, it would take a week or two for him to grasp the change of events, and in the meantime he made polite and civilized conversation based on what little he could remember about Nature and things.

On the lines of:

'I expect it must be a, mm, a change for you, mm,

sleeping in a real bed, instead of under the, mm, stars?'
And: 'These things, mm, here, are called knives and forks,
mm.' And: 'This, mm, *green* stuff on the scrambled egg,
mm, would it be parsley, do you think?'

But since the new Archchancellor never paid much
attention to anything anyone said while he was eating, and
Poons never noticed that he wasn't getting any answers,
they got along quite well.

Anyway, the Bursar had other problems.

The Alchemists, for one thing. You couldn't trust alchemists. They were too serious-minded.

Boom.

And that was the last one. Whole days went by without
being punctuated by small explosions. The city settled
down again, which was a foolish thing to do.

What the Bursar failed to consider was that no more
bangs doesn't mean they've stopped doing it, whatever it
is. It just means they're doing it *right*.

It was midnight. The surf boomed on the beach, and made
a phosphorescent glow in the night. Around the ancient
hill, though, the sound seemed as dead as if it was arriving
through several layers of velvet.

The hole in the sand was quite big now.

If you could put your ear to it, you might think you
could hear applause.

It was still midnight. A full moon glided above the smoke
and fumes of Ankh-Morpork, thankful that several thousand miles of sky lay between it and them.

The Alchemists' Guildhall was new. It was always new.
It had been explosively demolished and rebuilt four times
in the last two years, on the last occasion without a lecture
and demonstration room in the hope that this might be a
helpful move.

On this night a number of muffled figures entered the
building in a surreptitious fashion. After a few minutes the
lights in a window on the top floor dimmed and went out.

Well, nearly out.

Something was happening up there. A strange flickering filled the window, very briefly. It was followed by a ragged cheering.

And there was a noise. Not a bang this time, but a strange mechanical purring, like a happy cat at the bottom of a tin drum.

It went *clickaclickaclickaclicka . . . click.*

It went on for several minutes, to a background of cheers. And then a voice said:

'That's all, folks.'

'That's all what?' said the Patrician of Ankh-Morpork, next morning.

The man in front of him shivered with fear.

'Don't know, lordship,' he said. 'They wouldn't let me in. They made me wait outside the door, lordship.'

He twisted his fingers together nervously. The Patrician's stare had him pinned. It was a good stare, and one of the things it was good at was making people go on talking when they thought they had finished.

Only the Patrician knew how many spies he had in the city. This particular one was a servant in the Alchemists' Guild. He had once had the misfortune to come up before the Patrician accused of malicious lingering, and had then chosen of his own free will to become a spy.[3]

'That's *all*, lordship,' he whined. 'There was just this clicking noise and this sort of flickery *glow* under the door. And, er, they said the daylight here was wrong.'

'Wrong? How?'

'Er. Dunno, sir. Just wrong, they said. They ought to go somewhere where it was better, they said. Uh. And they told me to go and get them some food.'

The Patrician yawned. There was something infinitely boring about the antics of alchemists.

---

[3] The alternative was choosing of his own free will to be thrown into the scorpion pit.

'Indeed,' he said.

'But they'd had their supper only fifteen minutes before,' the servant blurted out.

'Perhaps whatever they were doing makes people hungry,' said the Patrician.

'Yes, and the kitchen was all shut up for the night and I had to go and buy a tray of hot sausages in buns from Throat Dibbler.'

'Indeed.' The Patrician looked down at the paperwork on his desk. 'Thank you. You may go.'

'You know what, lordship? They liked them. They actually liked them!'

That the Alchemists had a Guild at all was remarkable. Wizards were just as unco-operative, but they also were by nature hierarchical and competitive. They *needed* organization. What was the good of being a wizard of the Seventh Level if you didn't have six other levels to look down on and the Eighth Level to aspire to? You needed other wizards to hate and despise.

Whereas every alchemist was an alchemist alone, working in darkened rooms or hidden cellars and endlessly searching for the big casino – the Philosopher's Stone, the Elixir of Life. They tended to be thin, pink-eyed men, with beards that weren't really beards but more like groups of individual hairs clustering together for mutual protection, and many of them had that vague, unworldly expression that you get from spending too much time in the presence of boiling mercury.

It wasn't that alchemists hated other alchemists. They often didn't notice them, or thought they were walruses.

And so their tiny, despised Guild had never aspired to the powerful status of the Guilds of, say, the Thieves or the Beggars or the Assassins, but devoted itself instead to the aid of widows and families of those alchemists who had taken an overly relaxed attitude to potassium cyanide, for example, or had distilled some interesting fungi, drunk the result, and then stepped off the roof to play with the fairies.

There weren't actually very *many* widows and orphans, of course, because alchemists found it difficult to relate to other people long enough, and generally if they ever managed to marry it was only to have someone to hold their crucibles.

By and large, the only skill the alchemists of Ankh-Morpork had discovered so far was the ability to turn gold into less gold.

Until now . . .

Now they were full of the nervous excitement of those who have found an unexpected fortune in their bank account and don't know whether to draw people's attention to it or simply take the lot and run.

'The wizards aren't going to like it,' said one of them, a thin, hesitant man called Lully. 'They're going to call it magic. You know they get really *pissed* if they think you're doing magic and you're not a wizard.'

'There isn't any magic involved,' said Thomas Silverfish, the president of the Guild.

'There's the imps.'

'That's not magic. That's just ordinary occult.'

'Well, there's the salamanders.'

'Perfectly normal natural history. Nothing wrong with that.'

'Well, all right. But they'll *call* it magic. You know what they're like.'

The alchemists nodded gloomily.

'They're reactionaries,' said Sendivoge, the Guild secretary. 'Bloated thaumocrats. And the other Guilds, too. What do they know about the march of progress? What do they care? They could have been doing something like this for years, but did they? Not them! Just *think* how we can make people's lives so much . . . well, better. The possibilities are immense.'

'Educational,' said Silverfish.

'Historical,' said Lully.

'And of course there's entertainment,' said Peavie, the Guild treasurer. He was a small, nervous man. Most

24

alchemists were nervous, in any case; it came from not knowing what the crucible of bubbling stuff they were experimenting with was going to do next.

'Well, yes. Obviously some entertainment,' said Silverfish.

'Some of the great historical dramas,' said Peavie. 'Just picture the scene! You get some actors together, they act it just once, and people all over the Disc will be able to see it as many times as they like! A great saving in wages, by the way,' he added.

'But tastefully done,' said Silverfish. 'We have a great responsibility to see that nothing is done which is in any way . . . ' his voice trailed off, ' . . . you know . . . *coarse*.'

'They'll stop us,' said Lully darkly. 'I know those wizards.'

'I've been giving that some thought,' said Silverfish. 'The light's too bad here anyway. We agreed. We need clear skies. And we need to be a long way away. I think I know just the place.'

'You know, I can't believe we're doing this,' said Peavie. 'A month ago it was just a mad idea. And now it's all worked! It's just like magic! Only not magical, if you see what I mean,' he added quickly.

'Not just illusion, but *real* illusion,' said Lully.

'I don't know if anyone's thought about this,' said Peavie, 'but this could make us a bit of money. Um?'

'But that isn't important,' said Silverfish.

'No. No, of course not,' muttered Peavie. He glanced at the others.

'Shall we watch it again?' he said, shyly. 'I don't mind turning the handle. And, and . . . well, I know I haven't contributed very much to this project, but I did come up with this, er, this stuff.'

He pulled a very large bag from the pocket of his robe and dropped it on the table. It fell over, and a few fluffy, white mis-shapen balls rolled out.

The alchemists stared at it.

'What is it?' said Lully.

'Well,' said Peavie, uncomfortably, 'what you do is, you take some corn, and you put it in, say, a Number 3 crucible, with some cooking oil, you see, and then you put a plate or something on top of it, and when you heat it up it goes bang, I mean, not *seriously* bang, and when it's stopped banging you take the plate off and it's metamorphosed into these, er, things . . . ' He looked at their uncomprehending faces. 'You can eat it,' he mumbled apologetically. 'If you put butter and salt on it, it tastes like salty butter.'

Silverfish reached out a chemical-stained hand and cautiously selected a fluffy morsel. He chewed it thoughtfully.

'Don't really know why I did it,' said Peavie, blushing. 'Just sort of had an idea that it was *right*.'

Silverfish went on chewing.

'Tastes like cardboard,' he said, after a while.

'Sorry,' said Peavie, trying to scoop the rest of the heap back into the sack. Silverfish laid a gentle hand on his arm.

'Mind you,' he said, selecting another puffed morsel, 'it *does* have a certain something, doesn't it? They *do* seem right. What did you say it's called?'

'Hasn't really got a name,' said Peavie. 'I just call it banged grains.'

Silverfish took another one. 'Funny how you want to go on eating them,' he said. 'Sort of more-ish. Banged grains? Right. Anyway . . . gentlemen, let us turn the handle one more time.'

Lully started to wind the film back into the unmagical lantern.

'You were saying you knew a place where we could really build up the project and where the wizards wouldn't bother us?' he said.

Silverfish grabbed a handful of banged grains.

'It's along the coast a way,' he said. 'Nice and sunny and no-one ever goes there these days. Nothing there but some wind-blown old forest and a temple and sand dunes.'

'A temple? Gods can get really *pissed* if you—' Peavie began.

'Look,' said Silverfish, 'the whole area's been deserted for centuries. There's nothing there. No people, no gods, no nothing. Just lots of sunlight and land, waiting for us. It's our chance, lads. We're not allowed to make magic, we can't make gold, we can't even make a living – so let's make *moving pictures*. Let's make *history*!'

The alchemists sat back and looked more cheerful.

'Yeah,' said Lully.

'Oh. Right,' said Peavie.

'Here's to moving pictures,' said Sendivoge, holding up a handful of banged grains. 'How'd you hear about this place?'

'Oh, I—' Silverfish stopped. He looked puzzled. 'Don't know,' he said, eventually. 'Can't . . . quite remember. Must have heard about it once and forgot it, and then it just popped into my head. You know how these things happen.'

'Yeah,' said Lully. 'Like with me and the film. It was like I was *remembering* how to do it. Funny old tricks the mind can play.'

'Yeah.'

'Yeah.'

' 'S'n idea whose time has come, see.'

'Yeah.'

'Yeah.'

'That must be it.'

A slightly worried silence settled over the table. It was the sound of minds trying to put their mental fingers on something that was bothering them.

The air seemed to glitter.

'What's this place called?' said Lully, eventually.

'Don't know what it was called in the old days,' said Silverfish, leaning back and pulling the banged grains towards him. 'These days they call it the Holy Wood.'

'Holy Wood,' said Lully. 'Sounds . . . familiar.'

There was another silence while they thought about it.

27

It was broken by Sendivoge.

'Oh, well,' he said cheerfully, 'Holy Wood, here we come.'

'Yeah,' said Silverfish, shaking his head as if to dislodge a disquieting thought. 'Funny thing, really. I've got this feeling . . . that we've been going there . . . all this time.'

Several thousand miles under Silverfish, Great A'Tuin the world turtle sculled dreamily on through the starry night.

Reality is a curve.

That's not the problem. The *problem* is that there isn't as much as there should be. According to some of the more mystical texts in the stacks of the library of Unseen University –

– the Discworld's premier college of wizardry and big dinners, whose collection of books is so massive that it distorts Space and Time –

– at least nine-tenths of all the original reality ever created lies outside the multiverse, and since the multiverse by definition includes absolutely everything that is anything, this puts a bit of a strain on things.

Outside the boundaries of the universes lie the raw realities, the could-have-beens, the might-bes, the never-weres, the wild ideas, all being created and uncreated chaotically like elements in fermenting supernovas.

Just occasionally where the walls of the worlds have worn a bit thin, they can leak *in*.

And reality leaks out.

The effect is like one of those deep-sea geysers of hot water, around which strange submarine creatures find enough warmth and food to make a brief, tiny oasis of existence in an environment where there shouldn't be any existence at all.

The idea of Holy Wood leaked innocently and joyfully into the Discworld.

And reality leaked out.

And was found. For there are Things outside, whose ability to sniff out tiny frail conglomerations of reality made the thing with the sharks and the trace of blood seem very boring indeed.

They began to gather.

A storm slid in across the sand dunes but, where it reached the low hill, the clouds seemed to curve away. Only a few drops of rain hit the parched soil, and the gale became nothing more than a faint breeze.

It blew sand over the long-dead remains of a fire.

Further down the slope, near a hole that was now big enough for, say, a badger, a small rock dislodged itself and rolled away.

A month went by quickly. It didn't want to hang around.

The Bursar knocked respectfully at the Archchancellor's door and then opened it.

A crossbow bolt nailed his hat to the woodwork.

The Archchancellor lowered the bow and glared at him.

'Bloody dangerous thing to do, wasn't it?' he said. 'You could have caused a nasty accident.'

The Bursar hadn't got where he was today, or rather where he had been ten seconds ago, which was where a calm and self-assured personality was, rather than where he was now, which was on the verge of a mild heart attack, without a tremendous ability to recover from unexpected upsets.

He unpinned his hat from the target chalked on the ancient woodwork.

'No harm done,' he said. No voice could be as calm as that without tremendous effort. 'You can barely see the hole. Why, er, are you shooting at the door, Master?'

'Use your common sense, man! It's dark outside and the damn walls are made of stone. You don't expect me to shoot at the damn walls?'

'Ah,' said the Bursar. 'The door is, er, five hundred

years old, you know,' he added, with finely-tuned reproach.

'Looks it,' said the Archchancellor, bluntly. 'Damn great black thing. What we need around here, man, is a lot less stone and wood and a bit more jolliness. A few sportin' prints, yer know. An ornament or two.'

'I shall see to it directly,' lied the Bursar smoothly. He remembered the sheaf of papers under his arm. 'In the meantime, Master, perhaps you would care to—'

'Right,' said the Archchancellor, ramming his pointed hat on his head. 'Good man. Now, got a sick dragon to see to. Little devil hasn't touched his tar oil for days.'

'Your signature on one or two of—' the Bursar burbled hurriedly.

'Can't be havin' with all that stuff,' said the Archchancellor, waving him away. 'Too much damn paper around here as it is. And—' He stared through the Bursar, as if he had just remembered something. 'Saw a funny thing this mornin',' he said. 'Saw a monkey in the quad. Bold as brass.'

'Oh, yes,' said the Bursar, cheerfully. 'That would be the Librarian.'

'Got a pet, has he?'

'No, you misunderstand me, Archchancellor,' said the Bursar cheerfully. 'That *was* the Librarian.'

The Archchancellor stared at him.

The Bursar's smile began to glaze.

'The Librarian's a *monkey*?'

It took some time for the Bursar to explain matters clearly, and then the Archchancellor said: 'What yer tellin' me, then, is that this chap got himself turned into a monkey by magic?'

'An accident in the Library, yes. Magical explosion. One minute a human, next minute an orang-utan. And you mustn't call him a monkey, Master. He's an ape.'

'Same damn difference, surely?'

'Apparently not. He gets very, er, aggressive if you call him a monkey.'

'He doesn't stick his bottom out at people, does he?'

The Bursar closed his eyes and shuddered. 'No, Master. You're thinking of baboons.'

'Ah.' The Archchancellor considered this. 'Haven't got any of them workin' here, then?'

'No, Master. Just the Librarian, Master.'

'Can't have it. Can't have it, yer know. Can't have damn great hairy things shambling around the place,' said the Archchancellor firmly. 'Get rid of him.'

'Good grief, no! He's the best Librarian we've ever had. And tremendous value for money.'

'Why? What d'we pay him?'

'Peanuts,' said the Bursar promptly. 'Besides, he's the only one who knows how the Library actually works.'

'Turn him back, then. No life for a man, bein' a monkey.'

'*Ape*, Archchancellor. And he seems to prefer it, I'm afraid.'

'How d'yer know?' said the Archchancellor suspiciously. 'Speaks, does he?'

The Bursar hesitated. There was always this trouble with the Librarian. Everyone had got so accustomed to him it was hard to remember a time when the Library was *not* run by a yellow-fanged ape with the strength of three men. If the abnormal goes on long enough it becomes the normal. It was just that, when you came to explain it to a third party, it sounded odd. He coughed nervously.

'He says "oook", Archchancellor,' he said.

'And what's that mean?'

'Means "no", Archchancellor.'

'And how does he say "yes", then?'

The Bursar had been dreading this. ' "Oook", Archchancellor,' he said.

'That was the same oook as the other oook!'

'Oh, no. No. I assure you. There's a different inflection . . . I mean, when you get used to . . . ,' the Bursar shrugged. 'I suppose we've just got into the way of understanding him, Archchancellor.'

'Well, at least he keeps himself fit,' said the Archchancellor nastily. 'Not like the rest of you fellows. I went into the Uncommon Room this morning, and it was full of chaps snoring!'

'That would be the senior masters, Master,' said the Bursar. 'I would say they are supremely fit, myself.'

'*Fit?* The Dean looks like a man who's swallered a bed!'

'Ah, but Master,' said the Bursar, smiling indulgently, 'the word "fit", as I understand it, means "appropriate to a purpose", and I would say the body of the Dean is supremely appropriate to the purpose of sitting around all day and eating big heavy meals.' The Bursar permitted himself a little smile.

The Archchancellor gave him a look so old-fashioned it might have belonged to an ammonite.

'That a joke?' he said, in the suspicious tones of someone who wouldn't really understand the term 'sense of humour' even if you sat down for an hour and explained it to him with diagrams.

'I was just making an observation, Master,' said the Bursar cautiously.

The Archchancellor shook his head. 'Can't stand jokes. Can't stand chaps goin' around tryin' to be funny the whole time. Comes of spendin' too much time sitting indoors. A few twenty-mile runs and the Dean'd be a different man.'

'Well, yes,' said the Bursar. 'He'd be dead.'

'He'd be healthy.'

'Yes, but still dead.'

The Archchancellor irritably shuffled the papers on his desk.

'Slackness,' he muttered. 'Far too much of it going on. Whole place gone to pot. People goin' round sleepin' all day and turnin' into monkeys the whole time. We never even *thought* of turnin' into a monkey when I was a student.' He looked up irritably.

'What was it you wanted?' he snapped.

'What?' said the Bursar, unnerved.

'You wanted me to do somethin', didn't you? You came in to ask me to do somethin'. Probably because I'm the only feller here not fast asleep or sittin' in a tree whoopin' every mornin',' the Archchancellor added.

'Er. I think that's gibbons, Archchancellor.'

'What? What? Do try and make some sense, man!'

The Bursar pulled himself together. He didn't see why he had to be treated like this.

'In *fact*, I wanted to see you about one of the students, Master,' he said coldly.

'Students?' barked the Archchancellor.

'Yes, Master. You know? They're the thinner ones with the pale faces? Because we're a *university*? They come with the whole thing, like rats—'

'I thought we paid people to deal with 'em.'

'The teaching staff. Yes. But sometimes . . . well, I wonder, Archchancellor, if you would care to look at these examination results . . . '

It was midnight – not the same midnight as before, but a very similar midnight. Old Tom, the tongueless bell in the University bell tower, had just tolled its twelve sonorous silences.

Rainclouds squeezed their last few drops over the city. Ankh-Morpork sprawled under a few damp stars, as real as a brick.

Ponder Stibbons, student wizard, put down his book and rubbed his face.

'All right,' he said. 'Ask me anything. Go on. Anything at all.'

Victor Tugelbend, student wizard, picked up his battered copy of *Necrotelicomnicon Discussed for Students, with Practical Experiments* and turned the pages at random. He was lying on Ponder's bed. At least, his shoulder blades were. His body extended up the wall. This is a perfectly normal position for a student taking his ease.

'OK,' he said. 'Right. OK? What, right, what is the name of the outer-dimensional monster whose distinctive cry is "Yerwhatyerwhatyerwhat"?'

'Yob Soddoth,' said Ponder promptly.

'Yeah. How does the monster Tshup Aklathep, Infernal Star Toad with A Million Young, torture its victims to death?'

'It . . . don't tell me . . . it holds them down and shows them pictures of its children until their brains implode.'

'Yep. Always wondered how that happens, myself,' said Victor, flicking through the pages. 'I suppose after you've said "Yes, he's got your eyes" for the thousandth time you're about ready to commit suicide in any case.'

'You know an awful lot, Victor,' said Ponder admiringly. 'I'm amazed you're still a student.'

'Er, yes,' said Victor. 'Er. Just unlucky at exams, I guess.'

'Go on,' said Ponder, 'Ask me one more.'

Victor opened the book again.

There was a moment's silence.

Then he said, 'Where's Holy Wood?'

Ponder shut his eyes and pounded his forehead. 'Hang on, hang on . . . don't tell me . . . ' He opened his eyes. 'What do you mean, where's Holy Wood?' he added sharply. 'I don't remember anything about any Holy Wood.'

Victor stared down at the page. There was nothing about any Holy Wood there.

'I could have sworn I heard . . . I think my mind must be wandering,' he finished lamely. 'It must be all this revision.'

'Yes. It really gets to you, doesn't it? But it'll be worth it, to be a wizard.'

'Yes,' said Victor. 'Can't wait.'

Ponder shut the book.

'Rain's stopped. Let's go over the wall,' he said. 'We deserve a drink.'

Victor waggled a finger. 'Just one drink, then. Got to

keep sober,' he said. 'It's Finals tomorrow. Got to keep a clear head!'

'Huh!' said Ponder.

Of course, it is very important to be sober when you take an exam. Many worthwhile careers in the street-cleansing, fruit-picking and subway-guitar-playing industries have been founded on a lack of understanding of this simple fact.

But Victor had a special reason for keeping alert.

He might make a mistake, and pass.

His dead uncle had left him a small fortune not to be a wizard. He hadn't realized it when he'd drawn up the will, but that's what the old man had done. He *thought* he was helping his nephew through college, but Victor Tugelbend was a very bright young lad in an oblique sort of way and had reasoned thusly:

What are the advantages and disadvantages of being a wizard? Well, you got a certain amount of prestige, but you were often in dangerous situations and certainly always at risk of being killed by a fellow mage. He saw no future in being a well-respected corpse.

On the other hand . . .

What are the advantages and disadvantages of being a *student* wizard? You got quite a lot of free time, a certain amount of licence in matters like drinking a lot of ale and singing bawdy songs, no-one tried to kill you much except in the ordinary, everyday Ankh-Morpork way of things and, thanks to the legacy, you also got a modest but comfortable style of living. Of course, you didn't get much in the way of prestige but at least you were alive to know this.

So Victor had devoted a considerable amount of energy in studying firstly the terms of the will, the byzantine examination regulations of Unseen University, and every examination paper of the last fifty years.

The pass mark in Finals was 88.

Failing would be easy. Any idiot can *fail*.

Victor's uncle had been no fool. One of the conditions

of the legacy was that, should Victor ever achieve a mark of less than 80, the money supply would dry up like thin spit on a hot stove.

He'd won, in a way. Few students had ever studied as hard as Victor. It was said that his knowledge of magic rivalled that of some of the top wizards. He spent hours in a comfy chair in the Library, reading grimoires. He researched answer formats and exam techniques. He listened to lectures until he could quote them by heart. He was generally considered by the staff to be the brightest and certainly the busiest student for decades and, at every Finals, he carefully and competently got a mark of 84.

It was uncanny.

The Archchancellor reached the last page.

Eventually he said: 'Ah. I see. Feel sorry for the lad, do you?'

'I don't think you quite see what I mean,' said the Bursar.

'Fairly obvious to me,' said the Archchancellor. 'Lad keeps coming within an ace of passin'.' He pulled out one of the papers. 'Anyway, it says here he passed three years ago. Got 91.'

'Yes, Archchancellor. But he appealed.'

'*Appealed*? Against *passin'*?'

'He said he didn't think the examiners had noticed that he got the allotropes of octiron wrong in question six. He said he couldn't live with his conscience. He said it would haunt him for the rest of his days if he succeeded unfairly over better and more worthy students. You'll notice he got only 82 and 83 in the next two exams.'

'Why's that?'

'We think he was playing safe, Master.'

The Archchancellor drummed his fingers on the desk.

'Can't have this,' he said. 'Can't have someone goin' around *almost* bein' a wizard and laughin' at us up his, his – what's it that people laugh up?'

'My feelings exactly,' purred the Bursar.

'We should send him up,' said the Archchancellor firmly.

'*Down*, Master,' said the Bursar. 'Sending him up would mean making spiteful and satirical comments about him.'

'Yes. Good thinkin'. Let's do that,' said the Archchancellor.

'No, Master,' said the Bursar patiently. '*He's* sending *us* up, so *we* send *him* down.'

'Right. Balance things up,' said the Archchancellor. The Bursar rolled his eyes. 'Or down,' the Archchancellor added. 'So you want me to give him his marchin' orders, eh? Just send him along in the morning and—'

'No, Archchancellor. We can't do it just like that.'

'We can't? I thought we were in charge here!'

'Yes, but you have to be extremely careful when dealing with Master Tugelbend. He's an expert on procedures. So what I thought we could do is give him *this* paper in the finals tomorrow.'

The Archchancellor took the proferred document. His lips moved silently as he read it.

'Just one question.'

'Yes. And he'll either pass or fail. I'd like to see him manage 84 per cent on *that*.'

In a sense which his tutors couldn't quite define, much to their annoyance, Victor Tugelbend was also the laziest person in the history of the world.

Not simply, ordinarily lazy. Ordinary laziness was merely the absence of effort. Victor had passed through there a long time ago, had gone straight through commonplace idleness and out on the far side. He put more effort into avoiding work than most people put into hard labour.

He had never wanted to be a wizard. He'd never wanted much, except perhaps to be left alone and not woken up until midday. When he'd been small, people had said things like, 'And what do *you* want to be, little man?' and he'd said, 'I don't know. What have you got?'

They didn't let you get away with that sort of thing for

very long. It wasn't enough to be what you were, you had to be working to be something else.

He'd tried. For quite a long while he'd tried wanting to be a blacksmith, because that looked interesting and romantic. But it also involved hard work and intractable bits of metal. Then he'd tried wanting to be an assassin, which looked dashing and romantic. But it also involved hard work and, when you got right down to it, occasionally having to kill someone. Then he'd tried wanting to be an actor, which looked dramatic and romantic, but it had involved dusty tights, cramped lodgings and, to his amazement, hard work.

He'd allowed himself to be sent to the University because it was easier than not going.

He tended to smile a lot, in a faintly puzzled way. This gave people the impression that he was slightly more intelligent than they were. In fact, he was usually trying to work out what they had just said.

And he had a thin moustache, which in a certain light made him look debonair and, in another, made him look as though he had been drinking a thick chocolate milk shake.

He was quite proud of it. When you became a wizard you were expected to stop shaving and grow a beard like a gorse bush. Very senior wizards looked capable of straining nourishment out of the air via their moustaches, like whales.

It was now half-past one. He was ambling back from the Mended Drum, the most determinedly disreputable of the city's taverns. Victor Tugelbend always gave the impression of ambling, even when he was running.

He was also quite sober and a bit surprised, therefore, to find himself in the Plaza of Broken Moons. He'd been heading for the little alley behind the University and the piece of wall with the conveniently-spaced removable bricks where, for hundreds and hundreds of years, student wizards had quietly got around, or more precisely climbed over, Unseen University's curfew restrictions.

The plaza wasn't on the route.

He turned to amble back the way he had come, and then stopped. There was something unusual going on.

Usually there'd be a storyteller there, or some musicians, or an entrepreneur looking for prospective buyers of such surplus Ankh-Morpork landmarks as the Tower of Art or the Brass Bridge.

Now there were just some people putting up a big screen, like a bedsheet stretched between poles.

He sauntered over to them. 'What're you doing?' he said amiably.

'There's going to be a performance.'

'Oh. Acting,' said Victor, without much interest.

He mooched back through the damp darkness, but stopped when he heard a voice coming from the gloom between two buildings.

The voice said 'Help', quite quietly.

Another voice said, 'Just hand it over, right?'

Victor wandered closer, and squinted into the shadows. 'Hallo?' he said. 'Is everything all right?'

There was a pause, and then a low voice said, 'You don't know what's good for you, kid.'

He's got a knife, Victor thought. He's coming at me with a knife. That means I'm either going to get stabbed or I'm going to have to run away, which is a real waste of energy.

People who didn't apply themselves to the facts in hand might have thought that Victor Tugelbend would be fat and unhealthy. In fact, he was undoubtedly the most athletically-inclined student in the University. Having to haul around extra poundage was far too much effort, so he saw to it that he never put it on and he kept himself in trim because doing things with decent muscles was far less effort than trying to achieve things with bags of flab.

So he brought one hand round in a backhanded swipe. It didn't just connect, it lifted the mugger off his feet.

Then he looked for the prospective victim, who was still cowering against the wall.

'I hope you're not hurt,' he said.

'Don't move!'

'I wasn't going to,' said Victor.

The figure advanced from the shadows. It had a package under one arm, and its hands were held in front of its face in an odd gesture, each forefinger and thumb extended at right angles and then fitted together, so that the man's little weasely eyes appeared to be looking out through a frame.

He's probably warding off the Evil Eye, Victor thought. He looks like a wizard, with all those symbols on his dress.

'Amazing!' said the man, squinting through his fingers. 'Just turn your head slightly, will you? Great! Pity about the nose, but I expect we can do something about that.'

He stepped forward and tried to put his arm round Victor's shoulders. 'It's lucky for you', he said, 'that you met me.'

'It is?' said Victor, who had been thinking it was the other way around.

'You're just the type I'm looking for,' said the man.

'Sorry,' said Victor. 'I thought you were being robbed.'

'He was after this,' said the man, patting the package under his arm. It rang like a gong. 'Wouldn't have done him any good, though.'

'Not worth anything?' said Victor.

'Priceless.'

'That's all right, then,' said Victor.

The man gave up trying to reach across both of Victor's shoulders, which were quite broad, and settled for just one of them.

'But a lot of people would be disappointed,' he said. 'Now, look. You stand well. Good profile. Listen, lad, how would you like to be in moving pictures?'

'Er,' said Victor. 'No. I don't think so.'

The man gaped at him.

'You did hear what I said, didn't you?' he said. 'Moving pictures?'

'Yes.'

'Everyone wants to be in moving pictures!'

'No, thanks,' said Victor, politely. 'I'm sure it's a worthwhile job, but moving pictures doesn't sound very interesting to me.'

'I'm talking about *moving pictures*!'

'Yes,' said Victor mildly. 'I heard you.'

The man shook his head. 'Well,' he said, 'you've made my day. First time in weeks I've met someone who isn't desperate to get into moving pictures. I thought everyone wanted to get into moving pictures. I thought as soon as I saw you: he'll be expecting a job in moving pictures for this night's work.'

'Thanks all the same,' said Victor. 'But I don't think I'd take to it.'

'Well, I owe you something.' The little man fumbled in a pocket and produced a card. Victor took it. It read:

Thomas Silverfish

Interesting and Instructive Kinematography

One and Two Reelers   Nearly non-explosive Stock

1, Holy Wood

'That's if ever you change your mind,' he said. 'Everyone in Holy Wood knows me.'

Victor stared at the card. 'Thank you,' he said vaguely. 'Er. Are you a wizard?'

Silverfish glared at him.

'Whatever made you think that?' he snapped.

'You're wearing a dress with magic symbols—'

'*Magic symbols?* Look closely, boy! These are certainly not the credulous symbols of a ridiculous and outmoded belief system! These are the badges of an enlightened craft

41

whose clear, new dawn is just . . . er, dawning! Magic symbols!' he finished, in tones of withering scorn. 'And it's a robe, not a dress,' he added.

Victor peered at the collection of stars and crescent moons and things. The badges of an enlightened craft whose new dawn was just dawning looked just like the credulous symbols of a ridiculous and outmoded belief system to him, but this was probably not the time to say so.

'Sorry,' he said again. 'Couldn't see them clearly.'

'I'm an alchemist,' said Silverfish, only slightly mollified.

'Oh, lead into gold, that sort of thing,' said Victor.

'Not lead, lad. *Light*. It doesn't work with lead. *Light* into gold . . . '

'Really?' said Victor politely, as Silverfish started to set up a tripod in the middle of the plaza.

A small crowd was collecting. A small crowd collected very easily in Ankh-Morpork. As a city, it had some of the most accomplished spectators in the universe. They'd watch anything, especially if there was any possibility of anyone getting hurt in an amusing way.

'Why don't you stay for the show?' said Silverfish, and hurried off.

An alchemist. Well, everyone knew that alchemists were a little bit mad, thought Victor. It was perfectly normal.

Who'd want to spend their time moving pictures? Most of them looked all right where they were.

'Sausages inna bun! Get them while they're hot!' bellowed a voice by his ear. He turned.

'Oh, hallo, Mr Dibbler,' he said.

'Evening, lad. Want to get a nice hot sausage down you?'

Victor eyed the glistening tubes in the tray around Dibbler's neck. They smelled appetizing. They always did. And then you bit into them, and learned once again that Cut-me-own-Throat Dibbler could find a use for bits of an animal that the animal didn't know it had got. Dibbler had worked out that with enough fried onions and mustard people would eat *anything*.

'Special rate for students,' Dibbler whispered conspiratorially. 'Fifteen pence, and that's cutting my own throat.' He flapped the frying pan lid strategically, raising a cloud of steam.

The piquant scent of fried onions did its wicked work.

'Just one, then,' Victor said warily.

Dibbler flicked a sausage out of the pan and snatched it into a bun with the expertise of a frog snapping a mayfly.

'You won't live to regret it,' he said cheerfully,

Victor nibbled a bit of onion. That was safe enough.

'What's all this?' he said, jerking a thumb in the direction of the flapping screen.

'Some kind of entertainment,' said Dibbler. 'Hot sausages! They're lovely!' He lowered his voice again to its normal conspiratorial hiss.

'All the rage in the other cities, I hear,' he added. 'Some sort of moving pictures. They've been trying to get it right before coming to Ankh-Morpork.'

They watched Silverfish and a couple of associates fumble technically with the box on the tripod. White light suddenly appeared at a circular orifice on the front of it, and illuminated the screen. There was a half-hearted cheer from the crowd.

'Oh,' said Victor. 'I *see*. Is that all? It's just plain old shadow play. That's all it is. My uncle used to do it to amuse me. You know? You kind of move your hands in front of the light and the shadows make a kind of silhouettey picture.'

'Oh, yeah,' said Dibbler uncertainly. 'Like "Big Elephant", or "Bald Eagle". My grandad used to do that sort of stuff.'

'Mainly my uncle did "Deformed Rabbit",' said Victor. 'He wasn't very good at it, you see. It used to get pretty embarrassing. We'd all sit round desperately guessing things like "Surprised Hedgehog" or "Rabid Stoat" and he'd go off to bed in a sulk because we hadn't guessed he was really doing "Lord Henry Skipps and His Men beating the Trolls at the Battle of Pseudopolis". I can't see what's so special about shadows on a screen.'

43

'From what I hear it's not like that,' said Dibbler. 'I sold one of the men a Jumbo Sausage Special earlier on, and he said it's all down to showing pictures very fast. Sticking lots of pictures together and showing them one after another. Very, very fast, he said.'

'Not too fast,' said Victor severely. 'You wouldn't be able to see them go past if they were too fast.'

'He said that's the whole secret, not seeing 'em go past,' said Dibbler. 'You have to see 'em all at once, or something.'

'They'd all be blurred,' said Victor. 'Didn't you ask him about that?'

'Er, no,' said Dibbler. 'Point of fact, he had to rush off just then. Said he felt a bit odd.'

Victor looked thoughtfully at the remnant of his sausage in a bun and, as he did so, he was aware of being stared at in his turn.

He looked down. There was a dog sitting by his feet.

It was small, bow-legged and wiry, and basically grey but with patches of brown, white and black in outlying areas, and it was staring.

It was certainly the most penetrating stare Victor had ever seen. It wasn't menacing or fawning. It was just very slow and very thorough, as though the dog was memorizing details so that it could give a full description to the authorities later on.

When it was sure it had his full attention, it transferred its gaze to the sausage.

Feeling wretched at being so cruel to a poor dumb animal, Victor flicked the sausage downwards. The dog caught and swallowed it in one economical movement.

More people were drifting into the plaza now. Cut-me-own-Throat Dibbler had wandered off and was doing a busy trade with those late-night revellers who were too drunk to prevent optimism triumphing over experience; anyone who bought a meal at one a.m. after a night's revelling was probably going to be riotously ill anyway, so they might as well have something to show for it.

Victor was gradually surrounded by a large crowd. It didn't consist solely of humans. He recognized, a few feet away, the big rangy shape of Detritus, an ancient troll well known to all the students as someone who found employment anywhere people needed to be thrown very hard out of places for money. The troll noticed him, and tried to wink. This involved closing both eyes, because Detritus wasn't good at complicated things. It was widely believed that, if Detritus could be taught to read and write sufficiently to sit down and do an intelligence test, he'd prove to be slightly less intelligent than the chair.

Silverfish picked up a megaphone.

'Ladies and gentlemen,' he said, 'you are privileged tonight to witness a turning point in the history of the Century of—' he lowered the megaphone and Victor heard him whisper urgently to one of his assistants, 'What century is this? Is it?' and then raised the megaphone again and continued in the original plummily optimistic tones '—Century of the Fruitbat! No less than the birth of Moving Pictures! Pictures that move without magic!'

He waited for the applause. There wasn't any. The crowd just watched him. You needed to do more than end your sentences with exclamation marks to get a round of applause from an Ankh-Morpork crowd.

Slightly dispirited, he went on, 'Seeing is Believing, they say! But, ladies and gentlemen, you will not believe the Evidence of Your Own Eyes! What you are about to witness is a Triumph of Natural Science! A Marvel of the Age! A Discovery of World, nay, dare I say, Universe-Shaking Proportions!—'

' 'S got to be better than that bloody sausage, anyway,' said a quiet voice by Victor's knee.

'—Harnessing Natural Mechanisms to create Illusion! Illusion, Ladies and Gentlemen, without recourse to Magic!—'

Victor let his gaze slide downwards. There was nothing down there but the little dog, industriously scratching itself. It looked up slowly, and said 'Woof?'

'—Potential for Learning! The Arts! History! I thank

45

you, Ladies and Gentlemen! Ladies and Gentlemen, You Ain't Seen Nothing Yet!'

There was another hopeful break for applause.

Someone at the front of the crowd said, 'That's right. We ain't.'

'Yeah,' said the woman next to him. 'When're you goin' to stop goin' on like that and get on with the shadow play?'

'That's right,' snapped a second woman. 'Do "Deformed Rabbit". My kids always love that one.'

Victor looked away for a while, to lull the dog's suspicions, and then turned and glared hard at it.

It was amiably watching the crowd, and apparently taking no notice of him.

Victor poked an exploratory finger in his ear. It must have been a trick of an echo, or something. It wasn't that the dog had gone 'woof!', although that was practically unique in itself; most dogs in the universe *never* went 'woof!', they had complicated barks like 'whuuugh!' and 'hwhoouf!'. No, it was that it hadn't in fact *barked* at all. It had *said* 'woof'.

He shook his head, and looked back as Silverfish climbed down from the screen and motioned to one of his assistants to start turning a handle at the side of the box. There was a grinding noise that rose to a steady clicking. Vague shadows danced across the screen, and then . . .

One of the last things Victor remembered was a voice beside his knee saying, 'Could have bin worse, mister. I could have said "miaow".'

Holy Wood dreams . . .

And now it was now eight hours later.

A horribly overhung Ponder Stibbons looked guiltily at the empty desk beside him. It was unlike Victor to miss exams. He always said he enjoyed the challenge.

'Get ready to turn over your papers,' said the invigilator at the end of the hall. The sixty chests of sixty prospective wizards tightened with dark, unbearable tension. Ponder fumbled anxiously with his lucky pen.

The wizard on the dais turned over the hourglass. 'You may begin,' he said.

Several of the more smug students turned over their papers by snapping their fingers. Ponder hated them instantly.

He reached for his lucky inkwell, missed completely in his nervousness, and then knocked it over. A small black flood rolled over his question paper.

Panic and shame washed over him nearly as thoroughly. He mopped the ink up with the hem of his robe, spreading it smoothly over the desk. His lucky dried frog had been washed away.

Hot with embarrassment, dripping black ink, he looked up in supplication at the presiding wizard and then cast his eyes imploringly at the empty desk beside him.

The wizard nodded. Ponder gratefully sidled across the aisle, waited until his heart had stopped thumping and then, very carefully, turned over the paper on the desk.

After ten seconds, and against all reason, he turned it over again just in case there had been a mistake and the rest of the questions had somehow been on the top side after all.

Around him there was the intense silence of fifty-nine minds creaking with sustained effort.

Ponder turned the paper over again.

Perhaps it was some mistake. No . . . there was the University seal and the signature of the Archchancellor and everything. So perhaps it was some sort of special test. Perhaps they were watching him now to see what he'd do . . .

He peered around furtively. The other students seemed to be working hard. Perhaps it *was* a mistake after all. Yes. The more he came to think about it, the more logical it seemed. The Archchancellor had probably signed the papers and then, when the clerks had been copying them out, one of them had got as far as the all-important first question and then maybe had been called away or something, and no-one had noticed, and it'd got put on Victor's desk, but now he wasn't here and Ponder had got it which meant, he decided, in a sudden rush of piety, that the gods must have *wanted* him to get it. After all, it wasn't his fault if some sort of error gave him a paper like this. It was probably sacriligious or something to ignore the opportunity.

They had to accept what you put down. Ponder hadn't shared the room with the world's greatest authority on examination procedures without learning a thing or two.

He looked again at the question: 'What is your name?'

He answered it.

After a while he underlined it, several times, with his lucky ruler.

After a little while longer, to show willing, he wrote above it: 'The anser to questione One is:'.

After a further ten minutes he ventured 'Which is what my name is' on the line below, and underlined it.

Poor old Victor will be really sorry he missed this, he thought.

I wonder where he is?

There was no road to Holy Wood yet. Anyone trying to get there would take the highway to Quirm and, at some unmarked point out in the scrubby landscape, would turn off and strike out towards the sand dunes. Wild lavender and rosemary lined the banks. There was no sound but the buzzing of bees and the distant song of a skylark, which only made the silence more obvious.

Victor Tugelbend left the road at the point where the bank had been broken down and flattened by the passage of many carts and, by the look of it, an increasing number of feet.

There were still many miles to go. He trudged on.

Somewhere at the back of his mind a tiny voice was saying things like 'Where am I? Why am I doing this?' and another part of him knew that he didn't really have to do it at all. Like the hypnotist's victim who knows they're not really hypnotized and can snap out of it any time they like, but just happened not to feel like it right now, he let his feet be guided.

He wasn't certain why. He just knew that there was something that he had to be part of. Something that might never happen again.

Some way behind, but catching up fast, was Cut-me-own-Throat Dibbler, trying to ride a horse. He was not a natural horseman, and fell off occasionally, which was one reason why he hadn't overtaken Victor yet. The other was that he had paused, before leaving the city, to sell his sausage-in-a-bun business cheaply to a dwarf who could not believe his luck (after actually trying some of the sausages, would still not be able to believe his luck).

Something was calling Dibbler, and it had a golden voice.

A long way behind Throat, knuckles dragging in the sand, was Detritus the troll. It's hard to be certain of what he was thinking, any more than it's possible to tell what a homing pigeon is thinking. He just knew that where he ought to be was not where he was.

And finally, even further down the road, was an eight-horse wagon taking a load of lumber to Holy Wood. Its driver wasn't thinking about anything very much, although he was slightly puzzled by an incident that occurred just as he was leaving Ankh-Morpork in the darkness before dawn. A voice from the gloom by the road had shouted 'Stop in the name of the city guard!' and he had stopped, and when nothing further had transpired he had looked around, and there was no-one there.

The wagon rumbled past, revealing to the eye of the imaginative beholder the small figure of Gaspode the Wonder Dog, trying to make himself comfortable amongst the balks of timber at the rear. He was going to Holy Wood too.

And he also didn't know why.

But he was determined to find out.

*

No-one would have believed, in the final years of the Century of the Fruitbat, that Discworld affairs were being watched keenly and impatiently by intelligences greater than Man's, or at least much nastier; that their affairs were being scrutinized and studied as a man with a three-day appetite might study the All-You-Can-Gobble-For-A-Dollar menu outside Harga's House of Ribs . . .

Well, actually . . . most wizards would have believed it, if anyone had told them.

And the Librarian would certainly have believed it.

And Mrs Marietta Cosmopilite of 3 Quirm Street, Ankh-Morpork, would have believed it, too. But she believed the world was round, that a sprig of garlic in her underwear drawer kept away vampires, that it did you good to get out and have a laugh occasionally, that there was niceness in everyone if you only knew where to look, and that three horrible little dwarfs peered in at her undressing every night.[4]

Holy Wood! . . .

. . . was nothing very much, yet. Just a hill by the sea, and on the other side of the hill, a lot of sand dunes. It was that special sort of beautiful area which is only beautiful if you can leave after briefly admiring its beauty and go somewhere else where there are hot tubs and cold drinks. Actually staying there for any length of time is a penance.

Nevertheless, there was a town there . . . just. Wooden shacks had been built wherever someone had dropped a load of timber, and they were crude, as if the builders had resented the time taken from something more important that they'd much rather be doing. They were square plank boxes.

Except for the front.

If you wanted to understand Holy Wood, Victor said years afterwards, you had to understand its buildings.

---

[4] She was right about that, but only by coincidence.

You'd see a box on the sand. It'd have a roughly peaked roof, but that wasn't important, because it *never* rained in Holy Wood. There'd be cracks in the walls, stuffed with old rags. The windows would be holes – glass was too fragile to cart all the way from Ankh-Morpork. And, from behind, the front was just like a huge wooden billboard, held up by a network of struts.

From the front, it was a fretted, carved, painted, ornate, baroque architectural extravaganza. In Ankh-Morpork, sensible men built their houses plain, so as not to attract attention, and kept the decoration for inside. But Holy Wood wore its houses inside out.

Victor walked up what passed for the main street in a daze. He had woken up in the early hours out in the dunes. Why? He'd decided to come to Holy Wood, but why? He couldn't remember. All he *could* remember was that, at the time, it was the obvious thing to do. There had been hundreds of good reasons.

If only he could remember one of them.

Not that his mind had any room to review memories. It was too busy being aware that he was very hungry and acutely thirsty. His pockets had yielded a total of seven pence. That wouldn't buy a bowl of soup, let alone a good meal.

He needed a good meal. Things would look a lot clearer after a good meal.

He pushed through the crowds. Most of them seemed to be carpenters, but there were others, carrying carboys or mysterious boxes. And everyone was moving very quickly and resolutely, bent on some powerful purpose of their own.

Except him.

He trailed up the impromptu street, gawping at the houses, feeling like a stray grasshopper in an ant hill. And there didn't seem to—

'Why don't you look where you're going!'

He rebounded off a wall. When he got his balance the other party in the collision had already whirred off

51

into the crowd. He stared for a moment and then ran desperately after her.

'Hey!' he said, 'Sorry! Excuse me? Miss?'

She stopped, and waited impatiently as he caught up.

'Well?' she said.

She was a foot shorter than him and her shape was doubtful since most of her was covered in a ridiculously frilly dress, although the dress wasn't as ludicrous as the big blond wig full of ringlets. And her face was white with make-up apart from her eyes, which were heavily ringed in black. The general effect was of a lampshade that hadn't been getting much sleep lately.

'Well?' she repeated, 'Hurry up! They're shooting again in five minutes!'

'Er—'

She unbent slightly. 'No, don't tell me,' she said. 'You've just got here. It's all new to you. You don't know what to do. You're hungry. You haven't got any money. Right?'

'Yes! How did you *know*?'

'Everyone starts like that. And now you want to break into the clicks, right?'

'The clicks?'

She rolled her eyes, deep within their black circles.

'Moving pictures!'

'Oh—' I *do*, he thought. I didn't know it but I do. Yes. That's why I came here. Why didn't I think of that? 'Yes,' he said. 'Yes, that's what I want to do. I want to, er, break in. And how does one do that?'

'*One* waits for ever and ever. Until *one* is noticed.' The girl looked him up and down with unconcealed contempt. 'Take up carpentry, why don't you? Holy Wood always needs good wood butchers.'

And then she spun around and was gone, lost in a crowd of busy people.

'Er, thank you,' Victor called after her. 'Thank you.' He raised his voice and added, 'I hope your eyes get better!'

He jingled the coins in his pocket.

Well, carpentry was out. It sounded too much like

hard work. He'd tried it once, and wood and him had soon reached an agreement – he wouldn't touch it, and it wouldn't split.

Waiting for ever and ever had its attractions, but you needed money to do it with.

His fingers closed around a small, unexpected rectangle. He pulled it out and looked at it.

Silverfish's card.

No. 1 Holy Wood turned out to be a couple of shacks inside a high fence. There was a queue at the gate. It was made up of trolls, dwarfs and humans. They looked as though they had been there for some time; in fact, some of them had such a naturally dispirited way of sagging while remaining upright that they might have been specially-evolved descendants of the original prehistoric queuers.

At the gate was a large, heavy-set man, who was eyeing the queue with the smug look of minor power-wielders everywhere.

'Excuse me—' Victor began.

'Mister Silverfish ain't hiring any more people this morning,' said the man out of the corner of his mouth. 'So scram.'

'But he said that if ever I was in—'

'Did I just say scram, friend?'

'Yes, but—'

The door in the fence opened a fraction. A small pale face poked out.

'We need a troll and a coupla humans,' it said. 'One day, usual rates.' The gate shut again.

The man straightened up and cupped his scarred hands around his mouth.

'Right, you horrible lot!' he shouted. 'You heard the man!' He ran his eyes over the line with the practised gaze of a stock breeder. 'You, you and you,' he said, pointing.

'Excuse me,' said Victor helpfully, 'but I think that man over *there* was actually first in the—'

He was shoved out of the way. The lucky three shuffled

in. He thought he saw the glint of coins changing hands. Then the gatekeeper turned an angry red face towards him.

'*You*,' he said, 'get to the end of the queue. And stay there!'

Victor stared at him. He stared at the gate. He looked at the long line of dispirited people.

'Um, no,' he said. 'I don't think so. Thanks all the same.'

'Then beat it!'

Victor gave him a friendly smile. He walked to the end of the fence, and followed it. It turned, at the far end, into a narrow alley.

Victor searched among the usual alley debris for a while until he found a piece of scrap paper. Then he rolled up his sleeves. And only then did he inspect the fence carefully until he found a couple of loose boards that, with a bit of effort, let him through.

This brought him into an area stacked with lumber and piles of cloth. There was no-one around.

Walking purposefully, in the knowledge that no-one with their sleeves rolled up who walks purposefully with a piece of paper held conspicuously in their hand is ever challenged, he set out across the wood and canvas wonderland of Interesting and Instructive Kinematography.

There were buildings painted on the back of other buildings. There were trees that were trees, at the front, and just a mass of struts at the back. There was a flurry of activity although, as far as Victor could see, no-one was actually producing anything.

He watched a man in a long black cloak, a black hat and a moustache like a yard brush tie a girl to one of the trees. No-one seemed interested in stopping him, even though she was struggling. A couple of people were in fact watching disinterestedly, and there was a man standing behind a large box on a tripod, turning a handle.

She flung out an imploring arm and opened and shut her mouth soundlessly.

One of the watchers stood up, sorted through a stack of

boards beside him, and held one up in front of the box.

It was black. On it, in white, were the words 'Noe! Noe!'

He walked away. The villain twirled his moustache. The man walked back with a board. This time it said 'Ahar! My proude beauty!'

Another of the seated watchers picked up a megaphone.

'Fine, fine,' he said. 'OK, take a five minutes break and then everyone back here for the big fight scene.'

The villain untied the girl. They wandered off. The man stopped turning the handle, lit a cigarette, and then opened the top of the box.

'Everyone get that?' he said.

There was a chorus of squeaks.

Victor walked over and tapped the megaphone man on his shoulder.

'Urgent message for Mr Silverfish?' he said.

'He's in the offices over there,' said the man, jerking his thumb over his shoulder without looking around.

'Thank you.'

The first shed he poked his head into contained nothing but rows of small cages stretching away into the gloom. Indistinct things hurled themselves against the bars and chittered at him. He slammed the door hurriedly.

The next door revealed Silverfish, standing in front of a desk covered with bits of glassware and drifts of paper. He didn't turn around.

'Just put it over there,' he said absently.

'It's me, Mr Silverfish,' said Victor.

Silverfish turned around and peered vaguely at him, as if it was Victor's fault that his name meant nothing.

'Yes?'

'I've come because of that job,' said Victor. 'You know?'

'What job? What should I know?' said Silverfish. 'How the hell did you get in here?'

'I broke into moving pictures,' said Victor. 'But it's nothing that a hammer and a few nails won't put right.'

Panic bloomed on Silverfish's face. Victor pulled out the card and waved it in what he hoped was a reassuring way.

'In Ankh-Morpork?' he said. 'A couple of nights ago? You were being menaced?'

Realization dawned. 'Oh, yes,' said Silverfish faintly. 'And you were the lad who was of some help.'

'And you said to come and see you if I wanted to move pictures,' said Victor. 'I didn't, then, but I do now.' He gave Silverfish a bright smile.

But he thought: he's going to try and wriggle out of it. He's regretting the offer. He's going to send me back to the queue.

'Well, of course,' said Silverfish, 'a lot of very talented people want to be in moving pictures. We're going to have sound any day now. I mean, are you a carpenter? Any alchemical experience? Have you ever trained imps? Any good with your hands at all?'

'No,' Victor admitted.

'Can you sing?'

'A bit. In the bath. But not very well,' Victor conceded.

'Can you dance?'

'No.'

'Swords? Do you know how to handle a sword?'

'A little,' said Victor. He'd used one sometimes in the gym. He'd never in fact fought an opponent, since wizards generally abhor exercise and the only other University resident who ever entered the place was the Librarian, and then only to use the ropes and rings. But Victor had practised an energetic and idiosyncratic technique in front of the mirror, and the mirror had never beaten him yet.

'I see,' said Silverfish gloomily. 'Can't sing. Can't dance. Can handle a sword a little.'

'But I have saved your life twice,' said Victor.

'Twice?' snapped Silverfish.

'Yes,' said Victor. He took a deep breath. This was going to be risky. 'Then,' he said, 'and now.'

There was a long pause.

Then Silverfish said, 'I really don't think there's any call for that.'

'I'm sorry, Mr Silverfish,' Victor pleaded. 'I'm really not that kind of person but you did say and I've walked all this way and I haven't got any money and I'm hungry and I'll do anything you've got. Anything at all. *Please*.'

Silverfish looked at him doubtfully.

'Even acting?' he said.

'Pardon?'

'Moving about and pretending to do things,' said Silverfish helpfully.

'Yes!'

'Seems a shame, a bright, well-educated lad like you,' said Silverfish. 'What do you do?'

'I'm studying to be a w—,' Victor began. He remembered Silverfish's antipathy towards wizardry, and corrected himself, 'a clerk.'

'A waclerk?' said Silverfish.

'I don't know if I'd be any good at acting, though,' Victor confessed.

Silverfish looked surprised. 'Oh, you'll be OK,' he said. 'It's very hard to be bad at acting in moving pictures.'

He fumbled in his pocket and pulled out a dollar coin.

'Here,' he said, 'go and get something to eat.'

He looked Victor up and down.

'Are you waiting for something?' he said.

'Well,' said Victor, 'I was hoping you could tell me what's going on.'

'How do you mean?'

'A couple of nights ago I watched your, your *click*,' he felt slightly proud of remembering the term, 'back in the city and suddenly I wanted to be here more than anything else. I've never really wanted anything in my life before!'

Silverfish's face broke into a relieved grin.

'Oh, that,' he said. 'That's just the magic of Holy Wood. Not wizard's magic,' he added hastily, 'which is all superstition and mumbo-jumbo. No. This is magic

57

for ordinary people. Your mind is fizzing with all the possibilities. I know mine was,' he added.

'Yes,' said Victor uncertainly. 'But how does it work?'

Silverfish's face lit up.

'You want to know?' he said. 'You want to know how things work?'

'Yes, I—'

'You see, most people are so disappointing,' Silverfish said. 'You show them something really wonderful like the picture box, and they just go "oh". They never ask how it works. Mr Bird!'

The last word was a shout. After a while a door opened on the far side of the shack and a man appeared.

He had a picture box on a strap round his neck. Assorted tools hung from his belt. His hands were stained with chemicals and he had no eyebrows, which Victor was later to learn was a sure sign of someone who had been around octo-cellulose for any length of time. He also had his cap on back to front.

'This is Gaffer Bird,' beamed Silverfish. 'Our head handleman. Gaffer, this is Victor. He's going to act for us.'

'Oh,' said Gaffer, looking at Victor in the same way that a butcher might look at a carcass. 'Is he?'

'And he wants to know how things work!' said Silverfish.

Gaffer gave Victor another jaundiced look.

'String,' he said gloomily. 'It all works by string. You'd be amazed how things'd fall to bits around here,' he said, 'if it weren't for me and my ball of string.'

There was a sudden commotion from the box round his neck. He thumped it with the flat of his hand.

'You lot can cut that out,' he said. He nodded at Victor.

'They gets fractious if their routine is upset,' he said.

'What's in the box?' said Victor.

Gaffer winked at Silverfish. 'I bet you'd like to know,' he said.

58

Victor remembered the caged things he'd seen in the shed.

'They sound like common demons,' he said cautiously.

Gaffer gave him an approving look, such as might be given to a stupid dog who had just done a rather clever trick.

'Yeah, that's right,' he conceded.

'But how do you stop them escaping?' said Victor.

Gaffer leered. 'Amazin' stuff, string,' he said.

Cut-me-own-Throat Dibbler was one of those rare people with the ability to think in straight lines.

Most people think in curves and zig-zags. For example, they start from a thought like: I wonder how I can become very rich, and then proceed along an uncertain course which includes thoughts like: I wonder what's for supper, and: I wonder who I know who can lend me five dollars?

Whereas Throat was one of those people who could identify the thought at the other end of the process, in this case *I am now very rich*, draw a line between the two, and then think his way along it, slowly and patiently, until he got to the other end.

Not that it worked. There was always, he found, some small but vital flaw in the process. It generally involved a strange reluctance on the part of people to buy what he had to sell.

But his life savings were now resting in a leather bag inside his jerkin. He'd been in Holy Wood for a day. He'd looked at its ramshackle organization, such as it was, with the eye of a lifelong salesman. There seemed nowhere in it for him, but this wasn't a problem. There was always room at the top.

A day's enquiries and careful observation had led him to Interesting and Instructive Kinematography. Now he stood on the far side of the street, watching carefully.

He watched the queue. He watched the man on the gate. He reached a decision.

He strolled along the queue. He had brains. He *knew* he had brains. What he needed now was muscle. Somewhere here there was bound to—

'Aft'noon, Mister Dibbler.'

That flat head, those rangy arms, that curling lower lip, that croaking voice that bespoke an IQ the size of a walnut. It added up to—

'It's me. Detritus,' said Detritus. 'Fancy seein' you here, eh?'

He gave Dibbler a grin like a crack appearing in a vital bridge support.

'Hallo, Detritus. You working in films?' said Dibbler.

'Not exactly working,' said Detritus, bashfully.

Dibbler looked quietly at the troll, whose chipped fists were generally the final word in any street fight.

'I call that disgusting,' he said. He pulled out his money bag and counted out five dollars. 'How would you like to work for me, Detritus?'

Detritus touched his jutting brow respectfully.

'Right you are, Mr Dibbler,' he said.

'Just step this way.'

Dibbler strolled back up to the head of the queue. The man at the door thrust out an arm to bar his way.

'Where d'you think you're going, pal?' he said.

'I have an appointment with Mr Silverfish,' said Dibbler.

'And he knows about this, does he?' said the guard, in tones that suggested that he personally would not believe it even if he saw it written on the sky.

'Not yet,' said Dibbler.

'Well, my friend, in that case you can just get yourself to—'

'Detritus?'

'Yes, Mr Dibbler?'

'Hit this man.'

'Right you are, Mr Dibbler.'

Detritus's arm whirled round in a 180 degree arc with oblivion on the end of it. The guard was lifted off his feet and smashed through the door, coming to a stop in its wreckage twenty feet away. There was a cheer from the queue.

Dibbler looked approvingly at the troll. Detritus was wearing nothing except a ragged loincloth which covered whatever it was that trolls felt it necessary to conceal.

'Very good, Detritus.'

'Right you are, Mr Dibbler.'

'But we shall have to see about getting you a suit,' said Dibbler. 'Now, please guard the gate. Don't let anyone in.'

'Right you are, Mr Dibbler.'

Two minutes later a small grey dog trotted through the troll's short and bandy legs and hopped over the remains of the gate, but Detritus didn't do anything about this because everyone knew dogs weren't anyone.

'Mr Silverfish?' said Dibbler.

Silverfish, who had been cautiously crossing the studio with a box of fresh film stock, hesitated at the sight of a skinny figure bearing down on him like a long-lost weasel. Dibbler's expression was the expression worn by something long and sleek and white as it swims over the reef and into the warm shallow waters of the kiddies' paddling area.

'Yes?' said Silverfish. 'Who're you? How did you get—'

'Dibbler's the name,' said Dibbler. 'But I'd like you to call me Throat.'

He clasped Silverfish's unresisting hand and then placed his other hand on the man's shoulder and stepped forward, pumping the first hand vigorously. The effect was of acute affability, and it meant that if Silverfish backed away he would dislocate his own elbow.

'And I'd just like you to know', Dibbler went on, 'that we're all incredibly impressed at what you boys are doing here.'

Silverfish watched his own hand being strenuously made friends with, and grinned uncertainly.

'You are?' he ventured.

'All this—', Dibbler released Silverfish's shoulder just long enough to expansively indicate the energetic chaos around them. 'Fantastic!' he said. 'Marvellous! And that last thing of yours, what was it called now—?'

'*High Jinks at the Store*,' said Silverfish. 'That's the one where the thief steals the sausages and the shop-keeper chases him?'

'Yeah,' said Dibbler, his fixed smile glazing for only a second or two before becoming truly sincere again. 'Yeah. That was it. Amazing! True genius! A beautifully sustained metaphor!'

'That cost us nearly twenty dollars, you know,' said Silverfish, with shy pride. 'And another forty pence for the sausages, of course.'

'Amazing!' said Dibbler. 'And it must have been seen by hundreds of people, yes?'

'Thousands,' said Silverfish.

There was no analogy for Dibbler's grin now. If it had managed to be any wider, the top of his head would have fallen off.

'Thousands?' he said. 'Really? That many? And of course they all pay you, oh, how much—?'

'Oh, we just take up a collection at the moment,' said Silverfish. 'Just to cover costs while we're still in the experimental stage, you understand.' He looked down. 'I wonder,' he added, 'could you stop shaking my hand now?'

Dibbler followed his gaze. 'Of course!' he said, and let go. Silverfish's hand carried on going up and down for a while of its own accord, out of sheer muscular spasm.

Dibbler was silent for a moment, his expression that of a man in deep communion with some inner god. Then he said, 'You know, Thomas – may I call you Thomas? – when I saw that masterpiece I thought, Dibbler, behind all this is a creative artist—'

'—how did you know my name was—'

'—a creative artist, I thought, who should be free to

pursue his muse instead of being burdened with all the fussy details of management, am I right?'

'Well . . . it's true that all this paperwork is a bit—'

'My thoughts exactly,' said Dibbler, 'and I said, Dibbler, you should go there right now and offer him your services. You know. Administrate. Take the load off his shoulders. Let him get on with what he does best, am I right? Tom?'

'I, I, I, yes, of course, it's true that my forte is really more in—'

'Right! Right!' said Dibbler. 'Tom, I accept!'

Silverfish's eyes were glassy.

'Er,' he said.

Dibbler punched him playfully on the shoulder. 'Just you show me the paperwork,' he said, 'and then you can get right out there and do whatever it is you do so well.'

'Er. Yes,' said Silverfish.

Dibbler grasped him by both arms and gave him a thousand watts of integrity.

'This is a proud moment for me,' he said hoarsely. 'I can't tell you how much this means to me. I can honestly say this is the happiest day of my life. I want you to know that. Tommy. Sincerely.'

The reverential silence was broken by a faint sniggering.

Dibbler looked around slowly. There was no-one behind them apart from a small grey mongrel dog sitting in the shade of a heap of lumber. It noticed his expression and put its head on one side.

'Woof?' it said.

Cut-me-own-Throat Dibbler looked around momentarily for something to throw, realized that this would be out of character, and turned back to the imprisoned Silverfish.

'You know,' he said sincerely, 'it's really lucky for me that I met you.'

Lunch in a tavern had cost Victor the dollar plus a couple of pence. It was a bowl of soup. Everything cost a lot, said the soup-seller, because it all had to be brought a long way.

There weren't any farms around Holy Wood. Anyway, who'd grow things when they could be making movies?

Then he reported to Gaffer for his screen test.

This consisted of standing still for a minute while the handleman watched him owlishly over the top of a picture box. After the minute had passed Gaffer said, 'Right. You're a natural, kid.'

'But I didn't do anything,' said Victor. 'You just told me not to move.'

'Yeah. Quite right. That's what we need. People who know how to stand still,' said Gaffer. 'None of this fancy acting like in the theatre.'

'But you haven't told me what the demons *do* in the box,' said Victor.

'They do *this*,' said Gaffer, unclicking a couple of latches. A row of tiny malevolent eyes glared out at Victor.

'These six demons here', he said, pointing cautiously to avoid the claws, 'look out through the little hole in the front of the box and paint pictures of what they see. There has to be six of them, OK? Two to paint and four to blow on it to get it dry. On account of the next picture coming down, see. That's because every time this handle *here* is turned, the strip of transparent membrane is wound down one notch for the next picture.' He turned the handle. It went *clickaclicka*, and the imps gibbered.

'What did they do that for?' said Victor.

'Ah,' said Gaffer, *'that's* because the handle also drives this little wheel with whips on. It's the only way to get them to work fast enough. He's a lazy little devil, your average imp. It's all feedback, anyway. The faster you turn the handle, the faster the film goes by, the faster they have to paint. You got to get the speed just right. Very important job, handlemanning.'

'But isn't it all rather, well, *cruel*?'

Gaffer looked surprised. 'Oh, no. Not really. I gets a rest every half an hour. Guild of Handlemen regulations.'

He walked further along the bench, where another box

stood with its back panel open. This time a cageful of sluggish-looking lizards blinked mournfully at Victor.

'We ain't very happy with this,' said Gaffer, 'but it's the best we can do. Your basic salamander, see, will lie in the desert all day, absorbing light, and when it's frightened it excretes the light again. Self-defence mechanism, it's called. So as the film goes past and the shutter here clicks backwards and forwards, their light goes out *through* the film and these lenses *here* and on to the screen. Basically very simple.'

'How do you make them frightened?' said Victor.

'You see this handle?'

'Oh.'

Victor prodded the picture box thoughtfully.

'Well, all right,' he said. 'So you get lots of little pictures. And you wind them fast. So we ought to see a blur, but we don't.'

'Ah,' said Gaffer, tapping the side of his nose. 'Handle-men's Guild secret, that is. Handed down from initiate to initiate,' he added importantly.

Victor gave him a sharp look. 'I thought people'd only been making movies for a few months,' he said.

Gaffer had the decency to look shifty. 'Well, OK, at the moment we're more sort of handing it *round*,' he admitted. 'But give us a few years and we'll soon be handing it down *don't touch that!*'

Victor jerked his hand back guiltily from the pile of cans on the bench.

'That's actual film in there,' said Gaffer, pushing them gently to one side. 'You got to be very careful with it. You mustn't get it too hot because it's made of octo-cellulose, and it don't like sharp knocks either.'

'What happens to it, then?' said Victor, staring at the cans.

'Who knows? No-one's ever lived long enough to tell us.' Gaffer looked at Victor's expression and grinned.

'Don't worry about *that*,' he said. 'You'll be in front of the moving-picture box.'

'Except that I don't know how to act,' said Victor.

'Do you know how to do what you're told?' said Gaffer.

'What? Well. Yes. I suppose so.'

'That's all you need, lad. That's all you need. That and big muscles.'

They stepped out into the searing sunlight and headed for Silverfish's shed.

Which was occupied.

Cut-me-own-Throat Dibbler was meeting the movies.

'What I thought', said Dibbler, 'is that, well, look. Something like this.'

He held up a card.

On it was written, in shaky handwriting:

> After thys perfromans, Why Notte Visit
> Harga's Hous of Ribs,
> For the Best inne Hawt Cuisyne

'What's hawt cuisyne?' said Victor.

'It's foreign,' said Dibbler. He scowled at Victor. Some-one like Victor under the same roof wasn't part of the plan. He'd been hoping to get Silverfish alone. 'Means food,' he added.

Silverfish stared at the card.

'What about it?' he said.

'Why don't you', said Dibbler, speaking very carefully, 'hold this card up at the end of the performance?'

'Why should we do that?'

'Because someone like Sham Harga will pay you a lo— quite a lot of money,' said Dibbler.

They stared at the card.

'I've eaten at Harga's House of Ribs,' said Victor. 'I wouldn't say it's the best. Not the best. A long way from being the best.' He thought for a bit. 'About as far away from being the best as you can get, in fact.'

'That doesn't matter,' said Dibbler sharply. 'That's not *important*.'

'But,' Silverfish said, 'if we went around saying Harga's House of Ribs was the best place in the city, what would all the other restaurants think?'

Dibbler leaned across the table.

'They'd think,' he said, ' "Why didn't we think of it first?" '

He sat back. Silverfish flashed him a look of bright incomprehension.

'Just run that past me one more time, will you?' he said.

'They'll want to do exactly the same thing!' said Dibbler.

'I know,' said Victor. 'They'll want us to hold up cards with things on like "Harga's Isn't the Best Place in Town, Actually, Ours Is".'

'Something like that, something like that,' snapped Dibbler, glaring at him. 'Maybe we can work on the words, but something like that.'

'But, but,' Silverfish fought to keep ahead of the conversation, 'Harga won't like it, will he? If he pays us money to say his place is best, and then we take money from other people to say that *their* place is best, then he's bound to—'

'Pay us more money,' said Dibbler, 'to say it again, only in larger letters.'

They stared at him.

'You really think that will work?' said Silverfish.

'Yes,' said Dibbler flatly. 'You listen to the street traders any morning. They don't shout, "Nearly-fresh oranges, only slightly squashy, reasonable value", do they? No, they shout, "Git chore orinjes, they're luvverly". Good business sense.'

He leaned across the desk again.

'Seems to me', he said, 'that you could do with some of that around here.'

'So it appears,' said Silverfish weakly.

'And with the money,' said Dibbler, his voice a crowbar inserted in the cracks in reality, 'you could really get on with perfecting your art.'

Silverfish brightened a bit. 'That's true,' he said. 'For example, some way of getting sound on—'

Dibbler wasn't listening. He pointed to a stack of boards leaning against the wall.

'What are those?' he said.

'Ah,' said Silverfish. 'That was *my* idea. We thought it would be, er, good business sense', he savoured the words as if they were some rare new sweet, 'to tell people about the other moving pictures we were making.'

Dibbler picked up one of the boards and held it critically at arm's length.

It said:

Nexte weke wee will be Shewing
Pelias and Melisande,
A Romantick Tragedie in Two Reels.
Thank you.

'Oh,' he said, flatly.

'Isn't that all right?' said Silverfish, now thoroughly beaten. 'I mean, it tells them everything they should know, doesn't it?'

'May I?' said Dibbler, taking a piece of chalk from Silverfish's desk. He scribbled intently on the back of the card for a while, and then turned it around.

Now it read:

Goddes and Men Saide It Was Notte To Bee, But They
Would Notte Listen!

Pelias and Melisande, A Storie of Forbiden Love!

A searing Sarger of Passion that Bridged Spaes and Tyme!

Thys wille shok you!

With a 1,000 elephants!

Victor and Silverfish read it carefully, as one reads a dinner menu in an alien language. This *was* an alien language, and to make it worse it was also their own.

'Well, well,' said Silverfish. 'My word . . . I don't know if there was anything actually *forbidden*. Er. It was just very historical. I thought it would help, you know, children and so on. Learn about history. They never actually met, you know, which was what was so tragic. It was all very, er, sad.' He stared at the card. 'Though I must say, you've certainly got something there. Er.' He looked uncomfortable about something. 'I don't actually remember any elephants,' he said, as if it was his own fault. 'I was there the whole afternoon we made it, and I don't recall a thousand elephants at any point. I'm sure I would have noticed.'

Dibbler stared. He didn't know where they were coming from, but now he was putting his mind to it he was getting some very clear ideas about what you needed to put in movies. A thousand elephants was a good start.

'No elephants?' he said.

'I don't think so.'

'Well, are there any dancing girls?'

'Um, no.'

'Well, are there any wild chases and people hanging by their fingertips from the edge of a cliff?'

Silverfish brightened up slightly. 'I think there's a balcony at one point,' he said.

'Yes? Does anyone hang on it by their fingertips?'

'I don't think so,' said Silverfish. 'I believe Melisande leans over it.'

'Yes, but will the audience hold their breath in case she falls off?'

'I *hope* they'd be watching Pelias' speech,' said Silverfish testily. 'We had to put it on five cards. In small writing.'

Dibbler sighed.

'I think I know what people want,' he said, 'and they don't want to read lots of small writing. They want spectacles!'

'Because of the small writing?' said Victor, sarcastically.

'They want dancing girls! They want thrills! They want elephants! They want people falling off roofs! They want dreams! The world is full of little people with big dreams!'

'What, you mean like dwarfs and gnomes and so on?' said Victor.

'No!'

'Tell me, Mr Dibbler,' said Silverfish, 'what exactly is your profession?'

'I sell merchandise,' said Dibbler.

'Mostly sausages,' Victor volunteered.

'*And* merchandise,' said Dibbler, sharply. 'I only sells sausages when the merchandising trade is a bit slow.'

'And the sale of sausages leads you to believe you can make better moving pictures?' said Silverfish. 'Anyone can sell sausages! Isn't that so, Victor?'

'Well . . . ' said Victor, reluctantly. No-one except Dibbler could possibly sell Dibbler's sausages.

'There you are, then,' said Silverfish.

'The thing is', said Victor, 'that Mr Dibbler can even sell sausages to people that have bought them off him *before*.'

'That's right!' said Dibbler. He beamed at Victor.

'And a man who could sell Mr Dibbler's sausages twice could sell anything,' said Victor.

The next morning was bright and clear, like all Holy Wood days, and they made a start on *The Interestinge and Curious Adventures of Cohen the Barbarian*. Dibbler had worked on it all evening, he said.

The title, however, was Silverfish's. Although Dibbler had assured him that Cohen the Barbarian was practically historical and certainly educational, Silverfish had held out against *Valley of Blud!*

Victor was handed what looked like a leather purse but which turned out to be his costume. He changed behind a couple of rocks.

He was also given a large, blunt sword.

70

'Now,' said Dibbler, who was sitting in a canvas chair, 'what you do is, you fight the trolls, rush up and untie the girl from the stake, fight the other trolls, and then run off behind that other rock over there. That's the way I see it. What do you say, Tommy?'

'Well, I—' Silverfish began.

'That's great,' said Dibbler. 'OK. Yes, Victor?'

'You mentioned trolls. What trolls?' said Victor.

The two rocks unfolded themselves.

'Don't you worry about a fing, mister,' said the nearest one. 'Me and ole Galena over there have got this down pat.'

'Trolls!' said Victor, backing away.

'That's right,' said Galena. He flourished a club with a nail in it.

'But, but,' Victor began.

'Yeah?' said the other troll.

What Victor would like to have said was: but you're *trolls*, fierce animated rocks that live in the mountains and bash travellers with huge clubs very similar to the ones you're holding now, and *I* thought when they said trolls they meant ordinary men dressed up in, oh, I don't know, sacking painted grey or something.

'Oh, good,' he said weakly. 'Er.'

'And don't you go listening to them stories about us eatin' people,' said Galena. 'That's a slander, that is. I mean, we're made of rock, what'd we want to eat people—'

'Swaller,' said the other troll. 'You mean swaller.'

'Yeah. What's we want to swaller people for? We always spit out the bits. And anyway we're retired from all that now,' he added quickly. 'Not that we ever did it.' He nudged Victor in a friendly fashion, nearly breaking one of his ribs. 'It's good here,' he said conspiratorially. 'We get three dollars a day plus a dollar barrier cream allowance for daylight working.'

'On account of turning to stone until nightfall otherwise, what is a pain,' said his companion.

71

'Yeah, an' it holds up shooting and people strike matches on you.'

'Plus our contract says we get five pence extra for use of own club,' said the other troll.

'If we could just get started—' Silverfish began.

'Why's there only two trolls?' complained Dibbler. 'What's heroic about fighting two trolls? I asked for twenty, didn't I?'

'Two's fine by me,' Victor called out.

'Listen, Mr Dibbler,' said Silverfish, 'I know you're trying to help, but the basic economics—'

Silverfish and Dibbler started to argue. Gaffer the handleman sighed and took the back off the moving-picture-box to feed and water the demons, who were complaining.

Victor leaned on his sword.

'Do a lot of this sort of thing, do you?' he said to the trolls.

'Yeah,' said Galena. 'All the time. Like, in *A King's Ransom*, I play a troll who rushed out an' hit people. An' in *The Dark Forest*, I play a troll who rushed out an' hit people. An', an', in *Mystery Mountain* I play a troll who rushed out, an' jumped up an' down on people. It doesn't pay to get type-cast.'

'And do you do the same thing?' said Victor, to the other troll.

'Oh, Morraine's a character actor, ain't you?' said Galena. 'Best in the business.'

'What does he play?'

'Rocks.'

Victor stared.

'On account of his craggy features,' Galena went on. 'Not just rocks. You should see him do an ancient monolith. You'd be *amazed*. Go on, Morry, show 'im yer inscription.'

'Nah,' said Morraine, grinning sheepishly.

'I'm thinking of changing my name for movin' pictures,' Galena went on. 'Somethin' with a bit o' class. I thought

"Flint".' He gave Victor a worried look, insofar as Victor was any judge of the range of expressions available to a face that looked as though it had been kicked out of granite with a pair of steel-toed boots. 'What you fink?' he said.

'Er. Very nice.'

'More *dynamic*, I fought,' said the prospective Flint.

Victor heard himself say: 'Or Rock. Rock's a nice name.'

The troll stared at him, its lips moving soundlessly as it tried out the alias.

'Cor,' he said. 'Never *fought* of that. *Rock*. I *like* that. I reckon I'd be due more'n three dollars a day, with a name like Rock.'

'Can we make a start?' said Dibbler sternly. 'Maybe we'll be able to afford more trolls if this is a successful click, but it won't be if we go over budget, which means we ought to wrap it up by lunchtime. Now, Morry and Galena—'

'Rock,' corrected Rock.

'Really? Anyway, you two rush out and attack Victor, OK. Right . . . *turn it* . . . '

The handleman turned the handle of the picture box. There was a faint clicking noise and a chorus of small yelps from the demons. Victor stood looking helpful and alert.

'That means you start,' said Silverfish patiently. 'The trolls rush out from behind the rocks, and you valiantly defend yourself.'

'But I don't know how to fight trolls!' Victor wailed.

'Tell you what,' said the newly-christened Rock. 'You parry first, and we'll sort of arrange not to hit you.'

Light dawned.

'You mean it's all *pretending*?' said Victor.

The trolls exchanged a brief glance, which nevertheless contrived to say: amazing, isn't it, that things like this apparently rule the world?

'Yeah,' said Rock. 'That's it. Nuffin's real.'

'We ain't allowed to kill you,' said Morraine reassuringly.

'That's right,' said Rock. 'We wouldn't go round killin' *you*.'

73

'They stops our money if we does things like that,' said Morraine, morosely.

Outside the fault in reality They clustered, peering in with something approaching eyes at the light and warmth. There was a crowd of them by now.

There had been a way through, once. To say that they remembered it would be wrong, because they had nothing as sophisticated as memory. They barely had anything as sophisticated as heads. But they did have instincts and emotions.

They needed a way in.

They found it.

It worked quite well, the sixth time. The main problem was the trolls' enthusiasm for hitting each other, the ground, the air and, quite often, themselves. In the end, Victor just concentrated on trying to hit the clubs as they whirred past him.

Dibbler seemed quite happy with this. Gaffer wasn't.

'They moved around too much,' he said. 'They were out of the picture half the time.'

'It was a *battle*,' said Silverfish.

'Yeah, but I can't move the picture box around,' said the handleman. 'The imps fall over.'

'Couldn't you strap them in or something?' said Dibbler.

Gaffer scratched his chin. 'I suppose I could nail their feet to the floor,' he said.

'Anyway, it'll do for now,' said Silverfish. 'We'll do the scene where you rescue the girl. Where's the girl? I distinctly instructed her to be here. Why isn't she here? Why doesn't anyone ever do what I tell them?'

The handleman took his cigarette stub out of his mouth.

'She's filmin' *A Bolde Adventurer* over the other side of the hill,' he volunteered.

'But that ought to have been finished yesterday!' wailed Silverfish.

'Film exploded,' said the handleman.

'Blast! Well, I suppose we can do the next fight. She doesn't have to be in it,' said Silverfish grumpily. 'All right, everybody. We'll do the bit where Victor fights the dreaded Balgrog.'

'What's a Balgrog?' said Victor.

A friendly but heavy hand tapped him on the shoulder.

'It's a traditional evil monster what is basically Morry painted green with wings stuck on,' said Rock. 'I'll jus' go an' help him with the paintin'.'

He lumbered off.

No-one seemed to want Victor at the moment.

He stuck the ridiculous sword into the sand, wandered away and found a bit of shade under some scrubby olive trees. There were rocks here. He tapped them gently. They didn't appear to be anyone.

The ground formed a cool little hollow that was almost pleasant by the seared standards of Holy Wood hill.

There was even a draught blowing from somewhere. As he leaned back against the stones he felt a cool breeze coming from them. Must be full of caves under here, he thought.

– far away in Unseen University, in a draughty, many pillar'd corridor, a little device that no-one had paid much attention to for years started to make a noise –

So this was Holy Wood. It hadn't looked like this on the silver screen. It seemed that moving pictures involved a lot of waiting around and, if he was hearing things right, a mixing-up of time. Things happened before the things they happened after. The monsters were just Morry painted green with wings stuck on. Nothing was really real.

Funnily enough, that was exciting.

'I've just about had enough of this,' said a voice beside him.

He looked up. A girl had come down the other path. Her face was red with exertion under the pale make-up, her hair hung over her eyes in ridiculous ringlets, and she wore a dress which, while clearly made for her size, was designed for someone who was ten years younger and keen on lace edging.

She was quite attractive, although this fact was not immediately apparent.

'And you know what they say when you complain?' she demanded. This was not really addressed to Victor. He was just a convenient pair of ears.

'I can't imagine,' said Victor politely.

'They say, "There's plenty of other people out there just waiting for a chance to get into moving pictures". That's what they say.'

She leaned against a gnarled tree and fanned herself with her straw hat. 'And it's too hot,' she complained. 'And now I've got to do a ridiculous one-reeler for Silverfish, who hasn't got the faintest idea. And some kid probably with bad breath and hay in his hair and a forehead you could lay a table on.'

'And trolls,' said Victor mildly.

'Oh *gods*. Not Morry and Galena?'

'Yes. Only Galena's calling himself Rock now.'

'I thought it was going to be Flint.'

'He likes Rock.'

From behind the rocks came the plaintive bleat of Silverfish wondering where everyone had got to just when he needed them. The girl rolled her eyes.

'Oh *gods*. For this I'm missing lunch?'

'You could always eat it off my forehead,' said Victor, standing up.

He had the satisfaction of feeling her thoughtful gaze on the back of his neck as he retrieved his sword and gave it a few experimental swishes, with rather more force than was necessary.

'You're the boy in the street, aren't you?' she said.

'That's right. You're the girl who was going to be shot,' said Victor. 'I see they missed.'

She looked at him curiously. 'How did you get a job so quickly? Most people have to wait weeks for a chance.'

76

'Chances are where you find them, I've always said,' said Victor.

'But *how*—'

Victor had already strolled away with gleeful nonchalance. She trailed after him, her face locked in a petulant pout.

'Ah,' said Silverfish sarcastically, looking up. 'My word. Everyone where they should be. Very well. We'll go from the bit where he finds her tied to the stake. What *you* do,' he said to Victor, 'is untie her, then drag her off and fight the Balgrog, and *you*,' he pointed to the girl, 'you, you, you just follow him and look as, as *rescued* as you possibly can, OK?'

'I'm good at that,' she said, resignedly.

'No, no, no,' said Dibbler, putting his head in his hands. 'Not that again!'

'Isn't that what you wanted?' said Silverfish. 'Fights and rescues?'

'There's got to be more to it than that!' said Dibbler.

'Like what?' Silverfish demanded.

'Oh, I don't know. Razzmatazz. Oomph. The old zonkaroonie.'

'Funny noises? We haven't got sound.'

'*Everyone* makes clicks about people running around and fighting and falling over,' said Dibbler. 'There should be something more. I've been looking at the things you make here, and they all look the same to me.'

'Well, all sausages look the same to me,' snapped Silverfish.

'*They're* meant to! That's what people expect!'

'And I'm giving them what they expect, too,' said Silverfish. 'People like to see more of what they expect. Fights and chases, that sort of thing—'

' 'Scuse me, Mister Silverfish,' said the handleman, above the angry chattering of the demons.

'Yes?' snapped Dibbler.

' 'Scuse me, Mister Dibbler, but I got to feed 'em ina quarter of a hour.'

Dibbler groaned.

In retrospect, Victor was always a little unclear about those next few minutes. That's the way it goes. The moments that change your life are the ones that happen suddenly, like the one where you die.

There had been another stylized battle, he knew that much, with Morry and what would have been a fearsome whip if the troll hadn't kept tangling it round his own legs. And, when the dreadful Balgrog had been beaten and had slid out of shot mugging terribly and trying to hold its wings on with one hand, he'd turned and cut the ropes holding the girl to the stake and should have dragged her sharply to the right when—

—the whispering started.

There were no words but there was something that was the heart of words, that went straight through his ears and down his spinal column without bothering to make a stopover in his brain.

He stared into the girl's eyes and wondered if she was hearing it too.

A long way off, there *were* words. There was Silverfish saying, 'Come on, get on with it, what are you looking at her like that for?' and the handleman saying, 'They gets really fractious if they misses a meal,' and Dibbler saying, in a voice hissing like a thrown knife, 'Don't stop turning the handle.'

The edges of his vision went cloudy, and there were shapes in the cloud that changed and faded before he had a chance to examine them. Helpless as a fly in an amber flow, as much in control of his destiny as a soap bubble in a hurricane, he leaned down and kissed her.

There were more words beyond the ringing in his ears.

'Why's he *doing* that? Did I tell him to do that? No-one told him to do that!'

'—and then I have to muck 'em out afterwards, and let me tell you, it's no—'

'*Turn that handle! Turn that handle!*' screamed Dibbler.

'Now why's he looking like *that*?'

'Cor!'

'If you stop turning that handle you'll never work in this town again!'

'Listen, mister, I happen to belong to the Handlemen's Guild—'

'Don't stop! Don't *stop*!'

Victor surfaced. The whispering faded, to be replaced by the distant boom of the breakers. The real world was back, hot and sharp, the sun pinned to the sky like a medal awarded for being a great day.

The girl took a deep breath.

'I'm, gosh, I'm terribly sorry,' babbled Victor, backing away. 'I really don't know what happened—'

Dibbler jumped up and down.

'That's it, that's *it*!' he yelled. 'How soon can you have it ready?'

'Well, like I said, I got to feed the imps and muck 'em out—'

'Right, right – it'll give me time to get some posters drawn,' said Dibbler.

'I've already had some done,' said Silverfish coldly.

'I bet you have, I bet you have,' said Dibbler, excitedly. 'I bet you have. I bet they say things like "You mighte like to see a Quite Interestinge Moving Picture"!'

'What's wrong with it?' Silverfish demanded. 'It's a bloody sight better than hot sausage!'

'I *told* you, when you sell sausages you don't just hang around waiting for people to *want* sausage, you go out there and make them hungry. *And* you put mustard on 'em. And that's what your lad there has done.'

He clapped one hand on Silverfish's shoulder, and waved the other expansively.

'Can't you see it?' he said. He hesitated. Strange ideas were pouring into his head faster than he could think them. He felt dizzy with excitement and possibilities.

'Sword of Passione,' he said. 'That's what we'll call it. Not name it after some daft old bugger who's probably

not even alive any more. *Sword of Passione*. Yeah. A Tumultuous Saga of – of Desire an' Raw, Raw, Raw *wossname* in the Primal Heat of a Tortured Continent! Romance! Glamour! In three Searing Reels! *Thrill* to the Death Fight with Ravening Monsters! *Scream* as a thousand elephants—'

'It's only one reel,' muttered Silverfish testily.

'Shoot some more this afternoon!' crowed Dibbler, his eyes revolving. 'You just need more fights and monsters!'

'And there's certainly no elephants,' snapped Silverfish.

Rock put up a craggy arm.

'Yes?' demanded Silverfish.

'If you've got some grey paint an' stuff to make the ears out of, I'm sure me an' Morry could—'

'*No-one's* ever done a three-reeler,' said Gaffer reflectively. 'Could be really tricky. I mean, it'd be nearly ten minutes long.' He looked thoughtful. 'I suppose if I was to make the spools bigger—'

Silverfish knew he was cornered.

'Now *look here*,' he began.

Victor stared down at the girl. Everyone else was ignoring them.

'Er,' he said, 'I don't think we've been formally introduced?'

'You didn't seem to let that stop you,' she said.

'I wouldn't normally do something like that. I must have been . . . ill. Or something.'

'Oh, good. And that makes me feel a lot better, does it?'

'Shall we sit in the shade? It's very hot out here.'

'Your eyes went all . . . smouldery.'

'Did they?'

'They looked really odd.'

'I *felt* really odd.'

'I know. It's this place. It gets to you. D'you know,' she said, sitting down on the sand, 'there's all kind of rules for the imps and things, they mustn't be worn out, what kind of food they get, stuff like that. No-one cares about us, though. Even the trolls get better treatment.'

'It's the way they go around being seven foot tall and weighing 1,000 lbs all the time, I expect,' said Victor.

'My name's Theda Withel, but my friends call me Ginger,' she said.

'My name's Victor Tugelbend. Er. But my friends call me Victor,' said Victor.

'This is your first click, is it?'

'How can you tell?'

'You looked as though you were enjoying it.'

'Well, it's better than working, isn't it?'

'You wait until you've been in it as long as I have,' she said bitterly.

'How long's that?'

'Nearly since the start. Five weeks.'

'Gosh. It's all happened so *fast*.'

'It's the best thing that's *ever* happened,' said Ginger flatly.

'I suppose so . . . er, are we allowed to go and eat?' said Victor.

'No. They'll be shouting for us again any minute,' said Ginger.

Victor nodded. He had, on the whole, got through life quite happily by doing what he pleased in a firm yet easy-going sort of way, and he didn't see why he should stop that even in Holy Wood.

'Then they'll have to shout,' he said. 'I want something to eat and a cool drink. Maybe I've just caught a bit too much sun.'

Ginger looked uncertain. 'Well, there's the commissary, but—'

'Good. You can show me the way.'

'They fire people just like that—'

'What, before the third reel?'

'They say "There's plenty more people who're dying to break into moving pictures", you see—'

'Good. That means they'll have all afternoon to find two

81

of them who look just like us.' He strolled past Morry, who was also trying to keep in the shade of a rock.

'If anyone wants us,' he said, 'we'll be having some lunch.'

'What, right now?' said the troll.

'Yes,' said Victor firmly, and strode on.

Behind him he could see Dibbler and Silverfish locked in heated discussion, with occasional interruptions from the handleman, who spoke in the leisurely tones of one who knows he's going to get paid six dollars today regardless.

'—we'll call it an epic. People will talk about it for ages.'

'Yes, they'll say we went bankrupt!'

'Look, I know where I can get some coloured woodcuts done at practically cost—'

'*—I was finking, maybe if I got some string and tied the moving picture box on to wheels, so it can be moved around—*'

'People'll say, that Silverfish, there's a moving-picture-smith with the guts to give the people what they want, they'll say. A man to roll back the wossname of the medium—'

'*—maybe if I was to make a sort of pole and swivel arrangement, we could bring the picture box right up close to—*'

'What? You think they'll say that?'

'Trust me, Tommy.'

'Well . . . all right. All right. But no elephants. I want to make that absolutely clear. No elephants.'

'Looks weird to me,' said the Archchancellor. 'Looks like a bunch of pottery elephants. Thought you said it was a machine?'

'More . . . more of a *device*,' said the Bursar uncertainly. He gave it a prod. Several of the pottery elephants wobbled. 'Riktor the Tinkerer built it, I think. It was before my time.'

It looked like a large, ornate pot, almost as high as a man of large pot height. Around its rim eight pottery

elephants hung from little bronze chains; one of them
swung backwards and forwards at the Bursar's touch.

The Archchancellor peered down inside.

'It's all levers and bellows,' he said, distastefully.

The Bursar turned to the University housekeeper.

'Well, now, Mrs Whitlow,' he said, 'what exactly
happened?'

Mrs Whitlow, huge, pink and becorseted, patted her
ginger wig and nudged the tiny maid who was hovering
beside her like a tugboat.

'Tell his lordship, Ksandra,' she ordered.

Ksandra looked as though she was regretting the whole
thing.

'Well, sir, please, sir, I was dusting, you see—'

'She hwas dusting,' said Mrs Whitlow, helpfully. When
Mrs Whitlow was in the grip of acute class consciousness
she could create aitches where nature never intended
them to be.

'—and then it started me'king a noise—'

'Hit made hay hnoise,' said Mrs Whitlow. 'So she come
and told me, your lordship, h'as hper my instructions.'

'What kind of noise, Ksandra?' said the Bursar, as
kindly as he could.

'Please, sir, sort of—' she screwed up her eyes,
' "whumm . . . whumm . . . whumm . . . whumm . . .
whummwhumm*whumm* WHUMM*WHUMM* – plib",
sir.'

'Plib,' said the Bursar, solemnly.

'Yes, sir.'

'Hplib,' echoed Mrs Whitlow.

'That was when it spat at me, sir,' said Ksandra.

'*Hexpectorated*,' corrected Mrs Whitlow.

'Apparently one of the elephants spat out a little lead
pellet, Master,' said the Bursar. 'That was the, er, the
"plib".'

'Did it, bigods,' said the Archchancellor. 'Can't have
pots going around gobbin' all over people.'

Mrs Whitlow twitched.

'What'd it go and do that for?' Ridcully added.

'I really couldn't say, Master. I thought perhaps you'd know. I believe Riktor was a lecturer here when you were a student. Mrs Whitlow is very concerned', he added, in tones that made it clear that when Mrs Whitlow was concerned about something it would be an unwise Archchancellor who ignored her, 'about staff being magically interfered with.'

The Archchancellor tapped the pot with his knuckles. 'What, old "Numbers" Riktor? Same fella?'

'Apparently, Archchancellor.'

'Total madman. Thought you could measure everythin'. Not just lengths and weights and that kind of stuff, but everythin'. "If it exists," he said, "you ought to be able to measure it."' Ridcully's eyes misted with memory. 'Made all kinds of weird widgets. Reckoned you could measure truth and beauty and dreams and stuff. So this is one of old Riktor's toys, is it? Wonder what it measured?'

'Ay think', said Mrs Whitlow, 'that it should be put haway somewhere out of 'arm's way, if it's hall the hsame to you.'

'Yes, yes, yes, of course,' said the Bursar hurriedly. Staff were hard to keep at Unseen University.

'Get rid of it,' said the Archchancellor.

The Bursar was horrified. 'Oh, no, sir,' he said. 'We *never* throw things out. Besides, it is probably quite valuable.'

'Hmm,' said Ridcully. 'Valuable?'

'Possibly an important historical artifact, Master.'

'Shove it in my study, then. I said the place needs bright'nin' up. It'll be one of them conversation pieces, right? Got to go now. Got to see a man about trainin' a gryphon. Good day, ladies—'

'Er, Archchancellor, I wonder if you could just sign—' the Bursar began, but to a closing door.

No-one asked Ksandra which of the pottery elephants had spat the ball, and the direction wouldn't have meant anything to them anyway.

That afternoon a couple of porters moved the universe's only working resograph[5] into the Archchancellor's study.

No-one had found a way to add sound to moving pictures, but there was a sound that was particularly associated with Holy Wood. It was the sound of nails being hammered.

Holy Wood had gone critical. New houses, new streets, new *neighbourhoods*, appeared overnight. And, in those areas where the hastily-educated alchemical apprentices were not yet fully alongside the trickier stages of making octo-cellulose, disappeared even faster. Not that it made a lot of difference. Barely would the smoke have cleared before someone was hammering again.

And Holy Wood grew by fission. All you needed was a steady-handed, non-smoking lad who could read alchemical signs, a handleman, a sackful of demons and lots of sunshine. Oh, and some people. But there were plenty of those. If you couldn't breed demons or mix chemicals or turn a handle rhythmically, you could always hold horses or wait on tables and look interesting while you hoped. Or, if all else failed, hammer nails. Building after rickety building skirted the ancient hill, their thin planks already curling and bleaching in the pitiless sun, but there was already a pressing need for more.

Because Holy Wood was calling. More people arrived every day. They didn't come to be ostlers, or tavern wenches, or short-order carpenters. They came to make movies.

And they didn't know why.

As Cut-me-own-Throat Dibbler knew in his heart, wherever two or more people are gathered together, someone will be trying to sell them a suspicious sausage in a bun.

Now that Dibbler was in fact engaged elsewhere, others had arisen to fulfil that function.

One such was Nodar Borgle the Klatchian, whose huge

---

[5] Lit.: 'Thingness-writer', or device for detecting and measuring disturbances in the fabric of reality.

echoing shed wasn't so much a restaurant as a feeding factory. Great steaming tureens occupied one end. The rest of it was tables, and around the tables were –

Victor was astonished.

– there were trolls, humans and dwarfs. And a few gnomes. And perhaps even a few elves, the most elusive of Discworld races. And lots of other things, which Victor had to hope were trolls dressed up, because if they weren't, everyone was going to be in a lot of trouble. And they were all eating, and the amazing thing was that they were not eating one another.

'You take a plate and you queue up and then you pay for it,' said Ginger. 'It's called self-serf.'

'You pay for it before you eat it? What happens if it's dreadful?'

Ginger nodded grimly. 'That's why.'

Victor shrugged, and leaned down to the dwarf behind the lunch counter. 'I'd like—'

'It's stoo,' said the dwarf.

'What kind of stew?'

'There ain't more'n one kind. That's why it's stoo,' the dwarf snapped. 'Stoo's stoo.'

'What I meant was, what's in it?' said Victor.

'If you need to ask, you're not hungry enough,' said Ginger. 'Two stews, Fruntkin.'

Victor stared at the grey-brown stuff that was dribbled on to his plate. Strange lumps, carried to the surface by mysterious convection currents, bobbed for a moment, and then sank back down, hopefully forever.

Borgle belonged to the Dibbler school of cuisine.

'It's stoo or nuffin, boy.' The cook leered. 'Half a dollar. Cheap at half the price.'

Victor handed over the money with reluctance, and looked around for Ginger.

'Over here,' said Ginger, sitting down at one of the long tables. 'Hi, Thunderfoot. Hi, Breccia, how's it goin'? This is Vic. New boy. Hi, Sniddin, didn't see you there.'

Victor found himself wedged between Ginger and a

mountain troll in what looked like chain mail, but it turned out to be just Holy Wood chain mail, which was inexpertly knitted string painted silver.

Ginger started talking animatedly to a four-inch-high gnome and a dwarf in one half of a bear outfit, leaving Victor feeling a little isolated.

The troll nodded at him, and then grimaced at its plate.

'Dey call dis pumice,' he said. 'Dey never even bother to cut der lava off. And you can't even taste der sand.'

Victor stared at the troll's plate.

'I didn't know trolls ate rock,' he said, before he could stop himself.

'Why not?'

'Aren't you made of it?'

'Yeah. But you're made a meat, an' what do *you* eat?'

Victor looked at his own plate. 'Good question,' he said.

'Vic's doing a click for Silverfish,' said Ginger, turning around. 'It looks like they're going to make it a three-reeler.'

There was a general murmur of interest.

Victor carefully laid something yellow and wobbly on the side of his plate.

'Tell me,' he said thoughtfully, 'while you've been filming, have any of you had a . . . heard a sort of . . . felt that you were . . . ' He hesitated. They were all looking at him. 'I mean, did you ever feel something was acting through you? I can't think of any other way to put it.'

His fellow diners relaxed.

'Dat's just Holy Wood,' said the troll. 'It gets to you. It's all dis creativity sloshin' about.'

'That was a pretty bad attack you had, though,' said Ginger.

'Happens all the time,' said the dwarf reflectively. 'It's just Holy Wood. Last week, me and the lads were working on *Tales of the Dwarfes* and suddenly we all started singing.

87

Just like that. Just like this song came into our heads, all at once. What d'you think of that?'

'What song?' said Ginger.

'Search me. We just call it the "Hiho" song. That's all it was. Hihohiho. Hihohiho.'

'Sound like every other dwarf song I ever did hear,' rumbled the troll.

It was past two o'clock when they got back to the moving-picture-making place. The handleman had the back off the picture box and was scraping at its floor with a small shovel.

Dibbler was asleep in his canvas chair with a handkerchief over his face. But Silverfish was wide awake.

'Where have you two been?' he shouted.

'I was hungry,' said Victor.

'And you'll jolly well *stay* hungry, my lad, because—'

Dibbler lifted the corner of his handkerchief.

'Let's get started,' he muttered.

'But we can't have performers telling us—'

'Finish the click, and *then* sack him,' said Dibbler.

'Right!' Silverfish waved a threatening finger at Victor and Ginger. 'You'll never work in this town again!'

They got through the afternoon somehow. Dibbler made them bring a horse in, and cursed the handleman because the picture box still couldn't be moved around. The demons complained. So they put the horse head-on in front of the box and Victor bounced up and down in the saddle. As Dibbler said, it was good enough for moving pictures.

Afterwards, Silverfish very grudgingly paid them two dollars each and dismissed them.

'He'll tell all the other alchemists,' said Ginger dispiritedly. 'They stick together like glue.'

'I notice we only get two dollars a day but the trolls get three,' said Victor. 'Why's that?'

'Because there aren't so many trolls wanting to make moving pictures,' said Ginger. 'And a good handleman can

88

get six or seven dollars a day. Performers aren't important.'
She turned and glared at him.

'I was doing OK,' she said. 'Nothing special, but OK.
I was getting quite a lot of work. People thought I was
reliable. I was building a career—'

'You can't build a career on Holy Wood,' said Victor.
'That's like building a house on a swamp. Nothing's
real.'

'I liked it! And now you've spoilt it all! And I'll probably
have to go back to a horrible little village you've probably never even heard of! Back to bloody milkmaiding!
Thanks very much! Every time I see a cow's arse, I'll
think of you!'

She stormed off in the direction of the town leaving
Victor with the trolls. After a while Rock cleared his
throat.

'You got anywhere to stay?' he said.

'I don't think so,' said Victor, weakly.

'There's never enough places to stay,' said Morry.

'I thought I might sleep on the beach,' said Victor. 'It's
warm enough, after all. I think I really could do with a
good rest. Good night.'

He tottered off in that direction.

The sun was setting, and a wind off the sea had cooled
things a little. Around the darkening bulk of the hill the
lights of Holy Wood were being lit. Holy Wood only relaxed in the darkness. When your raw material is daylight,
you don't waste it.

It was pleasant enough on the beach. No-one much went
there. The driftwood, cracked and salt-crusted, was no
good for building. It was stacked in a long white row on
the tide line.

Victor pulled together enough to make a fire, and lay
back and watched the surf.

From the top of the next dune, hidden behind a dry
clump of grass, Gaspode the Wonder Dog watched him
thoughtfully.

*

It was two hours after midnight.

It had them now, and poured joyfully out of the hill, poured its glitter into the world.

Holy Wood dreams . . .

It dreams for everyone.

In the hot breathless darkness of a clapboard shack, Ginger Withel dreamed of red carpets and cheering crowds. And a grating. She kept coming back to a grating, in the dream, where a rush of warm air blew up her skirts . . .

In the not much cooler darkness of a marginally more expensive shack, Silverfish the moving picturesmith dreamed of cheering crowds, and someone giving him a prize for the best moving picture ever made. It was a great big statue.

Out in the sand dunes Rock and Morry dozed fitfully, because trolls are night creatures by nature and sleeping in darkness bruised the instincts of eons. They dreamed of mountains.

Down on the beach, under the stars, Victor dreamed of pounding hooves, flowing robes, pirate ships, sword fights, chandeliers . . .

On the next dune, Gaspode the Wonder Dog slept with one eye open and dreamed of wolves.

But Cut-me-own-Throat Dibbler was not dreaming, because he was not asleep.

It had been a long ride to Ankh-Morpork and he preferred selling horses to riding them, but he was there now.

The storms that so carefully avoided Holy Wood didn't worry about Ankh-Morpork, and it was pouring with rain. That didn't stop the city's night life, though – it just made it damper.

There was nothing you couldn't buy in Ankh-Morpork, even in the middle of the night. Dibbler had a lot of things to buy. He needed posters painted. He needed all sorts of things. Many of them involved ideas he'd had to invent in his head on the long ride, and now had to explain very carefully to other people. And he had to explain it fast.

The rain was a solid curtain when he finally staggered

out into the grey light of dawn. The gutters overflowed. Along the rooftops, repulsive gargoyles threw up expertly over passers-by although, since it was now five a.m., the crowds had thinned out a bit.

Throat took a deep breath of the thick city air. *Real* air. You would have to go a long way to find air that was realer than Ankh-Morpork air. You could tell just by breathing it that other people had been doing the same thing for thousands of years.

For the first time in days he felt that he was thinking clearly. That was the strange thing about Holy Wood. When you were there it all seemed natural, it all seemed just what life was all about, but when you got away from it and looked back, it was like looking at a brilliant soap bubble. It was as though, when you were in Holy Wood, you weren't quite the same person.

Well, Holy Wood was Holy Wood, and Ankh was Ankh, and Ankh was solid and proof, in Throat's opinion, against any Holy Wood weirdness.

He splashed through the puddles, listening to the rain.

After a while he noticed, for the first time in his life, that it had a rhythm.

Funny. You could live in a city all your life, and you had to go away and come back again before you noticed the way the rain dripping off the gutters had a rhythm all its own: DUMDi-dum-dum, dumdi-dumdi-DUM-DUM . . .

A few minutes later Sergeant Colon and Corporal Nobbs of the Night Watch were sharing a friendly roll-up in the shelter of a doorway and doing what the Night Watch was best at, which was keeping warm and dry and staying out of trouble.

They were the only witnesses to the manic figure which splashed down the dripping street, pirouetted through the puddles, grabbed a drainpipe to swing around the corner and, clicking its heels together merrily, disappeared from view.

Sgt Colon handed the soggy dog-end back to his companion.

'Was that old Throat Dibbler?' he said after a while.

'Yeah,' said Nobby.

'He looked happy, didn't he?'

'Must be off 'is nut, if you ask me,' said Nobby. 'Singing in the rain like that.'

Whumm . . . whumm . . .

The Archchancellor, who had been updating his dragon stud book and enjoying a late night drink in front of the fire, looked up.

. . . whumm . . . whumm . . . whumm . . .

'Bigods!' he muttered, and wandered over to the big pot. It was actually wobbling from side to side, as if the building was shaking.

The Archchancellor watched, fascinated.

. . . whumm . . . whumm*whummwhummWHUMM*.

It wobbled to a standstill, and went silent.

'Odd,' said the Archchancellor. 'Damned odd.'

Plib.

On the other side of the room, his brandy decanter shattered.

Ridcully the Brown took a deep breath.

'Burs*aar*!'

Victor was woken up by sandflies. The air was already warm. It was going to be another fine day.

He waded out into the shallows to wash and clear his head.

Let's see . . . he still had his two dollars from yesterday, plus a handful of pennies. He could afford to stay a while, especially if he slept on the beach. And Borgle's stoo, while only food in the technical sense, was cheap enough – although, come to think of it, eating there might involve embarrassing encounters with Ginger.

He took another step, and sank.

Victor hadn't swum in the sea before. He surfaced, half-drowned, treading water furiously. The beach was only a few yards away.

He relaxed, gave himself time to get his breath back, and swam a leisurely crawl out beyond the breakers. The water was crystal clear. He could see the bottom shelving away sharply to – he surfaced for a quick breath – a dim blueness in which it was just possible, through the teeming shoals of fish, to see the outline of pale, rectangular rocks scattered on the sand.

He tried a dive, fighting his way down until his ears clanged. The largest lobster he had ever seen waved its feelers at him from a rocky spire and snapped away into the depths.

Victor bobbed up again, gasping, and struck out for the shore.

Well, if you couldn't make it in moving pictures there was an opening here for a fisherman, that was certain.

A beachcomber would do all right, as well. There was enough wind-dried firewood piled up on the edge of the dunes to keep Ankh-Morpork's fires supplied for years. No-one in Holy Wood would dream of lighting a fire except for cooking or company.

And someone had been doing just that. As he waded ashore Victor realized that the wood further along the beach had been stacked not haphazardly but apparently by design, in neat piles. Further along, stones had been stacked into a crude fireplace.

It was clogged with sand. Maybe someone else had been living on the beach, waiting for their big chance in moving pictures. Come to think of it, the timber behind the half-buried stones had a dragged-together look. You could imagine, looking at it from the sea, that several balks of timber had been set up to form an arched doorway.

Perhaps they were still there. Perhaps they might have something to drink.

They were, indeed, still there. But they hadn't needed a drink for months.

It was eight in the morning. A thunderous knocking

awoke Bezam Planter, owner of the *Odium*, one of Ankh-Morpork's mushrooming crop of moving-picture pits.

He'd had a bad night. The people of Ankh-Morpork liked novelty. The trouble was that they didn't like novelty for long. The *Odium* had done great business for a week, had broken even for the next week, and was now dying. The late showing last night had been patronized by one deaf dwarf and an orang-utan, who'd brought along its own peanuts. Bezam relied on the sale of peanuts and banged grains for his profit, and wasn't in a good mood.

He opened the door and stared out blearily.

'We're shut 'til two o'clock,' he said. 'Mat'nee. Come back then. Seats in all parts.'

He slammed the door. It rebounded off Throat Dibbler's boot and hit Bezam on the nose.

'I've come about the special showing of *Sword of Passione*,' said Throat.

'Special showing? What special showing?'

'The special showing I'm about to tell you about,' said Throat.

'We ain't showing nothin' about any special passionate swords. We're showin' *The Exciting—*'

'Mister Dibbler says yore showing *Sword of Passione*,' rumbled a voice.

Throat leaned against the doorway. Behind him was a slab of rock. It looked as though someone had been throwing steel balls at it for thirty years.

It creased in the middle and leaned down towards Bezam.

He recognized Detritus. Everyone recognized Detritus. He wasn't a troll you forgot.

'But I haven't even *heard* of—' Bezam began.

Throat pulled a large tin from under his coat, and grinned.

'And here are some posters,' he added, producing a fat white roll.

'Mister Dibbler let me stick some up on walls,' said Detritus proudly.

Bezam unrolled the poster. It was in eye-watering

94

colours. It showed a picture of what might just possibly be Ginger pouting in a blouse too small for her, and Victor in the act of throwing her over one shoulder while fighting an assortment of monsters with the other hand. In the background, volcanoes were erupting, dragons were zooming through the sky, and cities were burning down.

' "The Motione-Picture They Coud Not Banne!" ', read Bezam hesitantly. ' "A Scorching Adventure In the White-Hotte Dawne of A New Continont! A Mann and a Womann Throne Together in the Wherlpool of a World Gone Madde!! STARING **Delores De Syn** as The Woman and **Victor Maraschino** as Cohen the Barbarian!!! THRILS! ADVENTURE!! ELEPHANTS!!! Cominge Soone to A Pit nr. You!!!!" '

He read it again.

'Who's Staring Delores De Syn?' he said, suspiciously.

'That's *starring*,' said Throat. 'That's why we've put stars against their names, see.' He leaned closer and lowered his voice to a piercing whisper. 'They do say', he said, 'that she's the daughter of a Klatchian pirate and his wild, headstrong captive, and *he's* the son of . . . the son of . . . a rogue wizard and a reckless gypsy flamenco dancer.'

'Cor!' said Bezam, impressed despite himself. Dibbler permitted himself a mental slap on the back. He'd been quite taken with it himself.

'I reckon you should start showing it in about an hour,' he said.

'At this time in the morning?' said Bezam. The click he had obtained for the day was *An Exciting Study of Pottery Making*, which had been worrying him. This seemed a much better proposition.

'Yes,' said Dibbler. 'Because a lot of people are going to want to watch it.'

'I dunno about that,' said Bezam. 'Houses have been falling off lately.'

'They'll want to watch this one,' said Throat. 'Trust me. Have I ever lied to you?'

Bezam scratched his head. 'Well, one night last month you sold me a sausage in a bun and you said—'

'I was speaking rhetorically,' snapped Throat.

'Yeah,' said Detritus.

Bezam sagged. 'Oh. Well. I dunno about rhetorically,' he said.

'Right,' said Throat, grinning like a predatory pumpkin. 'Just you open up, and you can sit back and rake in the money.'

'Oh. Good,' said Bezam weakly.

Throat put a friendly arm around the man's shoulders. 'And now,' he said, 'let's talk about percentages.'

'What're percentages?'

'Have a cigar,' said Throat.

Victor walked slowly up Holy Wood's nameless main street. There was packed sand under his fingernails.

He wasn't sure that he had done the right thing.

Probably the man had just been some old beachcomber who'd just gone to sleep one day and hadn't woken up, although the stained red and gold coat was unusual beachcombing wear. It was hard to tell how long he'd been dead. The dryness and salt air had been a preservative; they'd preserved him just the way he must have looked when he was alive, which was like someone who was dead.

By the look of his hut, he'd beachcombed some odd stuff.

It had occurred to Victor that someone ought to be told, but there was probably no-one in Holy Wood who would be interested. Probably only one person in the world had been interested in whether the old man lived or died, and he'd been the first to know.

Victor buried the body in the sand, landward of the driftwood hut.

He saw Borgle's ahead of him. He'd risk breakfast there, he decided. Besides, he needed somewhere to sit down and read the book.

It wasn't the sort of thing you expected to find on a beach, in a driftwood hut, clutched in the hand of a dead man.

On the cover were the words *The Boke of the Film*.

On the first page, in the neat round hand of someone to whom writing doesn't come easily, were the further words: This is the Chroncal of the Keeprs of the ParaMountain coppied out by me Deccan Beacuase Of the old onne it being fallin Apart.

He turned the stiff pages carefully. They seemed to be crammed with almost identical entries. They were all undated, but that wasn't very important, since one day had been pretty much like the other.

Gott up. Went to lavatry. Made up fire, announused the Matinee Performanse. Broke fast. Colected woode. Made up fire. Foraged on the hille. Chanted the Evening Performansee. Supper. Sed the Late-Nite Performanse chant. Wnet to lavatry. Bed.

Gott up. Went to lavatry. Made up fire, sed the Matinee Performanse. Broke fast. Crullet the fisheman from Jowser Cove have left 2 fyne see bass. Clected woode. Heralded the Evewning Performanse, made up fire. Howskeepeing. Supper. Chanted the Late Night performanse. Bed. Gott up at Midnigte, went to lavaotry, checked fire, but it was not Needful of Woode.

He saw the waitress out of the tail of his eye.

'I'd like a boiled egg,' he said.

'It's stew. Fish stew.'

He looked up into Ginger's blazing eyes.

'I didn't know you were a waitress,' he said.

She made a show of dusting the salt bowl. 'Nor did I until yesterday,' she said. 'Lucky for me Borgle's regular morning girl got a chance in the new moving picture that Untied Alchemists are making, isn't it?' She shrugged. 'If I'm really lucky, who knows? I might get to do the afternoon shift too.'

'Look, I didn't mean—'

'It's stew. Take it or leave it. Three customers this morning have done both.'

'I'll take it. Look, you won't believe it, but I found this book in the hands of—'

'I'm not allowed to dally with customers. This isn't the best job in town, but you're not losing it for me,' snapped Ginger. 'Fish stew, right?'

'Oh. Right. Sorry.'

He flicked backwards through the pages. Before Deccan there was Tento, who also chanted three times a day and also sometimes received gifts of fish and also went to the lavatory, although either he wasn't so assiduous about it as Deccan or hadn't thought it always worth writing down. Before that, someone called Meggelin had been the chanter. A whole string of people had lived on the beach, and then if you went back further there was a group of them, and further still the entries had a more official feel. It was hard to tell. They seemed to be written in code, line after line of little complex pictures . . .

A bowl of primal soup was plonked down in front of him.

'Look,' he said. 'What time do you get off—'

'Never,' said Ginger.

'I just wondered if you might know where—'

'No.'

Victor stared at the murky surface of the broth. Borgle worked on the principle that if you find it in water, it's a fish. There was something purple in there and it had at least ten legs.

He ate it anyway. It was costing him thirty pence.

Then, with Ginger resolutely busying herself at the counter with her back to him lighthouse-fashion, so that however he tried to attract her attention her back was still facing him without her apparently moving, he went to look for another job.

Victor had never worked for anything in his life. In his experience, jobs were things that happened to other people.

Bezam Planter adjusted the tray around his wife's neck.

'All right,' he said. 'Got everything?'

'The banged grains have gone soft,' she said. 'And there's no way to keep the sausages hot.'

'It'll be dark, love. No-one'll notice.' He tweaked the strap and stood back.

'There,' he said. 'Now, you know what to do. Halfway through I'll stop showing the film and put up the card that says "Wy not Try a Cool Refreshinge Drinke and Some Banged Grains?" and then you come out of the door over there and walk up the aisle.'

'You might as well mention cool refreshing sausages as well,' said Mrs Planter.

'And I reckon you should stop using a torch to show people to their seats,' said Bezam. 'You're starting too many fires.'

'It's the only way I can see in the dark,' she said.

'Yes, but I had to let that dwarf have his money back last night. You know how sensitive they are about their beards. Tell you what, love, I'll give you a salamander in a cage. They've been on the roof since dawn, they should be nice and ready.'

They were. The creatures lay dozing in the bottom of their cages, their bodies vibrating gently as they absorbed the light. Bezam selected six of the ripest, climbed heavily back down to the projection room, and tipped them into the showing-box. He wound Throat Dibbler's film on to a spool, and then peered out into the darkness.

Oh, well. Might as well see if there was anyone outside.

He shuffled to the front door, yawning.

He reached up, and slid the bolt.

He reached down, and slid the other bolt.

He pulled open the doors.

'All right, all right,' he grumbled. 'Let's be having you . . .'

He woke up in the projection room, with Mrs Planter fanning him desperately with her apron.

'What happened?' he whispered, trying to put out of his mind the memories of trampling feet.

'It's a full house!' she said. 'And they're still queueing

up outside! They're all down the street! It's them disgusting posters!'

Bezam got up unsteadily but with determination.

'Woman, shut up and get down to the kitchen and bang some more grains!' he shouted. 'And then come and help me repaint the signs! If they're queueing for the fivepenny seats, they'll queue for tenpence!'

He rolled up his sleeves and grasped the handle.

In the front row the Librarian sat with a bag of peanuts in his lap. After a few minutes he stopped chewing and sat with his mouth open, staring and staring and staring at the flickering images.

'Hold your horse, sir? Ma'am?'

'No!'

By mid-day Victor had earned tuppence. It wasn't that people didn't have horses that needed holding, it was just that they didn't seem to want him to hold them.

Eventually a gnarled little man from further along the street sidled up to him, dragging four horses. Victor had been watching him for hours, in frank astonishment that anyone should give the wizened homunculus a kindly smile, let alone a horse. But he'd been doing a brisk trade, while Victor's broad shoulders, handsome profile and honest, open smile were definitely a drawback in the horse-holding business.

'You're new to this, right?' said the little man.

'Yes,' said Victor.

'Ah. I could tell. Waitin' for yer big break in the clicks, right?' He grinned encouragingly.

'No. I've had my big break, in fact,' said Victor.

'Why you here then?'

Victor shrugged. 'I broke it.'

'Ah, is that so? Yessir, thank'ee sir, godsblessyousir, rightchewaresir,' said the man, accepting another set of reins.

'I suppose you don't need an assistant?' said Victor wistfully.

★

Bezam Planter stared at the pile of coins in front of him. Throat Dibbler moved his hands and it was a smaller pile of coins, but it was still a bigger pile of coins than Bezam had ever seen while in a waking state.

'And we're still showing it every quarter of an hour!' breathed Bezam. 'I've had to hire a boy to turn the handle! I don't know, what should I do with all this money?'

Throat patted him on the shoulder.

'Buy bigger premises,' he said.

'I've been thinking about that,' said Bezam. 'Yeah. Something with fancy pillars out in front. And my daughter Calliope plays the organ really nice, it'd make a good accompaniment. And there should be lots of gold paint and curly bits—'

His eyes glazed.

It had found another mind.

Holy Wood dreams.

– and make it a palace, like the fabulous Rhoxie in Klatch, or the richest temple there ever was, with slave girls to sell the banged grains and peanuts, and Bezam Planter walking about proprietorially in a red velvet jacket with gold string on it –

'Hmm?' he whispered, as the sweat beaded on his forehead.

'I said, I'm off,' said Throat. 'Got to keep moving in the moving-picture business, you know.'

'Mrs Planter says you've got to make more pictures with that young man,' said Bezam. 'The whole city's talking about him. She said several ladies swooned when he gave them that smouldery look. She watched it five times,' he added, his voice rimed with sudden suspicion. 'And that girl! Wow!'

'Don't you worry about a thing,' said Throat loftily. 'I've got them under contr—'

Sudden doubt drifted across his face.

'See you,' he said shortly, and scurried out of the building.

Bezam stood alone and looked around at the cobwebbed

101

interior of the *Odium*, his overheated imagination peopling its dark corners with potted palms, gold leaf and fat cherubs. Peanut shells and banged grain bags crunched under his feet. Have to get it cleaned up for the next house, he thought. I expect that monkey'll be first in the queue again.

Then his eye fell on the poster for *Sword of Passione*. Amazing, really. There hadn't been much in the way of elephants and volcanoes, and the monsters had been trolls with bits stuck on them, but in that close up . . . well . . . all the men had sighed, and then all the women had sighed . . . It was like magic. He grinned at the images of Victor and Ginger.

Wonder what those two're doing now? he thought. Prob'ly eating caviar off of gold plates and lounging around up to their knees in velvet cushions, you bet.

'You look up to your knees in it, lad,' said the horse-holder.

'I'm afraid I'm not getting the hang of this horse-holding,' said Victor.

'Ah, 'tis a hard trade, horse-holding,' said the man. 'It's learning the proper grovellin' and the irreverent-but-not-too-impudent cheery 'oss-'older's banter. People don't just want you to look after the 'oss, see. They want a 'oss-'olding hexperience.'

'They do?'

'They want an amusin' encounter and a soup-son of repartee,' said the little man. 'It's not just a matter of 'oldin' reins.'

Realization began to dawn on Victor.

'It's a performance,' he said.

The 'oss-'older tapped the side of his strawberry-shaped nose.

'That's right!' he said.

Torches flared in Holy Wood. Victor struggled through the crowds in the main street. Every bar, every tavern, every shop had its doors thrown open. A sea of people ebbed and flowed between them. Victor tried jumping up and down to search the mob of faces.

He was lonely and lost and hungry. He needed someone to talk to, and she wasn't there.

'Victor!'

He spun around. Rock bore down on him like an avalanche.

'Victor! My friend!' A fist the size and hardness of a foundation stone pounded him playfully on the shoulder.

'Oh, hi,' said Victor weakly. 'Er. How's it going, Rock?'

'Great! Great! Tomorrow we shoot *Bad Menace of Troll Valley*!'

'I'm very happy for you,' said Victor.

'You my lucky human!' Rock boomed. 'Rock! What a name! Come and have a drink!'

Victor accepted. He really didn't have much of a choice, because Rock gripped his arm and, ploughing through the crowds like an icebreaker, half-led, half-dragged him towards the nearest door.

A blue light illuminated a sign. Most Morporkians could read Troll, it was hardly a difficult language. The sharp runes spelled out *The Blue Lias*.

It was a troll bar.

The smoky glow from the furnaces beyond the slab counter was the only light. It illuminated three trolls playing – well, something percussive, but Victor couldn't quite make out what because the decibel level was in realms where the sound was a solid force, and it made his eyeballs vibrate. The furnace smoke hid the ceiling.

'What you havin'?' roared Rock.

'I don't have to drink molten metal, do I?' Victor quavered. He had to quaver at the top of his voice in order to be heard.

'We got all typer human drink!' shouted the female troll behind the bar. It had to be a female. There was no doubt about it. She looked slightly like the statues cavemen used to carve of fertility goddesses thousands of years ago, but mostly like a foothill. 'We very cosmopolitan.'

'I'll have a beer, then!'

'Ana flowers-of-sulphur onna rocks, Ruby!' added Rock.

Victor took the opportunity to look around the bar, now that he was getting accustomed to the gloom and his eardrums had mercifully gone numb.

He was aware of masses of trolls seated at long tables, with here and there a dwarf, which was astonishing. Dwarfs and trolls normally fought like, well, dwarfs and trolls. In their native mountains there was a state of unremitting vendetta. Holy Wood certainly changed things.

'Can I have a quiet word?' Victor shouted in Rock's pointed ear.

'Sure!' Rock put down his drink. It contained a purple paper umbrella, which was charring in the heat.

'Have you seen Ginger? You know? Ginger?'

'She working at Borgle's!'

'Only in the mornings! I've just been there! Where does she go when she's not working?'

'Who know where anyone go?'

There was a sudden silence from the combo in the smoke. One of the trolls picked up a small rock and started to pound it gently, producing a slow, sticky rhythm that clung to the walls like smoke. And from the smoke, Ruby emerged like a galleon out of the fog, with a ridiculous feather boa around her neck.

It was continental drift with curves.

She began to sing.

The trolls stood in respectful silence. After a while Victor heard a sob. Tears were rolling down Rock's face.

'What's the song about?' he whispered.

Rock leaned down.

'Is ancient folklorique troll song,' he said. 'Is about Amber and Jasper. They were—' he hesitated, and waved his hands about vaguely. 'Friends. Good friends?'

'I think I know what you mean,' said Victor.

'And one day Amber takes her troll's dinner down to the

cave and finds him—' Rock waved his hands in vague yet thoroughly descriptive motions '—with another lady troll. So she go home and get her club and come back and beat him to death, thump, thump, thump. 'Cos he was her troll and he done her wrong. Is very romantic song.'

Victor stared. Ruby undulated down from the tiny stage and glided among the customers, a small mountain in a four-wheel skid. She must weigh two tons, he thought. If she sits on my knee they'll have to roll me off the floor like a carpet.

'What did she just say to that troll?' he said, as a deep wave of laughter rolled across the room.

Rock scratched his nose. 'Is play on words,' he said. 'Very hard to translate. But basically, she say "Is that the legendary Sceptre of Magma who was King of the Mountain, Smiter of Thousands, Yea, Even Tens of Thousands, Ruler of the Golden River, Master of the Bridges, Delver in Dark Places, Crusher of Many Enemies",' he took a deep breath, '"in your pocket or are you just glad to see me?"'

Victor's forehead creased.

'I don't get it,' he said.

'Perhaps I not translate properly,' said Rock. He took a pull of molten sulphur. 'I hear Untied Alchemists is casting for—'

'Rock, there's something very odd about this place,' said Victor urgently. 'Can't you feel it?'

'What odd?'

'Everything seems to, well, *fizz*. No-one acts like they should. Did you know there was a great city here once? Where the sea is. A great city. And it's just gone!'

Rock rubbed his nose thoughtfully. It looked like a Neanderthal Man's first attempt at an axe.

'And there's the way everyone acts!' said Victor. 'As if who they are and what they want are the most important things in the world!'

'I'm wondering—' Rock began.

'Yes?' said Victor.

'I'm wondering, would it be worth takin' half a inch off my nose? My cousin Breccia knows this stonemason, fixed his ears a treat. What do you fink?'

Victor stared dully at him.

'I mean, on the one hand, it's too big, but on the other hand, it's definit'ly your stereotyped troll nose, right? I mean, maybe I'll *look* better, but in this business maybe it best to look just as troll as you can. Like, Morry's had his touched up with cement, now he got a face you wouldn't want to meet on a dark night. What you fink? I value your opinion, because you a human with ideas.'

He gave Victor a bright silicon smile.

Eventually Victor said: 'It's a great nose, Rock. With you behind it, it could go a long way.'

Rock gave a big grin, and took another pull of sulphur. He extracted a small steel swizzle stick and sucked the amethyst off it.

'You really fink—' he began, and was then aware of the small area of empty space. Victor had gone.

'I don't know nuffin about no-one,' said the horse-holder, looking shiftily at the looming presence of Detritus.

Dibbler chewed on his cigar. It had been a bumpy journey from Ankh, even in his new coach, and he'd missed lunch.

'Tall lad, bit dopey, thin moustache,' he said. 'He was working for you, right?' The horse-holder gave in.

'He'll never make a good 'oss-'older, anyway,' he said. 'Lets his work get on top of him. I think he went to get something to eat.'

Victor sat in the dark alley, his back pressed against the wall, and tried to think.

He remembered staying out in the sun too long, once, when he was a boy. The feeling he'd got afterwards was something like this.

There was a soft flopping noise in the packed sand by his feet.

Someone had dropped a hat in front of him. He stared at it.

Then someone started playing the harmonica. They weren't very good at it. Most of the notes were wrong, and those that were right were cracked. There was a tune in there somewhere, in the same way that there's a bit of beef in a hamburger grinder.

Victor sighed and fumbled in his pocket for a couple of pennies. He tossed them into the hat.

'Yeah, yeah,' he said. 'Very good. Now go away.'

He was aware of a strange smell. It was hard to place, but could perhaps have been a very old and slightly damp nursery rug.

He looked up.

'Woof bloody woof,' said Gaspode the Wonder Dog.

Borgle's commissary had decided to experiment with salads tonight. The nearest salad growing district was thirty slow miles away.

'What dis?' demanded a troll, holding up something limp and brown.

Fruntkin the short-order chef hazarded a guess.

'Celery?' he said. He peered closer. 'Yeah, celery.'

'It *brown*.'

' 'S'right. 'S'right! Ripe celery ort to be brown,' said Fruntkin, quickly. 'Shows it's ripe,' he added.

'It should be *green*.'

'Nah. Yore finking about the tomatoes,' said Fruntkin.

'Yeah, and what's this runny stuff?' said a man in the queue.

Fruntkin drew himself up to his full height.

'That', he said, 'is the mayonnaisey. Made it myself. Out of a *book*,' he added proudly.

'Yeah, I expect you did,' said the man, prodding it. 'Clearly oil, eggs and vinegar were not involved, right?'

'Specialitay de lar mayson,' said Fruntkin.

'Right, right,' said the man. 'Only it's attacking my lettuce.'

Fruntkin grasped his ladle angrily.

'Look—' he began.

'No, it's all right,' said the prospective diner. 'The slugs have formed a defensive ring.'

There was a commotion by the door. Detritus the troll waded through the diners, with Cut-me-own-Throat Dibbler strutting along behind him.

The troll shouldered the queue aside and glared at Fruntkin.

'Mr Dibbler want a word,' he said, and reached across the counter, lifted the dwarf up by his food-encrusted shirt, and dangled him in front of Throat.

'Anyone seen Victor Tugelbend?' said Throat. 'Or that girl Ginger?'

Fruntkin opened his mouth to swear, and thought better of it.

'The boy was in here half an hour ago,' he squeaked. 'Ginger works here mornings. Don't know where she goes.'

'Where'd *Victor* go?' said Throat. He pulled a bag out of his pocket. It jingled. Fruntkin's eyes swivelled towards it as though they were ball bearings and it was a powerful magnet.

'Dunno, Mr Throat,' he said. 'He just went out again when she wasn't here.'

'Right,' said Throat. 'Well, if you see him again, tell him I'm looking for him and I'm going to make him a star, right?'

'Star. Right,' said the dwarf.

Throat reached into his moneybag and produced a ten-dollar piece.

'And I want to order dinner for later on,' he added.

'Dinner. Right,' quavered Fruntkin.

'Steak and prawns, I think,' said Throat. 'With a choice of sunkissed vegetables in season, and then strawberries and cream.'

Fruntkin stared at him.

'Er—,' he began.

Detritus poked the dwarf so that he swung backwards and forwards.

'An' I', he said, 'will 'ave . . . er . . . a well-weathered basalt with a aggregate of fresh-hewn sandstone conglomerates. Right?'

'Er. Yes,' said Fruntkin.

'Put him down, Detritus. He doesn't want to be hanging around,' said Throat. 'And *gently*.' He looked around at the fascinated faces.

'Remember,' he said, 'I'm looking for Victor Tugelbend and I'm going to make him a star. If anyone sees him, you must tell him. Oh, and I'll have the steak rare, Fruntkin.'

He strode back to the door.

After he had gone the chattering flowed back like a tide.

'Make him a star? What'd he want a star for?'

'I didn't know you could make stars . . . I thought they were like, you know, stuck to the sky . . . '

'I think he meant make *him* a star. You know, him himself. Turn him *into* a star.'

'How can you make anyone into a star?'

'I dunno. I suppose you compress them right up small and they burst into this mass of flaming hydrogen?'

'Good grief!'

'Yeah! Is that troll *mean*, or what?'

Victor looked at the dog carefully.

It couldn't have spoken to him. It must have been his imagination. But he'd said that last time, hadn't he?

'I wonder what your name is?' said Victor, patting it on the head.

'Gaspode,' said Gaspode.

Victor's hand froze in mid-tousle.

'Tuppence,' said the dog, wearily. 'World's only bloody harmonica-playing dog. Tuppence.'

It *is* the sun, Victor thought. I haven't been wearing a hat. In a minute I'll wake up and there'll be cool sheets.

'Well, you didn't play very well. I couldn't recognize the tune,' he said, stretching his mouth into a terrible grin.

'You're not supposed to recognize the bloody tune,' said Gaspode, sitting down heavily and industriously scratching one ear with his hind leg. 'I'm a *dog*. You're supposed to be bloody amazed I can bloody well get a squeak out of the bloody thing.'

How shall I put it? Victor thought. *Do I just say: excuse me, you appear to be tal . . . No, probably not.*

'Er,' he said. *Hey, you're quite chatty for . . . no.*

'Fleas,' said Gaspode, changing ears and legs. 'Giving me gyp.'

'Oh dear.'

'And all these trolls. Can't stand 'em. They smell all wrong. Bloody walking stones. You try and bite 'em, next minute you're spittin' teef. It's not natural.'

Talking of natural, I can't help noticing that—

'Bloody desert, this place,' said Gaspode.

You're a talking dog.

'I expect you're wondering,' said Gaspode, turning his penetrating stare on Victor once again, 'how come I'm talking.'

'Hadn't given it a thought,' said Victor.

'Me neither,' said Gaspode. 'Until a couple of weeks ago. All my life, never said a bloody word. Worked for a bloke back in the big city. Tricks and that. Balancing a ball on my nose. Walkin' on me 'ind legs. Jumpin' through a 'oop. Carried the hat round in my mouf afterwards. You know. Show business. Then this woman pats me on me 'ead, says "Eow, wot a dear little doggy, he looks like he understands every word we say," and I thinks, "Ho, ho, I don't even bother to make the effort any more, missus," and then I realizes I can hear the words, and they're coming out of me own mouf. So I grabbed the 'at and had it away on my paws pretty damn quick, while they were still starin'.'

'Why?' said Victor.

Gaspode rolled his eyes. 'Exactly wot life do you fink a genuine talking dog is going to have?' he said. 'Shouldn't have opened my stupid mouth.'

'But you're talking to *me*,' said Victor.

Gaspode gave him a sly look.

'Yeah, but jus' you try tellin' anyone,' he said. 'Anyway, you're all right. You've got the look. I could tell it a mile orf.'

'What on earth do you mean?' said Victor.

'You don't fink you really belong to yourself, right?' said the dog. 'You've 'ad the feeling that something else is doin' your thinking for you?'

'Good grief.'

'Give you a kind of hunted look,' said Gaspode. He picked up the cap in his mouth. 'Tuppence,' he said indistinctly. 'I mean, it's not as if I've got any way of spending it, but . . . tuppence.' He gave a canine shrug.

'What do you mean by a hunted look?' said Victor.

'You've all got the look. Many are called and few are chosen, style of fing.'

'*What look?*'

'Like you've been called here and you don't know why.' Gaspode tried to scratch his ear again. 'Saw you acting Cohen the Barbarian,' he said.

'Er . . . what did you think of it?' said Victor.

'I reckon, so long as ole Cohen never gets to hear about it, you should be OK.'

'I *said*, how long ago was he in here?' shouted Dibbler. On the tiny stage, Ruby was crooning something in a voice like a ship in thick fog and bad trouble.

'GrooOOowwonnogghrhhooOOo—'[6]

---

[6] SUB-TITLE: 'Vunce again I am fallink in luf (lit., experiencing the pleasant feeling of being hit over the head with a rock by Chondrodite, the troll god of love).' Note: Chondrodite must not be confused with Gigalith, the troll god who gives trolls wisdom by hitting them on the head with a rock, or Silicarous, the troll god who brings trolls good fortune by hitting them on the head with a rock, or with the folk hero Monolith, who first wrested the secret of rocks from the gods.

'He only just went out!' bellowed Rock. 'I'm trying to listen to this song, all right?'

'—OowoowgrhhffrghooOOo—'[7]

Cut-me-own-Throat nudged Detritus, who was taking the weight off his knuckles and watching the floor show with his mouth open.

The old troll's life had, up to now, been very straightforward; people paid you money, and you hit other people.

Now it was beginning to get complicated. Ruby had winked at him.

Strange and unfamiliar emotions were rampaging through Detritus' battered heart.

'—groooOOOooohoofooOOoo—'[8]

'Come *on*,' snapped Throat.

Detritus lumbered to his feet and took one last longing look at the stage.

'—ooOOOgooOOmoo. OOhhhooo.'[9]

Ruby blew him a kiss. Detritus blushed the colour of fresh-cut garnet.

Gaspode led the way out of the alley and through the dark hinterland of scrubby bushes and sandgrass behind the town.

'There's definitely something wrong with this place,' he muttered.

'It's *different*,' said Victor. 'What do you mean, wrong?'

Gaspode looked as though he was going to spit.

'Now, take me,' he said, ignoring the interruption. 'A dog. Never dreamed in my life except about chasing fings. And sex, of course. Suddenly I'm dreaming these dreams. In *colour*. Frightened the bloody life out of me. Never seen colour before, right? Dogs see in black-an'-white, as

---

[7] SUB-TITLE: 'Vy iss it I now am a blue colour?'

[8] SUB-TITLE: 'Vot is the action I should take at this time?'

[9] SUB-TITLE: ' . . . I can't help it. Hiya, big boy.'

I expect you knows, you bein' a great reader. Red comes as a nasty shock, I can tell you. You fink your dinner is just this white bone with shades of grey on it, suddenly it turns out for years you bin eatin' this gharsteley red and purple stuff.'

'What kind of dreams?' said Victor.

'It's bloody embarrassing,' said Gaspode. 'Like, in one there's this bridge that's been washed away and I have to run and bark a warning, right? And there's another where this house is on fire and I drag these kids out. And there's one where some kids are lost in these caves and I find 'em and go and lead the search party to them . . . and I *hates* kids. Seems I can't get me 'ead down these days without rescuin' people or savin' people or foilin' robbers or sunnink. I mean, I'm seven years old, I got hardpad, I got scurf, I got fleas somethin' dreadful, I don't need to be a 'ero every time I go to sleep.'

'Gosh. Isn't life interesting,' said Victor, 'when you see it from someone else's perspective . . . ?'

Gaspode rolled a crusted yellow eye skyward.

'Er. Where are we going?' said Victor.

'We're goin' to see a few Holy Wood folk,' said Gaspode. ' 'Cos there's something *weird* goin' on.'

'Up on the hill? I didn't know there were any people on the hill.'

'They ain't people,' said Gaspode.

A little twig fire burned on the slope of Holy Wood Hill. Victor had lit it because – well, because it was reassuring. Because it was the sort of thing humans did.

He found it necessary to remember he was human, and probably not crazy.

It wasn't that he'd been talking to a dog. People often talked to dogs. The same applied to the cat. And maybe even the rabbit. It was the conversation with the mouse and the duck that might be considered odd.

'You think *we* wanted to talk?' snapped the rabbit. 'One

minute I'm just another rabbit and happy about it, next minute *whazaam*, I'm thinking. That's a major drawback if you're looking for happiness as a rabbit, let me tell you. You want grass and sex, not thoughts like "What's it all about, when you get right down to it?" '

'Yeah, but at least you eats grass,' Gaspode pointed out. 'At least grass don't talk back at you. The last thing you needs when you're hungry is a bloody ethical conundrum on your plate.'

'You think you've got problems,' said the cat, apparently reading his mind. '*I'm* reduched to eating fish. You put a paw on your dinner, it shoutsh "Help!", you got a major predicament.'

There was silence. They looked at Victor. So did the mouse. And the duck. The duck was looking particularly belligerent. It had probably heard about orange sauce.

'Yeah. Take us,' said the mouse. 'There's me, being chased by *this*,' it indicated the cat looming over it, 'around the kitchen. Scrabble, scrabble, squeak, panic. Then there's this sizzling noise in my head, I see a frying pan – you understand? A second ago I never knew what frying was, now I'm holding the handle, he comes around the corner, *clang*. Now he's staggering around saying "What hit me?" I say "Me." That's when we both realize. We're talking.'

'*Concheptualishing*,' said the cat. It was a black cat, with white paws, ears like shotgun targets, and the scarred face of a cat that has already lived eight lives to the full.

'You tell him, kid,' said the mouse.

'Tell him what you did next,' said Gaspode.

'We came here,' said the cat.

'From Ankh-Morpork?' said Victor.

'Yeah.'

'That's nearly thirty miles!'

'Yeah, and take it from me,' said the cat, 'it's hard to hitch-hike when you's a cat.'

'See?' said Gaspode. 'It's happening all the time. All sorts are turnin' up in Holy Wood. They don't know why they've come, only that it's important to be here. An' they don't act like they do anywhere else in the world. I bin watchin'. Somethin' weird's goin' on.'

The duck quacked. There were words in there somewhere, but so mangled by the incompatibility of beak and larynx that Victor couldn't understand a word.

The animals gave it a sympathetic audience.

'What's up, Duck?' said the rabbit.

'The duck says', translated Gaspode, 'that it's like a migratory thing. Just the same feelin' as a migration, he says.'

'Yeah? I didn't have far to come,' the rabbit volunteered. 'We lived on the dunes anyway.' It sighed. 'For three happy years and four miserable days,' it added.

A thought struck Victor. 'So you'd know about the old man on the beach?' he said.

'Oh, him. Yeah. Him. He was always coming up here.'

'What sort of person was he?' said Victor.

'Listen, buster, up to four days ago I had a vocabulary consisting of two verbs and one noun. What do *you* think I thought he was? All I know is, he didn't bother us. We probably thought he was a rock on legs, or something.'

Victor thought about the book in his pocket. Chanting and lighting fires. What sort of person did that?

'I don't know what's going on,' he said. 'I'd like to find out. Look, haven't you got names? I feel awkward, talking to people without names.'

'Only me,' said Gaspode. 'Bein' a dog. I'm named after the famous Gaspode, you know.'

'A kid called me Puss once,' said the cat doubtfully.

'I thought you had names in your own language,' said Victor. 'You know, like "Mighty Paws" or – or "Speedy Hunter". Or something.'

He smiled encouragingly.

The others gave him a long blank stare.

'He reads books,' explained Gaspode. 'See, the thing is,' he added, scratching himself vigorously, 'animals don't normally bother with names. I mean, we know who we are.'

'Mind you, I like "Speedy Hunter",' said the mouse.

'I was thinking that's more a cat's name,' said Victor, starting to sweat. 'Mice have friendly little names, like – like Squeak.'

'Squeak?' said the mouse, coldly.

The rabbit grinned.

'And, and I always thought rabbits were called Flopsy. Or Mr Thumpy,' Victor gabbled.

The rabbit stopped grinning and twitched its ears.

'Now *look*, pal—' it began.

'Y'know,' said Gaspode cheerfully, in an attempt to revive the conversation, 'I heard there's this legend where the first two people in the world named all the animals. Makes you fink, don't it.'

Victor pulled out the book to cover his embarrassment. Chanting and lighting fires. Three times a day.

'This old man—' he began.

'What's so important about him?' said the rabbit. 'He just used to come up on to the hill and make noises a couple of times every day. You could set your . . . your,' it hesitated. 'It was always the same times. Many times a day.'

'Three times. Three performances. Like a sort of theatre?' said Victor, running his finger down the page.

'We can't count up to three,' said the rabbit sourly. 'It goes one . . . many. Many times.' He glared at Victor. '*Mr Thumpy*,' it said, in withering tones.

'And people from other places brought him fish,' said Victor. 'There's no-one else living near here. They must have come from miles away. People sailed miles just to bring him fish. It's as though he didn't want to eat fish out of the bay here. And it's *teeming* with them. When I went swimming I saw lobsters you wouldn't believe.'

116

'What did you name them?' said Mr Thumpy, who wasn't the kind of rabbit that forgot a grudge. 'Mr Snappy?'

'Yeah, I want this cleared up right now,' squeaked the mouse. 'Back home I was top mouse. I could lick any other mouse in the house. I want a proper name, kid. Anyone calls me Squeaky Boots', he looked up at Victor, 'is asking for a head shaped like a frying pan, do I make myself clear?'

The duck quacked at length.

'Hold it,' said Gaspode. 'The thing is, the duck says,' said Gaspode, 'that all this is part of the same thing. Humans and trolls and everything coming here. Animals suddenly talking. The duck says he thinks it's caused by something here.'

'How does a duck know that?' said Victor.

'Look, friend,' said the rabbit, 'when *you* can fly all the way across the sea and even end up finding the same bloody *continent*, you can start badmouthing ducks.'

'Oh,' said Victor. 'You mean mysterious animal senses, yes?'

They glared at him.

'Anyway, it's got to stop,' said Gaspode. 'All this cogitatin' and talkin' is all right for you humans. You're used to it. Fing is, see, someone's got to find out what's causin' all this . . . '

They carried on glaring at him.

'Well,' he said, vaguely, 'maybe the book can help? The early bits are in some sort of ancient language. I can't—,' he paused. Wizards weren't welcomed in Holy Wood. It probably wasn't a good idea to mention the University, or his small part in it. 'That is,' he continued, choosing his words with care, 'I think I know someone in Ankh-Morpork who might be able to read it. He's an animal, too. An ape.'

'How's he in the mysterious senses department?' said Gaspode.

'He's red hot on mysterious senses,' said Victor.

'In that case—' said the rabbit.

'Hold it,' said Gaspode. 'Someone's coming.'

A moving torch was visible coming up the hill. The duck rocketed clumsily into the air and glided away. The others disappeared into the shadows. Only the dog didn't move.

'Aren't you going to make yourself scarce?' Victor hissed.

Gaspode raised an eyebrow.

'Woof?' he said.

The torch zig-zagged erratically among the scrub, like a firefly. Sometimes it would stop for a moment, and then wander away in some totally new direction. It was very bright.

'What is it?' said Victor.

Gaspode sniffed. 'Human,' he said. 'Female. Wearin' cheap scent.' His nose twitched again. 'It's called *Passion's Plaything*.' He sniffed again. 'Fresh laundry, no starch. Old shoes. Lot of studio make-up. She's been in Borgle's and had—' his nose twitched '—stoo. Not a big plate.'

'I suppose you can tell how tall she is, can you?' said Victor.

'She smells about five foot two, two and a half,' hazarded Gaspode.

'Oh, come *on*!'

'Walk a mile on these paws and call me a liar.'

Victor kicked sand over his little fire and strolled down the slope.

The light stopped moving as he approached it. For a moment he got a glimpse of a female figure clasping a shawl around her with one hand holding the torch high above her head. Then the light vanished so quickly it left blue and purple after-images dancing across his vision. Behind them, a small figure made a blacker shadow against the dusk.

It said, 'What are you doing in my . . . what am I . . . why are you in . . . where . . . ,' and then, as if it had finally got to grips with the situation, changed gear and in a much more familiar voice demanded, 'What are *you* doing here?'

'Ginger?' said Victor.

'Yes?'

Victor paused. What were you supposed to say in circumstances like this?

'Er . . . ' he said. 'It's nice up here in the evenings, don't you think?'

She glared at Gaspode.

'That's that horrible dog who's been hanging round the studio, isn't it?' she said. 'I can't stand small dogs.'

'Bark, bark,' said Gaspode. Ginger stared at him. Victor could almost read her thoughts: he said Bark, bark. And he's a dog, and that's the kind of noise dogs *make*, isn't it?

'I'm a cat person, myself,' she said, vaguely.

A low-level voice said: 'Yeah? Yeah? Wash in your own spit, do you?'

'*What* was that?'

Victor backed away, waving his hands frantically. 'Don't look at me!' he said. 'I didn't say it!'

'Oh? I suppose it was the dog, was it?' she demanded.

'Who, me?' said Gaspode.

Ginger froze. Her eyes swivelled around and down, to where Gaspode was idly scratching an ear.

'Woof?' he said.

'That dog spoke—' Ginger began, pointing a shaking finger at him.

'I know,' said Victor. 'That means he likes you.' He looked past her. Another light was coming up the hill.

'Did you bring someone with you?' he said.

'Me?' Ginger turned round.

Now the light was accompanied by the cracking of dry twigs, and Dibbler stepped out of the dusk with Detritus trailing behind like a particularly scary shadow.

'Ah-*ha*!' he said. 'The lovebirds surprised, eh?'

Victor gaped at him. 'The what?' he said.

'The *what*?' said Ginger.

'Been looking all over for you two,' said Dibbler. 'Someone said he'd seen you come up here. Very romantic. Could do something with that. Look good on the posters. Right.' He draped his arms around them. 'Come on,' he said.

'What for?' said Victor.

'We're shooting first thing in the morning,' said Dibbler.

'But Mr Silverfish said I wasn't going to work in this town again—' Victor began.

Dibbler opened his mouth, and hesitated just for a moment. 'Ah. Yes. But I'm going to give you another chance,' he said, speaking quite slowly for once. 'Yeah. A chance. Like, you're young people. Headstrong. Young once myself. Dibbler, I thought, even if it means cutting your own throat, give 'em a chance. Lower wages, of course. A dollar a day, how about that?'

Victor saw the look of sudden hope on Ginger's face.

He opened his mouth.

'Fifteen dollars,' said a voice. It wasn't his.

He shut his mouth.

'What?' said Dibbler.

Victor opened his mouth.

'Fifteen dollars. Renegot'ble after a week. Fifteen dollars or nuffin'.'

Victor shut his mouth, his eyes rolling.

Dibbler waved a finger under his nose, and then hesitated.

'I like it!' he said eventually. 'Tough bargainer! OK. Three dollars.'

'Fifteen.'

'Five's my last offer, kid. There's thousands of people down there who'd jump at it, right?'

'Name two, Mr Dibbler.'

Dibbler glanced at Detritus, who was lost in a reverie concerning Ruby, and then stared at Ginger.

'OK,' he said. 'Ten. Because I *like* you. But it's cutting my own throat.'

'Done.'

Throat held out a hand. Victor stared at his own as if he was seeing it for the first time, and then shook.

'And now let's get back down,' said Dibbler. 'Lot to organize.'

He strode off through the trees. Victor and Ginger followed meekly behind him, in a state of shock.

'Are you crazy?' Ginger hissed. 'Holding out like that! We could have lost our chance!'

'I didn't say anything! I thought it was you!' said Victor.

'It was you!' said Ginger.

Their eyes met.

They looked down.

'Bark, bark,' said Gaspode the Wonder Dog.

Dibbler turned round.

'What's that noise?' he said.

'Oh, it's – it's just this dog we found,' said Victor hurriedly. 'He's called Gaspode. After the famous Gaspode, you know.'

'He does tricks,' said Ginger, malevolently.

'A performing dog?' Dibbler reached down and patted Gaspode's bullet head.

'Growl, growl.'

'You'd be amazed, the things he can do,' said Victor.

'Amazed,' echoed Ginger.

'Ugly devil, though,' said Dibbler. He gave Gaspode a long, slow stare, which was like challenging a centipede to an arse-kicking contest. Gaspode could outstare a mirror.

Dibbler seemed to be turning an idea over in his mind. 'Mind you . . . bring him along in the morning. People like a good laugh,' said Dibbler.

'Oh, he's a laugh all right,' said Victor. 'A scream.'

As they walked off Victor heard a quiet voice behind him say, 'I'll get you for that. Anyway, you owe me a dollar.'

'What for?'

'Agent's fee,' said Gaspode the Wonder Dog.

Over Holy Wood, the stars were out. They were huge balls of hydrogen heated to millions of degrees, so hot they could not even burn. Many of them would swell enormously before they died, and then shrink to tiny, resentful dwarfs remembered only by sentimental astronomers. In the meantime, they glowed because of metamorphoses beyond the reach of alchemists, and turned mere boring elements into pure light.

Over Ankh-Morpork, it just rained.

The senior wizards crowded around the elephant vase. It had been put back in the corridor on Ridcully's strict orders.

'I remember Riktor,' said the Dean. 'Skinny man. Bit of a one-track mind. But clever.'

'Heh, heh. I remember his mouse counter,' said Windle Poons, from his ancient wheelchair. 'Used to count mice.'

'The pot itself is quite—' the Bursar began, and then said, 'What d'you mean, count mice? They were fed into it on a little belt or something?'

'Oh, no. You just wound it up, y'see, and it sat there whirring away, counting all the mice in the building, mm, and these little wheels with numbers on them came up.'

'Why?'

'Mm? I s'pose he just wanted to count mice.'

The Bursar shrugged. 'This pot', he said, peering closely, 'is actually quite an old Ming vase.'

He waited expectantly.

'Why's it called Ming?' said the Archchancellor, on cue.

The Bursar tapped the pot. It went *ming*.

'And they spit lead balls at people, do they?' said Ridcully.

'No, Master. He just used it to put the . . . the machinery in. Whatever it is. Whatever it's doing.'

. . . whumm . . .

'Hold on. It wobbled,' said the Dean.

. . . whumm . . . whumm . . .

The wizards stared at one another in sudden panic . . .

'What's happening? What's happening?' said Windle Poons. 'Why won't anyone, mm, tell me what's happening?'

. . . whumm . . . whumm . . .

'Run!' suggested the Dean.

'Which way?' quavered the Bursar.

. . . *whumm*WHUMM . . .

'I'm an old man and I *demand* someone tell me what's—'

Silence.

'Duck!' shouted the Archchancellor.

Plib.

A splinter of stone was knocked off the pillar behind him.

He raised his head.

'Bigods, that was a damn lucky es—'

Plib.

The second pellet knocked the tip off his hat.

The wizards lay trembling on the flagstones for several minutes. After a while the Dean's muffled voice, 'Was that all, do you think?'

The Archchancellor raised his head. His face, always red, was now incandescent.

'Bur*saar*!'

'Master?'

'That's what I call *shootin*'!'

Victor turned over.

'Wzstf,' he said.

'It's six aye-emm, rise and shine, Mr Dibbler says,' said Detritus, grasping the bedclothes in one hand and dragging them on to the floor.

'Six o'clock? That's *night-time*!' groaned Victor.

'It's going to be a long day, Mr Dibbler says,' said the troll. 'Mr Dibbler says you got to be on set by half past six. This is goin' to happen.'

Victor pulled on his trousers.

'I suppose I get to eat breakfast?' he said sarcastically.

'Mr Dibbler is havin' food laid on, Mr Dibbler says,' said Detritus.

There was a wheezing noise from under the bed. Gaspode

emerged, in a cloud of old-rugness, and had an early morning scratch.

'Wha—' he began, and then saw the troll. 'Bark, bark,' he corrected himself.

'Oh. A little dog. I like little dogs,' said Detritus.

'Woof.'

'Raw,' the troll added. But he couldn't get the right amount of statutory nastiness into his voice. Visions of Ruby in her feather boa and three acres of red velvet kept undulating across his mind.

Gaspode scratched his ear vigorously.

'Woof,' he said quietly. 'In tones of low menace,' he added, after Detritus had gone.

The slope of the hill was already alive with people when Victor arrived. A couple of tents had been erected. Someone was holding a camel. Several cages of demons gibbered in the shade of a thorn tree.

In the middle of all this were Dibbler and Silverfish, arguing. Dibbler had his arm around Silverfish's shoulder.

'A dead giveaway, is that,' said a voice from the level of Victor's knees. 'It means some poor bugger is about to be taken to the cleaners.'

'It'll be a step up for you, Tom!' Dibbler was saying. 'I mean, how many people in Holy Wood can call themselves Vice-President in Charge of Executive Affairs?'

'Yes, but it's my company!' Silverfish wailed.

'Right! Right!' said Dibbler. 'That's what a name like Vice-President of Executive Affairs *means*.'

'It does?'

'Have I ever lied to you?'

Silverfish's brow furrowed. 'Well,' he said, 'yesterday you said—'

'I mean *metaphorically*,' said Dibbler quickly.

'Oh. Well. Metaphorically? I suppose not—'

'There you are, then. Now, where's that artist?' Dibbler spun around, giving the impression that Silverfish had just been switched off.

A man scurried up with a folder under his arm.

'Yessir, Mr Dibbler?'

Throat pulled a scrap of paper out of his pocket.

'I want the posters ready by tonight, understand?' he warned. 'Here. This is the name of the click.'

'*Shadowe of the Dessert*,' the artist read. His brow furrowed. He had been educated beyond the needs of Holy Wood. 'It's about food?' he said.

But Dibbler wasn't listening. He was advancing on Victor.

'Victor!' he said. 'Baby!'

'It's got him,' said Gaspode quietly. 'Got him worse than anyone, I reckon.'

'What has? How can you tell?' Victor hissed.

'Partly a'cos of subtle signs what you don't seem to be abler recognize,' said Gaspode, 'and partly because he's actin' like a complete twerp, really.'

'Great to see you!' Dibbler enthused, his eyes glowing manically.

He put his arm round Victor's shoulder and half walked, half dragged him towards the tents.

'This is going to be a great picture!' he said.

'Oh, good,' said Victor weakly.

'You play this bandit chieftain,' said Dibbler, 'only a nice guy, too, kind to women and so forth, and you raid this village and you carry off this slave girl only when you look into her eyes, see, you fall for her, and then there's this raid and hundreds of men on elephants come charging—'

'Camels,' said a skinny youth behind Dibbler. 'It's camels.'

'I ordered elephants!'

'You got camels.'

'Camels, elephants,' said Dibbler dismissively. 'We're talking *exotic* here, OK? And—'

'And we've only got one,' said the youth.

'One what?'

'Camel. We could only find one camel,' said the youth. 'But I've got dozens of guys with bedsheets on their heads

125

waiting for camels!' shouted Dibbler, waving his hands in the air. 'Lots of camels, right?'

'We only got one camel 'cos there's only one camel in Holy Wood and that's only 'cos a guy from Klatch rode all the way here on it,' said the youth.

'You should have sent away for more!' snapped Dibbler.

'Mr Silverfish said I wasn't to.'

Dibbler growled.

'Maybe if it moves around a lot it'll look like more than one camel,' said the youth optimistically.

'Why not ride the camel past the picture box, and then get the handleman to stop the demons, and lead it back and put a different rider on it, then start up the box again and ride it past again?' said Victor. 'Would that work?'

Dibbler looked at him open-mouthed.

'What did I tell you?' he said, to the sky in general. 'The lad is a genius! That way we can get a hundred camels for the price of one, right?'

'It means the desert bandits ride in single file, though,' said the youth. 'It's not like, you know, a massed attack.'

'Sure, sure,' said Dibbler dismissively. 'Makes sense. We just put a card up where the leader says, he says—' He thought for a second. 'He says, "Follow me in single file, bwanas, to fool the hated enemy," OK?'

He nodded at Victor. 'Have you met my nephew Soll?' he said. 'Keen lad. Been nearly to school and everything. Brought him out here yesterday. He's Vice-President in Charge of Making Pictures.'

Soll and Victor exchanged nods.

'I don't think "bwanas" is the right word, Uncle,' said Soll.

'It's Klatchian, isn't it?' said Dibbler.

'Well, technically, but I think it's the wrong part of Klatch and maybe "effendies" or something—'

'Just so long as it's foreign,' said Dibbler with an air that suggested the matter was settled. He patted Victor on the back again. 'OK, kid, get into costume.' He chuckled. 'A hundred camels! What a mind!'

126

'Excuse me, Mr Dibbler,' said the poster artist, who had been hovering uneasily, 'I don't understand this bit here . . . '

Dibbler snatched the paper from him.

'Which bit?' he snapped.

'Where you're describing Miss De Syn—'

'It's obvious,' said Dibbler. 'What we want here is to conjure up the exotic, alluring yet distant romance of pyramid-studded Klatch, right, so nat'r'ly we gotta use the symbol of a mysterious and unscrutable continent, see? Do I have to explain everything to everyone all the time?'

'It's just that I thought—' the artist began.

'Just do it!'

The artist looked down at the paper. ' "She has the face",' he read, ' "of a Spink." '

'Right,' said Dibbler. 'Right!'

'I thought maybe Sphinx—'

'Will you listen to the man?' said Dibbler, talking to the sky again. He glared at the artist. 'She doesn't look like *two* of them, does she? One Spink, two Spinks. Now get on with it. I want those posters all round the city first thing tomorrow.'

The artist gave Victor an agonized look he was coming to recognize. Everyone around Dibbler wore them after a while.

'Right you are, Mr Dibbler,' he said.

'Right.' Dibbler turned to Victor.

'Why aren't you changed?' he said.

Victor ducked quickly into a tent. A little old lady[10] shaped like a cottage loaf helped him into a costume apparently made of sheets inexpertly dyed black, although given the current state of accommodation in Holy Wood

---

[10] Mrs Marietta Cosmopilite, former Ankh-Morpork seamstress until her dreams led her to Holy Wood, where she found her skill with a needle was highly prized. Once a darner of casual socks, now a knitter of fake chain mail for trolls and able to run up a pair of harem trousers in a trice.

they were probably just sheets taken off a bed at random. Then she handed him a curved sword.

'Why's it bent?' he asked.

'I think it's meant to be, dear,' she said doubtfully.

'I thought swords had to be straight,' said Victor. Outside, he could hear Dibbler asking the sky why everyone was so stupid.

'Perhaps they start out straight and go bendy with use,' said the old lady, patting him on the hand. 'A lot of things do.'

She gave him a bright smile. 'If you're all right, dear, I'd better go and help the young lady, in case any little dwarfs is peering in at her.'

She waddled out of the tent. From the tent next door came a metallic chinking noise and the sound of Ginger's voice raised in complaint.

Victor made a few experimental slashes with the sword. Gaspode watched him with his head on one side.

'What're you supposed to be?' he said at last.

'A leader of a pack of desert bandits, apparently,' said Victor. 'Romantic and dashing.'

'Dashing where?'

'Just dashing generally, I guess. Gaspode, what did you mean when you said it's got Dibbler?'

The dog gnawed at a paw.

'Look at his eyes,' he said. 'They're even worse than yours.'

'Mine? What's wrong with mine?'

Detritus the troll stuck his head through the tent flaps. 'Mr Dibbler says he wants you now,' he said.

'Eyes?' said Victor. 'Something about my eyes?'

'Woof.'

'Mr Dibbler says—' Detritus began.

'All right, all right! I'm coming!'

Victor stepped out of his tent at the same time as Ginger stepped out of hers. He shut his eyes.

'Gosh, I'm sorry,' he babbled. 'I'll go back and wait for you to get dressed . . . '

'I *am* dressed.'

'Mr Dibbler says—' said Detritus, behind them.

'Come on,' said Ginger, grabbing his arm. 'We mustn't keep everyone waiting.'

'But you're . . . your . . . ' Victor looked down, which wasn't a help. 'You've got a navel in your diamond,' he hazarded.

'I've come to terms with that,' said Ginger, flexing her shoulders in an effort to make everything settle. 'It's these two saucepan lids that are giving me problems. Makes you realize what those poor girls in the harems must suffer.'

'And you don't *mind* people seeing you like that?' said Victor, amazed.

'Why should I? This is moving pictures. It's not as if it's *real*. Anyway, you'd be amazed at what girls have to do for a lot less than ten dollars a day.'

'Nine,' said Gaspode, who was still trailing at Victor's heels.

'Right, gather round, people,' shouted Dibbler through a megaphone. 'Sons of the Desert over there, please. The slave girls – where are the slave girls? Right. Handlemen?—'

'I've never seen so many people in a click,' Ginger whispered. 'It must be costing more than a hundred dollars!'

Victor eyed the Sons of the Desert. It looked as though Dibbler had dropped in at Borgle's and hired the twenty people nearest the door, irrespective of their appropriateness, and had given them each Dibbler's idea of a desert bandit headdress. There were trollish Sons of the Desert – Rock recognized him, and gave him a little wave – dwarf Sons of the Desert and, shuffling into the end of the line, a small, hairy and furiously-scratching Son in a headdress that reached down to his paws.

' . . . grab her, become entranced by her beauty, and then throw her over your pommel.' Dibbler's voice intruded into his consciousness.

Victor desperately re-ran the half-heard instructions past his mind.

'My what?' he said.

'It's part of your saddle,' Ginger hissed.

'Oh.'

'And then you ride into the night, with all the Sons following you and singing rousing desert bandit songs—'

'No-one'll hear them,' said Soll helpfully. 'But if they open and shut their mouths it'll help create a, you know, amby-ance.'

'But it isn't night,' said Ginger. 'It's broad daylight.'

Dibbler stared at her.

His mouth opened once or twice.

'Soll!' he shouted.

'We can't *film* at night, Uncle,' said the nephew hurriedly. 'The demons wouldn't be able to *see*. I don't see why we can't put up a card saying "Night-time" at the start of the scene, so that—'

'That's not the magic of moving pictures!' snapped Dibbler. 'That's just messing about!'

'Excuse me,' said Victor. 'Excuse me, but surely it doesn't matter, because surely the demons can paint the sky black with stars on it?'

There was a moment's silence. Then Dibbler looked at Gaffer.

'Can they?' he said.

'Nah,' said the handleman. 'It's bloody hard enough to make sure they paint what they do see, never mind what they don't.'

Dibbler rubbed his nose.

'I might be prepared to negotiate,' he said.

The handleman shrugged. 'You don't understand, Mr Dibbler. What'd they want money for? They'd only eat it. We start telling them to paint what isn't there, we're into all sorts of—'

'Perhaps it's just a very bright full moon?' said Ginger.

'That's good thinking,' said Dibbler. 'We'll do a card where Victor says to Ginger something like: "How bright the moon is tonight, bwana".'

'Something like that,' said Soll diplomatically.

It was noon. Holy Wood Hill glistened under the sun, like a champagne-flavoured wine gum that had been half-sucked. The handlemen turned their handles, the extras charged enthusiastically backwards and forwards, Dibbler raged at everyone, and cinematographic history was made with a shot of three dwarfs, four men, two trolls and a dog all riding one camel and screaming in terror for it to stop.

Victor was introduced to the camel. It blinked its long eyelashes at him and appeared to chew soap. It was kneeling down and it looked like a camel that had had a long morning and wasn't about to take any shit from anyone. So far it had kicked three people.

'What's it called?' he said cautiously.

'We call it Evil-Minded Son of a Bitch,' said the newly-appointed Vice-President in Charge of Camels.

'That doesn't sound like a name.'

' 'S a good name for this camel,' said the handler fervently.

'There's nothin' wrong with bein' a son of a bitch,' said a voice behind him. 'I'm a son of a bitch. My *father* was a son of a bitch, you greasy nightshirt-wearin' bastard.'

The handler grinned nervously at Victor and turned around. There was no-one behind him. He looked down.

'Woof,' said Gaspode, and wagged what was almost a tail.

'Did you just hear someone say something?' said the handler carefully.

'No,' said Victor. He leaned close to one of the camel's ears and whispered, in case it was a special Holy Wood camel: 'Look, I'm a friend, OK?'

Evil-Minded Son of a Bitch flicked a carpet-thick ear.[11]

'How do you ride it?' he said.

'When you want to go forward you swear at it and hit it with a stick, and when you want to stop you swear at it and really hit it with a stick.'

'What happens if you want it to turn?'

---

[11] Camels are far too intelligent to admit to being intelligent.

'Ah, well, you're on to the Advanced Manual there. Best thing to do is get off and do it round by hand.'

'When you're ready!' Dibbler bellowed through his megaphone. 'Now, you ride up to the tent, leap off the camel, fight the huge eunuchs, burst into the tent, drag the girl out, get back on the camel and away. Got it? Think you can do that?'

'What huge eunuchs?' said Victor, as the camel unfolded itself upwards.

One of the huge eunuchs shyly raised a hand.

'It's me. Morry,' it said.

'Oh. Hi, Morry.'

'Hi, Vic.'

'And me, Rock,' said a second huge eunuch.

'Hi, Rock.'

'Hi, Vic.'

'Places, everyone,' said Dibbler. 'We'll – what is it, Rock?'

'Er, I was just wondering, Mr Dibbler . . . what is my motivation for this scene?'

'Motivation?'

'Yes. Er. I got to know, see,' said Rock.

'How about: I'll fire you if you don't do it properly?'

Rock grinned. 'Right you are, Mr Dibbler,' he said.

'OK,' said Dibbler. 'Everyone ready . . . *turn 'em!*'

Evil-minded Son of a Bitch turned awkwardly, legs flailing at odd camel angles, and then lumbered into a complicated trot.

The handle turned . . .

The air glittered.

And Victor awoke. It was like rising slowly out of a pink cloud, or a magnificent dream which, try as you might, drains out of your mind as the daylight shuffles in, leaving a terrible sense of loss; nothing, you know instinctively, nothing you're going to experience for the rest of the day is going to be one half as good as that dream.

He blinked. The images faded away. He was aware of

an ache in his muscles, as if he'd recently been really exerting himself.

'What happened?' he mumbled.

He looked down.

'Wow,' he said. An expanse of barely-clad buttock occupied a view recently occupied by the camel's neck. It was an improvement.

'Why', said Ginger icily, 'am I lying on a camel?'

'Search me. Didn't you want to?'

She slid down on to the sand and tried to adjust her costume.

At this point they both became aware of the audience.

There was Dibbler. There was Dibbler's nephew. There was the handleman. There were the extras. There were the assorted vice-presidents and other people who are apparently called into existence by the mere presence of moving-picture creation.[12] There was Gaspode the Wonder Dog.

And every one, except for the dog, who was sniggering, had his mouth open.

The handleman's hand was still turning the handle. He looked down at it as if its presence was new to him, and stopped.

Dibbler seemed to come out of whatever trance he was in.

'Whoo-*hoo*,' he said. 'Blimey.'

'*Magic*,' breathed Soll. 'Real *magic*.'

Dibbler nudged the handleman.

'Did you get all that?' he said.

'Get what?' said Ginger and Victor together.

Then Victor noticed Morry sitting on the sand. There was a sizeable chip out of his arm; Rock was trowelling something into it. The troll noticed Victor's expression and gave him a sickly grin.

'Fink you're Cohen the Barbarian, do you?' he said.

'Yeah,' said Rock. 'There was no call to go callin' him

---

[12] Some of them have clipboards.

wot you called him. An' if you're going to go doin' fancy swordwork, we're applyin' for an extra dollar a day Havin'-Bits-Chopped-Off allowance.'

Victor's sword had several nicks on the blade. For the life of him, he couldn't imagine how they had got there.

'Look,' he said desperately. 'I don't understand. I didn't call anyone anything. Have we started filming yet?'

'One minute I'm sitting in a tent, next minute I'm breathing camel,' said Ginger petulantly. 'Is it too much to ask what is going on?'

But no-one seemed to be listening to them.

'*Why* can't we find a way of getting sound?' said Dibbler. 'That was damn good dialogue there. Didn't understand a word of it, but I know good dialogue when I hear it.'

'Parrots,' said the handleman flatly. 'Your common Howondaland Green. Amazing bird. Memory like an elephant. Get a couple of dozen in different sizes and you've got a full vocal—'

That launched a detailed technical discussion.

Victor let himself slide off the camel's back and ducked under its neck to reach Ginger.

'Listen,' he said urgently. 'It was just like last time. Only stronger. Like a sort of dream. The handleman started to take pictures and it was just like a dream.'

'Yes, but what did we actually *do*?' she said.

'What you did,' said Rock, 'was gallop the camel up to the tent, leap off, come at us like a windmill—'

'—leapin' on rocks and laughin'—' said Morry.

'Yeah, you said to Morry, "Have at you, you Foul Black Guard," ' said Rock. 'And then you caught him a right ding on the arm, cut a hole in the tent—'

'Good sword work, though,' said Morry appraisingly. 'A bit showy, but pretty good.'

'But I don't know *how* to—' Victor began.

'—and she was lying there all longgrass,' said Rock. 'An' you swept her up, and she said—'

'Long grass?' said Ginger weakly.

'*Languorous*,' said Victor. 'I think he means languorous.'

134

'—she said, "Why, it is the Thief of . . . the Thief of . . . " ' Rock hesitated. 'Dad's Bag, I think you said.'

'Bagged Dad,' said Morry, rubbing his arm.

'Yeah, an' then she said, "You are in great danger, for my father has sworn to kill you", and Victor said "But now, o fairest rose, I can reveal that I am really the Shadow of the Dessert—" '

'What's languorous *mean*?' said Ginger suspiciously.

'An' he said, "Fly with me now to the casbah", or something like that, an' then he gave her this, this, thing humans do with their lips—'

'Whistle?' said Victor, with hopeless hope.

'Nah, the other thing. Sounds like a cork coming out of a bottle,' said Rock.

'Kiss,' said Ginger, coldly.

'Yeah. Not that I'm any judge,' said Rock, 'but it seemed to go on for a while. Definitely very, you know, kissy.'

'I thought it was going to be bucket-of-water time myself,' said a quiet canine voice behind Victor. He kicked out backwards, but failed to connect.

'And then he was back on the camel and dragged her up and Mr Dibbler shouted "Stop, stop, what the hell's going on, why won't anyone tell me what the hell's going on," ' said Rock. 'And then you said "What happened?" '

'Don't know when I last saw swordplay like that,' said Morry.

'Oh,' said Victor. 'Well. Thank you.'

'All that shouting "Ha!" and "Have at you, you dog". Very professional,' said Morry.

'I see,' said Victor. He reached sideways and grabbed Ginger's arm.

'We've got to talk,' he hissed. 'Somewhere quiet. Behind the tent.'

'If you think I'm going anywhere alone with you—' she began.

'Listen, this is no time to start acting like—'

A heavy hand settled on Victor's shoulder. He turned, and saw the shape of Detritus eclipsing the world.

135

'Mr Dibbler doesn't want anyone running off,' he said. 'Everyone has to stay until Mr Dibbler says.'

'You're a real pain, you know,' said Victor. Detritus gave him a big, gem-studded grin.[13]

'Mr Dibbler says I can be a *vice-president*,' he said proudly.

'In charge of what?' said Victor.

'Vice-presidents,' said Detritus.

Gaspode the Wonder Dog made a little growling sound at the back of his throat. The camel, which had been idly staring at the sky, sidled around a bit and suddenly lashed out with a kick that caught the troll in the small of the back. Detritus yelped. Gaspode gave the world a look of satisfied innocence.

'Come on,' said Victor grimly. 'While he's trying to find something to hit the camel with.'

They sat down in the shade behind the tent.

'I just want you to know', said Ginger coldly, 'that I have never attempted to look languorous in my life.'

'Could be worth a try,' said Victor, absently.

'What?'

'Sorry. Look, something made us act like that. I don't know how to use a sword. I've always just waved it around. What did you feel like?'

'You know how you feel when you hear someone say something and you realize you've been daydreaming?'

'It was like your own life fading away and something else filling up the space.'

They considered this in silence.

'Do you think it's something to do with Holy Wood?' she said.

Victor nodded. Then he threw himself sideways and landed on Gaspode, who had been watching them intently.

'Yelp,' said Gaspode.

'Now *listen*,' Victor hissed into his ear, 'No more of these hints. What is it that you noticed about us?

---

[13] Trolls' teeth are made of diamond.

Otherwise it's Detritus for you. With mustard.'

The dog squirmed in his grip.

'Or we could make you wear a muzzle,' said Ginger.

'I ain't dangerous!' wailed Gaspode, scrabbling with his paws in the sand.

'A talking dog sounds pretty dangerous to me,' said Victor.

'Dreadfully,' said Ginger. 'You never know what it might say.'

'See? See?' said Gaspode mournfully. 'I knew it'd be nothing but trouble, showin' I can talk. It shouldn't happen to a dog.'

'*But it's going to*,' said Victor.

'Oh, all right. All right. For what good it'll do,' muttered Gaspode.

Victor relaxed. The dog sat up and shook sand off himself.

'You won't understand it, anyway,' he grumbled. 'Another dog would understand, but you won't. It's down to species experience, see. Like kissing. *You* know what it's like, but I don't. It's not a canine experience.' He noticed the warning look in Victor's eyes, and plunged on, 'It's the way you look as if you belong here.' He watched them for a moment. 'See? See?' he said. 'I *tole* you you wouldn't understand. It's – it's *territory*, see? You got all the signs of bein' right where you should be. Nearly everyone else here is a stranger, but you aren't. Er. Like, you mus' have noticed where some dogs bark at you when you're new to a place? It's not jus' smell, we got this amazin' sense of displacement. Like, some humans get uncomfortable when they see a picture hung crooked? It's like that, only worse. It's kind of like the only place you ought to be now is *here*.' He looked at them again, and then industriously scratched an ear.

'What the hell,' he said. 'The trouble is, I can explain it in Dog but you only listen in Human.'

'It sounds a bit mystical to me,' said Ginger.

'You said something about my eyes,' said Victor.

'Yeah, well. Have you looked at your own eyes?' Gaspode nodded at Ginger. 'You too, miss.'

'Don't be daft,' said Victor. 'How can we look at our own eyes?'

Gaspode shrugged. 'You could look at each other's,' he suggested.

They automatically turned to face each other.

There was a long drawn-out moment. Gaspode employed it to urinate noisily against a tent peg.

Eventually Victor said, 'Wow.'

Ginger said, 'Mine, too?'

'Yes. Doesn't it hurt?'

'You should know.'

'There you are, then,' said Gaspode. 'And you look at Dibbler next time you see him. Really *look*, I mean.'

Victor rubbed his eyes, which were beginning to water. 'It's as though Holy Wood has called us here, is doing something to us and has, has—'

'—*branded* us,' said Ginger bitterly. 'That's what it's done.'

'It, er, it does look quite attractive, actually,' said Victor gallantly. 'Gives them a sort of sparkle.'

A shadow fell across the sand.

'Ah, there you are,' said Dibbler. He put his arms around their shoulders as they stood up, and gave them a sort of hug. 'You young people, always going off alone together,' he said archly. 'Great business. Great business. Very romantic. But we've got a click to make, and I've got lots of people standing around waiting for you, so let's do it.'

'See what I mean?' muttered Gaspode, very quietly.

When you knew what you were looking for, you couldn't miss it.

In the centre of both of Dibbler's eyes was a tiny golden star.

In the heartlands of the great dark continent of Klatch the air was heavy and pregnant with the promise of the coming monsoon.

Bullfrogs croaked in the rushes[14] by the slow brown river. Crocodiles dozed on the mudflats.

Nature was holding its breath.

A cooing broke out in the pigeon loft of Azhural N'choate, stock dealer. He stopped dozing on the veranda, and went over to see what had caused the excitement.

In the vast pens behind the shack a few threadbare bewilderbeests, marked down for a quick sale, yawning and cudding in the heat, looked up in alarm as N'choate leapt the veranda steps in one bound and tore towards them.

He rounded the zebra pens and homed in on his assistant M'Bu, who was peacefully mucking out the ostriches.

'How many—' he stopped, and began to wheeze.

M'Bu, who was twelve years old, dropped his shovel and patted him heavily on the back.

'How many—' he tried again.

'You been overdoing it again, boss?' said M'Bu in a concerned voice.

'How many elephants we got?'

'I just done them,' said M'Bu. 'We got three.'

'Are you sure?'

'Yes, boss,' said M'Bu, evenly. 'It's *easy* to be sure, with elephants.'

Azhural crouched in the red dust and hurriedly began to scrawl figures with a stick.

'Old Muluccai's bound to have half a dozen,' he muttered. 'And Tazikel's usually got twenty or so, and then the people on the delta generally have—'

'Someone want elephants, boss?'

'—got fifteen head, he was telling me, plus also there's a load at the logging camp probably going cheap, call it two dozen—'

'Someone want a *lot* of elephants, boss?'

'—was saying there's a herd over T'etse way, shouldn't be a problem, then there's all the valleys over towards—'

M'Bu leaned on the fence and waited.

---

[14] But were edited out of the finished production.

'Maybe two hundred, give or take ten,' said Azhural, throwing down the stick. 'Nowhere near enough.'

'You can't give or take ten elephants, boss,' said M'Bu firmly. He knew that counting elephants was a precision job. A man might be uncertain about how many wives he had, but never about elephants. Either you had one, or you didn't.

'Our agent in Klatch has an order for', Azhural swallowed, 'a thousand elephants. A thousand! Immediately! Cash on delivery!'

Azhural let the paper drop to the ground. 'To a place called Ankh-Morpork,' he said despondently. He sighed. 'It would have been nice,' he said.

M'Bu scratched his head and stared at the hammerhead clouds massing over Mt F'twangi. Soon the dry veldt would boom to the thunder of the rains.

Then he reached down and picked up the stick.

'What're you doing?' said Azhural.

'Drawing a map, boss,' said M'Bu.

Azhural shook his head. 'Not worth it, boy. Three thousand miles to Ankh, I reckon. I let myself get carried away. Too many miles, not enough elephants.'

'We could go across the plains, boss,' said M'Bu. 'Lot of elephants on the plains. Send messengers ahead. We could pick up plenty more elephants on the way, no problem. That whole plain just about covered in damn elephants.'

'No, we'd have to go around on the coast,' said the dealer, drawing a long curving line in the sand. 'The reason being, there's the jungle just *here*,' he tapped on the parched ground, 'and *here*,' he tapped again, slightly concussing an emerging locust that had optimistically mistaken the first tap for the onset of the rains. 'No roads in the jungle.'

M'Bu took the stick and drew a straight line through the jungle.

'Where a thousand elephants want to go, boss, they don't need no roads.'

Azhural considered this. Then he took the stick and drew a jagged line by the jungle.

140

'But here's the Mountains of the Sun,' he said. 'Very high. Lots of deep ravines. And no bridges.'

M'Bu took the stick, indicated the jungle, and grinned.

'I know where there's a lot of prime timber just been uprooted, boss,' he said.

'Yeah? OK, boy, but we've still got to get it into the mountains.'

'It just so happen that a t'ousand real strong elephants'll be goin' that way, boss.'

M'Bu grinned again. His tribe went in for sharpening their teeth to points.[15] He handed back the stick.

Azhural's mouth opened slowly.

'By the seven moons of Nasreem,' he breathed. 'We could do it, you know. It's only, oh, thirteen or fourteen hundred miles that way. Maybe less, even. Yeah. We could really do it.'

'Yes, boss.'

'Y'know, I've always wanted to do something big with my life. Something *real*,' said Azhural. 'I mean, an ostrich here, a giraffe there . . . it's not the sort of thing you get remembered for . . . ' He stared at the purple-grey horizon. 'We *could* do it, couldn't we?' he said.

'Sure, boss.'

'Right over the mountains!'

'Sure, boss.'

If you looked really hard, you could just see that the purple-grey was topped with white.

'They're pretty high mountains,' said Azhural, his voice now edged with doubt.

'Slope go up, slope go down,' said M'Bu gnomically.

'That's true,' said Azhural. 'Like, on *average*, it's flat all the way.'

He gazed at the mountains again.

'A thousand elephants,' he muttered. 'D'you know, boy, when they built the Tomb of King Leonid of Ephebe they

---

[15] Not for any particular religious reason. They just rather liked the effect when they grinned.

used a hundred elephants to cart the stone? And two hundred elephants, history tells us, were employed in the building of the palace of the Rhoxie in Klatch city.'

Thunder rumbled in the distance.

'A thousand elephants,' Azhural repeated. 'A thousand elephants. I wonder what they want them for?'

The rest of the day passed in a trance for Victor.

There was more galloping and fighting, and more rearranging of time. Victor still found that hard to understand. Apparently the film could be cut up and then stuck together again later, so that things happened in the right order. And some things didn't have to happen at all. He saw the artist draw one card which said 'In thee Kinges' Palace, One Houre Latre.'

One hour of Time had been vanished, just like that. Of course, he knew that it hadn't really been surgically removed from his life. It was the sort of thing that happened all the time in books. And on the stage, too. He'd seen a group of strolling players once, and the performance had leapt magically from 'A Battlefield in Tsort' to 'The Ephebian Fortresse, That Nighte' with no more than a brief descent of the sackcloth curtain and a lot of muffled bumping and cursing as the scenery was changed.

But this was different. Ten minutes after doing a scene, you'd do another scene that was taking place the day before, somewhere else, because Dibbler had rented the tents for both scenes and didn't want to have to pay any more rent than necessary. You just had to try and forget about everything but Now, and that was hard when you were also waiting every moment for that fading sensation . . .

It didn't come. Just after another half-hearted fight scene Dibbler announced that it was all finished.

'Aren't we going to do the ending?' said Ginger.

'You did that this morning,' said Soll.

'Oh.'

There was a chattering noise as the demons were let out of their box and sat swinging their little legs on the edge of the lid and passing a tiny cigarette from hand to hand. The extras queued up for their wages. The camel kicked the Vice-President in Charge of Camels. The handlemen wound the great reels of film out of the boxes and went away to whatever arcane cutting and gluing the handlemen got up to in the hours of darkness. Mrs Cosmopilite, Vice-President in Charge of Wardrobe, gathered up the costumes and toddled off, possibly to put them back on the beds.

A few acres of scrubby backlot stopped being the rolling dunes of the Great Nef and went back to being scrubby backlot again. Victor felt that much the same thing was happening to him.

In ones and twos, the makers of moving-picture magic departed, laughing and joking and arranging to meet at Borgle's later on.

Ginger and Victor were left alone in a widening circle of emptiness.

'I felt like this the first time the circus went away,' said Ginger.

'Mr Dibbler said we were going to do another one tomorrow,' said Victor. 'I'm sure he just makes them up as he goes along. Still, we got ten dollars each. Minus what we owe Gaspode,' he added conscientiously. He grinned foolishly at her. 'Cheer up,' he said. 'You're doing what you've always wanted to do.'

'Don't be stupid. I didn't even *know* about moving pictures a couple of months ago. There weren't any.'

They strolled aimlessly towards the town.

'What *did* you want to be?' he ventured.

She shrugged. 'I didn't know. I just knew I didn't want to be a milkmaid.'

There had been milkmaids at home. Victor tried to recollect anything about them. 'It always looked quite an interesting job to me, milkmaiding,' he said vaguely. 'Buttercups, you know. And fresh air.'

'It's cold and wet and just as you've finished the bloody cow kicks the bucket over. Don't tell me about

143

milking. Or being a shepherdess. Or a goosegirl. I really hated our farm.'

'Oh.'

'And they expected me to marry my cousin when I was fifteen.'

'Is that allowed?'

'Oh, yes. Everyone marries their cousins where I come from.'

'Why?' said Victor.

'I suppose it saves having to worry about what to do on Saturday nights.'

'Oh.'

'Didn't *you* want to be anything?' said Ginger, putting a whole sentence-worth of disdain in a mere three letters.

'Not really,' said Victor. 'Everything looks interesting until you do it. Then you find it's just another job. I bet even people like Cohen the Barbarian get up in the morning thinking, "Oh, *no*, not another day of crushing the jewelled thrones of the world beneath my sandalled feet."'

'Is that what he does?' said Ginger, interested despite herself.

'According to the stories, yes.'

'Why?'

'Search me. It's just a job, I guess.'

Ginger picked up a handful of sand. There were tiny white shells in it, which stayed behind as it trickled away between her fingers.

'I remember when the circus came to our village,' she said. 'I was ten. There was this girl with spangled tights. She walked a tightrope. She could even do somersaults on it. Everybody cheered and clapped. They wouldn't let *me* climb a tree, but they cheered *her*. That's when I decided.'

'Ah,' said Victor, trying to keep up with the psychology of this. 'You decided you wanted to be someone?'

'Don't be silly. That's when I decided I was going to be a lot more than just someone.'

She threw the shells towards the sunset and laughed. 'I'm

going to be the most famous person in the world, everyone will fall in love with me, and I shall live forever.'

'It's always best to know your own mind,' said Victor diplomatically.

'You know what the greatest tragedy is in the whole world?' said Ginger, not paying him the least attention. 'It's all the people who never find out what it is they really want to do or what it is they're really good at. It's all the sons who become blacksmiths because their fathers were blacksmiths. It's all the people who could be really fantastic flute players who grow old and die without ever seeing a musical instrument, so they become bad ploughmen instead. It's all the people with talents who never even find out. Maybe they are never even *born* in a time when it's even possible to find out.'

She took a deep breath. 'It's all the people who never get to know what it is they can really be. *It's all the wasted chances*. Well, Holy Wood is *my* chance, do you understand? This is my time for getting!'

Victor nodded. 'Yes,' he said. Magic for ordinary people, Silverfish had called it. A man turned a handle, and your life got changed.

'And not just for me,' Ginger went on. 'It's a chance for all of *us*. The people who aren't wizards and kings and heroes. Holy Wood's like a big bubbling stew but this time different ingredients float to the top. Suddenly there's all these *new* things for people to do. Do you know the theatres don't allow women to act? But Holy Wood does. And in Holy Wood there's jobs for trolls that don't just involve hitting people. And what did the handlemen do before they had handles to turn?'

She waved a hand vaguely in the direction of Ankh-Morpork's distant glow.

'Now they're trying to find ways of adding sound to moving pictures,' she said, 'and out *there* are people who'll turn out to be amazingly good at making, making . . . making *soundies*. They don't even know it yet – but they're out there. I can feel them. They're out there.'

Her eyes were glowing gold. It might just be the sunset, Victor thought, but . . .

'Because of Holy Wood, hundreds of people are finding out what it is they really want to be,' said Ginger. 'And thousands and thousands are getting a chance to forget themselves for an hour or so. This whole damn world is being given a shake!'

'That's it,' said Victor. 'That's what worries me. It's as though we're being slotted in. You think we're using Holy Wood, but Holy Wood is using us. All of us.'

'How? Why?'

'I don't know, but—'

'Look at wizards,' Ginger went on, vibrating with indignation. 'What good has their magic ever done anyone?'

'I think it sort of holds the world together—' Victor began.

'They're pretty good at magic flames and things, but can they make a loaf of bread?' Ginger wasn't in the mood for listening to anyone.

'Not for very long,' said Victor helplessly.

'What does that mean?'

'Something *real* like a loaf of bread contains a lot of . . . well . . . I suppose you'd call it energy,' said Victor. 'It takes a massive amount of power to create that amount of energy. You'd have to be a pretty good wizard to make a loaf that'd last in this world for more than a tiny part of a second. But that's not what magic is really about, you see,' he added quickly, 'because this world is—'

'Who cares?' said Ginger. 'Holy Wood's really doing things for ordinary people. Silver screen magic.'

'What's come over you? Last night—'

'That was then,' said Ginger impatiently. 'Don't you see? We could be going somewhere. We could be becoming *someone*. Because of Holy Wood. The world is our—'

'Lobster,' said Victor.

She waved a hand irritably. 'Any shellfish you like,' she said. 'I was thinking of oysters, actually.'

'Were you? I was thinking of lobsters.'

*

'Bur*saar*!'

I shouldn't have to run around like this at my age, thought the Bursar, scurrying down the corridor in answer to the Archchancellor's bellow. Why's he so interested in the damn thing, anyway? Wretched pot!

'Coming, Master,' he trilled.

The Archchancellor's desk was covered with ancient documents.

When a wizard died, all his papers were stored in one of the outlying reaches of the Library. Shelf after shelf of quietly mouldering documents, the haunt of mysterious beetles and dry rot, stretched away into an unguessable distance. Everyone kept telling everyone that there was a wealth of material here for researchers, if only someone could find the time to do it.

The Bursar was annoyed. He couldn't find the Librarian anywhere. The ape never seemed to be around these days. He'd had to scrabble among the stuff *himself*.

'I think this is the last, Archchancellor,' he said, tipping an avalanche of dusty paperwork on to the desk. Ridcully flailed at a cloud of moths.

'Paper, paper, paper,' he muttered. 'How many damn bits of paper in his stuff, eh?'

'Er . . . 23,813, Archchancellor,' said the Bursar. 'He kept a record.'

'Look at this,' said the Archchancellor. ' "Star Enumerator" . . . "Rev Counter for Use in Ecclesiastical Areas" . . . "Swamp Meter" . . . Swamp meter! The man was mad!'

'He had a very tidy mind,' said the Bursar.

'Same thing.'

'Is it, er, really important, Archchancellor?' the Bursar ventured.

'Damn thing shot pellets at me,' said Ridcully. 'Twice!'

'I'm sure it wasn't, er, intended—'

'I want to see how it was made, man! Just think of the sportin' possibilities!'

The Bursar tried to think of the possibilities.

'I'm sure Riktor didn't intend to make any kind of offensive device,' he ventured, hopelessly.

'Who gives a damn what *he* intended? Where is the thing now?'

'I had a couple of servants put sandbags around it.'

'Good idea. It's—'

. . . whumm . . . whumm . . .

It was a muffled sound from the corridor. The two wizards exchanged a meaningful glance.

. . . whumm . . . *whumm*WHUMM.

The Bursar held his breath.

Plib.

Plib.

Plib.

The Archchancellor peered at the hourglass on the mantelpiece. 'It's doin' it every five minutes now,' he said.

'And it's up to three shots,' said the Bursar. 'I'll have to order some more sandbags.'

He flicked through a heap of paper. A word caught his eye.

Reality.

He glanced at the handwriting that flowed across the page. It had a very small, cramped, deliberate look. Someone had told him that this was because Numbers Riktor had been an anal retentive. The Bursar didn't know what that meant, and hoped never to find out.

Another word was: Measurement. His gaze drifted upwards, and took in the underlined title: *Some Notes on the Objective Measurement of Reality*.

Over the page was a diagram. The Bursar stared at it.

'Found anything?' said the Archchancellor, without looking up.

The Bursar shoved the paper up the sleeve of his robe.

'Nothing important,' he said.

Down below, the surf boomed on the beach. (. . . and

148

below the surface, the lobsters walked backwards along the deep, drowned streets . . .)

Victor threw another piece of driftwood on to the fire. It burned blue with salt.

'I don't understand her,' he said. 'Yesterday she was quite normal, today it's all gone to her head.'

'Bitches!' said Gaspode, sympathetically.

'Oh, I wouldn't go that far,' said Victor. 'She's just aloof.'

'Loofs!' said Gaspode.

'That's what intelligence does for your sex life,' said Don't-call-me-Mr-Thumpy. 'Rabbits never have that sort of trouble. Go, Sow, Thank You Doe.'

'You could try offering her a moushe,' said the cat. 'Preshent company exchepted, of course,' it added guiltily, trying to avoid Definitely-Not-Squeak's glare.

'Being intelligent hasn't done *my* social life any favours, either,' said Mr Thumpy bitterly. 'A week ago, no problems. Now suddenly I want to make conversation, and all they do is sit there wrinklin' their noses at you. You feel a right idiot.'

There was a strangulated quacking.

'The duck says, have you done anything about the book?' said Gaspode.

'I had a look at it when we broke for lunch,' said Victor.

There was another irritable quack.

'The duck says, yes, but what have you *done* about it?' said Gaspode.

'Look, I can't go all the way to Ankh-Morpork just like that,' snapped Victor. 'It takes hours! We film all day as it is!'

'Ask for a day off,' said Mr Thumpy.

'No-one asks for a day off in Holy Wood!' said Victor. 'I've been fired once, thank you.'

'And he took you on again at more money,' said Gaspode. 'Funny, that.' He scratched an ear. 'Tell him your contract says you can have a day off.'

'I haven't got a contract. You *know* that. You work, you get paid. It's simple.'

'Yeah,' said Gaspode. 'Yeah. Yeah? A verbal contract. It's simple. I *like* it.'

Towards the end of the night Detritus the troll lurked awkwardly in the shadows by the back door of the Blue Lias. Strange passions had wracked his body all day. Every time he'd shut his eyes he kept seeing a figure shaped like a small hillock.

He had to face up to it.

Detritus was in love.

Yes, he'd spent many years in Ankh-Morpork hitting people for money. Yes, it had been a friendless, brutalizing life. And a lonely one, too. He'd been resigned to an old-age of bitter bachelorhood and suddenly, now, Holy Wood was handing him a chance he'd never dreamed of.

He'd been strictly brought up and he could dimly remember the lecture he'd been given by his father when he was a young troll. If you saw a girl you liked, you didn't just rush at her. There were proper ways to go about things.

He'd gone down to the beach and found a rock. But not any old rock. He'd searched carefully, and found a large sea-smoothed one with veins of pink and white quartz. Girls liked that sort of thing.

Now he waited, shyly, for her to finish work.

He tried to think of what he would say. No-one had ever told him what to *say*. It wasn't as if he was a smart troll like Rock or Morry, who had a way with words. Basically, he'd never needed much of what you might call a vocabulary. He kicked despondently at the sand. What chance did he have with a smart lady like her?

There was a thump of heavy feet, and the door opened. The object of desire stepped out into the night and took a deep breath, which had the same effect on Detritus as an ice cube down the neck.

He gave his rock a panicky look. It didn't seem anything

like big enough now, when you saw the size of her. But maybe it was what you did with it that mattered.

Well, this was it. They said you never forgot your first time . . .

He wound up his arm with the rock in it and hit her squarely between the eyes.

That's when it all started to go wrong.

Tradition said that the girl, when she was able to focus again, and if the rock was of an acceptable standard, should immediately be amenable to whatever the troll suggested, i.e., a candle-lit human for two, although of course that sort of thing wasn't done any more now, at least if there was any chance of being caught.

She shouldn't narrow her eyes and catch him a ding across the ear that made his eyeballs rattle.

'You stupid troll!' she shouted, as Detritus staggered around in a circle. 'What you do that for? You think I unsophisticated girl just off mountain? Why you not do it right?'

'But, but,' Detritus began, in terror at her rage, 'I not able to ask father permission to hit you, not know where he living—'

Ruby drew herself up haughtily.

'All that old-fashioned stuff very uncultured now,' she sniffed. 'It's not the modern way. I not interested in any troll', she added, 'that not up-to-date. A rock on the head may be quite sentimental,' she went on, the certainty draining out of her voice as she surveyed the sentence ahead of her, 'but diamonds are a girl's best friend.' She hesitated. That didn't sound right, even to her.

It certainly puzzled Detritus.

'What? You want I should knock my teeth out?' he said.

'Well, all right, not diamonds,' Ruby conceded. 'But there proper modern ways now. You got to court a girl.'

Detritus brightened. 'Ah, but I—' he began.

'That's court, not caught,' said Ruby wearily. 'You got to, to, to—' She paused.

151

She wasn't all that sure what you had to do. But Ruby had spent some weeks in Holy Wood, and if Holy Wood did anything, it *changed* things; in Holy Wood she'd plugged into a vast cross-species female freemasonry she hadn't suspected existed, and she was learning fast. She'd talked at length to sympathetic human girls. And dwarfs. Even *dwarfs* had better courtship rituals, for gods' sake.[16] And what humans got up to was *amazing*.

Whereas all a female troll had to look forward to was a quick thump on the head and the rest of her life subduing and cooking anything the male dragged back to the cave.

Well, there were going to be changes. Next time Ruby went home the troll mountains were going to receive their biggest shake-up since the last continental collision. In the meantime, she was going to start with her own life.

She waved a massive hand in a vague way.

'You got to, to sing outside a girl's window,' she said, 'and, and you got to give her *oograah*.'

'Oograah?'

'Yeah. *Pretty* oograah.'[17]

Detritus scratched his head.

'Why?' he said.

Ruby looked panicky for a moment. She also couldn't for the life of her imagine why the handing over of inedible vegetation was so important, but she wasn't about to admit it.

'Fancy you not knowing that,' she said scathingly.

The sarcasm was lost on Detritus. Most things were.

'Right,' he said. 'I not so uncultured as you think,' he added. 'I bang up to date. You wait and see.'

*

---

[16] All dwarfs have beards and wear many layers of clothing. Their courtships are largely concerned with finding out, in delicate and circumspect ways, what sex the other dwarf is.

[17] Trolls have 5,400 words for rocks and one for vegetation. 'Oograah' means everything from moss to giant redwoods. The way trolls see it, if you can't eat it, it's not worth naming it.

Hammering filled the air. Buildings were spreading backwards from the nameless main street into the dunes. No-one *owned* any land in Holy Wood; if it was empty, you built on it.

Dibbler had two offices now. There was one where he shouted at people, and a bigger one just outside it where people shouted at each other. Soll shouted at handlemen. Handlemen shouted at alchemists. Demons wandered over every flat surface and drowned in the coffee cups and shouted at one another. A couple of experimental green parrots shouted at themselves. People wearing odd bits of costume wandered in and just shouted. Silverfish shouted because he couldn't quite work out why he now had a desk in the outer office even though he owned the studio.

Gaspode sat stolidly by the door to the inner office. In the past five minutes he had attracted one half-hearted kick, a soggy biscuit and a pat on the head. He reckoned he was ahead of the game, dogwise.

He was trying to listen to all the conversations at once. It was extremely instructive. For one thing, some of the people coming in and shouting were carrying bags of money . . .

'You what?'

The shout had come from the inner office. Gaspode cocked the other ear.

'I, er, want a day off, Mr Dibbler,' said Victor.

'A day *off*? You don't want to work?'

'Just for the day, Mr Dibbler.'

'But you don't think I'm going to go around paying people to have days off, do you? I'm not made of money, you know. It's not as if we make a profit, even. Hold a crossbow to my head, why don't you.'

Gaspode looked at the bags in front of Soll, who was furiously adding up piles of coins. He raised a cynical eyebrow.

There was a pause. Oh, no, thought Gaspode. The young idiot's forgetting his lines.

'I don't want paying, Mr Dibbler.'

Gaspode relaxed.

'You don't want paying?'

'No, Mr Dibbler.'

'But you want a job when you get back, I suppose?' said Dibbler sarcastically.

Gaspode tensed. Victor had taken a lot of coaching.

'Well, I hope so, Mr Dibbler. But I was thinking of going to see what Untied Alchemists had to offer.'

There was a sound exactly like the sound of a chairback striking the wall. Gaspode grinned evilly.

Another bag of money was dropped in front of Soll.

'*Untied Alchemists!*'

'They really look as if they're making progress with sou*n*dies, Mr Dibbler,' said Victor meekly.

'But they're amateurs! *And* crooks!'

Gaspode frowned. He hadn't been able to coach Victor past this stage.

'Well, that's a relief, Mr Dibbler.'

'Why's that?'

'Well, it'd be dreadful if they were crooks and *professional*.'

Gaspode nodded. Nice one. Nice one.

There was the sound of footsteps hurrying around a desk. When Dibbler spoke next, you could have sunk a well in his voice and sold it at ten dollars a barrel.

'Victor! Vic! Haven't I been like an uncle to you?'

Well, yes, thought Gaspode. He's like an uncle to most people here. That's because they're his nephews.

He stopped listening, partly because Victor was going to get his day off and was very likely going to get paid for it as well, but mainly because another dog had been led into the room.

It was huge and glossy. Its coat shone like honey.

Gaspode recognized it as pure-bred Ramtop hunting dog. When it sat down beside him, it was as if a beautifully sleek racing yacht had slipped into a berth alongside a coal barge.

He heard Soll say, 'So that is Uncle's latest idea, is it? What's it called?'

'Laddie,' said the handler.

'How much was it?'

'Sixty dollars.'

'For a *dog*? We're in the wrong business.'

'It can do all kinds of tricks, the breeder said. Bright as a button, he said. Just what Mr Dibbler is looking for.'

'Well, tie it up there. And if that other mutt starts a fight, kick it out.'

Gaspode gave Soll a long, thoughtful scrutiny. Then, when the attention was no longer on them, he sidled closer to the newcomer, looked it up and down, and spoke quietly out of the corner of his mouth.

'What you here for?' he said.

The dog gave him a look of handsome incomprehension.

'I mean, do you b'long to someone or what?' said Gaspode.

The dog whined softly.

Gaspode tried Basic Canine, which is a combination of whines and sniffs.

'*Hallo?*' he ventured. '*Anyone in there?*'

The dog's tail thumped uncertainly.

'*The grub here's ruddy awful,*' said Gaspode.

The dog raised its highly-bred muzzle.

'*What dis place?*' it said.

'*This is Holy Wood,*' said Gaspode conversationally. '*I'm Gaspode. Named after the famous Gaspode, you know. Anythin' you want to know, you just—*'

'*All dese two-legs here. Dur . . . What dis place?*'

Gaspode stared.

At that moment Dibbler's door opened. Victor emerged, coughing, at one end of a cigar.

'Great, great,' said Dibbler, following him out. 'Knew we could sort it out. Don't waste it, boy, don't waste it. They cost a dollar a box. Oh, I see you brought your little doggie.'

'Woof,' said Gaspode, irritably.

The other dog gave a short sharp bark and sat up with obedient alertness radiating from every hair.

'Ah,' said Dibbler, 'and I see we've got our wonder dog.'

Gaspode's apology for a tail twitched once or twice.

Then the truth dawned.

He glared at the larger dog, opened his mouth to speak, caught himself just in time, and managed to turn it into a *'Bark?'*

'I got the idea the other night, when I saw your dog,' said Dibbler. 'I thought, people *like* animals. Me, I like dogs. Good image, the dog. Saving lives, Man's best friend, that kind of stuff.'

Victor looked at Gaspode's furious expression.

'Gaspode's *quite* bright,' he said.

'Oh, I expect you think he is,' said Dibbler. 'But you've just got to look at the two of them. On the one hand there's this bright, alert, handsome animal, and on the other there's this dust ball with a hangover. I mean, no contest, am I right?'

The wonder dog gave a brisk yap.

'What dis place? Good boy Laddie!'

Gaspode rolled his eyes.

'See what I mean?' said Dibbler. 'Give him the right name, a bit a training, and a star is born.' He slapped Victor on the back again. 'Nice to see you, nice to see you, drop in again any time, only not too frequently, let's have lunch sometime, now get out, *Soll!*'

'Coming, Uncle.'

Victor was suddenly alone, apart from the dogs and the room full of people. He took the cigar out of his mouth, spat on the glowing end, and carefully hid it behind a potted plant.

'A star is whelped,' said a small, withering voice from below.

'What he say? Where dis place?'

'Don't look at me,' said Victor. 'Nothing to do with me.'

'Will you just look at it? I mean, are we talking Thicko City here or what?' sneered Gaspode.

'*Good boy Laddie!*'

'Come on,' said Victor. 'I'm supposed to be on set in five minutes.'

Gaspode trailed after him, muttering under his horrible breath. Victor caught the occasional 'old rug' and 'Man's best friend' and 'bloody wonder bloody dog'. Finally, he couldn't stand it any longer.

'You're just jealous,' he said.

'What, of an overgrown puppy with a single-figure IQ?' sneered Gaspode.

'*And* a glossy coat, cold nose and probably a pedigree as long as your ar – as my arm,' said Victor.

'Pedigree? *Pedigree?* What's a pedigree? It's just breedin'. I had a father too, you know. And two grandads. And *four* great grandads. And many of 'em were the same dog, even. So don't you tell me I'm from no pedigree,' said Gaspode.

He paused to cock a leg against one of the supports of the new 'Home of Century of the Fruitbat Moving Pictures' sign.

That was something else that had puzzled Thomas Silverfish. He'd come in this morning, and the hand-painted sign saying 'Interesting and Instructive Films' had gone and had been replaced by this huge billboard. He was sitting back in the office with his head in his hands, trying to convince himself that it had been his idea.

'*I'm* the one Holy Wood called,' Gaspode muttered, in a self-pitying voice. 'I came all the way here, and then they chose that great hairy thing. Probably it'll work for a plate of meat a day, too.'

'Well, look, maybe you weren't called to Holy Wood to be a wonder dog,' said Victor. 'Maybe it's got something else in mind for you.'

This is ridiculous, he thought. Why are we talking about it like this? A place hasn't got a mind. It can't call people to it . . . well, unless you count things like homesickness. But you can't be homesick for a place you've never been to before, it stands to reason. The last time people were here must have been thousands of years ago.

Gaspode sniffed at a wall.

'Did you tell Dibbler everything I told you?' he said.

'Yes. He was very upset when I mentioned about going to Untied Alchemists.'

Gaspode sniggered.

'An' you told him what I said about a verbal contract not being worth the paper it's printed on?'

'Yes. He said he didn't understand what I meant. But he gave me a cigar. And he said he'd *pay* for me and Ginger to go to Ankh-Morpork soon. He said he's got a really big picture planned.'

'What is it?' said Gaspode suspiciously.

'He didn't say.'

'Listen, lad,' said Gaspode, 'Dibbler's making a fortune. I counted it. There were five thousand, two hundred and seventy-three dollars and fifty-two pence on Soll's desk. And you earned it. Well, you and Ginger did.'

'Gosh!'

'Now, there's some new words I want you to learn,' said Gaspode. 'Think you can?'

'I hope so.'

' "Per-cent-age of the gross" ', said Gaspode. 'There. Think you can remember it?'

' "Per-cent-age of the gross",' said Victor.

'Good lad.'

'What does it mean?'

'Don't you worry about that,' said Gaspode. 'You just have to say it's what you want, OK. When the time's right.'

'When will the time be right, then?' said Victor.

Gaspode grinned nastily. 'Oh, I reckon when Dibbler's just got a mouthful of food'd be favourite.'

Holy Wood Hill bustled like an ant heap. On the seaward side Fir Wood Studios were making *The Third Gnome*. Microlithic Pictures, which was run almost entirely by the dwarfs, was hard at work on *Golde Diggers of 1457*, which was going to be followed by *The Golde Rushe*. Floating

Bladder Pictures was hard at work with *Turkey Legs*. And Borgle's was packed out.

'I don't know what it's called, but we're doing one about going to see a wizard. Something about following a yellow sick toad,' a man in one half of a lion suit explained to a companion in the queue.

'No wizards in Holy Wood, I thought.'

'Oh, this one's all right. He's not very good at the wizarding.'

'So what's new?'

Sound! That was the problem. Alchemists toiled in sheds all over Holy Wood, screaming at parrots, pleading with mynah birds, constructing intricate bottles to trap sound and bounce it around harmlessly until it was time for it to be let out. To the sporadic boom of octo-cellulose exploding was added the occasional sob of exhaustion or scream of agony as an enraged parrot mistook a careless thumb for a nut.

The parrots weren't the success they'd hoped for. It was true that they could remember what they heard and repeat it after a fashion, but there was no way to turn them off and they were in the habit of ad-libbing other sounds they'd heard or, Dibbler suspected, had been taught by mischievous handlemen. Thus, brief snatches of romantic dialogue would be punctuated with cries of 'Waaaarrrk! Showusyerknickers!' and Dibbler said he had no intention of making that kind of picture, at least at the moment.

Sound! Whoever got sound first would rule Holy Wood, they said. People were flocking to the clicks now, but people were fickle. Colour was different. Colour was just a matter of breeding demons who could paint fast enough. It was sound that meant something new.

In the meantime, there were stop-gap measures. The dwarfs' studio had shunned the general practice of putting the dialogue on cards between scenes and had invented sub-titles, which worked fine provided the performers remembered not to step too far forward and knock over the letters.

But if sound was missing, then the screen had to be filled from side to side with a feast for the eyes. The sound of hammering was always Holy Wood's background noise, but it redoubled now . . .

The cities of the world were being built in Holy Wood. Untied Alchemists started it, with a one-tenth-size wood and canvas replica of the Great Pyramid of Tsort. Soon the backlots sprouted whole streets in Ankh-Morpork, palaces from Pseudopolis, castles from the Hublands. In some cases, the streets were painted on the back of the palaces, so that princes and peasants were separated by one thickness of painted sacking.

Victor spent the rest of the morning working on a one-reeler. Ginger hardly said a word to him, even after the obligatory kiss when he rescued her from whatever it was Morry was supposed to be today. Whatever magic Holy Wood worked on them it wasn't doing it today. He was glad to get away.

Afterwards he wandered across the backlot to watch them putting Laddie the Wonder Dog through his paces.

There was no doubt, as the graceful shape streaked like an arrow over obstacles and grabbed a trainer by a well-padded arm, that here was a dog almost designed by Nature for moving pictures. He even barked photogenically.

'An' do you know what he's sayin'?' said a disgruntled voice beside Victor. It was Gaspode, a picture of bow-legged misery.

'No. What?' said Victor.

'"*Me Laddie. Me good boy. Good boy Laddie*,"' said Gaspode. 'Makes you want to throw up, doesn't it?'

'Yes, but could you leap a six-foot hurdle?' said Victor.

'That's intelligent, is it?' said Gaspode. 'I always walk *around* – what's that they're doing now?'

'Giving him his lunch, I think.'

'They call that lunch, do they?'

Victor watched Gaspode stroll over and peer into the dog's bowl. Laddie gave him a sideways look. Gaspode barked quietly. Laddie whined. Gaspode barked again.

There was a lengthy exchange of yaps.

Then Gaspode strolled back, and sat down beside Victor.

'Watch this,' he said.

Laddie took the food bowl in his mouth, and turned it upside down.

'Disgustin' stuff,' said Gaspode. 'All tubes and innards. I wouldn't give it to a dog, and I *am* one.'

'You made him tip out his own dinner?' said Victor, horrified.

'Very obedient lad, I thought,' said Gaspode smugly.

'What a *nasty* thing to do!'

'Oh, no. I give 'im some advice, too.'

Laddie barked peremptorily at the people clustering around him. Victor heard them muttering.

'*Dog don't eat his dinner,*' came Detritus' voice, '*dog go hungry.*'

'*Don't be daft. Mr Dibbler says he's worth more than we are!*'

'*Perhaps it's not what he's used to. I mean, a posh dog like him an' all. It's a bit yukky, isn't it?*'

'*It dog food! That what dogs are supposed to eat!*'

'*Yeah, but is it* wonder *dog food? What're* wonder *dogs fed on?*'

'*Mr Dibbler'll feed you* to *him if there's any trouble.*'

'*All right, all right. Detritus, go around to Borgle's. See what he's got. Not the stuff he gives to the usual customers, mind.*'

'*That IS the stuff he give to usual customers.*'

'*That's what I mean.*'

Five minutes later Detritus trailed back carrying about nine pounds of raw steak. It was dumped in the dog bowl. The trainers looked at Laddie.

Laddie cocked an eye towards Gaspode, who nodded almost imperceptibly.

The big dog put one foot on one end of the steak, took the other end in his mouth, and tore off a lump. Then he padded over the compound and dropped it respectfully in front of Gaspode, who gave it a long, calculating stare.

161

'Well, I dunno,' he said at last. 'Does that look like ten per cent to you, Victor?'

'You *negotiated* his *dinner*?'

Gaspode's voice was muffled by meat. 'I reckon ten per cent is ver' fair. Very fair, in the circumstances.'

'You know, you really *are* a son of a bitch,' said Victor.

'Proud of it,' said Gaspode, indistinctly. He bolted the last of the steak. 'What shall we do now?'

'I'm supposed to get an early night. We're starting for Ankh very early tomorrow,' said Victor doubtfully.

'Still not made any progress with the book?'

'No.'

'Let me have a look, then.'

'Can you read?'

'Dunno. Never tried.'

Victor looked around them. No-one was paying him any attention. They never did. Once the handles stopped turning, no-one bothered about performers; it was like being temporarily invisible.

He sat down on a pile of lumber, opened the book randomly at an early page, and held it out in front of Gaspode's critical stare.

Eventually the dog said, 'It's got all marks on it.'

Victor sighed. 'That's writing,' he said.

Gaspode squinted. 'What, all them little pictures?'

'Early writing was like that. People drew little pictures to represent ideas.'

'So . . . if there's a lot of one picture, it means it's an important idea?'

'What? Well, yes. I suppose so.'

'Like the dead man.'

Victor was lost.

'The dead man on the beach?'

'No. The dead man on the pages. See? Everywhere, there's the dead man.'

Victor gave him an odd look, and then turned the book around and peered at it.

'Where? I don't see any dead men.'

Gaspode snorted.

'Look, all over the page,' he said. 'He looks just like those tombs you get in old temples and stuff. You know? Where they do this statchoo of the stiff lyin' on top of the tomb, with his arms crossed an' holdin' his sword. Dead noble.'

'Good grief! You're right! It does look sort of . . . dead . . . '

'Prob'ly all the writing's goin' on about what a great guy he was when he was alive,' said Gaspode knowledgeably. 'You know, "Slayer of thousands" stuff. Prob'ly he left a lot of money for priests to say prayers and light candles and sacrifice goats and stuff. There used to be a lot of that sort of thing. You know, you'd get dese guys whorin' and drinkin' and carryin' on regardless their whole life, and then when the old Grim Reaper starts sharpenin' his scythe they suddenly becomes all pious and pays a lot of priests to give their soul a quick wash-and-brush-up and gen'rally keep on tellin' the gods what a decent chap they was.'

'Gaspode?' said Victor levelly.

'What?'

'You were a performing dog. How come you know all this stuff?'

'I ain't just a pretty face.'

'You aren't *even* a pretty face, Gaspode.'

The little dog shrugged. 'I've always had eyes and ears,' he said. 'You'd be amazed, the stuff you see and hear when you're a dog. I dint know what any of it meant at the time, of course. Now I do.'

Victor stared at the pages again. There certainly was a figure which, if you half-closed your eyes, looked very much like a statue of a knight with his hands resting on his sword.

'It might not *mean* a man,' he said. 'Pictographic writing doesn't work like that. It's all down to context, you see.' He racked his brains to think of some of the books he'd seen. 'For example, in the Agatean language the signs for "woman" and "slave" written down together actually mean "wife".'

He looked closely at the page. The dead man – or the sleeping man, or the standing man resting his hands on his sword, the figure was so stylized it was hard to be sure – seemed to appear beside another common picture. He ran his finger along the line of pictograms.

'See,' he said, 'it could be the man figure is only part of a word. See? It's always to the right of this other picture, which looks a bit like – a bit like a doorway, or something. So it might really mean—' he hesitated. ' "Doorway/man",' he hazarded.

He turned the book slightly.

'Could be some old king,' said Gaspode. 'Could mean something like The Man with the Sword is Imprisoned, or something. Or maybe it means Watch Out, There's a Man with a Sword behind the Door. Could mean anything, really.'

Victor squinted at the book again. 'It's funny,' he said. 'It doesn't look dead. Just . . . not alive. Waiting to be alive? A waiting man with a sword?'

Victor peered at the little man-figure. It had hardly any features, but still managed to look vaguely familiar.

'You know,' he said, 'it looks just like my Uncle Osric . . . '

Clickaclickaclicka. Click.

The film spun to a standstill. There was a thunder of applause, a stamping of feet and a barrage of empty banged grain bags.

In the very front row of the *Odium* the Librarian stared up at the now-empty screen. It was the fourth time that afternoon he'd watched *Shadow of the Dessert*, because there's something about a 300lb orang-utan that doesn't encourage people to order it out of the pit between houses. A drift of peanut shells and screwed up paper bags lay around his feet.

The Librarian loved the clicks. They spoke to something

in his soul. He'd even started writing a story which he thought would make a very good moving picture.[18] Everyone he showed it to said it was jolly good, often even before they'd read it.

But something about this click was worrying him. He'd sat through it four times, and he was still worried.

He eased himself out of the three seats he was occupying and knuckled his way up the aisle and into the little room where Bezam was rewinding the film.

Bezam looked up as the door opened.

'Get out—' he began, and then grinned desperately and said, 'Hallo, sir. Pretty good click, eh? We'll be showing it again any minute now and – *what the hell are you doing? You can't do that!*'

The Librarian ripped the huge roll of film off the projector and pulled it through his leathery fingers, holding it up to the light. Bezam tried to snatch it back and got a palm in his chest that sat him firmly on the floor, where great coils of film piled up on top of him.

He watched in horror as the great ape grunted, grasped a piece of the film in both hands and, with two bites, edited it. Then the Librarian picked him up, dusted him off, patted him on the head, thrust the great pile of unwound click into his helpless arms, and ambled swiftly out of the room with a few frames of film dangling from one paw.

Bezam stared helplessly after him.

'You're banned!' he shouted, when he judged the ape to be safely out of earshot.

Then he looked down at the two severed ends.

Breaks in films weren't unusual. Bezam had spent many a flustered few minutes feverishly cutting and pasting while the audience cheerfully stamped its feet and high-spiritedly threw peanuts, knives and double-headed axes at the screen.

He let the coils fall around him and reached for the

---

[18] It was about a young ape who is abandoned in the big city and grows up being able to speak the language of humans.

scissors and glue. At least – he found, after holding the two ends up to the lantern – the Librarian hadn't taken a very interesting bit. Odd, that. Bezam wouldn't have put it past the ape to have taken a bit where the girl was definitely showing too much chest, or one of the fight scenes. But all he'd wanted was a piece that showed the Sons galloping down from their mountain fastness, in single file, on identical camels.

'Dunno what he wanted that for,' he muttered, taking the lid off the glue pot. 'It just shows a lot of rocks.'

Victor and Gaspode stood among the sand dunes near the beach.

'That's where the driftwood hut is,' said Victor, pointing, 'and then if you look hard you can see there's a sort of road pointing straight towards the hill. But there's nothing on the hill but the old trees.'

Gaspode looked back at Holy Wood Bay.

'Funny it bein' circular,' he said.

'I thought so,' said Victor.

'I heard once where there was this city that was so wicked that the gods turned it into a puddle of molten glass,' said Gaspode, apropos of nothing. 'And the only person who saw it happen was turned into a pillar of salt by day and a cheese shaker by night.'

'Gosh. What had the people been doing?'

'Dunno. Prob'ly not much. It doesn't take much to annoy gods.'

'Me good boy! Good boy Laddie!'

The dog came streaking over the dunes, a comet of gold and orange hair. It skidded to a halt in front of Gaspode, and then began to dance around excitedly, yapping.

'He's escaped and he wants me to play with him,' said Gaspode despondently. 'Ridiculous, ain't it? *Laddie drop dead.*'

Laddie rolled over obediently, all four legs in the air.

'See? He understands every word I say,' muttered Gaspode.

'He likes you,' said Victor.

'Huh,' sniffed Gaspode. 'How're dogs ever goin' to amount to anything if they bounce around worshipping people just 'cos they've been given a meal? What's he want me to do with this??'

Laddie had dropped a stick in front of Gaspode and was looking at him expectantly.

'He wants you to throw it,' said Victor.

'What for?'

'So he can bring it back.'

'What I don't understand,' said Gaspode, as Victor picked up the stick and hurled it away, Laddie racing along underneath it, 'is how come we're descended from wolves. I mean, your average wolf, he's a bright bugger, know what I mean? Chock full of cunnin' an' like that. We're talking grey paws racing over the trackless tundra, is what I'm getting at.'

Gaspode looked wistfully at the distant mountains. 'And suddenly a handful of generations later we've got Percy the Pup here with a cold nose, bright eyes, glossy coat and the brains of a stunned herring.'

'And you,' said Victor. Laddie whirled back in a storm of sand and dropped the damp stick in front of him. Victor picked it up and threw it again. Laddie bounded off, yapping himself sick with excitement.

'Well, yeah,' said Gaspode, ambling along in a bow-legged swagger. 'Only I can look after myself. It's a dog-eat-dog world out there. You think Dopey the Mutt there would last five minutes in Ankh-Morpork? He set one paw in some o' the streets, he's three sets of fur gloves an' Crispy Fried No. 27 at the nearest Klatchian all-night carry-out.'

Victor threw the stick again.

'Tell me,' he said, 'who *was* the famous Gaspode you're named after?'

'You never heard of him?'

'No.'

'He was dead famous.'

'He was a dog?'

'Yeah. It was years and years ago. There was this ole bloke in Ankh who snuffed it, and he belonged to one of them religions where they bury you after you're dead, an' they did, and he had this ole dog—'

'—called Gaspode—?'

'Yeah, and this ole dog had been his only companion and after they buried the man he lay down on his grave and howled and howled for a couple of weeks. Growled at everybody who came near. An' then died.'

Victor paused in the act of throwing the stick again.

'That's very sad,' he said. He threw. Laddie tore along underneath it, and disappeared into a stand of scrubby trees on the hillside.

'Yeah. Everyone says it demonstrates a dog's innocent and undyin' love for 'is master,' said Gaspode, spitting the words out as if they were ashes.

'You don't believe that, then?'

'Not really. I b'lieve any bloody dog will stay still an' howl when you've just lowered the gravestone on his tail,' said Gaspode.

There was a ferocious barking.

'Don't worry about it. He's probably found a threatening rock or something,' said Gaspode.

He'd found Ginger.

The Librarian knuckled purposefully through the maze of Unseen University's library and descended the steps towards the maximum-security shelves.

Nearly all the books in the Library were, being magical, considerably more dangerous than ordinary books; most of them were chained to the bookcases to stop them flapping around.

But the lower levels . . .

. . . there they kept the *rogue* books, the books whose behaviour or mere contents demanded a whole shelf, a whole *room* to themselves. Cannibal books, books which, if left on a shelf with their weaker brethren, would be found looking considerably fatter and more smug in the smoking ashes next morning. Books whose mere contents pages could reduce the unprotected mind to grey cheese. Books that were not just books of magic, but magical books.

There's a lot of loose thinking about magic. People go around talking about mystic harmonies and cosmic balances and unicorns, all of which is to real magic what a glove puppet is to the Royal Shakespeare Company.

Real magic is the hand around the bandsaw, the thrown spark in the powder keg, the dimension-warp linking you straight into the heart of a star, the flaming sword that burns *all the way down to the pommel*. Sooner juggle torches in a tar pit than mess with real magic. Sooner lie down in front of a thousand elephants.

At least, that's what wizards say, which is why they charge such swingeingly huge fees for getting involved with the bloody stuff.

But down here, in the dark tunnels, there was no hiding behind amulets and starry robes and pointy hats. Down here, you either had it or you didn't. And if you hadn't got it, you'd had it.

There were sounds from behind the heavily barred doors as the Librarian shuffled along. Once or twice something heavy threw itself against a door, making the hinges rattle.

There were noises.

The orang-utan stopped in front of an arched doorway that was blocked with a door made not of wood but of stone, balanced so that it could easily be opened from outside but could withstand massive pressure from within.

He paused for a moment, and then reached into a little alcove and removed a mask of iron and smoked glass, which he put on, and a pair of heavy leather gloves reinforced with steel mesh. There was also a torch made of oil-soaked rags; he lit this from one of the flickering braziers in the tunnel.

At the back of the alcove was a brass key.

He took the key, and then he took a deep breath.

All the Books of Power had their own particular natures. *The Octavo* was harsh and imperious. *The Bumper Fun Grimoire* went in for deadly practical jokes. *The Joy of Tantric Sex* had to be kept under iced water. The Librarian knew them all, and how to deal with them.

This one was different. Usually people saw only tenth- or twelfth-hand copies, as like the real thing as a painting or an explosion was to, well, to an explosion. This was a book that had absorbed the sheer, graphite-grey evil of its subject matter.

Its name was hacked in letters over the arch, lest men and apes forget.

NECROTELICOMNICON.

He put the key in the lock, and offered up a prayer to the gods.

'Oook,' he said fervently. 'Oook.'

The door swung open.

In the darkness within, a chain gave a faint clink.

'She's still breathing,' said Victor. Laddie leapt around them, barking furiously.

'Maybe you should loosen her clothing or something,' said Gaspode. 'It's just a thought,' he added. 'You don't have to glare at me like that. I'm a dog, what do I know?'

'She seems all right, but . . . look at her hands,' said Victor. 'What the hell has she been trying to do?'

'Tryin' to open that door,' said Gaspode.

'What door?'

'That door *there*.'

Part of the hill had slipped away. Huge blocks of masonry protruded from the sand. There were the stubs of ancient pillars, sticking up like fluoridated teeth.

Between two of them was an arched doorway, three times as high as Victor. It was sealed with a pair of pale grey doors, either of stone or of wood that had become as hard as stone over the years. One of them was slightly open, but had been prevented from opening further by the drifts of sand in front of it. Frantically scrabbled furrows had been dug deep into the sand. Ginger had been trying to shift it with her bare hands.

'Stupid thing to do in this heat,' said Victor, vaguely. He looked from the door to the sea, and then down at Gaspode.

Laddie scrambled up the sand and barked excitedly at the crack between the doors.

'What's he doing that for?' said Victor, suddenly feeling spooked. 'All his hair is standing up. You don't think he's got one of those mysterious animal premonitions of evil, do you?'

'I think he's a pillock,' said Gaspode. '*Laddie shut up!*'

There was a yelp. Laddie recoiled from the door, lost his balance on the shifting sand, and rolled down the slope. He leapt to his feet and started barking again; not ordinary stupid-dog barking this time, but the genuine treed-cat variety.

Victor leaned forward and touched the door.

It felt very cold, despite the perpetual heat of Holy Wood, and there was just the faint suspicion of vibration.

He ran his fingers over the surface. There was a roughness there, as though there had been a carving that had been worn into obscurity over the years.

'A door like that,' said Gaspode, behind him, 'a door like that, if you want my opinion, a door like that, a door like that,' he took a deep breath, '*bodes.*'

'Hmm? What? Bodes what?'

'It don't have to bode anything,' said Gaspode. 'Just basic bodingness is bad enough, take it from me.'

'It must have been important. Looks a bit temple-ish,' said Victor. 'Why'd she want to open it?'

'Bits of cliff sliding down an' mysterious doors appearin',' said Gaspode, shaking his head. 'That's a lot of boding. Let's go somewhere far away and really think about it, eh?'

Ginger gave a groan. Victor crouched down.

'What'd she say?'

'Dunno,' said Gaspode.

'It sounded like "I want to be a lawn", I thought?'

'Daft. Touch of the sun there, I reckon,' said Gaspode knowledgeably.

'Maybe you're right. Her head certainly feels very hot.' He picked her up, staggering a little under the weight.

'Come on,' he managed. 'Let's get down into the town. It'll be getting dark soon.' He looked around at the stunted trees. The door lay in a sort of hollow, which presumably caught enough dew to make the growth there slightly less desiccated than elsewhere.

'You know, this place looks familiar,' he said. 'We did our first click here. It's where I first met her.'

'Very romantic,' said Gaspode distantly, hurrying away with Laddie bounding happily around him. 'If something 'orrible comes out of that door, you can fink of it as Our Monster.'

'Hey! Wait!'

'Hurry up, then.'

'What would she want to be a lawn for, do you think?'

'Beats me . . . '

After they had gone silence poured back into the hollow.

A little later, the sun set. Its long light hit the door, turning the merest scratches into deep relief. With the help of imagination, they might just have formed the image of a man.

With a sword.

There was the faintest of noises as, grain by grain, sand trickled away from the door. By midnight it had opened by at least a sixteenth of an inch.

Holy Wood dreamed.

It dreamed of waking up.

Ruby damped down the fires under the vats, put the benches on the tables, and prepared to shut the Blue Lias. But just before blowing out the last lamp she hesitated in front of the mirror.

He'd be waiting out there again tonight. Just like every

172

night. He'd been in during the evening, grinning to him-self. He was planning something.

Ruby had been taking advice from some of the girls who worked in the clicks, and in addition to her feather boa she'd now invested in a broad-rimmed hat with some sort of oograah, cherries she thought they were called, in it. She'd been assured that the effect was stunning.

The trouble, she had to admit, was that he was, well, a very hunky troll. For millions of years troll women had been naturally attracted to trolls built like a monolith with an apple on top. Ruby's treacherous instincts were firing messages up her spine, insidiously insisting that in those long fangs and bandy legs was everything a troll girl could wish for in a mate.

Trolls like Rock or Morry, of course, were far more modern and could do things like use a knife and fork, but there was something, well, *reassuring* about Detritus. Perhaps it was the way his knuckles touched the ground so dynamically. And apart from anything else, she was sure she was brighter than he was. There was a sort of gormless unstoppability about him that she found rather fascinating. That was the instincts at work again – intelligence has never been a particularly valuable survival trait in a troll.

And she had to admit that, whatever she might attempt in the way of feather boas and fancy hats, she was pushing 140 and was 400 lbs above the fashionable weight.

If only he'd buck his ideas up.

Or at least, buck one idea up.

Maybe this make-up the girls had been talking about could be worth a try.

She sighed, blew out the lamp, opened the door and stepped out into a maze of roots.

A gigantic tree stretched the whole length of the alley. He must have dragged it for miles. The few surviving branches poked through windows or waved forlornly in the air.

In the middle of it all was Detritus, perched proudly on the trunk, his face split in a watermelon grin, his arms spread wide.

'Tra-laa!' he said.

Ruby heaved a gigantic sigh. Romance wasn't easy, when you were a troll.

The Librarian forced the page open and chained it down. The book tried to snap at him.

Its contents had made it what it was. Evil and treacherous.

It contained forbidden knowledge.

Well, not actually *forbidden*. No-one had ever gone so far as forbidding it. Apart from anything else, in order to forbid it you'd have to know what it was, which was forbidden. But it definitely contained the sort of information which, once you knew it, you wished you hadn't.[19]

Legend said that any mortal man who read more than a few lines of the original copy would die insane.

This was certainly true.

Legend also said that the book contained illustrations that would make a strong man's brain dribble out of his ears.

This was probably true, too.

Legend went on to say that merely opening the *Necrotelicomnicon* would cause a man's flesh to crawl off his hand and up his arm.

---

[19] The *Necrotelicomnicon* was written by a Klatchian necromancer known to the world as Achmed the Mad, although he preferred to be called Achmed the I Just Get These Headaches. It is said that the book was written in one day after Achmed drank too much of the strange thick Klatchian coffee which doesn't just sober you up, but takes you through sobriety and *out the other side*, so that you glimpse the real universe beyond the clouds of warm self-delusion that sapient life usually generates around itself to stop it turning into a nutcake. Little is known about his life prior to this event, because the page headed 'About The Author' spontaneously combusted shortly after his death. However, a section headed 'Other Books By the Same Author' indicates that his previous published work was *Achmed the I Just Get These Headaches's Book of Humorous Cat Stories*, which might explain a lot.

No-one actually knew if this was true, but it sounded horrible enough to be true and no-one was about to try any experiments.

Legend had a lot to say about the *Necrotelicomnicon*, in fact, but absolutely nothing to say about orang-utans, who could tear the book into little bits and chew it for all legend cared. The worst that had ever happened to the Librarian after looking at it was a mild migraine and a touch of eczema, but that was no reason to take chances. He adjusted the smoked glass of the visor and ran one black-leather finger down the Index; the words bridled as the digit slid past, and tried to bite it.

Occasionally he'd hold the strip of film up to the light of the flickering torch.

The wind and sand had blurred them, but there was no doubt that there were carvings on the rock. And the Librarian had seen designs like that before.

He found the reference he was looking for and, after a brief struggle during which he had to threaten the *Necrotelicomnicon* with the torch, forced the book to turn to the page.

He peered closer.

Good old Achmed the I Just Get These Headaches . . .

' . . . and in that hill, it is said, a Door out of the World was found, and people of the city watched What was Seen therein, knowing not that Dread waited between the universes . . . '

The Librarian's fingertip dragged from right to left across the pictures, and skipped to the next paragraph.

' . . . for *Others* found the Gate of Holy Wood and fell upon the World, and in one nighte All Manner of Madnesse befell, and Chaos prevailed, and the City sank beneath the Sea, and all became one withe the fishes and the lobsters save for the few who fled . . . '

He curled a lip, and looked further down the page.

' . . . a Golden Warrior, who drove the Fiends back and saved the World, and said, Where the Gate is, There Am I Also; I Am He that was Born of Holy Wood, to guard the

Wild Idea. And they said, What must we do to Destroy the Gate Forever, and he said unto them, This you Cannot Do, for it is Not a Thing, but I will Guard the Gate for you. And they, not having been Born yesterday, and fearing the Cure more than the Malady, said to him, What will you Take from Us, that you will Guard the Door. And he grew until he was the height of a tree and said, Only your Remembrance, that I do Not Sleep. Three times a day will you remember Holy Wood. Else The Cities of the World Will Tremble and Fall, and you will See the Greatest of them All in Flames. And with that the Golden Man took up his golden sword and went into the Hill and stood at the Gate, forever.

'And the People said to one another, Funny, he lookes just like my Uncle Osbert . . .'

The Librarian turned the page.

' . . . But there were among them, humans and animals alike, those touched by the magic of Holy Wood. It goeth through the generations like an ancient curse, until the priests cease in their Remembrance and the Golden Man sleepeth. Then let the world Beware . . .'

The Librarian let the book snap shut.

It wasn't an uncommon legend. He'd read it before – at least, had read most of it – in books considerably less dangerous than this. You came across variants in all the cities of the Sto Plain. There had been a city once, in the mists of pre-history – bigger than Ankh-Morpork, if that were possible. And the inhabitants had done *something*, some sort of unspeakable crime not just against Mankind or the gods but against the very nature of the universe itself, which had been so dreadful that it had sunk beneath the sea one stormy night. Only a few people had survived to carry to the barbarian peoples in the less-advanced parts of the Disc all the arts and crafts of civilization, such as usury and macrame.

No-one had ever really taken it seriously. It was just one of those usual 'If you don't stop it you'll go blind' myths that civilizations tended to hand on to their descendants.

176

After all, Ankh-Morpork itself was generally considered as wicked a city as you could hope to find in a year of shore leaves, and seemed to have avoided any kind of supernatural vengeance, although it was always possible that it had taken place and no-one had noticed.

Legend had always put the nameless city far away and long ago.

No-one knew where it was, or even if it had existed.

The Librarian glanced at the symbols again.

They were very familiar. They were on the old ruins all over Holy Wood.

Azhural stood on a low hill, watching the sea of elephants move below him. Here and there a supply wagon bobbed between the dusty grey bodies like a rudderless boat. A mile of veldt was being churned into a soggy mud wallow, bare of grass – although, by the smell of it, it'd be the greenest patch on the Disc after the rains came.

He dabbed at his eyes with a corner of his robe.

Three hundred and sixty-three! Who'd have thought it?

The air was solid with the piqued trumpeting of three hundred and sixty-three elephants. And with the hunting and trapping parties already going on ahead, there should be plenty more. According to M'Bu, anyway. And he wasn't going to argue.

Funny, that. For years he'd thought of M'Bu as a sort of mobile smile. A handy lad with a brush and shovel, but not what you might call a major achiever.

And then suddenly someone somewhere wanted a thousand elephants, and the lad had raised his head and a gleam had come into his eye and you could *see* that under that grin was a skilled kilopachydermatolist ready to answer the call. Funny. You could know someone for their whole life and not realize that the gods had put them in this world to move a thousand elephants around the place.

Azhural had no sons. He'd already made up his mind to leave everything to his assistant. Everything he had at this point amounted to three hundred and sixty-three elephants and, ahaha, a mammoth overdraft, but it was the thought that counted.

M'Bu trotted up the path towards him, his clipboard held firmly under one arm.

'Everything ready, boss,' he said. 'You just got to say the word.'

Azhural drew himself up. He looked around at the heaving plain, the distant baobab trees, the purple mountains. Oh, yes. The mountains. He'd had misgivings about the mountains. He'd mentioned them to M'Bu, who said, 'We'll cross them bridges when we get to 'em, boss,' and when Azhural had pointed out that there *weren't* any bridges, had looked him squarely in the eye and said firmly, 'First we build them bridge, then we cross 'em.'

Far beyond the mountains was the Circle Sea and Ankh-Morpork and this Holy Wood place. Far-away places with strange sounding names.

A wind blew across the veldt, carrying faint whispers, even here.

Azhural raised his staff.

'It's fifteen hundred miles to Ankh-Morpork,' he said. 'We've got three hundred and sixty-three elephants, fifty carts of forage, the monsoon's about to break and we're wearing . . . we're wearing . . . sort of things, like glass, only dark . . . dark glass things on our eyes . . . ' His voice trailed off. His brow furrowed, as if he'd just been listening to his own voice and hadn't understood it.

The air seemed to glitter.

He saw M'Bu staring at him.

He shrugged. 'Let's go,' he said.

M'Bu cupped his hands. He'd spent all night working out the order of the march.

'Blue Section bilong Uncle N'gru – *forward!*' he shouted. 'Yellow Section bilong Aunti Googool – *forward!* Green Section bilong Second-cousin! Kck! – *forward* . . . '

An hour later the veldt in front of the low hill was

deserted except for a billion flies and one dung beetle who couldn't believe his luck.

Something went 'plop' on the red dust, throwing up a little crater.

And again, and again.

Lightning split the trunk of a nearby baobab.

The rains began.

Victor's back was beginning to ache. Carrying young women to safety looked a good idea on paper, but had major drawbacks after the first hundred yards.

'Have you any idea where she lives?' he said. 'And is it somewhere close?'

'No idea,' said Gaspode.

'She once said something about it being over a clothes shop,' said Victor.

'That'll be in the alley alongside Borgle's then,' said Gaspode.

Gaspode and Laddie led the way through the alleys and up a rickety outside staircase. Maybe they smelled out Ginger's room. Victor wasn't going to argue with mysterious animal senses.

Victor went up the back stairs as quietly as possible. He was dimly aware that where people stayed was often infested by the Common or Greatly Suspicious Landlady, and he felt that he had enough problems as it was.

He used Ginger's feet to push open the door.

It was a small room, low-ceilinged and furnished with the sad, washed-out furniture found in rented rooms across the multiverse. At least, that's how it had started out.

What it was furnished with now was Ginger.

She had saved every poster. Even those from early clicks, when she was just in very small print as A Girl. They were thumb-tacked to the walls. Ginger's face – and his own – stared at him from every angle.

There was a large mirror at one end of the poky room, and a couple of half-burned candles in front of him.

Victor deposited the girl carefully on the narrow bed and then stared around him, very carefully. His sixth, seventh and eighth senses were screaming at him. He was in a place of magic.

'It's like a sort of temple,' he said. 'A temple to . . . herself.'

'It gives me the willies,' said Gaspode.

Victor stared. Maybe he'd always successfully avoided being awarded the pointy hat and big staff, but he had acquired wizard instincts. He had a sudden vision of a city under the sea, with octopuses curling stealthily through the drowned doorways and lobsters watching the streets.

'Fate don't like it when people take up more space than they ought to. Everyone knows that.'

I'm going to be the most famous person in the whole world, thought Victor. *That's what she said.* He shook his head.

'No,' he said aloud. 'She just likes posters. It's just ordinary vanity.'

It didn't sound believable, even to him. The room fairly hummed with . . .

. . . what? He hadn't felt anything like it before. Power of some sort, certainly. Something that was brushing tantalizingly against his senses. Not exactly magic. At least, not the kind he was used to. But something that seemed similar while not being the same, like sugar compared with salt; the same shape and the same colour, but . . .

Ambition wasn't magical. Powerful, yes, but not magical . . . surely?

Magic wasn't difficult. That was the big secret that the whole baroque edifice of wizardry had been set up to conceal. Anyone with a bit of intelligence and enough perseverance could do magic, which was why the wizards cloaked it with rituals and the whole pointy-hat business.

The trick was to do magic and *get away with it*.

Because it was as if the human race was a field of corn and magic helped the users grow just that bit taller, so that they stood out. That attracted the attention of the gods and – Victor hesitated – other Things outside this world.

180

People who used magic without knowing what they were doing usually came to a sticky end.

All over the entire room, sometimes.

He pictured Ginger, back on the beach. *I want to be the most famous person in the whole world*. Perhaps that was something new, come to think of it. Not ambition for gold, or power, or land or all the things that were familiar parts of the human world. Just ambition to be yourself, as big as possible. Not ambition *for*, but to *be*.

He shook his head. He was just in some room in some cheap building in some town that was about as real as, as, as, well, as the thickness of a click. It wasn't the place to have thoughts like this.

The important thing was to remember that Holy Wood wasn't a real place at all.

He stared at the posters again. You just get one chance, she said. You live for maybe seventy years, and if you're lucky you get one chance. Think of all the natural skiers who are born in deserts. Think of all the genius blacksmiths who were born hundreds of years before anyone invented the horse. All the skills that are never used. All the wasted chances.

How lucky for me, he thought gloomily, that I happen to be alive at this time.

Ginger turned over in her sleep. At least her breathing was more regular now.

'Come *on*,' said Gaspode. 'It's not right, you being alone in a lady's boodwah.'

'I'm not alone,' Victor said. 'She's with me.'

'That's the point,' said Gaspode.

'Woof,' Laddie added, loyally.

'You know,' said Victor, following the dogs down the stairs, 'I'm beginning to feel there's something *wrong* here. There's something going on and I don't know what it is. Why was she trying to get into the hill?'

'Prob'ly in league with dread Powers,' said Gaspode.

'The city and the hill and the old book and everything,'

said Victor, ignoring this. 'It all makes sense if only I knew what was connecting it.'

He stepped out into the early evening, into the lights and noise of Holy Wood.

'Tomorrow we'll go up there in the daylight and sort this out once and for all,' he said.

'No, we won't,' said Gaspode. 'The reason being, tomorrow we're goin' to Ankh-Morpork, remember?'

'We?' said Victor. 'Ginger and I are going. I didn't know about you.'

'Laddie goin', too,' said Gaspode. 'I—'

'Good boy Laddie!'

'Yeah, yeah. I heard the trainers say. So I've got to go with him to see he don't get into any trouble, style of fing.'

Victor yawned. 'Well, I'm going to go to bed. We'll probably have to start early.'

Gaspode looked innocently up and down the alley. Somewhere a door opened and there was the sound of drunken laughter.

'I fought I might have a bit of a stroll before turnin' in,' he said. 'Show Laddie—'

'Laddie good boy!'

'—the sights and that.'

Victor looked doubtful.

'Don't keep him out too late,' he said. 'People will worry.'

'Yeah, right,' said Gaspode. 'G'night.'

He sat and watched Victor wander off.

'Huh,' he said, under his dreadful breath. 'Catch anyone worryin' about *me*.' He glared up at Laddie, who sprang to obedient attention.

'Right, young fella-me-pup,' he said. ' 'S time you got educated. Lesson One, Glomming Free Drinks in Bars. It's lucky for you', he added, 'that you met me.'

Two canine shapes staggered uncertainly up the midnight street.

'We're poor li'l lambs', Gaspode howled, 'wot have loorst our way . . . '

'*Woof! Woof! Woof!*'

'We're li'l loorst sheeps wot have – wot have . . . ' Gaspode sagged down, and scratched an ear, or at least where he vaguely thought an ear might be. His leg waved uncertainly in the air. Laddie gave him a sympathetic look.

It had been an amazingly successful evening. Gaspode had always got his free drinks by simply sitting and staring intently at people until they got uncomfortable and poured him some beer in a saucer in the hope that he would drink it and go away. It was slow and tedious, but as a technique it had served him well. Whereas Laddie . . .

Laddie did *tricks*. Laddie could drink out of bottles. Laddie could bark the number of fingers people held up; so could Gaspode, of course, but it had never occurred to him that such an activity could be rewarded.

Laddie could home in on young women who were being taken out for the evening by a hopeful swain and lay his head on their lap and give them such a soulful look that the swain would buy him a saucer of beer and a bag of goldfish-shaped biscuits just in order to impress the prospective loved-one. Gaspode had never been able to do that, because he was too short for laps and, anyway, got nothing but disgusted screams if he tried it.

He'd sat under the table in perplexed disapproval to begin with, and then in alcoholic perplexed disapproval, because Laddie was generosity itself when it came to sharing saucers of beer.

Now, after they'd both been thrown out, Gaspode decided it was time for a lecture in true dogness.

'You don't want to go himblong. Umlong. *Humbling* yourself to 'umans,' he said. 'It's letting everyone down. We'll never frow off the shackles of dependency on mankind if dogs like you go aroun' bein' glad to see people the whole time. I was person'ly disgusted when you did that Lyin'-on-your-back-and-playin'-dead routine, let me tell you.'

'*Woof.*'

'You're just a running dog of the human imperialists,' said Gaspode severely.

Laddie put his paws over his nose.

Gaspode tried to stand up, tripped over his legs, and sat down heavily. After a while a couple of huge tears coursed down his fur.

'O'course,' he said, 'I never had a chance, you know.' He managed to get back on all four feet. 'I mean, look at the start I had in life. Frone inna river inna sack. An actual sack. Dear little puppy dog opens his eyes, look out in wonder at the world, style of fing, he's in this sack.' The tears dripped off his nose. 'For two weeks I thought the brick was my mother.'

'*Woof,*' said Laddie, with uncomprehending sympathy.

'Just my luck they threw me in the Ankh,' Gaspode went on. 'Any other river, I'd have drowned and gone to doggy heaven. I heard where this big black ghostly dog comes up to you when you die an' says, your time has gome. Cone. Come.'

Gaspode stared at nothing much. 'Can't sink in the Ankh, though,' he said thoughtfully. 'Ver' tough river, the Ankh.'

'*Woof.*'

'It shouldn't happen to a dog,' said Gaspode. 'Metaphorically.'

'*Woof.*'

Gaspode peered blearily at Laddie's bright, alert and irrevocably stupid face.

'You don't understand a bloody word I've been saying, do you?' he muttered.

'*Woof!*' said Laddie, begging.

'Lucky bugger,' sighed Gaspode.

There was a commotion at the other end of the alley. He heard a voice say, 'There he is! Here, Laddie! Here, boy!' The words dripped relief.

'It's the Man,' growled Gaspode. 'You don't have to go.'

'*Good boy Laddie! Laddie good boy!*' barked Laddie, trotting forward obediently, if a little unsteadily.

'We've been looking for you everywhere!' muttered one of the trainers, raising a stick.

'Don't hit it!' said the other trainer. 'You'll ruin everything.' He peered into the alley, and met Gaspode's stare coming the other way.

'That's the fleabag that's been hanging around,' he said. 'It gives me the creeps.'

'Heave something at it,' suggested the other man.

The trainer reached down and picked up a stone. When he stood up again the alley was empty. Drunk or sober, Gaspode had perfect reflexes in certain circumstances.

'See?' the trainer said, glaring at the shadows. 'It's like it's some kind of mind reader.'

'It's just a mutt,' said his companion. 'Don't worry about it. Come on, get the leash on this one and let's get him back before Mr Dibbler finds out.'

Laddie followed them obediently back to Century of the Fruitbat, and allowed himself to be chained up to his kennel. Possibly he didn't like the idea, but it was hard to be sure in the network of duties, obligations and vague emotional shadows that made up what, for want of a better word, had to be called his mind.

He pulled experimentally on the chain once or twice, and then lay down, awaiting developments.

After a while a small hoarse voice on the other side of the fence said, 'I could send you a bone with a file in it, only you'd eat it.'

Laddie perked up.

'*Good boy Laddie! Good boy Gaspode!*'

'Ssh! Ssh! At least they ort to let you speak to a lawyer,' said Gaspode. 'Chaining someone up's against human rights.'

'*Woof!*'

'Anyway, I paid 'em back. I followed the 'orrible one

185

back to his house an' piddled all down his front door.'

'*Woof!*'

Gaspode sighed, and waddled away. Sometimes, in his heart of hearts, he wondered whether it wouldn't after all be nice to *belong* to someone. Not just be owned by them or chained up by them, but actually *belong*, so that you were glad to see them and carried their slippers in your mouth and pined away when they died, etc.

Laddie actually liked that kind of stuff, if you could call it 'liked'; it was more like something built into his bones. Gaspode wondered darkly if this was true dogness, and growled deep in his throat. It wasn't, if he had anything to do with it. Because true dogness wasn't about slippers and walkies and pining for people, Gaspode was sure. Dogness was about being tough and independent and mean.

Yeah.

Gaspode had heard that all canines could interbreed, even back to the original wolves, so that must mean that, deep down inside, every dog was a wolf. You could make a dog out of a wolf, but you couldn't take the wolf out of a dog. When the hardpad was acting up and the fleas were feisty and acting full of plumptiousness, it was a comforting thought.

Gaspode wondered how you went about mating with a wolf, and what happened to you when you stopped.

Well, that didn't matter. What mattered was that true dogs didn't go around going mad with pleasure just because a human said something to them.

Yeah.

He growled at a pile of trash and dared it to disagree.

Part of the pile moved, and a feline face with a defunct fish in its mouth peered out at him. He was just about to bark half-heartedly at it, for tradition's sake, when it spat the fish out and spoke to him.

'Hallo, Gathpode.'

Gaspode relaxed. 'Oh. Hallo, cat. No offence meant. Didn't know it was you.'

'I hateth fisth,' said the cat, 'but at leasth they don't talk back.'

Another part of the trash moved and Squeak the mouse emerged.

'What're you two doin' down here?' said Gaspode. 'I thought you said it was safer on the hill.'

'Not any more,' said the cat. 'It'sh getting too *shpooky*.'

Gaspode frowned. 'You're a cat,' he said disapprovingly. 'You ort to be right alongside the idea of spooky.'

'Yeah, but that doesh'nt exhtend to having golden sparks crackling off your fur and the ground shaking the whole time. And weird voices that you think must be happening in your own head,' said cat. 'It's becoming *eldritch* up there.'

'So we all came down,' said Squeak. 'Mr Thumpy and the duck are hiding out in the dunes—'

Another cat dropped off the fence beside them. It was large and ginger and not blessed with Holy Wood intelligence. It stared at the sight of a mouse looking relaxed in the presence of a cat.

Squeak nudged cat on the paw. 'Get rid of it,' he said.

Cat glared at the newcomer. 'Sod off,' he said. 'Go on, beat it. Gods, thish ish so *humiliating*.'

'Not just for you,' said Gaspode, as the new cat trotted away shaking its head. 'If some of the dogs in this town see me chatting to a cat, my street cred is going to go *way* down.'

'We were reckoning', said the cat, with the occasional nervous glance towards Squeak, 'that maybe we ought to give in and see if, see if, see if—'

'He's trying to say there might be a place for us in moving pictures,' said Squeak. 'What do you think?'

'As a double act?' said Gaspode. They nodded.

'Not a chance,' he said. 'Who's going to pay good money to see cats and mice chasing one another? They're only interested even in dogs if they jus' pander to humans the whole time, so they certainly ain't going to watch a cat chase a mouse. Take it from me. I know about movin' pictures.'

'Then it's about time your humans got it sorted out so we can go home,' snapped the mouse. 'The boy isn't doing anything.'

'He's *useless*,' said the mouse.

'He's in love,' said Gaspode. 'It's very tricky.'

'Yeah, I know how it ish,' said the cat sympathetically. 'People throwing old boots and things at you.'

'Old boots?' said the mouse.

'That'sh what's always happened to *me* when I've been in love,' said cat wistfully.

'It's different for humans,' said Gaspode uncertainly. 'You don't get so many boots and buckets of water thrown at you. It's more, er, flowers and arguing and stuff.'

The animals looked glumly at one another.

'I've watched 'em,' said Squeak. 'She thinks he's a idiot.'

'That's all part of it,' added Gaspode. 'They call it romance.'

Cat shrugged. 'Give me a boot every time. You know where you stand, with a boot.'

The glittering spirit of Holy Wood streamed out into the world, no longer a trickle but a flood. It bubbled in the veins of people, even of animals. When the handlemen turned their handles, it was there. When the carpenters hammered their nails, they hammered for Holy Wood. Holy Wood was in Borgle's stew, in the sand, in the air. It was growing.

And it was going to flower . . .

Cut-me-own-Throat Dibbler, or C.M.O.T. as he liked to be called, sat up in bed and stared at the darkness.

In his head a city was on fire.

He fumbled hurriedly beside his bed for the matches, managed to light the candle, and eventually located a pen.

There was no paper. He specifically told everyone there ought to be some paper by his bed, in case he woke up with an idea. That's when you got the best ideas, when you were asleep.

At least there was a pen and ink . . .

Images sleeted past his eyes. Catch them now, or let them go forever . . .

He snatched up the pen and started to scribble on the bedsheets.

A Man and A Woman Aflame With Passione in A Citie Riven by Sivil War!

The pen scritched and spluttered its way across the coarse linen.

Yes! Yes! This was it!

He'd show 'em, with their silly plaster pyramids and penny-and-dime palaces. *This* was the one they'd have to look up to! When the history of Holy Wood was written *this* was the one they'd point to and say: That was the Moving Picture to End all Moving Pictures!

Trolls! Battles! Romance! People with thin moustaches! Soldiers of fortune! And one woman's fight to keep the – Dibbler hesitated – something-or-other she loves, we'll think about this later, in a world gone mad!

The pen jerked and tore and raced onwards.

Brother against brother! Women in crinoline dresses slapping people's faces! A mighty dynasty brought low!

A great city aflame! Not with passione, he made a note in the margin, but with flame.

Possibly even—

He bit his lip.

Yeah. He'd been waiting for this! *Yeah!*

A thousand elephants!

(Later Soll Dibbler said, 'Look, Uncle, the Ankh-Morpork civil war – great idea. No problem with that. Famous historical occurrence, no problem. It's just that none of the historians mentioned seeing any elephants.'

'It was a big war,' said Dibbler defensively. 'You're bound to miss things.'

'Not a thousand elephants, I think.'

'Who's running this studio?'

189

'It's just that—'

'*Listen*,' said Dibbler. 'Maybe they didn't have a thousand elephants, but *we're* going to have a thousand elephants, 'cos a thousand elephants is more *real*, OK?')

The sheet gradually filled up with Dibbler's excited scrawl. He reached the bottom and continued over the woodwork of the bed.

By the gods, this was the real stuff! No fiddly little battles here. They'd need just about every handleman in Holy Wood!

He sat back, panting with exhilarated exhaustion.

He could see it now. It was as good as made.

All it needed was a title. Something with a ring to it. Something that people would remember. Something – he scratched his chin with the pen – that said that the affairs of ordinary people were so much chaff in the great storms of history. Storms, that was it. Good imagery, a storm. You got thunder. Lightning. Rain. Wind.

Wind. That was it!

He crawled up to the top of the sheet and, with great care, wrote:

  BLOWN AWAY.

Victor tossed and turned in his narrow bed, trying to get to sleep. Images marched through his half-dozing mind. There were chariot races and pirate ships and things he couldn't identify, and in the middle of it all this *thing*, climbing a tower. Something huge and terrible, grinning defiance at the world. And someone screaming . . .

He sat up, drenched in sweat.

After a few minutes he swung his legs out of bed and went to the window.

Above the lights of the town Holy Wood Hill brooded in the first dim light of dawn. It was going to be another fine day.

Holy Wood dreams surged through the streets, in great invisible golden waves.

And Something came with it.

Something that never, never dreamed at all. Something that never went to sleep.

Ginger got out of bed and also looked towards the hill, although it is doubtful if she saw it. Moving like a sightless person in a familiar room, she padded across to the door, down the steps, and out into the tail of the night.

A small dog, a cat and a mouse watched from the shadows as she moved silently down the alley and headed for the hill.

'Did you see her *eyes*?' said Gaspode.

'Glowing,' said the cat. 'Yukth!'

'She's going to the hill,' said Gaspode. 'I don't like that.'

'So what?' said Squeak. 'She's always around the hill somewhere. Goes up there every night and moons around looking dramatic.'

'What?'

'Every night. We thought it was all this romance stuff.'

'But you can see by the way she's movin' that somethin's not right,' said Gaspode desperately. 'That's not walkin', that's lurchin'. Like she's bein' pulled along by a inner voice, style of fing.'

'Don't look like that to me,' said Squeak. 'Walking on two legs *is* lurching, in my book.'

'You've only got to look at her face to see there's somethin' wrong!'

'Of course there's something wrong. She's a *human*,' said Squeak.

Gaspode considered the options. There weren't many. The obvious one was to find Victor and get him to come back here. He rejected it. It sounded too much like the silly, bouncy sort of thing that Laddie would do. It suggested that the best a dog could think of when confronted with a puzzle was to find a human to solve it.

He trotted forward and gripped the trailing hem of the sleepwalker's nightdress firmly in his jaws. She walked on, pulling him off his feet. The cat laughed, far too sarcastically for Gaspode's liking.

'Time to wake up, miss,' he growled, letting the night-dress go. Ginger strode onwards.

'See?' said the cat. 'Give them an opposed thumb and they think they're something shpecial.'

'I'm going to follow her,' said Gaspode. 'A girl could come to harm out by herself at night.'

'That's dogs for you,' said the cat to Squeak. 'Alwaysh fawning on people. It'll be diamante collars and a bowl with his name on it nexsht, I'm telling you.'

'If you're lookin' to lose a mouthful of fur you've come to the right place, kitty,' snarled Gaspode, baring his rotting teeth again.

'I don't have to tolerate that short of thing,' said the cat, lifting its nose haughtily. 'Come, Squeak. Let us hie us to a garbage heap where there ain't sho much *rubbish*.'

Gaspode scowled at their departing backs.

'Pussy!' he yelled after them.

Then he trotted after Ginger, hating himself. If I was a wolf, which technic'ly I am, he thought, there'd definitely be a rending of jaws and similar. Any girl wandering around by herself would be in dead trouble. I *could* attack, I *could* attack any time I liked, I'm jus' choosing not to. One thing I'm not doin', I'm *not* sort of keepin' an eye on her. I know Victor told me to keep an eye on her, but catch me goin' around doin' what humans tell me. I'd like to see humans that could give *me* orders. Tear his froat out, jus' like that. Hah.

An' if anything happened to her he'd go around moonin' for days and prob'ly forget to feed me. Not that dogs like me needs humans to feed 'em, I could be out bringing down reindeers just by leaping on their backs and bitin' their jugulars off, but it's damn convenient getting it all on a plate.

She was moving quite fast. Gaspode's tongue hung out as he strove to keep up. His head was aching.

He risked a few sideways squints to see if any other dogs

were watching. If they were, he thought, he could pretend he was chasin' her. Which was what he was doing, anyway. Yeah. The trouble was, he never had much breath at the best of times, and it was getting hard to keep pace. She ought to have the decency to slow down a bit.

Ginger began to climb the lower slopes of the hill.

Gaspode considered barking loudly, and then if anyone drew attention to this afterwards he could always say it was to frighten her. Trouble was, he had about enough wind left for a threatening wheeze.

Ginger topped a rise and went down into the little dell among the trees.

Gaspode staggered after her, righted himself, opened his mouth to whimper a warning, and almost swallowed his tongue.

The door had opened several inches. More sand rolled down the heap even as Gaspode watched.

And he could hear voices. They didn't seem to be speaking words but the *bones* of words, meaning without disguise. They hummed around his bullet head like mendicant mosquitoes, begging and cajoling and—

—he was the most famous dog in the world. The knots unravelled from his coat, the frayed patches sprouted glossy curls, his fur grew on his suddenly-supple frame and withdrew from his teeth. Plates appeared in front of him not laden with the multi-coloured and mysterious organs that he was normally expected to eat but with dark red steak. There was sweet water, no, there was beer in a bowl with his name on it. Tantalizing odours on the air suggested that a number of lady dogs would be happy to make his acquaintance after he had drunk and dined. Thousands of people thought he was marvellous. He had a collar with his name on it, and—

No, that couldn't be right. Not a collar. It'd be a squeaky toy next, if you dint draw the line at collars.

The image collapsed in confusion, and now—

— the pack bounded through the dark, snow-covered trees, falling in behind him, red mouths agape, long legs eating up the road. The fleeing humans on the sledge didn't have a

chance; one was thrown aside when a runner bounced off a
branch, and lay screaming in the road as Gaspode and the
wolves fell upon—

No, that wasn't right, he thought wretchedly. You dint actually *eat* humans. They got up your nose all right, the gods knew, but you couldn't acktually *eat* 'em.

A confusion of instincts threatened to short-circuit his schizophrenically doggy mind.

The voices gave up their assault in disgust and turned their attention to Ginger, who was methodically trying to shift more sand.

One of Gaspode's fleas bit him sharply. It was probably dreaming of being the biggest flea in the world. His leg came up automatically to scratch it, and the spell faded.

He blinked.

'Bloody hell,' he whined.

This is what's happening to the humans! Wonder what they're making *her* dream?

The hairs rose along Gaspode's back.

You didn't need any special mysterious animal instincts here. Perfectly generalized everyday instincts were enough to horrify him. There was something dreadful on the other side of the door.

She was trying to let it out.

He had to wake her up.

Biting wasn't really a good idea. His teeth weren't that good these days. He doubted very much if barking would be any better. That left one alternative . . .

The sand moved eerily under his paws; maybe it was dreaming of being rocks. The scrawny trees around the hollow were wrapped in sequoia fantasies. Even the air that curled around Gaspode's bullet head moved sluggishly, although it's anyone's guess what the air dreams about.

Gaspode trotted up to Ginger and pushed his nose against her leg.

The universe contains any amount of horrible ways to be woken up, such as the noise of the mob breaking down the front door, the scream of fire engines, or the realization that today is the Monday which on Friday night was a comfortably long way off. A dog's wet nose is not strictly speaking the worst of the bunch, but it has its own peculiar dreadfulness which connoisseurs of the ghastly and dog owners everywhere have come to know and dread. It's like having a small piece of defrosting liver pressed lovingly against you.

Ginger blinked. The glow faded from her eyes. She looked down, her expression of horror turning to astonishment and then, when she saw Gaspode leering up at her, back to a more mundane horror.

' 'Allo,' Gaspode said, ingratiatingly.

She backed away, bringing her hands up protectively. Sand dribbled between her fingers. Her eyes flickered towards it in bewilderment, and then back to Gaspode.

'Gods, that's *horrible*,' she said. 'What's going *on*? Why am I *here*?' Her hands flew to her mouth. 'Oh no,' she whispered, 'not again!'

She stared at him for a moment, glared up at the doorway, then turned, hitched up her nightdress, and hurried back to town through the morning mists.

Gaspode struggled after her, aware cf anger in the air, desperately trying to put as much space as possible between the door and himself.

Sunnink dreadful in there, he thought. Prob'ly tentacled fings that rips your face off. I mean, when you finds mysterious doors in old hills, stands to reason wot comes out ain't going to be pleased to see you. Evil creatures wot Man shouldn't wot of, and here's one dog wot don't want to wot of them either. Why couldn't she . . .

He grumbled on towards the town.

Behind him the door moved the tiniest fraction of an inch.

Holy Wood was awake long before Victor, and the hammering from Century of the Fruitbat echoed around the sky. Waggonloads of timber were queuing up to enter the archway. He was buffeted and pushed aside by a hurrying stream of plasterers and carpenters. Inside, crowds of workmen scurried around the arguing figures of Silverfish and C.M.O.T. Dibbler.

Victor reached them just as Silverfish said, in astonished tones, 'The whole city?'

'You can leave out the bits round the edge,' said Dibbler. 'But I want the whole of the centre. The palace, the University, the Guilds – everything that makes it a real city, understand? It's got to be right!'

He was red in the face. Behind him loomed Detritus the troll, patiently holding what appeared to be a bed over his head on one massive hand, like a waiter with a tray. Dibbler had the sheets in one hand. Then Victor realized that the whole bed, not just the sheets, was covered in writing.

'But the cost—' Silverfish protested.

'We'll find the money somehow,' said Dibbler calmly.

Silverfish couldn't have looked more horrified if Dibbler had worn a dress. He tried to rally.

'Well, if you're *determined*, Throat—'

'Right!'

'—I suppose, come to think of it, maybe we could amortize the cost over several clicks, maybe even hire it out afterwards—'

'What are you talking about?' demanded Dibbler. 'We're building it for *Blown Away*!'

'Yes, yes, of course,' said Silverfish soothingly. 'And then afterwards, we can—'

'Afterwards? There won't be any afterwards! Haven't you read the script? Detritus, show him the script!'

Detritus obligingly dropped the bed between them.

'It's your *bed*, Throat.'

'Script, bed, what's the difference? Look . . . here . . . just above the carving . . .'

There was a pause while Silverfish read. It was quite a long one. Silverfish wasn't used to reading matter that didn't come in columns with totals at the bottom.

Eventually he said, 'You're going . . . to . . . set it on fire?'

'It's historical. You can't argue with history,' said Dibbler smugly. 'The city was burned down in the civil war, everyone knows that.'

Silverfish drew himself up. 'The city might have been,' he said stiffly, 'but I didn't have to find the budget for it! It's recklessly extravagant!'

'I'll pay for it somehow,' said Dibbler, calmly.

'In a word – im-possible!'

'That's two words,' said Dibbler.

'There's no way I can work on something like this,' said Silverfish, ignoring the interruption. 'I've tried to see your point of view, haven't I? But you've taken moving pictures and you're trying to turn them into, into, into *dreams*. I never wanted them to be like this! Include me out!'

'OK.' Dibbler looked up at the troll.

'Mr Silverfish was just leaving,' he said. Detritus nodded, and then slowly and firmly picked up Silverfish by his collar.

Silverfish went white. 'You can't get rid of me like that,' he said.

'You want to bet?'

'There won't be an alchemist in Holy Wood who'll work for you! We'll take the handlemen with us! You'll be finished!'

'Listen! After this click the whole of Holy Wood will be coming to me for a job! Detritus, throw this bum out!'

'Right you are, Mr Dibbler,' rumbled the troll, gripping Silverfish's collar.

'You haven't heard the last of this, you – you scheming, devious megalomaniac!'

Dibbler removed his cigar.

'That's *Mister* Megalomaniac to you,' he said.

He replaced the cigar, and nodded significantly to the troll, who gently but firmly grasped Silverfish by a leg as well.

'You lay a finger on me and you'll never work in this town again!' shouted Silverfish.

'I got a job anyway, Mr Silverfish,' said Detritus calmly, carrying Silverfish towards the gate. 'I'm Vice-President of Throwing Out People Mr Dibbler Doesn't like the Face Of.'

'Then you'll have to take on an assistant!' snarled Silverfish.

'I got a nephew looking for a career,' said the troll. 'Have a nice day.'

'Right,' said Dibbler, rubbing his hands briskly. 'Soll!'

Soll appeared from behind a trestle table loaded with rolled-up plans, and took a pencil out of his mouth.

'Yes, Uncle?'

'How long will it take?'

'About four days, Uncle.'

'That's too long. Hire more people. I want it done by tomorrow, right?'

'But, Uncle—'

'Or you're sacked,' said Dibbler. Soll looked frightened.

'I'm your nephew, Uncle,' he protested. 'You can't sack nephews.'

Dibbler looked around and appeared to notice Victor for the first time.

'Ah, Victor. You're good at words,' he said. 'Can I sack a nephew?'

'Er. I don't think so. I think you have to disown them, or something,' said Victor lamely. 'But—'

'Right! Right!' said Dibbler. 'Good man. I knew it was some kind of a word like that. Disown. Hear that, Soll?'

'Yes, Uncle,' said Soll dispiritedly. 'I'll go and see if I can find some more carpenters, then, shall I?'

'Right.' Soll flashed Victor a look of terrified astonishment as he scurried away. Dibbler started haranguing a group of handlemen. Instructions spouted out of the man like water from a fountain.

'I reckon no-one's goin' to Ankh-Morpork this morning, then,' said a voice by Victor's knee.

'He's certainly very, er, ambitious today,' said Victor. 'Not like himself at all.'

Gaspode scratched an ear. 'There was sunnink I got to tell you. What was it, now? Oh, yeah. I remember. Your girlfriend is an agent of demonic powers. That night we saw her on the hill she was prob'ly on her way to commune with evil. What d'you fink of that, eh?'

He grinned. He was rather proud of the way he'd introduced the subject.

'That's nice,' said Victor abstractedly. Dibbler was certainly acting even stranger than usual. Even stranger than usual for Holy Wood, even . . .

'Yeah,' said Gaspode, slightly annoyed at this reception. 'A-cavortin' at night with eldritchly occult Intelligences from the Other Side, I shouldn't wonder.'

'Good,' said Victor. You didn't normally burn things in Holy Wood. You saved them and painted on the other side. Despite himself, he began to get interested.

'—a cast of thousands,' Dibbler was saying. 'I don't care where you get them from, we'll hire everyone in Holy Wood if we have to, right? And I want—'

'A-helpin' them in their evil attempts to take over the whole world, if I'm any judge,' said Gaspode.

'Does she?' said Victor. Dibbler was talking to a couple of apprentice alchemists now. What was that. A *twenty*-reeler? But no-one had ever dreamed of going above five!

'Yeah, a-diggin' away to rouse them from their ancient slumber to reek havoc, style of fing,' said Gaspode. 'Prob'ly aided by cats, you mark my—'

'Look, just shut up a minute, will you?' said Victor, irritably. 'I'm trying to hear what they're saying.'

'Well, 'scuse *me*. I was jus' tryin' to save the world,' muttered Gaspode. 'If *gharstely* creatures from Before the Dawna Time starts wavin' at you from under your bed, jus' you don't come complainin' to me.'

'What *are* you going on about?' said Victor.

'Oh, nothin'. Nothin'.'

Dibbler looked up, caught sight of Victor's craning face, and waved at it.

'You, lad! Come here! Have I got a part for you!'

'Have you?' said Victor, pushing his way through the crowd.

'That's what I said!'

'No, you asked if—' Victor began, and gave up.

'And where's Miss Ginger, may I ask?' said Dibbler. 'Late again?'

' . . . *prob'ly sleepin' in . . .* ' grumbled a sullen and totally ignored voice from down below in the sea of legs, '. . . *prob'ly takes it out of you, messin' with the occult . . .* '

'Soll, send someone to fetch her here—'

'Yes, Uncle.'

' . . . *wot can you expect, huh, people who like cats're capable of anythin', you can't trust 'em . . .*'

'And find someone to transcribe the bed.'

'Yes, Uncle.'

' . . . *but do they listen! Not them. Bet if I had a glossy coat an' ran aroun' yappin' they'd listen all right . . .* '

Dibbler opened his mouth to speak, and then frowned and raised a hand.

'Where's that muttering coming from?' he said.

' . . . *prob'ly saved the whole world for 'em, by rights I'd get a statchoo put up to me nose but no, oh no, not for you Mr Gaspode, on account of you not bein' the right kinda person, so . . .* '

The whine stopped. The crowd shuffled aside, revealing a small bow-legged grey dog, which looked up impassively at Dibbler.

'Bark?' it said, innocently.

Events always moved fast in Holy Wood, but the work on *Blown Away* sped forward like a comet. The other Fruitbat clicks were halted. So were most of the others in the town, because Dibbler was hiring actors and handlemen at twice what anyone else would pay.

And a sort of Ankh-Morpork rose among the dunes. It would have been cheaper, Soll complained, to have risked the wrath of the wizards, sneaked some filming in Ankh-Morpork itself, and then slipped someone a fistful of dollars to put a match to the place.

Dibbler disagreed.

'Apart from anything else,' he declared, 'it wouldn't look right.'

'But it's the real Ankh-Morpork, Uncle,' said Soll. 'It's got to look *exactly* right. How can it not look right?'

'Ankh-Morpork doesn't look all that genuine, you know,' said Dibbler thoughtfully.

'Of course it's bloody genuine!' snapped Soll, the bonds of kinship stretching to snapping point. 'It's really there! It's really itself! You can't make it any more genuine! It's as genuine as it can get!'

Dibbler took his cigar out of his mouth.

'No, it isn't,' he said. 'You'll see.'

Ginger turned up around lunchtime, looking so pale that even Dibbler didn't shout at her. She kept glaring at Gaspode, who tried to stay out of her way.

Dibbler was preoccupied, anyway. He was in his office, explaining The Plot.

It was basically quite simple, running on the familiar lines of Boy Meets Girl, Girl Meets Another Boy, Boy Loses Girl, except that on this occasion there was a civil war in the middle of it . . .

The origins of the Ankh-Morpork Civil War (8.32 p.m., Grune 3, 432 – 10.45 a.m., Grune 4, 432) have always been a subject of heated debate among historians. There are two main theories: 1. The common people, having been heavily taxed by a particularly stupid and unpleasant king, decided that enough was enough and that it was time to do away with the outmoded concept of monarchy and replace it with, as it turned out, a series of despotic overlords who still taxed heavily but at least had the decency not to pretend the gods had given them the

201

right to do it, which made everyone feel a bit better OR 2. One of the players in a game of Cripple Mr Onion in a tavern had accused another of palming more than the usual number of aces, and knives had been drawn, and then someone had hit someone with a bench, and then someone else had stabbed someone, and arrows started to fly, and someone had swung on the chandelier, and a carelessly-hurled axe had hit someone in the street, and then the Watch had been called in, and someone had set fire to the place, and someone had hit a lot of people with a table, and then everyone lost their tempers and commenced to start fighting.

Anyway, it all caused a civil war, which is something every mature civilization needs to have had . . . [20]

'The way I see it,' said Dibbler, 'there's this high-born girl living all by herself in this big house, right, and her young man goes off to fight for the rebels, you see, and she meets this other guy, and there's the chemistry between them—'

'They blow up?' said Victor.

'He means they fall in love,' said Ginger coldly.

'That sort of thing,' nodded Dibbler. 'Eyes meeting across a crowded room. And she's all alone in the world except for the servants and, let's see, yeah, perhaps her pet dog—'

'This'll be Laddie?' said Ginger.

'Right. And of course she's going to do everything she can to preserve the family mine, so she's kind of flirting with 'em both, the men, not the dog, and then one of them gets killed in the war and the other one throws her over but it's all OK because she's tough at heart.' He sat back. 'What d'you think?' he said.

The people sitting around the room looked uneasily at one another.

---

[20] Apart from anything else, it gives brother a rather better excuse to fight brother than the normal one, viz, what his wife said about our Mam at Auntie Vera's funeral.

There was a fidgety silence.

'It sounds great, Uncle,' said Soll, who wasn't looking for any more problems today.

'Technically very challenging,' said Gaffer.

There was a chorus of relieved assent from the rest of the team.

'I don't know,' said Victor slowly.

Everyone else's eyes turned on him in the same way that spectators at the lion pit watch the first condemned criminal to be pushed out through the iron gate. He went on: 'I mean, is that all? It doesn't sound, well, very complicated for such a long click. People sort of falling in love while a civil war is going on in the background . . . I don't see how you can make much of a picture out of that.'

There was another troubled silence. A couple of people near Victor moved away. Dibbler was staring at him.

Victor could hear, coming from under his chair, an almost inaudible little voice.

' . . . *oh, of course, there's always a part for Laddie . . . wot's he got that I haven't got, that's wot I'd like to . . . '*

Dibbler was still staring fixedly at Victor.

Then he said, 'You're right. You're right. Victor's right. Why didn't anyone else spot it?'

'That's just what I was thinking, Uncle,' said Soll hurriedly. 'We need to flesh it out a bit.'

Dibbler waved his cigar vaguely. 'We can think up some more stuff as we go, no problem. Like . . . like . . . how about a chariot race? People always like a chariot race. It's gripping. Will he fall out, will the wheels come off? Yeah. A chariot race.'

'I've, er, been reading a bit about the Civil War,' said Soll cautiously, 'and I don't think there's any mention of—'

'Of there *not* being chariot races, am I right?' said Dibbler, in soapy tones containing the razor blade of menace. Soll sagged.

'Since you put it like that, Uncle,' he said, 'you're right.'

'And . . . ' Dibbler stared reflectively, ' . . . we could

try . . . a great big shark?' Even Dibbler sounded slightly surprised at his own suggestion.

Soll looked hopefully at Victor.

'I'm almost certain sharks didn't fight in the Civil War,' said Victor.

'You sure?'

'I'm sure people would have noticed,' said Victor.

'They'd have got trampled by the elephants,' muttered Soll.

'Yeah,' said Dibbler, sadly. 'It was just a thought. Don't know why I said it, really.'

He stared at nothing for a while, and then shook his head briskly.

A shark, Victor thought. All the little golden fishes of your own thoughts are swimming away happily, and then the water *moves* and this great shark of a thought comes in from outside. As if someone's doing our thinking for us.

'You just don't know how to behave,' Victor told Gaspode, when they were alone. 'I could hear you grumbling under the chair the whole time.'

'I might not know how to behave, but at least I don't go mooning around over some girl who's letting dretful Creatures of the Night into the world,' said Gaspode.

'I should hope not,' said Victor, and then, 'What do you mean?'

'Aha! *Now* he listens! Your girlfriend—'

'She's not my girlfriend!'

'*Would-be* girlfriend,' said Gaspode, 'is goin' out every night and tryin' to open that door in the hill. She tried it again last night, after you'd gone. I saw her. I *stopped* her,' he added, defiantly. 'Not that I expect any credit, of course. There's something dretful in there, an' she's lettin' it out. No wonder she's always late and tired in the mornings, what with spendin' the whole night diggin'.'

'How do you know they're dreadful?' said Victor weakly.

'Put it like this,' said Gaspode. 'If something's shoved

in a cave under a hill behind great big doors, it's not 'cos people want it to come out every night to wash the dishes, is it? 'Corse,' he added charitably, 'I'm not sayin' she *knows* she's doing it. Prob'ly they've got a grip of her weak an' feeble cat-lovin' female mind and are twisting it to their evil will.'

'You do talk a lot of crap sometimes,' said Victor, but he didn't sound very convincing even to himself.

'Ask her, then,' said the dog, smugly.

'I will!'

'Right!'

Exactly how, though? thought Victor, as they trudged out into the sunshine. Excuse me, miss, my dog says that you . . . no. I say, Ginger, I understand that you're going out and . . . no. Hey, Ginj, how come my dog saw . . . no.

Perhaps he should just start up a conversation and wait until it got around naturally to monstrosities from Beyond the Void.

But it would have to wait, because of the row that was going on.

It was over the third major part in *Blown Away*. Victor was of course the dashing but dangerous hero, Ginger was the only possible choice for the female lead, but the second male role – the dull but dutiful one – was causing trouble.

Victor had never seen anyone stamp their foot in anger before. He'd always thought it was something they did only in books. But Ginger was doing it.

'Because I'd look an idiot, that's why!' she was saying.

Soll, who was by now feeling like a lightning rod on a stormy day, waved his hand frantically.

'But he's ideal for the role!' he said. 'It calls for a solid character—'

'Solid? Of course he's solid! He's made of *stone*!' shouted Ginger. 'He might have a suit of chain mail and a false moustache but he's still a troll!'

Rock, looming monolithically over the pair of them, cleared his throat noisily.

'Excuse me,' he said, 'I hope we're not going to get elementalist about this?'

Now it was Ginger's turn to wave her hands. 'I *like* trolls,' she said. 'As trolls, that is. But you can't seriously mean me to do a romantic scene with a, a, a cliff face.'

'Now look here,' said Rock, his voice winding up like a pitcher's arm. 'What you're saying is, is OK for trolls to be shown bashing people with clubs, is not OK to show trolls have finer feelings like squashy humans?'

'She's not saying that at all,' said Soll desperately. 'She's not—'

'If you cut me, do I not bleed?' said Rock.

'No, you don't,' said Soll, 'but—'

'Ah, yes, but I *would*. If I had blood, I'd bleed all over the place.'

'And another thing,' said a dwarf, prodding Soll in the knee. 'It says in the script that she owns a mine full of happy, laughing, singing dwarfs, right?'

'Oh, yes,' said Soll, putting the troll problem on one side. 'What about it?'

'It's a bit stereotypical, isn't it?' said the dwarf. 'I mean, it's a bit dwarfs = miners. I don't see why we have to be type-cast like this all the time.'

'But most dwarfs *are* miners,' said Soll desperately.

'Well, OK, but they're not happy about it,' said another dwarf. 'And they don't sing the whole time.'

'That's right,' said a third dwarf. ' 'Cos of safety, see? You can bring the whole roof down on you, singing.'

'*And* there's no mines anywhere near Ankh-Morpork,' said possibly the first dwarf, although they all looked identical to Soll. 'Everyone knows that. It's on loam. We'd be a laughing stock, if our people saw us mining for jewels anywhere near Ankh-Morpork.'

'I wouldn't say I've got a cliff face,' rumbled Rock,

who sometimes took a little time to digest things. 'Craggy, maybe. But not cliffy.'

'The fact is,' said one of the dwarfs, 'we don't see why humans get all the good roles and we get all the titchy bit parts.'

Soll gave the jolly little laugh of someone in a corner who hopes that a joke will lighten the atmosphere a bit.

'Ah,' he said, 'that's because you—'

'*Yes?*' said the dwarfs in unison.

'Um,' said Soll, and struck out quickly for a change of subject. 'You see, the whole point, as I understand it, is that Ginger will do absolutely anything to keep the mansion and the mine and—'

'I hopes we can get on,' said Gaffer, 'only I've got to muck the imps out in an hour.'

'Oh, I see,' said Rock. 'I'm absolutely anything, am I?'

'You don't keep mines,' said one of the dwarfs. 'Mines keep you. You take the treasure out. You don't put it in. That's fundamental to the whole mine business.'

'Well, perhaps this mine is worked out,' said Soll quickly. 'Anyway, she—'

'Well, in that case, you don't keep it,' said another dwarf, in the expansive manner of one about to settle down to a good long explanation. 'You abandon it, propping and shoring where necessary, and sink another shaft on a line with the major seam—'

'Allowing for fault escarpments and uniclinal structures,' said another dwarf.

'Of course, allowing for fault escarpments and uniclinal structures, and then—'

'And general crustal shifting.'

'All right, and then—'

'Unless you're just cutting and filling, of course.'

'Granted, but—'

'I don't see', Rock began, 'that my face could be called—'

'SHUT UP!' screamed Soll. 'Everyone shut up! SHUT

UP! The next person who doesn't shut up will never work in this town again! Understand? Do I make myself CLEAR? Right.' He coughed, and continued in a more normal voice: 'Very well. Now, I want it understood that this is a Breathtaking, Block-busting Romantic film about a woman's fight to save the—' he consulted his clipboard, and went on valiantly, '—everything she loves against the background of a World Gone Mad, and I don't want any more trouble from anyone.'

A dwarf tentatively raised his hand.

' 'Scuse me?'

'Yes?' said Soll.

'Why is it all Mr Dibbler's films are set against the background of a world gone mad?' said the dwarf.

Soll's eyes narrowed. 'Because Mr Dibbler', he growled, 'is a very observant man.'

Dibbler had been right. The new city was the old city distilled. Narrow alleys were narrower, tall buildings taller. Gargoyles were more fearsome, roofs more pointed. The towering Tower of Art in Unseen University was, here, even taller and more precariously towering even though it was at the same time only one quarter the size; the Unseen University was more baroque and buttressed; the Patrician's Palace more pillar'd. Carpenters swarmed over a construction that, when it was finished, would make Ankh-Morpork look like a very indifferent copy of itself, except that the buildings in the original city were not, by and large, painted on canvas stretched over timber and didn't have the dirt carefully sprayed on. Ankh-Morpork's buildings had to get dirty all by themselves.

It looked far more like Ankh-Morpork than Ankh-Morpork ever had.

Ginger had been ushered off to the changing tents before Victor had a chance to speak to her, and then shooting started and it was too late.

Century of the Fruitbat (and now it said on the sign, in slightly smaller type: More Stars than There Are in the Heavens[21]) believed that a click should be made in less than ten times the time it took to watch. *Blown Away* was going to be different. There were battles. There were night scenes, the imps painting away furiously by torchlight. Dwarfs worked merrily in a mine never seen before or since, where fake gold nuggets the size of chickens had been stuck in the plaster walls. Since Soll demanded that their lips should be seen to move they sang a *risqué* version of the 'Hihohiho' song, which had rather caught on among Holy Wood's dwarf population.

It was just possible that Soll knew how it all fitted together. Victor didn't. It was always best, he had learned, never to try to follow the plot of any click you were in, and in any case Soll wasn't just shooting back to front but sides to middle as well. It was totally confusing, just like real life.

When he did get a chance to talk to Ginger, two handlemen and everyone else in the cast who currently had nothing to do were watching them.

'OK, people,' said Soll. 'This is the scene near the end where Victor meets Ginger after all they've been through together, and on the card he'll be saying—' He stared at the big black oblong handed to him. 'Yes, he'll be saying "Frankly, my dear, I'd give anything for one of . . . Harga's . . . prime . . . pork . . . ribs . . . in . . . special . . . curry . . . sauce . . . " '

Soll's voice slowed and stopped. When he breathed in, it was like a whale surfacing.

'*Who* wrote THIS?'

One of the artists cautiously raised a hand.

'Mr Dibbler told me to,' he said quickly.

Soll leafed through the big heap of cards that represented the dialogue for a large part of the click. His lips tightened.

---

[21] 49,873, according to Numbers Riktor's clockwork Celestial Enumerator.

He nodded to one of the people with clipboards and said, 'Could you just run over to the office and ask my uncle to stroll over here, if he's got a moment?'

Soll pulled a card out of the stack and read, ' "I sure miss the old mine but for a taste of real country cooking I always . . . go . . . to . . . Harga's . . . House . . . Of . . ." I *see*.'

He selected another at random. 'Ah. I see here a wounded Royalist soldier's last words are "What I wouldn't give right now for a $1 Eat-Till-It-Hurts special at . . . Harga's . . . House . . . of . . . Ribs . . . Mother!" '

'I think it's very moving,' said Dibbler, behind him. 'There won't be a dry eye in the house, you'll see.'

'Uncle—' Soll began.

Dibbler raised his hands. 'I said I'd raise the money somehow,' he said, 'and Sham Harga's even helping us with the food for the barbecue scene.'

'You said you weren't going to interfere with the script!'

'That's not interfering,' said Dibbler stolidly. 'I don't see how *that* could be considered interfering. I just polished it up here and there. I think it's rather an improvement. Besides, Harga's All-You-Can-Gobble-For-A-Dollar is amazing value these days.'

'But the click is set hundreds of years ago!' shouted Soll.

'We-ell,' said Dibbler. 'I suppose someone could say, "I wonder if the food at Harga's House of Ribs will still be as good in hundreds of years' time—" '

'That isn't moving pictures. That is crass commerce!'

'I hope so,' said Dibbler. 'We're in real trouble if it isn't.'

'Now look—' Soll began, threateningly.

Ginger turned to Victor.

'Can we go somewhere and talk?' she said, quietly. 'Without your dog,' she added, in her normal voice. 'Definitely without your dog.'

'You want to talk to *me*?' said Victor.

'There hasn't been much of a chance, has there?'

'Right. Certainly. Gaspode, *stay*. There's a good dog.' Victor derived a quiet satisfaction from the brief look of pure disgust that flashed across Gaspode's face.

Behind them the eternal Holy Wood argument had wound up to cruising speed, with Soll and C.M.O.T. standing nose to nose and arguing in a circle of amused and interested staff.

'*I don't have to take this, you know! I can resign!*'

'*No, you can't! You're my nephew! You can't resign from being a nephew—!*'

Ginger and Victor sat down on the steps of a canvas and wood mansion. They had absolute privacy. No-one was going to bother to watch them with a rip-snorter of a row going on a few yards away.

'Er,' said Ginger. Her fingers twisted among themselves. Victor couldn't help noticing that the nails were worn down.

'Er,' she said again. Her face was a picture of anguish, and pale under the make-up. She isn't beautiful, Victor felt himself think, but you could have real trouble believing it.

'I, er, don't know how to say this,' she said, 'but, er, has anyone noticed me walking in my sleep?'

'To the hill?' said Victor.

Her head whipped around like a snake.

'You know? How do you know? Have you been spying on me?' she snapped. It was the old Ginger again, all fire and venom and the aggressiveness of paranoia.

'Laddie found you . . . asleep yesterday afternoon,' said Victor, leaning back.

'During the *day*?'

'Yes.'

She put her hands to her mouth. 'It's worse than I thought,' she whispered. 'It's getting worse! You know when you met me up the hill? Just before Dibbler found us, and thought we were . . . spooning . . . ' she blushed. 'Well, I didn't even know how I'd got there!'

211

'And you went back last night,' said Victor.

'The dog told you, did he?' she said, dully.

'Yes. Sorry.'

'It's every night now,' moaned Ginger. 'I know, because even if I go back to bed there's sand all over the floor and my nails are all broken! I go there every night and I don't know why!'

'You're trying to open the door,' said Victor. 'There's this big ancient door now, where part of the hill has slid away, and—'

'Yes, I've seen it, but *why*?'

Well, I've got a couple of ideas,' said Victor cautiously.

'Tell me!'

'Um. Well, have you heard of something called a *genius loci*?'

'No.' Her brow wrinkled. 'It's clever, is it?'

'It's the sort of soul of a place. It can be quite strong. It can be *made* strong, by worship or love or hate, if it goes on long enough. And I'm wondering if the spirit of a place can call to people. And animals, too. I mean, Holy Wood is a different sort of place, isn't it? People act differently here. Everywhere else, the most important things are gods or money or cattle. Here, the most important thing is to be important.'

He had her full attention. 'Yes?' she said encouragingly, and, 'It doesn't sound too bad so far.'

'I'm getting to the bad bit.'

'Oh.'

Victor swallowed. His brain was bubbling like a bouillon. Half-remembered facts surfaced tantalizingly and sank again. Dry old tutors in high old rooms had been telling him dull old things which were suddenly as urgent as a knife, and he dredged desperately for them.

'I'm not—' he croaked. He cleared his throat. 'I'm not sure it's right, though,' he managed. 'It's come from *somewhere else*. It can happen. You've heard of ideas whose time has come?'

'Yes.'

'Well, they're the tame ones. There's other ones. Ideas so full of vigour they don't even wait for their time. Wild ideas. Escaped ideas. And the trouble is, when you get something like that, you get a hole—'

He looked at her polite, blank expression. Analogies bubbled to the surface like soggy croutons. Imagine all the worlds that have ever been are in one sense pressed together like a sandwich . . . a pack of cards . . . a book . . . a folded sheet . . . if conditions are right, things can go *through* rather than *along* . . . but if you open a gate between worlds, there are terrible dangers, as for instance . . .

As for instance . . .

As for instance . . .

As for instance what?

It rose up in his memory like the suddenly-discovered bit of suspicious tentacle just when you thought it was safe to eat the paella.

'It could be that something else is trying to come through the same way,' he ventured. 'In the, uh, in the nowhere between the somewhere there are creatures which on the whole I'd rather not describe to you.'

'You already have,' said Ginger, in a tense voice.

'And, uh, they're generally quite keen to get into the real worlds and perhaps they're somehow making contact with you when you're asleep and . . . ' He gave up. He couldn't bear her expression any more.

'I could be entirely wrong,' he said quickly.

'You've got to stop me opening the door,' she whispered. 'I could be one of Them.'

'Oh, I don't think so,' said Victor loftily. 'They've generally got too many arms, I think.'

'I tried putting tacks on the floor to wake myself up,' said Ginger.

'Sounds awful. Did it work?'

'No. They were all back in their bag in the morning. I must have picked them up again.'

Victor pursed his lips. 'That could be a good sign,' he said.

'Why?'

'If you were being summoned by, uh, unpleasant things, I think they wouldn't bother what you walked over.'

'Urgh.'

'You haven't got any idea why it's all happening, have you?' Victor said.

'No! But I always get the same dream.' Her eyes narrowed. 'Hey, how come you know all this stuff?'

'I – a wizard told me, once,' said Victor.

'You're not a wizard yourself?'

'Absolutely not. No wizards in Holy Wood. And this dream?'

'Oh, it's too strange to mean anything. Anyway, I used to dream it even when I was small. It starts off with this mountain, only it's not a normal mountain, because—'

Detritus the troll loomed over them.

'Young Mr Dibbler says it's time to start shooting again,' he rumbled.

'Will you come to my room tonight?' hissed Ginger. 'Please? You can wake me up if I start sleepwalking again.'

'Well, er, yes, but your landlady might not like it—' Victor began.

'Oh, Mrs Cosmopilite is very broadminded,' said Ginger.

'She is?'

'She'll just think we're having sex,' said Ginger.

'Ah,' said Victor hollowly. 'That's all right, then.'

'Young Mr Dibbler don't like being kept waiting,' said Detritus.

'Oh, shut up,' said Ginger. She stood up and brushed the dust off her dress. Detritus blinked. People didn't usually tell him to shut up. A few worried fault-lines appeared on his brow. He turned and tried another loom, this time aimed at Victor.

'Young Mr Dibbler don't like—'

'Oh, go away,' snapped Victor, and wandered off after her.

Detritus stood alone and screwed up his eyes in the effort of thought.

Of course, people did occasionally say things like 'Go away' and 'Shut up' to him, but always with the tremor of terrified bravado in their voice, and so naturally he always riposted 'Hur hur' and hit them. But no-one had ever spoken to him as if his existence was the last thing in the world they could possibly be persuaded to worry about. His massive shoulders sagged. Perhaps all this hanging around Ruby was bad for him.

Soll was standing over the artist who lettered the cards. He looked up as Victor and Ginger approached.

'Right,' he said, 'places, everyone. We'll go straight on to the ballroom scene.' He looked pleased with himself.

'Are the words all sorted out?' said Victor.

'*No* problem,' said Soll proudly. He glanced at the sun. 'We've lost a lot of time,' he added, 'so let's not waste any more.'

'Fancy you being able to get C.M.O.T. to give in like that,' said Victor.

'He had no argument at all. He's gone back to his office to sulk, I expect,' said Soll loftily. 'OK, everyone, let's all get—'

The lettering artist tugged at his sleeve.

'I was just wondering, Mr Soll, what you wanted me to put in the big scene now Victor doesn't mention ribs—'

'Don't worry me now, man!'

'But if you could just give me an idea—'

Soll firmly unhooked the man's hand from his sleeve. 'Frankly,' he said, 'I don't give a damn,' and he strode off towards the set.

The artist was left alone. He picked up his paintbrush. His lips moved silently, shaping themselves around the words.

Then he said, 'Hmm. Nice one.'

Banana N'Vectif, cunningest hunter in the great yellow plains of Klatch, held his breath as he tweezered the last piece into place. Rain drummed on the roof of his hut.

There. That was it.

He'd never done anything like this before, but he knew he was doing it *right*.

He'd trapped everything from zebras to thargas in his time, and what had he got to show for it? But yesterday, when he'd taken a load of skins into N'kouf, he'd heard a trader say that if any man ever built a better mousetrap, then the world would beat a path to his door.

He'd lain awake all night thinking about this. Then, in the first light of dawn, he scratched a few designs on the hut wall with a stick and got to work. He had taken the opportunity to look at a few mousetraps while he was in the town, and they were definitely less than perfect. They hadn't been built by hunters.

Now he picked up the twig and pushed it gently into the mechanism.

Snap.

Perfect.

Now, all he had to do was take it into N'kouf and see if the merchant—

The rain was very loud indeed. In fact, it sounded more like—

When Banana woke up he was lying in the ruins of his hut and they were in a half-mile wide swathe of trodden mud.

He looked muzzily at what remained of his home. He looked at the brown scar that stretched from horizon to horizon. He looked at the dark, muddy cloud just visible at one end of it.

Then he looked down. The better mousetrap was now a rather nice two-dimensional design, squashed into the middle of an enormous footprint.

He said, 'I didn't know it was *that* good.'

According to the history books, the decisive battle that ended the Ankh-Morpork Civil War was fought between two handfuls of bone-weary men in a swamp early one misty morning and, although one side claimed victory, ended with a practical score of Humans 0, ravens 1,000, which is the case with most battles.

Something that both Dibblers were agreed on was that, if they'd been in charge, no-one would have been able to get away with such a low-grade war. It was a crime that people should have been allowed to stage a major turning-point in the history of the city without using thousands of people and camels and ditches and earthworks and siege-engines and trebuckets and horses and banners.

'And in a bloody fog, too,' said Gaffer. 'No thought about light levels.'

He surveyed the proposed field of battle, shading his eyes from the sun with one hand. There would be eleven handlemen working on this one, from every conceivable angle. One by one they held up their thumbs.

Gaffer rapped on the picture box in front of him.

'Ready, lads?' he said.

There was a chorus of squeaks.

'Good lads,' he said. 'Get this one right and thee can have an extra lizard for thy tea.'

He grasped the handle with one hand and picked up a megaphone with the other.

'Ready when you are, Mr Dibbler!' he yelled.

C.M.O.T. nodded and was about to raise his hand when Soll's arm shot out and grabbed it. The nephew was staring intently at the ranged ranks of horsemen.

'Just one moment,' he said levelly, and then cupped his hands and raised his voice to a shout. 'Hey, you there! Fifteenth knight along! Yes, you! Would you mind unfurling your banner, please? Thank you. Could you please report to Mrs Cosmopilite for a new one. Thank you.'

Soll turned to his uncle, his eyebrows raised.

'It's . . . it's a heraldic device,' said Dibbler quickly.

'Crossed spare ribs on a bed of lettuce?' said Soll.

'Very keen on their food, those old knights—'

'And I liked the motto,' said Soll. ' "Every (k)night is Gormay Night At Harga's House of Ribs." If we had sound, I wonder what his battle cry would have been?'

'You're my own flesh and blood,' said Dibbler, shaking his head. 'How can you do this to me?'

'Because I'm your own flesh and blood,' said Soll.

Dibbler brightened. Of course, when you looked at it like that, it didn't seem so bad.

This is Holy Wood. To pass the time quickly, you just film the clock hands moving fast . . .

In Unseen University, the resograph is already recording seven plibs a minute.

And, towards the end of the afternoon, they burned Ankh-Morpork.

The real city had been burned down many times in its long history – out of revenge, or carelessness, or spite, or even just for the insurance. Most of the big stone buildings that actually made it a *city*, as opposed simply to a load of hovels all in one place, survived them intact and many people[22] considered that a good fire every hundred years or so was essential to the health of the city since it helped to keep down the rats, roaches, fleas and, of course, people not rich enough to live in stone houses.

The famous Fire during the Civil War had been noteworthy simply because it was started by both sides *at the same time* in order to stop the city falling into enemy hands.

It had not otherwise, according to the history books, been very impressive. The Ankh had been particularly high that summer, and most of the city had been too damp to burn.

This time it was a lot better.

Flames poured into the sky. Because this was Holy Wood, *everything* burned, because the only difference between the stone buildings and the wooden buildings was what was painted on the canvas. The two-dimensional Unseen University burned. The Patrician's backless palace burned. Even the scale-model Tower of Art gushed flames like a roman candle.

Dibbler watched it with concern.

---

[22] The ones living in stone buildings, anyway.

After a while Soll, behind him, said, 'Waiting for something, Uncle?'

'Hmm? Oh, no. I hope Gaffer's concentrating on the tower, that's all,' said Dibbler. 'Very important symbolic landmark.'

'It certainly is,' said Soll. 'Very important. So important, in fact, that I sent some lads up it at lunchtime just to make sure it was all OK.'

'You did?' said Dibbler, guiltily.

'Yes. And do you know what they found? They found someone had nailed some fireworks to the outside. Lots and lots of fireworks, on fuses. It's a good thing they found them because if the things had gone off it would have *ruined* the shot and we'd never be able to do it again. And, do you know, they said it looked as though the fireworks would spell out words?' Soll added.

'What words?'

'Never crossed my mind to ask them,' said Soll. 'Never crossed my mind.'

He stuck his hands in his pockets and began to whistle under his breath. After a while he glanced sidelong at his uncle.

' "Hottest ribs in town",' he muttered. 'Really!'

Dibbler looked sulky. 'It would have got a laugh, anyway,' he said.

'Look, Uncle, this can't go on,' said Soll. 'No more of this commercial messing about, right?'

'Oh, all right.'

'Sure?'

Dibbler nodded. 'I've said all right, haven't I?'

'I want a bit more than that, Uncle.'

'I solemnly promise not to do any more meddling in the click,' said Dibbler gravely. 'I'm your uncle. I'm *family*. Is that good enough for you?'

'Well. All right.'

When the fire had died down they raked some of the ashes together for a barbecue at the end-of-shooting party, under the stars.

★

The velvet sheet of the night drapes itself over the parrot cage that is Holy Wood, and on warm nights like this there are many people with private business to pursue.

A young couple, strolling hand in hand across the dunes, were frightened to near insensibility when an enormous troll jumped out at them from behind a rock waving its arms and shouting 'Aaaargh!'

'Scared you, did I?' said Detritus, hopefully.

They nodded, white-faced.

'Well, that's a relief,' said the troll. He patted them on the heads, forcing their feet a little way into the sand. 'Thanks very much. Much obliged. Have a nice night,' he added mournfully.

He watched them walk off hand in hand, and then burst into tears.

In the handlemen's shed, C.M.O.T. Dibbler stood watching thoughtfully as Gaffer pasted together the day's footage. The handleman was feeling very gratified; Mr Dibbler had never shown the slightest interest in the actual techniques of film handling before now. This may have explained why he was a little freer than usual with Guild secrets that had been handed down sideways from one generation to the same generation.

'Why are all the little pictures alike?' said Dibbler, as the handleman wound the film on to its spool. 'Seems to me that's wasting money.'

'They're not really alike,' said Gaffer. 'Each one's a bit different, see? And so people's eyes see a lot of little slightly different pictures very fast and their eyes think they're watching something move.'

Dibbler took his cigar out of his mouth. 'You mean it's all a trick?' he said, astonished.

'Yeah, that's right.' The handleman chuckled and reached for the paste pot.

Dibbler watched in fascination.

'I thought it was all a special kind of magic,' he said,

a shade disappointed. 'Now you tell me it's just a big Find-the-Lady game?'

'Sort of. You see, people don't actually *see* any one picture. They see a lot of them at once, see what I mean?'

'Hey, I got lost at see there.'

'Every picture adds to the general *effect*. People don't see, sorry, any one picture, they just see the effect caused by a lot of them moving past very quickly.'

'Do they? That's very interesting,' said Dibbler. 'Very interesting indeed.' He flicked the ash from his cigar towards the demons. One of them caught it and ate it.

'So what would happen', he said slowly, 'if, say, just one picture in the whole click was different.'

'Funny you should ask,' said Gaffer. 'It happened the other day when we were patching up *Beyond the Valley of the Trolls*. One of the apprentices had stuck in just one picture from *The Golde Rush* and we all went around all morning thinking about gold and not knowing why. It was as if it'd gone straight into our heads without our eyes seeing it. Of course, I took my belt to the lad when we spotted it, but we'd never have found out if I hadn't happened to look at the click slowly.'

He picked up the paste brush again, squared up a couple of strips of film, and fixed them together. After a while he became aware that it had gone very quiet behind him.

'You all right, Mr Dibbler?' he said.

'Hmm? Oh.' Dibbler was deep in thought. 'Just one picture had all that effect?'

'Oh, yes. Are you all right, Mr Dibbler?'

'Never felt better, lad,' Dibbler said. 'Never felt better.'

He rubbed his hands together. 'Let's you and me have a little chat, man to man,' he added. 'Because, you know . . . ' he laid a friendly hand on Gaffer's shoulder, ' . . . I've a feeling that this could be your *lucky* day.'

And in another alleyway Gaspode sat muttering to himself.

'Huh. Stay, he says. Givin' me *orders*. Jus' so's his

221

girlfriend doesn't have to have a horrid smelly dog in her room. So here's me, man's best friend, sittin' out in the rain. If it was rainin', anyway. Maybe it ain't rainin', but if it was rainin', I'd be soaked by now. Serve him right if I just upped and walked away. I could do it, too. Any time I wanted. I don't have to sit here. I hope no-one's thinkin' I'm sittin' here because I've been told to sit here. I'd like to see the human who could give *me* orders. I'm sittin' here 'cos I *want* to. Yeah.'

Then he whined for a bit and shuffled into the shadows, where there was less chance of being seen.

In the room above, Victor was standing facing the wall. This was humiliating. It had been bad enough bumping into a grinning Mrs Cosmopilite on the stairs. She had given him a big smile and a complicated, elbow-intensive gesture that, he felt certain, sweet little old ladies shouldn't know.

There were clinks and the occasional rustle behind him as Ginger got ready for bed.

'She's really very nice. She told me yesterday that she had had four husbands,' said Ginger.

'What did she do with the bones?' said Victor.

'I'm sure I don't know what you mean,' said Ginger, sniffing. 'All right, you can turn around now. I'm in bed.'

Victor relaxed, and turned round. Ginger had drawn the covers up to her neck and was holding them there like a besieged garrison manning the barricades.

'You've got to promise me,' she said, 'that if anything happens, you won't try to take advantage of the situation.'

Victor sighed. 'I promise.'

'It's just that I've got a career to think about, you see.'

'Yes, I see.'

Victor sat by the lamp and took the book out of his pocket.

'I'm not trying to be ungrateful or anything like that,' Ginger went on.

Victor ruffled through the yellowing pages, looking for the place he'd got to. Scores of people had spent their lives by Holy Wood Hill, apparently just to keep a fire alight and chant three times a day. Why?

'What are you reading?' said Ginger, after a while.

'It's an old book I found,' said Victor, shortly. 'It's about Holy Wood.'

'Oh.'

'I should get some sleep if I were you,' he said, twisting so that he could make out the crabby script in the lamp light.

He heard her yawn.

'Did I finish telling you about the dream?' she said.

'I don't think so,' said Victor, in what he hoped was a politely discouraging voice.

'It always starts off with this mountain—'

'Look, you really shouldn't be talking—'

'—and there are stars around it, you know, in the sky, but one of them comes down and it's not a star at all, it's a woman holding a torch over her head—'

Victor slowly turned back to the front of the book.

'Yes?' he said, carefully.

'And she keeps on trying to tell me something, something I can't make out, about waking something, and then there are a lot of lights and this roar, like a lion or a tiger or something, you know? And then I wake up.'

Victor's finger idly traced the outline of the mountain under the stars.

'It's probably just a dream,' he said. 'It probably doesn't mean anything.'

Of course, Holy Wood Hill wasn't pointed. But perhaps it was once, in the days when there had been a city where now there was a bay. Good grief. Something must have really *hated* this place.

'You don't remember anything else about the dream, by any chance?' he asked, with feigned casualness.

223

There was no answer. He crept to the bed.

She was asleep.

He went back to the chair, which was promising to become annoyingly uncomfortable within half an hour, and turned down the lamp.

Something in the hill. That was the danger.

The more immediate danger was that he was going to fall asleep, too.

He sat in the dark and worried. How did you wake up a sleepwalker, anyway? He recalled vaguely that it was said to be a very dangerous thing to do. There were stories about people dreaming about being executed and then, when someone had touched them on the shoulder to wake them up, their heads had fallen off. How anyone ever knew what a dead person had been dreaming wasn't disclosed. Perhaps the ghost came back afterwards and stood at the end of the bed, complaining.

The chair creaked alarmingly as he shifted position. Perhaps if he stuck one leg out like *this* he could rest it on the end of the bed, so that even if he did fall asleep she wouldn't be able to get past without waking him.

Funny, really. For weeks he'd spent the days sweeping her up in his arms, defending her bravely from whatever it was Morry was dressed up as today, kissing her, and generally riding off into the sunset to live happily, and possibly even ecstatically, ever after. There was probably no-one who'd ever watched one of the clicks who would possibly believe that he'd spend the night sitting in her room on a chair made out of splinters. Even he found it hard to believe, and here he was. You didn't get this sort of thing in clicks. Clicks were all Passione in a Worlde Gone Madde. If this was a click, he certainly wouldn't be sitting around in the dark on a hard chair. He'd be . . . well, he wouldn't be sitting around in the dark on a hard chair, that was for sure.

The Bursar locked his study door behind him. You had to do that. The Archchancellor thought that knocking on doors was something that happened to other people.

At least the horrible man seemed to have lost interest in the resograph, or whatever Riktor had called it. The Bursar had had a dreadful day, trying to conduct University business while knowing that the document was hidden in his room.

He pulled it out from under the carpet, turned up the lamp, and began to read.

He'd be the first to admit that he wasn't any good at mechanical things. He gave up quickly on the bits about pivots, octiron pendulums, and air being compressed in bellows.

He homed in again on the paragraph that said: 'If, then, disturbances in the fabric of reality cause ripples to spread out from the epicentre, then the pendulum will tilt, compress the air in the relevant bellows, and cause the ornamental elephant closest to the epicentre to release a small lead ball into a cup. And thus the direction of the disturbance—'

. . . whumm . . . whumm . . .

He could hear it even up here. They'd just heaped more sandbags around it. No-one dared move it now. The Bursar tried to concentrate on his reading.

'—can be estimated by the number and force—'

. . . whumm . . . *whumm*WHUMM*WHUMM*.

The Bursar found himself holding his breath.

'—of the expelled pellets, which I estimate in serious disturbances—'

Plib.

'—may well exceed two pellets—'

Plib.

'—expelled several inches—'

Plib.

'—during the—'

Plib.

'—course—'

Plib.

'—of—'

Plib.
'—one—'
Plib.
'—month.'
Plib.

Gaspode woke up and quickly hauled himself into what he
hoped looked like an alert position.

Someone was shouting, but politely, as if they wanted
to be helped but only if it wouldn't be too much trouble.

He trotted up the steps. The door was ajar. He pushed
it open with his head.

Victor was lying on his back, tied to a chair. Gaspode
sat down and watched him intently, in case he was about
to do something interesting.

'All right, are we?' he said, after a while.

'Don't just sit there, idiot! Untie these knots,' said
Victor.

'Idiot I may be, but tied up I ain't,' said Gaspode evenly.
'Got the jump on you, did she?'

'I must have nodded off for a moment,' said Victor.

'Long enough for her to get up, rip up a sheet, and tie
you to the chair,' said Gaspode.

'Yes, all right, all right. Can't you gnaw through it, or
something?'

'With these teeth? I could fetch someone, though,' said
Gaspode, and grinned.

'Er, I'm not sure that's a very good—'

'Don't worry. I'll be right back,' said Gaspode, and
padded out.

'It might be a bit difficult to explain—' Victor called
after him, but the dog was down the stairs and ambling
along through the maze of backlots and alleys to the rear
of Century of the Fruitbat.

He shuffled up to the high fence. There was the gentle
clink of a chain.

'Laddie?' he whispered hoarsely.

There was a delighted bark.

'Good boy Laddie!'

'Yeah,' said Gaspode. 'Yeah.' He sighed. Had *he* ever been like that? If he had, thank goodness he hadn't known about it.

'Me good boy!'

'Sure, sure. Laddie be quiet,' muttered Gaspode, and squeezed his arthritic body under the fence. Laddie licked his face as he emerged.

'I'm too old for this sort of stuff,' he muttered, and peered at the kennel.

'A choke chain,' he said. 'A bloody choke chain. Stop pulling on it, you daft idiot. Back up. *Back up*. Right.'

Gaspode shoved a paw into the loop and eased it over Laddie's head.

'There,' he said. 'If we all knew how to do that, we'd be runnin' the world. Now stop kiddin' around. We need you.'

Laddie sprang to tongue-lolling attention. If dogs could salute, he would have done.

Gaspode wriggled under the fence again, and waited. He could hear Laddie's footsteps the other side, but the big dog seemed to be padding away from the fence.

'No!' hissed Gaspode. 'Follow *me*!'

There was a scurry of paws, a swishing noise, and Laddie cleared the high fence and did a four-point landing in front of him.

Gaspode unpeeled his tongue from the back of his throat.

'Good boy,' he muttered. 'Good boy.'

Victor sat up, rubbing his head.

'I caught myself a right crack when the chair fell backwards,' he said.

Laddie sat looking expectantly, with the remains of the sheet in his mouth.

'What's he waiting for?' said Victor.

'You've got to tell him he's a good boy,' sighed Gaspode.

'Doesn't he expect some meat or a sweet or something?'

Gaspode shook his head. 'Jus' tell him what a good boy he is. It's better'n hard currency, for dogs.'

'Oh? Well, then: good boy, Laddie.'

Laddie bounced up and down excitedly. Gaspode swore under his breath.

'Sorry about this,' he said. 'Pathetic, isn't it?'

'Good boy, find Ginger,' said Victor.

'Look, *I* can do that,' said Gaspode desperately, as Laddie started snuffling at the floor. 'We all know where she's headed. You don't have to go and—'

Laddie dashed out of the door, but gracefully. He paused at the bottom of the stairs and gave an eager, follow-me bark.

'Pathetic,' said Gaspode, miserably.

The stars always seemed to shine more brightly over Holy Wood. Of course, the air was clearer than Ankh, and there wasn't much smoke, but even so . . . they were somehow bigger, too, and closer, as if the sky was a vast lens.

Laddie streaked over the dunes, pausing occasionally for Victor to catch up. Gaspode followed on some way behind, rolling from side to side and wheezing.

The trail led to the hollow, which was empty.

The door was open about a foot. Scuffed sand around it indicated that, whatever may or may not have come out, Ginger had gone in.

Victor stared at it.

Laddie sat by the door, staring hopefully at Victor.

'He's waitin',' said Gaspode.

'What for?' said Victor apprehensively.

Gaspode groaned. 'What do you think?' he said.

'Oh. Yes. There's a *good* boy, Laddie.'

Laddie yapped and tried to turn a somersault.

'What do we do next?' said Victor. 'I suppose we go in, do we?'

'Could be,' said Gaspode.

'Er. Or we could wait till she comes out. The fact is, I've never been very happy about darkness,' said Victor.

'I mean, night-time is OK, but pitch darkness—'

'I bet Cohen the Barbarian isn't afraid of the dark,' said Gaspode.

'Well, yes—'

'And the Black Shadow of the Desert, he's not afraid of the dark either.'

'OK, but—'

'And Howondaland Smith, Balgrog Hunter, practic'ly eats the dark for his tea,' said Gaspode.

'Yes, but I'm not those people!' wailed Victor.

'Try tellin' that to all those people who handed over their pennies to watch you bein' 'em,' said Gaspode. He scratched at an insomniac flea. 'Cor, it'd be a laugh to have a handleman here now, wouldn't it?' he said, cheerfully. 'Wot a comedy feature it'd make. *Mr Hero Not Goin' Into the Dark*, we could call it. It'd be better'n *Turkey Legs*. It'd be funnier'n *A Night At The Arena*. I reckon people'd queue fo—'

'All right, all right,' said Victor. 'I'll go a little way in, perhaps.' He looked around desperately at the dried-up trees around the hollow. 'And I'll make a torch,' he added.

He'd expected spiders and dampness and possibly snakes, if nothing worse . . .

Instead, there was just a dry, roughly square passageway, leading slightly downwards. The air had a slightly salty smell, suggesting that somewhere the tunnel was connected to the sea.

Victor took a few paces along it, and stopped.

'Hang on,' he said. 'If the torch goes out, we could get horribly lost.'

'No, we can't,' said Gaspode. 'Sense of smell, see?'

'Gosh, that's clever.'

Victor went on a little further. The walls were covered with big versions of the square ideograms that featured in the book.

'You know,' he said, pausing to run his fingers over

one, 'these aren't really like a written language. It's more as if—'

'Keep movin' and stop makin' excuses,' said Gaspode behind him.

Victor's foot kicked against something which bounced away into the darkness.

'What was it?' he quavered.

Gaspode snuffled off into the darkness, and returned.

'Don't worry about it,' he said.

'Oh?'

'It's just a skull.'

'*Whose?*'

'He dint say,' said Gaspode.

'Shut up!'

Something crunched under Victor's sandal.

'An' *that*—' Gaspode began.

'I don't want to know!'

'It was a seashell, in fact,' said Gaspode.

Victor peered into the moving square of darkness ahead of them. The makeshift torch flared in the draught and, if he strained his ears, he could hear a rhythmic sound; it was either a beast roaring in the distance, or the sound of the sea moving in some underground tunnel. He opted for the second suggestion.

'Something's been calling her,' he said. 'In dreams. Someone that wants to be let out. I'm afraid she's going to get hurt.'

'She's not worth it,' said Gaspode. 'Messin' around with girls who're in thrall to Creatures from the Void never works out, take my word for it. You'd never know what you were going to wake up next to.'

'Gaspode!'

'You'll see I'm right.'

The torch went out.

Victor waved it desperately and blew on it in a last attempt to rekindle it. A few sparks flared and faded. There simply wasn't enough torch left.

The darkness flowed back. Victor had never known

darkness like it. No matter how long you looked into it, your eyes wouldn't grow accustomed to it. There was nothing to become accustomed *to*. It was darkness and mother of darkness, darkness absolute, the darkness under the earth, darkness so dense as to be almost tangible, like cold velvet.

'It's bloody dark,' volunteered Gaspode.

I've broken out into what they call a cold sweat, thought Victor. So that's what it feels like. I'd always wondered.

He eased himself sideways until he reached the wall.

'We'd better go back,' he said, in what he hoped was a matter-of-fact voice. 'There could be anything ahead of us. Ravines or anything. We could get more torches and more people and come back.'

There was a flat sound from far down the passage.

Whoomph.

It was followed by a light so harsh that it projected the image of Victor's eyeballs on the back of his skull. It faded after a few seconds, but was still almost painfully bright. Laddie whimpered.

'There you are,' said Gaspode hoarsely. 'You've got some light now, so everything's all right.'

'Yes, but what's making it?'

'I'm supposed to know, am I?'

Victor inched forward, his shadow dancing behind him.

After a hundred yards or so the passageway opened out in what had perhaps once been a natural cave. The light was coming from an arch high up at one end, but it was bright enough to reveal every detail.

It was bigger even than the Great Hall at the University, and must once have been even more impressive. The light gleamed off baroque gold ornamentation, and on the stalactites that ribbed the roof. Stairs wide enough for a regiment rose from a wide shadowy hole in the floor; a regular thud and boom and a smell of salt said that the sea had found an entrance somewhere below. The air was clammy.

'Some kind of a temple?' muttered Victor.

Gaspode sniffed at a dark red drapery hung on one side of the entrance. At his touch it collapsed into a mess of slime.

'Yuk,' he said. 'The whole place is mouldy!' Something many-legged scuttled hastily across the floor and dropped into the stairwell.

Victor reached out gingerly and prodded a thick red rope, slung between gold-encrusted posts. It disintegrated.

The cracked stairway carried on up to the distant lighted arch. They climbed it, scrambling over heaps of crumbling seaweed and driftwood flung up by some past high tide.

The arch opened out into another vast cavern, like an amphitheatre. Rows of seats stretched down towards a – – a wall?

It shimmered like mercury. If you could fill an oblong pool of mercury the size of a house, and then tip it on its side without any of it spilling, then it would look something like this.

Only not so malevolent.

It was flat and blank but Victor suddenly felt he was being stared at, like something under a lens.

Laddie whined.

Then Victor realized what it was that was making him uneasy.

It *wasn't* a wall. A wall was attached to something. That thing was attached to nothing. It just hung in the air, billowing and rippling like an image in a mirror, but without the mirror.

The light was coming from somewhere on the other side of it. Victor could see it now, a bright pinpoint moving around in the shadow at the far end of the chamber.

He set off down the sloping aisle between the rows of stone seats, the dogs plodding along beside him with their ears flat and their tails between their legs. They waded through something that might once have been carpet; it tore wetly and disintegrated under their feet.

After they'd gone a few yards Gaspode said, 'I don't know if you've noticed, but some of—'

'I know,' said Victor, grimly.

'—the seats, they're still—'

'I know.'

'—occupied.'

'I *know.*'

All these people – these things who *had been* people – sitting in rows. It's as though they were watching a click.

He'd almost reached it now. It shimmered above him, a rectangle with length and height but no thickness.

Just in front of it, almost underneath the silver screen, a smaller flight of steps led him down into a circular pit half filled with debris. By climbing on to it he could see behind the screen, to where the light was.

It was Ginger. She was standing with one hand held above her head. The torch in it burned like phosphorus.

She was staring up at a body on a slab. It was a giant. Or, at least, something like a giant. It might just have been a suit of armour with a sword laid on top of it, half buried in dust and sand.

'It's the thing from the book!' he hissed. 'Ye gods, what does she think she's doing?'

'I don't think she's thinkin' anythin',' said Gaspode.

Ginger half turned and Victor saw her face. She was smiling.

Behind the slab Victor could make out some kind of big, corroded disc. At least it was hanging from the ceiling by proper chains, and not defying gravity in such a disconcerting way.

'Right,' he said, 'I'm going to put a stop to this right now. *Ginger!*'

His voice boomed back at him from the distant walls. He could hear it bouncing away along caverns and corridors – *er, er, er.* There was a thud of falling rock somewhere far behind him.

'Keep it quiet!' said Gaspode. 'You'll have the whole place down on us!'

'Ginger!' Victor hissed. 'It's me!'

She turned and looked at him, or through him, or into him.

'Victor,' she said sweetly. 'Go away. Far away. Go away now or great harm will befall.'

'Great harm will befall,' muttered Gaspode. 'That's boding talk, that is.'

'You don't know what you're doing,' said Victor. 'You *asked* me to stop you! Come back. Come back with me now.'

He tried to climb up . . .

. . . and something sank under his foot. There was a faraway gurgling noise, a metallic clonk, and then one watery musical note billowed up around him and echoed around the cavern. He moved his foot hurriedly, but only on to another part of the ledge which sank like the first, producing a different note.

Now there was a scraping sound as well. Victor had been standing in a small sunken pit. Now to his horror he realized that it was rising slowly, to the accompaniment of blaring notes and the whirr and wheeze of ancient machinery. He thrust out his hands and hit a corroded lever, which produced a different chord and then snapped off. Laddie was howling. Victor saw Ginger drop her torch and clap her hands over her ears.

A block of masonry leaned slowly out of the wall and smashed on the seats. Fragments of rock pattered down, and a rumbling counterpoint to the blare suggested that the noise was rearranging the shape of the whole cavern.

And then it died, with a long strangulated gurgle and a final gasp. A series of jerks and creaks indicated that whatever prehistoric machinery had been activated by Victor had given of its all before collapsing.

Silence returned.

Victor eased himself carefully out of the music pit, which was now several feet in the air, and ran over to Ginger. She was on her knees, and sobbing.

'Come on,' he said. 'Let's get out of here.'

'Where am I? What's happening?'

'I couldn't even begin to explain.'

The torch was spluttering on the floor. It wasn't an actinic fire now, it was just a piece of charred and nearly extinguished driftwood. Victor grabbed it and waved it around until a dull yellow flame appeared.

'Gaspode?' he snapped.

'Yeah?'

'You two dogs lead the way.'

'Oh, thank you very much.'

Ginger clung to him as they lurched back up the aisle. Despite the incipient terror, Victor had to admit that it was a very pleasant sensation. He looked around at the occasional occupants of the seats and shuddered.

'It looks as though they died watching a click,' he said.

'Yeah. A comedy,' said Gaspode, trotting ahead of him.

'Why do you say that?'

'They're all grinnin'.'

'Gaspode!'

'Well, you've got to look on the bright side, haven't you?' sneered the dog. 'Can't go around bein' miserable jus' because you're in some lost underground tomb with a mad cat lover an' a torch that's goin' to go out any minute—'

'Keep going! Keep going!'

They half-fell, half ran down the steps, skidded unpleasantly on the seaweed at the bottom, and headed for the little archway that led to the wonderful prospect of living air and bright daylight. The torch was beginning to scorch Victor's hand. He let it go. At least there had been no problems in the passage; if they kept to one wall and didn't do anything stupid they couldn't help but reach the door. And it must be dawn by now, which meant that it shouldn't be long before they could see the light.

Victor straightened up. This was pretty heroic, really. There hadn't been any monsters to fight, but probably even monsters would have rotted away centuries ago. Of course it had been creepy, but really it was only, well, archaeology. Now it was all behind him it didn't seem so bad at all . . .

Laddie, who had been running ahead of them, barked sharply.

'What's he saying?' said Victor.

'He's saying', said Gaspode, 'that the tunnel's blocked.'

'Oh, no!'

'It was prob'ly your organ recital that did it.'

'Really blocked?'

Really blocked. Victor crawled over the heap. Several large roof slabs had come down, bringing tons of broken rock with them. He pulled and pushed at one or two pieces, but this produced only further falls.

'Perhaps there's another way out?' he said. 'Perhaps you dogs could go and—'

'Forget it, pal,' said Gaspode. 'Anyway, the only other way must be down those steps. They connect with the sea, right? All you have to do is swim down there and hope your lungs hold out.'

Laddie barked.

'Not *you*,' said Gaspode. 'I wasn't talking to you. *Never* volunteer for anything.'

Victor continued his burrowing among the rocks.

'I don't know,' he said, after a while, 'but it seems to me I can see a bit of light here. What do you think?'

He heard Gaspode scramble over the stones.

'Could be, could be,' said the dog grudgingly. 'Looks like a couple of blocks have wedged up and left a space.'

'Big enough for someone small to crawl through?' said Victor encouragingly.

'I knew you were going to say that,' said Gaspode.

Victor heard the scrabble of paws on loose rock. Eventually a muffled voice said, 'It opens up a bit . . . tight squeeze here . . . blimey . . . '

There was silence.

'Gaspode?' said Victor apprehensively.

'It's OK. I'm through. An' I can see the door.'

'Great!'

Victor felt the air move and there was a scratching noise. He reached out carefully and his hand met a ferociously hairy body.

'Laddie's trying to follow you!'

'He's too big. He'll get stuck!'

There was a canine grunt, a frantic kicking which showered Victor with gravel, and a small bark of triumph.

'O'corse, he's a bit skinnier'n me,' said Gaspode, after a while.

'Now you two run and fetch help,' said Victor. 'Er. We'll wait here.'

He heard them disappear into the distance. Laddie's faraway barking indicated that they had reached the outside air.

Victor sat back.

'Now all we have to do is wait,' he said.

'We're in the hill, aren't we?' said Ginger's voice in the darkness.

'Yes.'

'How did we get here?'

'I followed you.'

'I told you to *stop* me.'

'Yes, but then you tied me up.'

'I did no such thing!'

'You tied me up,' repeated Victor. 'And then you came here and opened the door and made a torch of some sort and went all the way into that – that place. I dread to think of what you'd have done if I hadn't woken you up.'

There was a pause.

'I really did all that?' said Ginger uncertainly.

'You really did.'

'But I don't remember any of it!'

'I *believe* you. But you still did it.'

'What – what was that place, anyway?'

Victor shifted in the darkness, trying to make himself comfortable.

'I don't know,' he confessed. 'At first I thought it was a

237

temple. And it looked as though people used it for watching moving pictures.'

'But it looked hundreds of years old!'

'Thousands, I expect.'

'But look, that can't be right,' said Ginger, in the small voice of one trying to be reasonable while madness is breaking down the door with a cleaver. 'The alchemists only got the idea a few months ago.'

'Yes. It's something to think about.'

He reached out and found her. Her body was ramrod stiff and flinched at his touch.

'We're safe enough here,' he added. 'Gaspode will soon bring back some help. Don't you worry about that.'

He tried not to think about the sea slapping at the stairs, and the many-legged things that scuttled over the midnight floor. He tried to put out of his mind the thought of octopi slithering silently over the seats in front of that living, shifting screen. He tried to forget the patrons who had been sitting in the darkness while, above them, centuries passed. Perhaps they were waiting for the lady to come around with the banged grains and hot sausages.

The whole of life is just like watching a click, he thought. Only it's as though you always get in ten minutes after the big picture has started, and no-one will tell you the plot, so you have to work it all out yourself from the clues.

And you never, never get a chance to stay in your seat for the second house.

Candlelight flickered in the University corridor.

The Bursar did not think of himself as a brave man. The most he felt happy about tackling was a column of numbers, and being good at numbers had taken him further up the hierarchy of Unseen University than magic had ever done. But he couldn't let this pass.

... whumm ... whumm ... whumm*whumm*whumm-WHUMM *WHUMM*.

He crouched behind a pillar and counted eleven pellets.

238

Little jets of sand puffed out of the bags. They were coming at two-minute intervals now.

He ran to the heap of sandbags and tugged at them.

Reality wasn't the same everywhere. Well, of course, every wizard knew *that*. Reality wasn't very thick anywhere on the Discworld. In some places it was very thin indeed. That was why magic *worked*. What Riktor thought he could measure was *changes* in reality, places where the real was rapidly becoming unreal. And every wizard knew what could happen if things became unreal enough to form a hole.

But, he thought, as he clawed at the bags, you'd need massive amounts of magic. We'd be *bound* to spot that amount of magic. It'd stand out like . . . well, like a lot of magic.

I must have taken at least fifty seconds so far.

He peered at the vase in its bunker.

Oh.

He'd been hoping he might be wrong.

All the pellets had been expelled in one direction. Half a dozen sandbags had been shot full of holes. And Numbers had thought that a couple of pellets in a month indicated a dangerous build-up of unreality . . .

The Bursar mentally drew a line from the vase, through the damaged sandbags, to the far end of the corridor.

. . . whumm . . . whumm . . .

He jerked back, and then realized that there was no need to worry. All the pellets were being shot out of the ornamental elephant's head opposite him. He relaxed.

. . . whumm . . . whumm . . .

The vase rocked violently as mysterious machinery swung around inside it. The Bursar put his head closer to it. Yes, there was definitely a hissing sound, like air being squeezed—

Eleven pellets slammed at high speed into the sandbags.

The vase recoiled back, in accordance with the famous principle of reaction. Instead of hitting a sandbag, it hit the Bursar.

Ming-ng-ng.

He blinked. He took a step backwards. He fell over.

Because Holy Wood's disturbances in reality were extending weak but opportunist tendrils even as far as Ankh-Morpork, a couple of little bluebirds flew around his head for a moment and went 'tweet-tweet-tweet' before vanishing.

Gaspode lay on the sand and wheezed. Laddie danced around him, barking urgently.

'We're well out of that,' he managed, and stood up and shook himself.

Laddie barked and looked incredibly photogenic.

'All right, all right,' sighed Gaspode. 'How about if we go and find some breakfast and maybe catch up on our sleep and then we'll—'

Laddie barked again.

Gaspode sighed.

'Oh, all *right*,' he said. 'Have it your way. But you won't get any thanks, you know.'

The dog whizzed away across the sand. Gaspode followed at a more leisurely, ambling pace, and was very surprised when Laddie doubled back, picked him up gently by the scruff of the neck, and bounded off again.

'You're only doin' this to me 'cos I'm small,' Gaspode complained, as he swung from side to side, and 'No, not that way! Humans'll be no good at this time o' the morning. We want trolls. They'll still be up and about and they're dab hands at the underground stuff. Take the next right. We want the Blue Lias and – oh, *bugger*.'

It had suddenly dawned on him that he was going to be required to talk.

And in public.

You could spend ages carefully concealing your vocal abilities from people and then, bingo, you were on the spot and you had to talk. Otherwise young Victor and Cat Woman would be moulderin' down there forever. Young Laddie was going to drop him in front of someone and look expectant and he'd have to *explain*. And afterwards spend his whole life as some sort of freak.

Laddie trotted up the street and into the smoky portals of the Blue Lias, which was crowded. He threaded his way through a maze of treetrunk legs to the bar, barked sharply, and dropped Gaspode on the floor.

He looked expectant.

The buzz of conversation stopped.

'Is that Laddie?' said a troll. 'What he want?'

Gaspode wandered groggily to the nearest troll and tugged politely at a trailing strip of rusty chain mail.

' 'Scuse me,' he said.

'He bloody intelligent dog,' said another troll, idly kicking Gaspode aside. 'I see him in click yesterday. He can play dead and count up to five.'

'That two more than you can, then.' This got a round of laughter.[23]

'No, shut up. I reckon', said the first troll, 'he trying to tell us something.'

'—'scuse me—'

'You only got to look at the way he leaping about and barking.'

'That right. I saw him in this click, he showing people where to find lost children in caves.'

'—'scuse me—'

A troll brow wrinkled. 'To eat 'em, you mean?'

'No, to bring 'em outside.'

'What, like for a barbecue sort of thing?'

'—*'scuse* me—'

Another foot caught Gaspode on the side of his bullet head.

'Could be he found some more. Look at the way he running back and forwards to the door. He one clever dog.'

'We could go look,' said the first troll.

'Good idea. It seem like ages since I had my tea.'

'Listen, you not *allowed* to eat people in Holy Wood. It

---

[23] By troll standards, this was Oscar Wilde at his best.

get us bad name! Also Silicon Anti-Defamation League be down on you like a ton of rectangular building things.'

'Yeah, but could be a reward or something.'

'—'SCUSE ME—'

'Right! Also, big improvement for troll image viz-ah-viz public relations if we find lost children.'

'And even if we don't, we can eat the dog, right?'

The bar emptied, leaving only the usual clouds of smoke, cauldrons of molten troll drinks, Ruby idly scraping the congealed lava off the mugs, and a small, weary, moth-eaten dog.

The small, weary, moth-eaten dog thought hard about the difference between looking and acting like a wonder dog and merely being one.

It said 'Bugger.'

Victor remembered being frightened of tigers when he was young. In vain did people point out that the nearest tiger was three thousand miles away. He'd say, 'Is there any sea between where they live and here?' and people would say, 'Well, no, but—' and he'd say, 'Then it's just a matter of distance.'

Darkness was the same thing. All dreadful dark places were connected by the nature of darkness itself. Darkness was everywhere, all the time, just waiting for the lights to go out. Just like the Dungeon Dimensions, really. Just waiting for reality to snap.

He held on tight to Ginger.

'You needn't,' she said. 'I've got a grip on myself now.'

'Oh, good,' he said weakly.

'The trouble is, so have you.'

He relaxed.

'Are you cold?' she said.

'A bit. It's very clammy down here.'

'Is it your teeth I can hear chattering?'

'Who else's? No,' he added hurriedly, 'don't even think about it.'

'You know,' she said, after a while, 'I don't remember anything about tying you up. I'm not even very good at knots.'

'These were pretty good,' said Victor.

'I just remember the dream. There was this voice telling me that I must wake the – the sleeping man?'

Victor thought of the armoured figure on the slab.

'Did you get a good look at it?' he said. 'What was it like?'

'I don't know about tonight,' said Ginger cautiously. 'But in my dreams it's always looked a bit like my Uncle Oswald.'

Victor thought of a sword taller than he was. You couldn't parry a slash from something like that, it'd cut through anything. Somehow it was hard to think of anything looking like an Oswald with a sword like that.

'Why's he remind you of your Uncle Oswald?' he said.

'Because my Uncle Oswald lay quite still like that. Mind you, I only ever saw him once. And that was at his funeral.'

Victor opened his mouth – and there were distant, blurred voices. A few stones moved. A voice, a little closer now, trilled, 'Hallo, little children. This way, little children.'

'That's Rock!' said Ginger.

'I'd know that voice anywhere,' said Victor. 'Hey! Rock! It's me! Victor!'

There was a worried pause. Then Rock's voice bellowed: 'It's my friend Victor!'

'That mean we can't eat him?'

'No-one is to eat my friend Victor! We dig him out with speed!'

There was the sound of crunching. Then another troll's voice complained, 'They call this limestone? I call it tasteless.'

There was some more scrabbling. A third voice said, 'Don't see why we can't eat him. Who'd know?'

243

'You uncivilized troll,' scolded Rock. 'What you thinking of? You eat people, everyone laugh at you, say, "He very defective troll, do not know how to behave in polite society" and stop paying you three dollar a day and send you back to mountains.'

Victor gave what he hoped would sound like a light chuckle.

'They're a lot of laughs, aren't they?' he said.

'Heaps,' said Ginger.

'Of course, all that stuff about eating people is just bravado. They hardly ever do it. You shouldn't worry about it.'

'I'm not. I'm worried because I walk around all the time when I'm asleep and I don't know why. You make it sound as if I was going to wake up that sleeping creature. It's a horrible thought. Something's inside my head.'

There was a crash as more rocks were pulled aside.

'That's the odd thing,' said Victor. 'When people are, er, possessed, the, er, possessing thing doesn't usually care much about them or anyone else. I mean, it wouldn't have just tied me up. It would have hit me over the head with something.'

He reached for her hand in the dark.

'That thing on the slab,' he said.

'What about it?'

'I've seen it before. It's in the book I found. There's dozens of pictures of it, and they must have thought it was very important to keep it behind the gate. That's what the pictograms say, I think. Gate . . . man. The man behind the gate. The prisoner. You see, I'm sure the reason why all the priests or whoever they were had to go and chant there every day was—'

A slab by his head was pulled aside and weak daylight poured through. It was very closely followed by Laddie, who tried to lick Victor's face and bark at the same time.

'Yes, yes! Well done, Laddie,' said Victor, trying to fight him off. 'Good dog. Good boy, Laddie.'

'*Good boy Laddie! Good boy Laddie!*'

244

The bark brought several small shards of stone down from the ceiling.

'Aha!' said Rock. Several other troll heads appeared behind him as Victor and Ginger stared out of the hole.

'They not little children,' muttered the one who had been complaining about the eating ban. 'They look stringy.'

'I tell you before,' said Rock menacingly, 'no eating people. It cause no end of trouble.'

'Why not just one leg? Then everyone'll be—'

Rock picked up a half-ton slab in one hand, weighed it thoughtfully, and then hit the other troll so hard with it that it broke.

'I tell you before,' he told the recumbent figure, 'it trolls like you getting us a bad name. How can we take rightful place in brotherhood of sapient species with defective trolls like you letting side down aller time?'

He reached through the hole and pulled Victor out bodily.

'Thanks, Rock. Er. There's Ginger in there, too.'

Rock gave him a crafty nudge that bruised a couple of ribs.

'So I see,' he said. 'And she wearing very pretty silk neggleliggle. You find nice place to indulge in bit of "What is the health of your parent?" and the Disc move for you, yeah?' The other trolls grinned.

'Uh, yes, I suppose—' Victor began.

'That's not true at all!' snapped Ginger, as she was helped through the hole. 'We weren't—'

'Yes, it is!' said Victor, making furious signals with his hands and eyebrows. 'It's absolutely true! You're absolutely right, Rock!'

'Yeah,' said one of the trolls behind Rock. 'I seen them on the clicks. He kissing her and carrying her off the whole time.'

'Now *listen*,' Ginger began.

'And now we get out of here fast,' said Rock. 'This whole ceiling looking very defective to me. Could go at any time.'

Victor glanced up. Several of the blocks were dipping ominously.

'You're right,' he said. He grabbed the arm of the protesting Ginger and hustled her along the passage. The trolls gathered up the fallen compatriot who did not know how to behave in polite company and plodded after them.

'That was *disgusting*, giving them the impression that—' Ginger hissed.

'Shut up!' snapped Victor. 'What did you want me to say, hmm? I mean, what sort of explanation do you think would fit? What would you like people to know?'

She hesitated.

'Well, all right,' she conceded. 'But you could have thought of something else. You could have said we were exploring, or looking for, for fossils—' her voice trailed off.

'Yes, in the middle of the night with you in a silk neggleliggle,' said Victor. 'What *is* a neggleliggle, anyway?'

'He meant negligee,' said Ginger.

'Come on, let's get back to town. Afterwards I might just have time to have a couple of hours' sleep.'

'What do you mean, afterwards?'

'We're going to have to buy these lads a big drink—'

There was a low rumble from the hill. A cloud of dust billowed out of the doorway and covered the trolls. The rest of the roof had gone.

'And that's it,' said Victor. 'It's over. Can you make the sleepwalking part of you understand that? It's no good trying to get in any more, there isn't any way. It's buried. It's over. Thank goodness.'

There's a bar like it in every town. It's dimly-lit and the drinkers, although they talk, don't address their words to one another and they don't listen, either. They just talk the hurt inside. It's a bar for the derelict and the unlucky and all of those people who have been temporarily flagged off the racetrack of life and into the pits.

It always does a brisk trade.

On this dawn the mourners sat ranged along the counter,

each in his cloud of gloom, each certain that he was the most unfortunate individual in the whole world.

'I *created* it,' said Silverfish, morosely. 'I thought it would be educational. It could broaden people's horizons. I didn't intend for it to be a, a, a *show*. With a thousand elephants!' he added nastily.

'Yeah,' said Detritus. 'She don't know what she wants. I do what she want, then she say, that not right, you a troll with no finer feelin', you do not understand what a girl wants. She say, Girl want sticky things to eat in box with bow around, I make box with bow around, she open box, she scream, she say flayed horse not what she mean. She don't know what she wants.'

'Yeah,' said a voice from under Silverfish's stool. 'It'd serve 'em all right if I went off an' joined the wolves.'

'I mean, take this *Blown Away* thing,' said Silverfish. 'It's not even real. It's not like things really were. It's just lies. Anyone can tell lies.'

'Yeah,' said Detritus. 'Like, she say, Girl want music under window, I play music under window, everyone in street wake up and shouting out of house, You bad troll, what you hitting rocks this time of night? And she never even wake up.'

'Yeah,' said Silverfish.

'Yeah,' said Detritus.

'Yeah,' said the voice under the stool.

The man who ran the bar was naturally cheerful. It wasn't hard to be cheerful, really, when your customers acted like lightning rods for any misery that happened to be floating around. He'd found that it wasn't a good idea to say things like, 'Never mind, look on the bright side,' because there never was one, or 'Cheer up, it may never happen,' because often it already had. All that was expected of him was to keep the drink coming.

He was a little puzzled this morning, though. There seemed to be an extra person in the bar, quite apart from whoever it was speaking up from the floor. He kept getting the feeling that he was serving an extra drink, and even getting paid for it, and even talking to the mysterious purchaser. But he couldn't see him. In fact he wasn't quite sure what he was seeing, or who he was talking to.

He wandered down to the far end of the bar.

A glass slid towards him.

SAME AGAIN, said a voice out of the shadows.

'Er,' said the barman. 'Yeah. Sure. What was it?'

ANYTHING.

The barman filled it with rum. It was pulled away.

The barman sought for something to say. For some reason, he was feeling terrified.

'Don't see you in here, much,' he managed.

I COME FOR THE ATMOSPHERE. SAME AGAIN.

'Work in Holy Wood, do you?' said the barman, topping up the glass quickly. It vanished again.

NOT FOR SOME TIME. SAME AGAIN.

The barman hesitated. He was, at heart, a kindly soul.

'You don't think you've had enough, do you?' he said.

I KNOW EXACTLY WHEN I'VE HAD ENOUGH.

'Everyone says that, though.'

I KNOW WHEN EVERYONE'S HAD ENOUGH.

There was something very odd about that voice. The barman wasn't quite sure that he was hearing it with his ears. 'Oh. Well, er,' he said. 'Same again?'

NO. BUSY DAY TOMORROW. KEEP THE CHANGE.

A handful of coins slid across the counter. They felt icy cold, and most of them were heavily corroded.

'Oh, er—' the barman began.

The door opened and shut, letting in a cold blast of air despite the warmth of the night.

The barman wiped the top of the bar in a distracted way, carefully avoiding the coins.

'You see some funny types, running a bar,' he muttered.

A voice by his ear said, I FORGOT. A PACKET OF NUTS, PLEASE.

Snow glittered on the rimward outriders of the Ramtop mountains, that great world-spanning range which, where it curves around the Circle Sea, forms a natural wall between Klatch and the great flat Sto plains.

It was the home of rogue glaciers and prowling avalanches and high, silent fields of snow.

And yetis. Yetis are a high-altitude species of troll, and quite unaware that eating people is out of fashion. Their view is: if it moves, eat it. If it doesn't, then wait for it to move. And then eat it.

They'd been listening all day to the sounds. Echoes had bounced from peak to peak along the frozen ranges until, now, it was a steady dull rumble.

'My cousin', said one of them, idly probing a hollow tooth with a claw, 'said they was enormous grey animals. Elephants.'

'Bigger'n us?' said the other yeti.

'Nearly as bigger'n us,' said the first yeti. 'Loads of them, he said. More than he could count.'

The second yeti sniffed the wind and appeared to consider this.

'Yeah, well,' he said, gloomily. 'Your cousin can't count above one.'

'He said there was lots of big ones. Big fat grey elephants, all climbing, all roped together. Big and slow. All carrying lots of oograah.'

'Ah.'

The first yeti indicated the vast sloping snowfield.

'Good and deep today,' he said. 'Nothing's gonna move fast in this, right? We lie down in the snow, they won't see us till they're right on top of us, we panic 'em, it's Big Eats time.' He waved his enormous paws in the air. 'Very heavy, my cousin said. They'll not move fast, you mark my words.'

The other yeti shrugged.

'Let's do it,' he said, against the sound of distant, terrified trumpeting.

They lay down in the snow, their white hides turning them into two unsuspicious mounds. It was a technique that had worked time and again, and had been handed down from yeti to yeti for thousands of years, although it wasn't going to be handed much further.

They waited.

There was a distant bellowing as the herd approached.

Eventually the first troll said, very slowly, because it had been working this out for a long time. 'What do you get, right, what do you get if, you cross . . . a mountain with a elephant?'

It never got an answer.

The yetis had been right.

When five hundred crude two-elephant bobsleighs crested the ridge ten feet away at sixty miles an hour, their strapped-on occupants trumpeting in panic, they never saw the yetis until they were right on top of them.

Victor got only two hours' sleep but got up feeling remarkably refreshed and optimistic.

It was all over. Things were going to be a whole lot better now. Ginger had been quite nice to him last night – well, a few hours ago – and whatever it was in the hill had been well and truly buried.

You got that sort of thing sometimes, he thought, as he poured some water into the cracked basin and had a quick wash. Some wicked old king or wizard gets buried and their spirit creeps about, trying to put things right or something. Well-known effect. But now there must be a million tons of rock blocking the tunnel, and I can't see anyone doing any creeping through that.

The unpleasantly alive screen surfaced briefly in his memory, but even that didn't seem so bad now. It had been dark in there, there had been lots of moving shadows, he had been wound up like a spring in any case, no wonder his eyes had played tricks on him. There had been the skeletons, too, but even they now lacked the power to terrify. Victor had heard of tribal leaders up on the cold plains who'd be buried with whole armies of mounted horsemen, so that their souls would live on in the next world. Maybe there was something like that here, once. Yes, it all seemed much less horrifying in the cold light of day.

And that's just what it was. Cold light.

The room was full of the kind of light you got when you woke up on a winter's morning and *knew*, by the light, that it had snowed. It was a light without shadows.

He went to the window and looked out on a pale silver glow.

Holy Wood had vanished.

The visions of the night fountained up in his mind again, as the darkness returns when the light goes out.

Hang on, hang on, he thought, fighting the panic. It's only fog. You're bound to get fog sometimes, this close to the sea. And it's glowing like that because the sun's out. There's nothing occult about fog. It's just fine drops of water floating in the air. That's *all* it is.

He dragged his clothes on and threw open the door to the passage and almost tripped over Gaspode, who had been lying full length in front of the door like the world's most unwashed draught excluder.

The little dog raised himself unsteadily on his front paws, fixed Victor with a yellow eye and said, 'I jus' want you to know, right, that I ain't lyin' in front of your door 'cos of any of this loyal-dog-protectin'-his-master nonsense, OK, it's jus' that when I got back here—'

'Shut up, Gaspode.'

Victor opened the outer door. Fog drifted in. It seemed to have an exploratory feel to it; it came in as if it had been waiting for just this opportunity.

'Fog's just fog,' he said aloud. 'Come on. We're going to Ankh-Morpork today, remember?'

'My head,' said Gaspode, 'my head feels like the bottom of a cat's basket.'

'You can sleep on the coach. *I* can sleep on the coach, if it comes to that.'

He took a few steps into the silvery glow, and was almost immediately lost. Buildings loomed vaguely at him in the thick clammy air.

'Gaspode?' he said hesitantly. Fog's just fog, he repeated. But it feels crowded. It feels like that, if it suddenly went away, I'd see lots of people watching me. From outside. And that's ridiculous, because I *am* outside, so there's nothing outside of outside. And it's flickering.

'I expect you'll be wantin' me to lead the way,' said a smug voice by his knee.

'It's very quiet, isn't it?' said Victor, trying to sound nonchalant. 'I expect it's the fog muffling everything.'

'O'corse, maybe gharstely creatures have come up out o' the sea and murthered every mortal soul except us,' said Gaspode conversationally.

'Shut up!'

Something loomed up out of the brightness. As it got closer it got smaller, and the tentacles and antennae that Victor's imagination had been furnishing became the more-or-less ordinary arms and legs of Soll Dibbler.

'Victor?' he said uncertainly.

'Soll?'

Soll's relief was visible. 'Can't see a thing in this stuff,' he said. 'We thought you'd got lost. Come on, it's nearly noon. We're more or less ready to go.'

'I'm ready.'

'Good.' Fog droplets had condensed on Soll's hair and clothing. 'Er,' he said. 'Where are we, exactly?'

Victor turned around. His lodgings *had* been behind him.

'The fog changes everything, doesn't it?' said Soll unhappily. 'Er, do you think your little dog can find his way to the studio? He seems quite bright.'

'Growl, growl,' said Gaspode, and sat up and begged in what Victor at least recognized as a sarcastic way.

'My word,' said Soll. 'It's as if he understands, isn't it?'

Gaspode barked sharply. After a second or two there was a barrage of excited answering barks.

252

'Of course, that'll be Laddie,' said Soll. 'What a clever dog!'

Gaspode looked smug.

'Mind you, that's Laddie in a nutshell,' said Soll, as they set off towards the barking. 'I expect he could teach your dog a few tricks, eh?'

Victor didn't dare look down.

After a few false turns the archway of Century of the Fruitbat passed overhead like a ghost. There were more people here; the site seemed to be filling up with lost wanderers who didn't know where else to go.

There was a coach waiting outside Dibbler's office and Dibbler himself stood beside it, stamping his feet.

'Come on, come on,' he said, 'I've sent Gaffer ahead with the film. Get in, the pair of you.'

'Can we travel in this?' said Victor.

'What's to go wrong?' said Dibbler. 'There's one road to Ankh-Morpork. Anyway, we'll probably be well out of this stuff when we leave the coast. I don't see why everyone's so nervy. Fog's fog.'

'That's what I say,' said Victor, climbing into the coach.

'It's just a mercy we finished *Blown Away* yesterday,' said Dibbler. 'All this is probably just something seasonal. Nothing to worry about at all.'

'You said that before,' said Soll. 'You said it at least five times so far this morning.'

Ginger was hunched on one seat, with Laddie lying underneath it. Victor slid along until he was next to her.

'Did you get any sleep?' he whispered.

'Just an hour or two, I think,' she said. 'Nothing happened. No dream or anything.'

Victor relaxed.

'Then it really is over,' he said. 'I wasn't sure.'

'And the fog?' she demanded.

'Sorry?' said Victor guiltily.

'What's causing the *fog*?'

'Well,' said Victor, 'as I understand it, when cool

253

air passes over warm ground, water is precipitated out of—'

'You know what I mean! It's not like normal fog at all! It – sort of drifts oddly,' she finished lamely. 'And you can nearly hear voices,' she added.

'You can't nearly hear voices,' said Victor, in the hope that his own rational mind would believe him. 'You either hear them or you don't. Listen, we're both just tired. That's all it is. We've been working hard and, er, not getting much sleep, so it's understandable that we think we're nearly hearing and seeing things.'

'Oh, so you're nearly seeing things, are you?' said Ginger triumphantly. 'And don't you go around using that calm and reasonable tone of voice on me,' she added. 'I hate it when people go around being calm and reasonable at me.'

'I hope you two lovebirds aren't having a tiff?'

Victor and Ginger stiffened. Dibbler clambered up into the opposite seat, and leered encouragingly at them. Soll followed. There was a slam as the driver shut the carriage door.

'We'll stop for a meal when we're halfway,' said Dibbler, as they lurched forward. He hesitated, and then sniffed suspiciously.

'What's that smell?' he said.

'I'm afraid my dog is under your seat,' said Victor.

'Is it ill?' said Dibbler.

'I'm afraid it always smells like that.'

'Don't you think it would be a good idea to give it a bath?'

A mutter on the edge of hearing said: 'Do you think it would be a good idea to have your feet bitten right orf?'

Meanwhile, over Holy Wood, the fog thickened . . .

The posters for *Blown Away* had been circulating in Ankh-Morpork for several days, and interest was running at fever pitch.

They'd even got as far as the University this time. The Librarian had one pinned up in the fetid, book-lined nest he called home,[24] and various others were surreptitiously circulating among the wizards themselves.

The artist had produced a masterpiece. Held in Victor's arms, against the background of the flaming city, Ginger was portrayed as not only showing nearly all she had but quite a lot of what she had not, strictly speaking, got.

The effect on the wizards was everything that Dibbler could possibly have hoped for. In the Uncommon Room, the poster was passed from hand to shaking hand as if it might explode.

'There's a girl who's got It,' said the Chair of Indefinite Studies. He was one of the fattest wizards, and so over-stuffed that he seemed to be living up to his title. He looked as though horsehair should be leaking from frayed patches. People felt an overpowering urge to rummage down the side of him for loose change.

'What's "It", Chair?' said another wizard.

'Oh, *you* know. It. Oomph. The old way-hey-hey.'

They watched him politely and expectantly, like people awaiting the punch line.

'Good grief, do I have to spell it out?' he said.

'He means sexual magnetism,' said the Lecturer in Recent Runes, happily. 'The lure of wanton soft bosoms and huge pulsating thighs, and the forbidden fruits of desire which—'

A couple of wizards carefully moved their chairs away from him.

'Ah, *sex*,' said the Dean of Pentacles, interrupting the Lecturer in Recent Runes in mid-sigh. 'Far too much of it these days, in my opinion.'

'Oh, I don't know,' said the Lecturer in Recent Runes. He looked wistful.

The noise woke up Windle Poons, who had been dozing

---

[24] In fact he *called* it 'oook'. But probably, in translation, it *meant* 'home'.

in his wheelchair by the fire. There was always a roaring fire in the Uncommon Room, summer or winter.

'Wassat?' he said.

The Dean leaned towards an ear.

'I was saying', he said loudly, 'that we didn't know the meaning of the word "sex" when we were young.'

'That's true. That's very true,' said Poons. He stared reflectively at the flames. 'Did we ever, mm, find out, do you remember?'

There was a moment's silence.

'Say what you like, she's a fine figure of a young woman,' said the Lecturer in Recent Runes defiantly.

'Several young women,' said the Dean.

Windle Poons focused unsteadily on the poster.

'Who's the young feller?' he said.

'What young feller?' said several wizards.

'He's in the middle of the picture,' said Poons. 'He's holding her in his arms.'

They looked again. 'Oh, him,' said the Chair, dismissively.

'Seems to me I've, mm, seen him before,' said Poons.

'My dear Poons, I hope you haven't been sneaking off to the moving pictures,' said the Dean, grinning at the others. 'You know it's demeaning for a wizard to patronize the common entertainments. The Archchancellor would be very angry with us.'

'Wassat?' said Poons, cupping a hand to his ear.

'He does look a bit familiar, now that you mention it,' said the Dean, peering at the poster.

The Lecturer in Recent Runes put his head on one side.

'It's young Victor, isn't it?' he said.

'Eh?' said Poons.

'You know, you could be right,' said the Chair of Indefinite Studies. 'He had the same type of weedy moustache.'

'Who's this?' said Poons.

'But he was a student. He could have been a wizard,' said the Dean. 'Why would he want to go off and fondle young women?'

'It's a Victor all right, but not our Victor. Says here he's "Victor Maraschino",' said the Chair.

'Oh, that's just a click name,' said the Lecturer in Recent Runes airily. 'They all have funny names like that. Delores De Syn and Blanche Languish and Rock Cliffe and so on . . . ' He realized that they were looking at him accusingly. 'Or so I'm told,' he added lamely. 'By the porter. He goes to see a click nearly every night.'

'What're you on about?' said Poons, waving his walking stick in the air.

'The cook goes every night, too,' said the Chair. 'So do most of the kitchen staff. You just try getting so much as a ham sandwich after nine o'clock.'

'Just about everyone goes,' said the Lecturer. 'Except us.'

One of the other wizards peered intently at the bottom of the poster.

'It says here,' he said, ' "A Sarger of Passione and Broad Staircases in Ankh-Morpork's Turbelent Histry!" '

'Ah. It's historical, then, is it?' said the Lecturer.

'And it says "A Epic Love Story that Astoundede Goddes and Menne!!" '

'Oh? Religious, as well.'

'And it says, "Withe a 1,000 elephants!!!" '

'Ah. Wildlife. Always very educational, wildlife,' said the Chair, looking speculatively at the Dean. The other wizards were doing so, too.

'It seems to me', said the Lecturer, slowly, 'that no-one could possibly object to senior wizards viewing a work of historical, religious and, er, wildliforific interest.'

'University rules are very specific,' said the Dean, but not very enthusiastically.

'But surely only meant for the students,' said the Lecturer. 'I can quite understand that students shouldn't be allowed to watch something like this. They'd probably whistle and throw things at the screen. But it couldn't be seriously suggested, could it, that senior wizards such as ourselves shouldn't examine this popular phenomenon?'

Poons' flailing walking stick caught the Dean sharply across the back of his legs.

'I demand to know what everyone's talking about!' he snapped.

'We don't see why senior wizards shouldn't be allowed to watch moving pictures!' bellowed the Chair.

'Jolly good thing, too!' snapped Poons. 'Everyone likes to look at a pretty woman.'

'No-one mentioned anything about any pretty women. We were far more interested in examining popular phenomenons,' said the Chair.

'Call it what you like, mm?' cackled Windle Poons.

'If people see wizards strolling out of the gate and going into a common moving-picture pit they'll lose all respect for the profession,' said the Dean. 'It's not even as if it's proper magic. It's just trickery.'

'Y'know,' said one of the lesser wizards, thoughtfully, 'I've always wondered exactly what these wretched clicks *are*. Some kind of puppet show, are they? Are these people acting on a stage? Or a shadow play?'

'See?' said the Chair. 'We're supposed to be wise, and we don't even *know*.'

They all looked at the Dean.

'Yes, but who wants to see a lot of young women dancing around in tights?' he said, hopelessly.

Ponder Stibbons, luckiest post-graduate wizard in the history of the University, sauntered happily towards the secret entrance over the wall. His otherwise uncrowded mind was pleasantly awash with thoughts of beer and maybe a visit to the clicks and maybe a Klatchian extra-hot curry to round off the evening, and then—

It was the second worst moment in his life.

They were *all* there. All the senior staff. Even the Dean. Even old Poons in his wheelchair. All standing there in the shadows, looking at him very sternly. Paranoia exploded its dark fireworks in the dustbin of his mind. *They were all waiting just for him.*

He froze.

The Dean spoke.

'Oh. Oh. Oh. Er. Ah. Um. Um,' he began, and then seemed to catch up with his tongue. '*Oh*. What's this? Forward this minute, that man!'

Ponder hesitated. Then he ran for it.

After a while the Lecturer in Recent Runes said, 'That was young Stibbons, wasn't it? Has he gone?'

'I think so.'

'He's bound to say something to someone.'

'No he won't,' said the Dean.

'Do you think he saw where we'd taken out the bricks?'

'No, I was standing in front of the holes,' said the Chair.

'Come on, then. Where were we?'

'Look, I really think this is most unwise,' said the Dean.

'Just shut up, old chap, and hold this brick.'

'Very well, but tell me this; how do you propose to get the wheelchair over?'

They looked at Poons' wheelchair.

There are wheelchairs which are lightweight and built to let their owners function fully and independently in modern society. To the thing inhabited by Poons, they were as gazelles to a hippopotamus. Poons was well aware of his function in modern society, and as far as he was concerned it was to be pushed everywhere and generally pandered to.

It was wide and long and steered by means of a little front wheel and a long cast-iron handle. Cast iron, in fact, featured largely in its construction. Bits of baroque ironwork adorned its frame, which seemed to have been made of iron drainpipes welded together. The rear wheels did not in fact have blades affixed to them, but looked as though these were optional extras. There were various dread levers which only Poons knew the purpose of. There was a huge oilskin hood that could be erected in a matter of hours to protect its occupant from showers, storms and, probably, meteor strikes and falling buildings. By way of light relief, the front handle was adorned with a selection of trumpets, hooters and whistles, with which Poons was wont to announce his progress around the passages and quadrangles of the University. For the fact was that although the wheelchair needed all the efforts of one strong man to get it moving it had, once actually locomotive, a sort of ponderous unstoppability; it may have had brakes, but Windle Poons had never bothered to find out. Staff and students alike knew that the only hope of survival, if they heard a honk or a blast at close range, was to flatten themselves against the nearest wall while the dreaded conveyance rattled by.

'We'll never get that over,' said the Dean firmly. 'It must weigh at least a ton. We ought to leave him behind, anyway. He's too old for this sort of thing.'

'When I was a lad I was over this wall, mm, every night,' said Poons, resentfully. He chuckled. 'We had some scrapes in those days, I can tell you. If I had a penny, mm, for every time the Watch chased me home,' his ancient lips moved in a sudden frenzy of calculation, 'I'd have fivepence-ha'penny.'

'Maybe if we—' the Chair began, and then said 'What do you mean, fivepence-ha'penny?'

'I recall once they gave up halfway,' said Poons, happily. 'Oh, those were great times. I remember me and old "Numbers" Riktor and "Tudgy" Spold climbed up on the Temple of Small Gods, you see, in the middle of a service, and Tudgy had got this piglet in a sack, and he—'

'See what you've done?' complained the Lecturer in Recent Runes. 'You've set him off now.'

'We could try lifting it by magic,' said the Chair. 'Gindle's Effortless Elevator should do the trick.'

'—and then the high priest turned around and, heh, the look on his face! And then old Numbers said, let's—'

'It's hardly a very dignified use of magic,' sniffed the Dean.

'Considerably more dignified than heaving the bloody

thing over the wall ourselves, wouldn't you say?' said the Lecturer in Recent Runes, rolling up his sleeves. 'Come on, lads.'

'—and next thing, Pimple was hammering on the door of the Assassins' Guild, and then old Scummidge, who was the porter there, heehee, he was a right terror, anyway, he came out, mm, and then the guards come around the corner—'

'All ready? Right!'

'—which puts me in mind of the time me and "Cucumber" Framer got some glue and went round to—'

'Up your end, Dean!'

The wizards grunted with effort.

'—and, mm, I can remember it as if it was only yesterday, the look on his face when—'

'Now lower away!'

The iron-shod wheels clanged gently on the cobbles of the alley.

Poons nodded amiably. 'Great times. Great times,' he muttered, and fell asleep.

The wizards climbed slowly and unsteadily over the wall, ample backsides gleaming in the moonlight, and stood wheezing gently on the far side.

'Tell me, Dean,' said the Lecturer, leaning on the wall to stop the shaking in his legs, 'have we made . . . the wall . . . higher in the last fifty years?'

'I . . . don't . . . think . . . so.'

'Odd. Used to go up it like a gazelle. Not many years ago. Not many at all, really.'

The wizards wiped their foreheads and looked sheepishly at one another.

'Used to nip over for a pint or three most nights,' said the Chair.

'*I* used to study in the evenings,' said the Dean, primly.

The Chair narrowed his eyes.

'Yes, you always did,' he said. 'I recall.'

It was dawning on the wizards that they were outside the University, at night and without permission, for the first time in decades. A certain suppressed excitement crackled from man to man. Any watcher trained in reading body language would have been prepared to bet that, after the click, someone was going to suggest that they might as well go somewhere and have a few drinks, and then someone else would fancy a meal, and then there was always room for a few more drinks, and then it would be 5 a.m. and the city guards would be respectfully knocking on the University gates and asking if the Archchancellor would care to step down to the cells to identify some alleged wizards who were singing an obscene song in six-part harmony, and perhaps he would also care to bring some money to pay for all the damage. Because inside every old person is a young person wondering what happened.

The Chair reached up and grasped the brim of his tall, wide and floppy wizarding hat.

'Right, boys,' he said. 'Hats off.'

They de-hatted, but with reluctance. A wizard gets very attached to his pointy hat. It gives him a sense of identity. But, as the Chair had pointed out earlier, if people knew you were a wizard because you were wearing a pointy hat, then if you took the pointy hat *off*, they'd think you were just some rich merchant or something.

The Dean shuddered. 'It feels like I've taken all my clothes off,' he said.

'We can tuck them in under Poons' blanket,' said the Chair. 'No-one'll know it's us.'

'Yes,' said the Lecturer in Recent Runes, 'but will we?'

'They'll just think we're, well, solid burghers.'

'That's just what I feel like,' said the Dean. 'A solid burgher.'

'Or merchants,' said the Chair. He smoothed back his white hair.

'Remember,' he said, 'if anyone says anything, we're *not wizards*. Just honest merchants out for an enjoyable evening, right?'

'What does an honest merchant look like?' said a wizard.

'How should I know?' said the Chair. 'So no-one is to do any magic,' he went on. 'I don't have to tell you what'll happen if the Archchancellor hears that his staff has been seen at the common entertainments.'

'I'm more worried about our students finding out,' shuddered the Dean.

'False beards,' said the Lecturer in Recent Runes, triumphantly. 'We should wear false beards.'

The Chair rolled his eyes.

'We've all GOT beards,' he said. 'What kind of disguise would *false* beards be?'

'Ah! That's the clever bit,' said the Lecturer. 'No-one would suspect that anyone wearing a false beard would have a *real* beard underneath, would they?'

The Chair opened his mouth to refute this, and then hesitated.

'Well—' he said.

'But where'd we get false beards at this time of night?' said a wizard doubtfully.

The Lecturer beamed, and reached into his pocket. 'We don't have to,' he said. 'That's the *really* clever bit. I brought some wire with me, you see, and all you need do is break two bits off, twiddle them into your sideburns, then loop them over your ears rather clumsily like this,' he demonstrated, 'and there you are.'

The Chair stared.

'Uncanny,' he said, at last. 'It's true! You look just like someone wearing a very badly-made false beard.'

'Amazing, isn't it?' said the Lecturer happily, passing out the wire. 'It's headology, you know.'

There were a few minutes of busy twanging and the occasional whimper as a wizard punctured himself with wire, but eventually they were ready. They looked shyly at one another.

'If we got a pillow case without a pillow in it and shoved it down inside the Chair's robe so the top was showing, he'd look just like a thin man making himself tremendously fat with a huge pillow,' said one of them enthusiastically. He caught the Chair's eye, and went quiet.

A couple of wizards grasped the handles of Poons' terrible wheelchair and started it rumbling over the damp cobbles.

'Wassat? What's everyone doing?' said Poons, suddenly waking up.

'We're going to play solid burghers,' said the Dean.

'That's a good game,' said Poons.

'Can you hear me, old chap?'

The Bursar opened his eyes.

The University sanitarium wasn't very big, and was seldom used. Wizards tended to be either in rude health, or dead. The only medicine they generally required was an antacid formula and a dark room until lunch.

'Brought you something to read,' said the voice, diffidently.

The Bursar managed to focus on the spine of *Adventures with Crossbow and Rod*.

'Nasty knock you had there, Bursar. Been asleep all day.'

The Bursar looked blearily at the pink and orange haze, which gradually refined itself into the Archchancellor's pink and orange face.

Let's see, he thought, exactly how did I—

He sat bolt upright and grabbed the Archchancellor's robe and screamed into the big pink and orange face: 'Something dreadful's going to happen!'

The wizards strolled through the twilight streets. So far the disguise was working perfectly. People were even jostling them. No-one ever knowingly jostled a wizard. It was a whole new experience.

There was a huge crowd of people outside the entrance to the *Odium*, and a queue that stretched down the street. The Dean ignored it, and led the party straight up to the doors, whereupon someone said 'Oi!'

He looked up at a red-faced troll in an ill-fitting military-looking outfit that included epaulettes the size of kettle-drums and no trousers.

'Yes?' he said.

'There *are* a queue, you know,' said the troll.

The Dean nodded politely. In Ankh-Morpork a queue was, almost by definition, something with a wizard at the head of it. 'So I see,' he said. 'And a very good thing, too. And if you will be so good as to stand aside, we'd like to take our seats.'

The troll prodded him in the stomach.

'What you fink you are?' he said. 'A wizard or something?' This got a laugh from the nearest queuers.

The Dean leaned closer.

'As a matter of fact, we *are* wizards,' he hissed.

The troll grinned at him.

'Don't come the raw trilobite with me,' he said. 'I can see your false beard!'

'Now listen—' the Dean began, but his voice became an incoherent squeak as the troll picked him up by the collar of his robe and propelled him out into the road.

'You get in queue like everyone else,' he said. There was a chorus of jeers from the queue.

The Dean growled and raised his right hand, fingers spread—

The Chair grabbed his arm.

'Oh, yes,' he hissed. 'That'd do a lot of good, wouldn't it? Come on.'

'Where to?'

'To the back of the queue!'

'But we're *wizards*! Wizards never stand in line for anything!'

'We're honest merchants, remember?' said the Chair. He glanced at the nearest click-goers, who were giving them odd looks. 'We're honest merchants,' he repeated loudly. He nudged the Dean. 'Go on,' he hissed.

'Go on what?'

'Go on and say something merchanty.'

'What sort of thing is that?' said the Dean, mystified.

'Say *something*! Everyone's looking at us!'

'Oh.' The Dean's face creased in panic, and then salvation dawned. 'Lovely apples,' he said. 'Get them while they're hot. They're luvverly . . . Will this do?'

'I suppose so. Now let's go to the end—'

There was a commotion at the other end of the street. People surged forward. The queue broke ranks and charged. The honest merchants were suddenly surrounded by a desperately-pushing crowd.

'I say, there *is* a queue, you know,' said the Honest Merchant in Recent Runes diffidently, as he was shoved aside.

The Dean grabbed the shoulder of a boy who was ferociously elbowing him aside.

'What is going on, young man?' he demanded.

'They're a-coming!' shouted the boy.

'Who are?'

'The stars!'

The wizards, as one man, looked upwards.

'No, they're not,' said the Dean, but the boy had shaken himself free and disappeared in the press of people.

'Strange primitive superstition,' said the Dean, and the wizards, with the exception of Poons, who was complaining and flailing around with his stick, craned forward to see.

The Bursar met the Archchancellor in a corridor.

'There's no-one in the Uncommon Room!' screamed the Bursar.

'The Library's empty!' bellowed the Archchancellor.

'I've heard about that sort of thing,' the Bursar whimpered. 'Spontaneous something-or-other. They've all gone spontaneous!'

'Calm down, man. Just because—'

'I can't even find any of the servants! You know what happens when reality gives way! Even now giant tentacles are probably—'

There was a distant *whumm . . . whumm* noise, and the sound of pellets bouncing off the wall.

'Always the same direction,' the Bursar muttered.

'What direction is that, then?'

'The direction They'll be coming from! I think I'm going mad!'

'Now, now,' said the Archchancellor, patting him on the shoulder. 'You don't want to go around talking like that. That's crazy talk.'

Ginger stared, panic-stricken, out of the carriage window.

'Who are all these people?' she said.

'They're fans,' said Dibbler.

'But I'm not hot!'

'Uncle means that they're people who like seeing you in the clicks,' said Soll. 'Er. Like you a *lot*.'

'There's women out there too,' said Victor. He gave a cautious wave. In the crowd, a woman swooned.

'You're famous,' he said. 'You said you always wanted to be famous.'

Ginger looked out at the crowd again. 'I never thought it would be like this, though. They're all shouting our names!'

'We've put a lot of effort into telling people about *Blown Away*,' said Soll.

'Yes,' said Dibbler. 'We said it was the greatest click in the entire history of Holy Wood.'

'But we've been making clicks for only a couple of months,' Ginger pointed out.

'So what? That's still a history,' said Dibbler.

Victor saw the look in Ginger's face. Exactly how long was Holy Wood's real history? Perhaps there was some ancient stone calendar, down there on the sea bed, among the lobsters. Perhaps there was no way it could be measured. How did you measure the age of an idea?

'A lot of civic dignitaries are going to be there, too,' said Dibbler. 'The Patrician and the nobles and the Guild heads and some of the high priests. Not the wizards, of course,

267

the stuck-up old idiots. But it'll be a night to remember right enough.'

'Will we have to be introduced to them all?' said Victor.

'No. *They'll* be introduced to *you*,' said Dibbler. 'It'll be the biggest thrill of their lives.'

Victor stared out at the crowds again.

'Is it my imagination,' he said, 'or is it getting foggy?'

Poons hit the Chair across the back of the legs with his stick.

'What's going on?' he said. 'Why's everyone cheering?'

'The Patrician's just got out of his carriage,' said the Chair.

'Don't see what's so wonderful about that,' said Poons. 'I've got out of carriages hundreds of times. There's no trick to it at all.'

'It's a bit odd,' the Chairman admitted. 'And they cheered the head of the Assassins' Guild and the High Priest of Blind Io, too. And now someone's rolled out a red carpet.'

'What, in the street? In *Ankh-Morpork*?'

'Yes.'

'Wouldn't like to have *their* cleaning bill,' said Poons.

The Lecturer in Recent Runes nudged the Chair heavily in the ribs, or at least at the point where the ribs were overlaid by the strata of fifty years of very good dinners.

'Quiet!' he hissed. 'They're coming!'

'Who?'

'Someone important, by the look of it.'

The Chair's face creased in panic behind his false real beard. 'You don't think they've invited the Archchancellor, do you?'

The wizards tried to shrink inside their robes, like upright turtles.

In fact it was a far more impressive coach than any of the crumbling items in the University's mews. The crowd surged forward against the line of trolls and city guards and stared expectantly at the carriage door; the very air hummed with anticipation.

Mr Bezam, his chest so inflated with self-importance that he appeared to be floating across the ground, bobbed towards the carriage door and opened it.

The crowd held its collective breath, except for a small part of it that hit surrounding people with its stick and muttered, 'What's happening? What's going on? Why won't anyone tell me what's *happening*? I *demand* someone tell me, mm, what's *happening*?'

The door stayed shut. Ginger was gripping the handle as if it was a lifeline.

'There's *thousands* of them out there!' said Ginger. 'I can't go out there!'

'But they all watch your clicks,' pleaded Soll. 'They're your public.'

'No!'

Soll threw up his hands. 'Can't you persuade her?' he said to Victor.

'I'm not even sure I can persuade myself,' said Victor.

'But you've spent days in front of these people,' said Dibbler.

'No I haven't,' said Ginger. 'It was just you and the handlemen and the trolls and everyone. That was different. Anyway, that wasn't really me,' she added. 'That was Delores De Syn.'

Victor bit his lip thoughtfully.

'Maybe you ought to send Delores de Syn out there, then,' he said.

'How can I do that?' she demanded.

'Well . . . why not pretend it's a click . . . ?'

The Dibblers, uncle and nephew, exchanged glances. Then Soll cupped his hands around his face like the eye of a picture box and Dibbler, after a prompting nudge, placed one hand on his nephew's head and turned an invisible handle in his ear.

'Action!' he directed.

269

The carriage door swung open.

The crowd gasped, like a mountain breathing in. Victor stepped out, reached up, took Ginger's hand . . .

The crowd cheered, madly.

The Lecturer in Recent Runes bit his fingers in sheer excitement. The Chair made a strange hoarse noise in the back of his throat.

'You know you said what could a boy find to do that was better than being a wizard?' he said.

'A true wizard should only be interested in one thing,' muttered the Dean. 'You know that.'

'Oh, I *know* it.'

'I was referring to magic.'

The Chair peered at the advancing figures.

'You know, that *is* young Victor. I'll swear it,' he said.

'That's disgusting,' said the Dean. 'Fancy choosing to hang around young women when he could have been a wizard.'

'Yeah. What a fool,' said the Lecturer in Recent Runes, who was having trouble with his breathing.

There was a sort of communal sigh.

'You got to admit she's a bit of a corker, though,' said the Chair.

'I'm an old man and if someone doesn't let me see *very soon*,' said a cracked voice behind them, 'someone's going to be feeling the wrong end of, mm, my stick, all right?'

Two of the wizards edged aside and eased the wheelchair through. Once moving, it coasted right up to the edge of the carpet, bruising any knees or ankles that stood in its way.

Poons' mouth fell open.

Ginger gripped Victor's hand.

'There's a group of fat old men in false beards waving at you over there,' she said through clenched and grinning teeth.

'Yes, I think they're wizards,' Victor grinned back.

'One of them keeps bouncing up and down in his wheel-chair and shouting things like "Way-hey!" and "Whoop-whoop!" and "Hubba-hubba!" '

'That's the oldest wizard in the world,' said Victor. He waved at a fat lady in the crowd, who fainted.

'Good grief! What was he like fifty years ago?'

'Well, for one thing he was eighty.[25] *Don't blow him a kiss!*'

The crowd roared its approval.

'He looks sweet.'

'Just keep smiling and waving.'

'Oh, *gods*, look at all those people waiting to be introduced to us!'

'I can see 'em,' said Victor.

'But they're *important*!'

'Well, so are we. I guess.'

'Why?'

'Because we're us. It's like you said, that time on the beach. We're us, just as big as we can be. It's just what you wanted. We're—'

He stopped.

The troll at the door of the *Odium* gave him a hesitant salute. The thump as its hand smacked into its ear was quite audible above the roar of the crowd . . .

Gaspode waddled at high speed down an alleyway, with Laddie trotting obediently at his heels. No-one had paid them any attention when they jumped, or in Gaspode's case plopped, down from the carriage.

'All evening in some stuffy pit ain't my idea of a good night out,' muttered Gaspode. 'This is the big city. This ain't Holy Wood. You stick by me, pup, and you'll be *all* right. First stop, the back door of Harga's House of Ribs. They know me there. OK?'

---

[25] Wizards who manage to avoid the ambitious attentions of other wizards tend to live for a long time. It seems even longer.

'*Good boy Laddie!*'

'Yeah,' said Gaspode.

'Look at what it's wearing!' said Victor.

'Red velvet jacket with gold frogging,' said Ginger out of the corner of her mouth. 'So what? A pair of trousers would have been a good idea.'

'Oh, gods,' breathed Victor.

They stepped into the brightly-lit foyer of the *Odium*.

Bezam had done his best. Trolls and dwarfs had worked overnight to finish it.

There were red plush drapes, and pillars, and mirrors.

Plump cherubs and miscellaneous fruit, all painted gold, seemed to cover every surface.

It was like stepping into a box of very expensive chocolates.

Or a nightmare. Victor half expected to hear the roar of the sea, to see drapes fall away with a smear of black slime.

'Oh, gods,' he repeated.

'What's the matter with you?' said Ginger, grinning fixedly at the line of civic dignitaries waiting to be introduced to them.

'Wait and see,' said Victor hoarsely. 'It's Holy Wood! Holy Wood's been brought to Ankh-Morpork!'

'Yes, but—'

'Don't you remember anything? That night in the hill? Before you woke up?'

'No. I *told* you.'

'Wait and see,' Victor repeated. He glanced at a decorated easel against one wall.

It said: 'Three showings a day!'

And he thought of sand dunes, and ancient myths, and lobsters.

Map-making had never been a precise art on the Discworld. People tended to start off with good intentions and then get so carried away with the spouting whales, monsters, waves and other twiddly bits of cartographic furniture that they often forgot to put the boring mountains and rivers in at all.

The Archchancellor put an overflowing ashtray on a corner that threatened to roll up. He dragged a finger across the grubby surface.

'Says here "Here be Dragons",' he said. 'Right inside the city, too. Odd, that.'

'That's just Lady Ramkin's Sunshine Sanctuary for Sick Dragons,' said the Bursar, distractedly.

'And here there's "Terra Incognita",' said the Archchancellor. 'Why's that?'

The Bursar craned to see. 'Well, it's probably more interesting than putting in lots of cabbage farms.'

'And there's "Here be Dragons" *again*.'

'I think that's just a lie, in fact.'

The Archchancellor's horny thumb continued in the direction they'd worked out. He brushed aside a couple of fly specks.

'Nothing here at all,' he said, peering closer. 'Just the sea. And—' he squinted – 'The Holy Wood. Mean anything?'

'Isn't that where the alchemists all went?' said the Bursar.

'Oh, *them*.'

'I suppose', said the Bursar slowly, 'they wouldn't be doing some kind of magic out there?'

'Alchemists. Doing *magic*?'

'Sorry. Ridiculous idea, I know. The porter told me they do some sort of, oh, shadow play or something. Or puppets. Or something similar. Pictures. Or something. I wasn't really paying attention. I mean . . . *alchemists*. Really! I mean, assassins . . . *yes*. Thieves . . . *yes*. Even merchants . . . merchants can be really devious, sometimes. But alchemists – show me a more unworldly, bumbling, well-meaning . . . '

His voice trailed off as his ears caught up with his mouth.

'They wouldn't dare, would they?' he said.

'Would they?'

The Bursar gave a hollow laugh. 'No-o-o. They wouldn't dare! They know we'd be down on them like a ton of bricks if they tried any magic round here . . . ' His voice trailed off again.

'I'm sure they wouldn't,' he said.

'I mean, even that far away,' he said.

'They wouldn't dare,' he said.

'Not magic. Surely not?' he said.

'I've *never* trusted those grubby-handed bastards!' he said. 'They're not like us, you know. They've got no idea of proper dignity!'

The crowd surging around the box office was getting deeper and more angry by the minute.

'Well, have you gone through *all* your pockets?' demanded the Chair.

'Yes!' muttered the Dean.

'Have another look, then.'

As far as wizards were concerned, paying to get into anything was something that happened to other people. A pointy hat usually did nicely.

While the Dean struggled, the Chair beamed madly at the young woman who was selling tickets. 'But I assure you, dear lady,' he said desperately, 'we *are* wizards.'

'I can see your false beards,' said the girl, and sniffed. 'We get all sorts in here. How do I know you aren't three little boys in your dad's coat?'

'Madam!'

'I've got two dollars and fifteen pence,' said the Dean, picking the coins out of a handful of fluff and mysterious occult objects.

'That's two in the stalls, then,' said the girl, grudgingly unreeling two tickets. The Chair scooped them up.

'Then I'll take Windle in,' he said quickly, turning to the others. 'I'm afraid the rest of you had better get *back* to your honest trading.' He moved his eyebrows up and down suggestively.

'I don't see why we should—' the Dean began.

'Otherwise we'll be in arrears,' the Chair went on, mugging furiously. 'If you don't get back.'

'See here, that was my money, and—' the Dean said, but the Lecturer in Recent Runes grabbed his arm.

'Just come along,' he said, winked slowly and deliberately at the Chair. 'Time we were getting back.'

'I don't see why—' the Dean gurgled, as they dragged him off.

Grey clouds swirled in the Archchancellor's magic mirror. Many wizards had them, but not many ever bothered to use them. They were quirky and unreliable. They weren't even much good for shaving in.

Ridcully was surprisingly adept at using one.

'Stalkin',' he offered as a brief explanation. 'Couldn't be having with all that crawlin' around in damp bracken for hours, bigods. Help yourself to a drink, man. And one for me.'

The clouds flickered.

'Can't seem to see anything else,' he said. 'Odd, that. Just fog, flashing away.

The Archchancellor coughed. It was beginning to dawn on the Bursar that, against all expectation, the Archchancellor was quite bright.

'Ever seen one of these shadow moving puppet play picture things?' Ridcully asked.

'The servants go,' said the Bursar. This, Ridcully decided, meant 'no'.

'I think we should have a look,' he said.

'Very well, Archchancellor,' said the Bursar, meekly.

An inviolable rule about buildings for the showing of moving pictures, applicable throughout the multiverse, is that the ghastliness of the architecture around the back is inversely proportional to the gloriousness of the architecture in the front. At the front: pillars, arches, gold leaf, lights. At the back: weird ducts, mysterious prolapses of pipework, blank walls, fetid alleys.

And the window to the lavatories.

'There's no reason at all why we should have to do this,' moaned the Dean, as the wizards struggled in the darkness.

'Shut up and keep pushing,' muttered the Lecturer in Recent Runes, from the other side of the window.

'We should have changed something into money,' said the Dean. 'Just a quick illusion. Where's the harm in that?'

'It's called watering the currency,' said the Lecturer in Recent Runes. 'You can get thrown into the scorpion pit for stuff like that. Where am I putting my feet? *Where* am I putting my *feet*?'

'You're fine,' said a wizard. 'Right, Dean. Up you come.'

'Oh, dear,' moaned the Dean, as he was dragged through the narrow window into the unmentionable gloom beyond. 'No good will come of this.'

'Just watch where you're putting your feet. Now see what you've done? Didn't I *tell* you to watch where you were putting your feet? Anyway, come on.'

The wizards skulked, or in the Dean's case, squelched furtively through the backstage area and into the darkened, bustling auditorium, where Windle Poons was keeping some seats free by the simple expedient of waving his stick at anyone who came near them. They sidled in, tripping over one another's legs, and sat down.

They stared at the shadowy grey rectangle at the other end of the hall.

After a while the Chair said, 'Can't see what people see in it, myself.'

'Has anyone done "Deformed Rabbit"?' said the Lecturer in Recent Runes.

'It hasn't started yet,' hissed the Dean.

'I'm hungry,' complained Poons. 'I'm an old man, mm, and I'm hungry.'

'Do you know what he did?' said the Chair. 'Do you know what the old fool did? When a young lady with a torch was showing us to our seats he pinched her on the . . . the fundament!'

Poons sniggered. 'Hubba-hubba! Does your mother know you're out?' he cackled.

'It's all too much for him,' the Chair complained. 'We never should have brought him.'

'Do you realize we're missing our dinner?' said the Dean.

The wizards fell silent at this. A stout woman edging past Poons' wheelchair suddenly started and looked around suspiciously and saw nothing except a dear old man, obviously fast asleep.

'And it's goose on Tuesdays,' said the Dean.

Poons opened one eye and honked the horn on his wheelchair.

'Tantarabobs! How's your granny off for soap!' he muttered triumphantly.

'See what I mean?' said the Chair. 'He doesn't know what century it is.'

Poons turned a beady black eye on him.

'Old I am, mm, and daft I may be,' he said, 'but I ain't goin' to be hungry.' He rummaged around in the unspeakable depths of the wheelchair and produced a greasy black bag. It jingled. 'I saw a young lady up the front a-selling of special moving-picture food,' he said.

'You mean you had money all the time?' said the Dean. 'And you never told us?'

'You never asked,' said Poons.

The wizards stared hungrily at the bag.

'They be having buttered banged grains and sausages in buns and chocolate things with things on and things,' said Poons. He gave them a toothless and crafty look. 'You can have some too, if you like,' he added graciously.

The Dean ticked off his purchases. 'Now,' he said, 'that's six Patrician-sized tubs of banged grains with

277

extra butter, eight sausages in a bun, a jumbo cup of fizzy drink, and a bag of chocolate-covered raisins.' He handed over the money.

'Right,' said the Chair, gathering up the containers. 'Er. Do you think we should get something for the others?'

In the picture-throwing room Bezam cursed as he threaded the huge reel of *Blown Away* into the picture-throwing box.

A few feet away, in a roped-off section of the balcony, the Patrician of Ankh-Morpork, Lord Vetinari, was also ill at ease.

They were, he had to admit, a pleasant enough young couple. He just wasn't sure why he was sitting next to them, and why they were so important.

He was used to important people, or at least to people who thought they were important. Wizards became important through high deeds of magic. Thieves became important for daring robberies and so, in a slightly different way, did merchants. Warriors became important through winning battles and staying alive. Assassins became important through skilful inhumations. There were many roads to prominence, but you could *see* them, you could work them out. They made some sort of sense.

Whereas these two people had merely moved interestingly in front of this new-fangled moving-picture machinery. The rankest actor in the city's theatre was a multi-skilled master of thespianism by comparison to them, but it wouldn't occur to anyone to line the streets and shout out his name.

The Patrician had never visited the clicks before. As far as he could ascertain, Victor Maraschino was famous for a sort of smouldering look that had middle-aged ladies who should know better swooning in the aisles, and Miss De Syn's forte was acting languidly, slapping faces, and looking fantastic while lying among silken cushions.

While *he*, Patrician of Ankh-Morpork, ruled the city,

preserved the city, loved the city, hated the city and had spent a lifetime in the service of the city . . .

And, as the common people had been filing into the stalls, his razor-keen hearing had picked up the conversation of two of them:

'Who's that up there?'

'That's Victor Maraschino and Delores De Syn! Do you know *nothing*?'

'I mean the tall guy in black.'

'Oh, dunno who *he* is. Just some bigwig, I expect.'

Yes, it was fascinating. You could become famous just for being, well, famous. It occurred to him that this was an extremely dangerous thing and he might probably have to have someone killed one day, although it would be with reluctance.[26] In the meantime, there was a kind of secondary glory that came from being in the company of the truly celebrated, and to his astonishment he was enjoying it.

Besides he was also sitting next to Miss de Syn, and the envy of the rest of the audience was so palpable he could taste it, which was more than he could do with the bagful of fluffy white starchy things he'd been given to eat.

On his other side, the horrible Dibbler man was explaining the mechanics of moving pictures in the utterly mistaken belief that the Patrician was listening to a word of it.

There was a sudden roar of applause.

The Patrician leaned sideways to Dibbler.

'Why are all the lamps being turned down?' he said.

'Ah, sir,' said Dibbler, 'that is so you can see the pictures better.'

'Is it? One would imagine it would make the pictures harder to see,' said the Patrician.

'It's not like that with the *moving* pictures, sir,' said Dibbler.

'How very fascinating.'

---

[26] On his part, that is. Their reluctance probably goes without saying.

The Patrician leaned the other way, to Ginger and Victor. To his mild surprise they were looking extremely tense. He'd noticed that as soon as they had walked into the *Odium*. The boy looked at all the ridiculous ornamentation as if it was something dreadful, and when the girl had stepped into the pit proper he'd heard her gasp.

They looked as though they were in shock.

'I expect this is all perfectly commonplace to you,' he said.

'No,' said Victor. 'Not really. We've never been in a proper picture pit before.'

'Except once,' said Ginger grimly.

'Yes. Except once.'

'But, ah, you *make* moving pictures,' said the Patrician kindly.

'Yes, but we never *see* them. We just see bits of them, when the handlemen are gluing it all together. The only clicks I've ever seen were on an old sheet outdoors,' said Victor.

'So this is all new to you?' said the Patrician.

'Not exactly,' said Victor, grey-faced.

'*Fascinating*,' said the Patrician, and went back to not listening to Dibbler. He had not got where he was today by bothering how things worked. It was how people worked that intrigued him.

Further along the row Soll leaned across to his uncle and dropped a small coil of film in his lap.

'This belongs to you,' he said sweetly.

'What is it?' said Dibbler.

'Well I thought I'd have a quick look at the click before it got shown—'

'You did?' said Dibbler.

'And what did I find, in the middle of the burning city scene, but *five minutes* showing nothing but a plate of spare ribs in Harga's Special Peanut Sauce. I know *why*, of course. I just want to know why *this*.'

Dibbler grinned guiltily. 'The way I see it,' he said, 'if one little quick picture can make people want to go and buy things, just think what five minutes' worth could do.'

Soll stared at him.

'I'm really hurt by this,' said Dibbler. 'You didn't trust me. Your own uncle. After I gave you my solemn promise not to try anything again, you didn't *trust* me? That wounds me, Soll. I'm really wounded. Whatever happened to integrity round here?'

'I think you probably sold it to someone, Uncle.'

'I'm really *hurt*,' said Dibbler.

'But you didn't *keep* your promise, Uncle.'

'That's got nothing to do with it. That's just business. We're talking *family* here. You got to learn to trust family, Soll. Especially me.'

Soll shrugged. 'OK. OK.'

'Right?'

'Yes, Uncle.' Soll grinned. 'You've got my solemn promise on that.'

'That's my boy.'

At the other end of the row, Victor and Ginger were staring at the blank screen in sullen horror.

'You know what's going to happen now, don't you,' said Ginger.

'Yes. Someone's going to start playing music out of a hole in the floor.'

'Was that cave *really* a picture pit?'

'Sort of, I think,' said Victor, carefully.

'But the screen here is just a screen. It's not . . . well, it's just a screen. Just a better class of sheet. It's not—'

There was a blast of sound from the front of the hall. With a clanking and the hiss of desperately escaping air, Bezam's daughter Calliope rose slowly out of the floor, attacking the keys on a small organ with all the verve of several hours' practice and the combined efforts of two strong trolls working the bellows behind the scenes. She was a beefy young woman and, whatever piece of music she was playing, it was definitely losing.

Down in the stalls, the Dean passed a bag along to the Chair.

'Have a chocolate-covered raisin,' he said.

'They look like rat droppings,' said the Chair.

The Dean peered at them in the gloom.

'So that's it,' he said. 'The bag fell on the floor a minute ago, and I *thought* there seemed rather a lot.'

'Shsss!' said a woman in the row behind. Windle Poons' scrawny head turned like a magnet.

'Hoochie koochie!' he cackled. 'Twopence more and up goes the donkey!'

The lights went down further. The screen flickered. Numbers appeared and blinked briefly, counting down.

Calliope peered intently at the score in front of her, rolled up her sleeves, pushed her hair out of her eyes, and launched a spirited attack on what was just discernible as the old Ankh-Morporkian civic anthem.[27]

The lights went out.

The sky flickered. It wasn't like proper fog at all. It shed a silvery, slatey light, flickering internally like a cross between the Aurora Coriolis and summer lightning.

In the direction of Holy Wood the sky blazed with light. It was visible even in the alley behind Sham Harga's House of Ribs, where two dogs were enjoying the All-You-Can-Drag-Out-Of-The-Midden-For-Free Special.

Laddie looked up and growled.

'I don't blame you,' said Gaspode. 'I *said* it boded. Didn't I say there was boding happening?'

Sparks crackled off his fur.

'Come on,' he said. 'We'd better warn people. You're *good* at that.'

Clickaclickaclicka . . .

It was the only noise inside the *Odium*. Calliope had stopped playing and was staring up at the screen.

Mouths hung open, and closed only to bite on handfuls of banged grains.

---

[27] 'We Can Rule You Wholesale'.

Victor was dimly aware that he'd fought it. He'd tried to look away. Even now, a little voice in his own head was telling him that things were wrong, but he ignored it. Things were clearly right. He'd shared in the sighs as the heroine tried to preserve the old family mine in a Worlde Gonne Madde . . . He'd shuddered at the fighting in the war. He'd watched the ballroom scene in a romantic haze. He . . .

. . . was aware of a cold sensation against his leg. It was as though a half-melted ice cube was soaking through his trousers. He tried to ignore it, but it had a definite unignorable quality.

He looked down.

' 'Scuse me,' said Gaspode.

Victor's eyes focused. Then his eyes found themselves being dragged back to the screen, where a huge version of himself was kissing a huge version of Ginger.

There was another feeling of sticky coldness. He surfaced again.

'I can bite your leg if you like,' said Gaspode.

'I, er, I—' Victor began.

'I can bite it quite hard,' Gaspode added. 'Just say the word.'

'No, er—'

'Something's boding, just like I said. Bode, bode, bode. Laddie's tried barkin' until he's hoarse and no-one's listenin'. So I fort I'd try the old cold nose technique. Never fails.'

Victor looked around him. The rest of the audience were staring at the screen as if they were prepared to remain in their seats for . . . for . . .

. . . *forever*.

When he lifted up his arms from his seat, sparks crackled from his fingers, and there was a greasy feel to the air that even student wizards soon learned to associate with a vast accumulation of magical potential. And there was fog in the pit. It was ridiculous, but there it was, covering the floor like a pale silver tide.

He shook Ginger's shoulder. He waved a hand in front of her eyes. He shouted in her ear.

Then he tried the Patrician, and Dibbler. They yielded to pressure but swayed gently back into position again.

'The film's doing something to them,' he said. 'It must be the film. But I can't see *how*. It's a perfectly ordinary film. We don't use magic in Holy Wood. At least . . . not normal magic . . .'

He struggled over unyielding knees until he reached the aisle, and ran up it through the tendrils of fog. He hammered on the door of the picture-throwing room. When that got no answer he kicked it down.

Bezam was staring intently at the screen through a small square hole cut in the wall. The picture-thrower was clicking away happily by itself. No-one was turning the handle. At least, Victor corrected himself, no-one he could see.

There was a distant rumble, and the ground shook.

He stared at the screen. He recognized this bit. It was just before the Burning of Ankh-Morpork scene.

His mind raced. What was it they said about the gods? They wouldn't exist if there weren't people to believe in them? And that applied to everything. Reality was what went on inside people's heads. And in front of him were hundreds of people really *believing* what they were seeing . . .

Victor scrabbled among the rubbish on Bezam's bench for some scissors or a knife, and found neither. The machine whirred on, winding reality from the future to the past.

In the background, he could hear Gaspode saying, 'I expect I've saved the day, right?'

The brain normally echoes with the shouts of various inconsequential thoughts seeking attention. It takes a real emergency to get them to shut up. It was happening now. One clear thought that had been trying to make itself heard for a long time rang out in the silence.

Supposing there *was* somewhere where reality was a little thinner than usual? And supposing you did something there that weakened reality even more. Books wouldn't do it. Even ordinary theatre wouldn't do it, because in your heart you knew it was just people in funny clothes on a stage. But Holy Wood went straight from the eye into the brain. In your heart you thought it was real. The clicks would do it.

That was what was under Holy Wood Hill. The people of the old city had used the hole in reality for *entertainment*. And then the Things had found them.

And now people were doing it again. It was like learning to juggle lighted torches in a firework factory. And the Things had been waiting . . .

But why was it still happening? He'd *stopped* Ginger.

The film clicked on. There seemed to be a fog around the picture throwing box, blurring its outline.

He snatched at the spinning handle. It resisted for a moment, and then broke. He gently pushed Bezam off his chair, picked it up and hit the throwing box with it. The chair exploded into splinters. He opened the cage at the back and took out the salamanders, and still the film danced on the distant screen.

The building shook again.

You only get one chance, he thought, and then you die.

He pulled off his shirt and wrapped it around his hand. Then he reached out for the flashing line of the film itself, and gripped it.

It snapped. The box jerked backwards. Film went on unreeling in glittering coils which lunged at him briefly and then slithered down to the floor.

Clickaclick . . . a . . . click.

The reels spun to a halt.

Victor cautiously stirred the heap of film with his foot. He'd been half expecting it to attack him like a snake.

'Have we saved the day?' prompted Gaspode. 'I'd appreciate knowing.'

Victor looked at the screen.

'No,' he said.

There were still images there. They weren't very clear, but he could still make out the vague shapes of himself and Ginger, hanging on to existence. And the screen itself was moving. It bulged here and there, like ripples of a pool of dull mercury. It looked unpleasantly familiar.

'They've found us,' he said.

'Who have?' said Gaspode.

'You know those ghastly creatures you were talking about?'

Gaspode's brow furrowed. 'The ones from before the dawnatime?'

'Where *they* come from, there is no time,' said Victor. The audience was stirring.

'We must get everyone out of here,' he said. 'But without panicking—'

There was a chorus of screams. The audience was waking up.

The screen Ginger was climbing out. She was three times normal size and flickered visibly. She was also vaguely transparent, but she had weight, because the floor buckled and splintered under her feet.

The audience was climbing over itself to get away. Victor fought his way down the aisle just as Poons' wheelchair went past backwards in the flow of people, its occupant flailing desperately and shouting, 'Hey! Hey! It's just getting good!'

The Chair grabbed Victor's arm urgently.

'Is it meant to do this?' he demanded.

'No!'

'It's not some sort of special kinematographic effect, then?' said the Chair hopefully.

'Not unless they've got *really* good in the last twenty-four hours,' said Victor. 'I think it's the Dungeon Dimensions.'

The Chair stared intently at him.

'You *are* young Victor, aren't you,' he said.

'Yes. Excuse me,' said Victor. He pushed past the astonished wizard and climbed over the seats to where Ginger was still sitting, staring at her own image. The monster Ginger was looking around and blinking very slowly, like a lizard.

'That's *me*?'

'No!' said Victor. 'That is, yes. Maybe. Not really. Sort of. Come on.'

'But it looks just like me!' said Ginger, her voice modulated with hysteria.

'That's because they're having to use Holy Wood! It . . . it *defines* how they can appear, I think,' said Victor hurriedly. He tugged her out of the seat and into the air, his feet kicking up mist and scattering banged grains. She stumbled along after him, looking over her shoulder.

'There's another one trying to come out of the screen,' she said.

'Come *on*!'

'It's you!'

'*I'm* me! It's . . . something else! It's just having to use my shape!'

'What shape does it normally use?'

'You don't want to know!'

'Yes I do! Why do you think I asked?' she yelled, as they stumbled through the broken seats.

'It looks worse than you can imagine!'

'I can imagine some pretty bad things!'

'That's why I said *worse*!'

'Oh.'

The giant spectral Ginger passed them, flickering like a strobe light, and smashed its way out through the wall. There were screams from the outside.

'It looks like it's getting bigger,' whispered Ginger.

'Go outside,' said Victor. 'Get the wizards to stop it.'

'What're you going to do?'

Victor drew himself up to his full height. 'There are some Things', he said, 'that a man has to do by himself.'

She gave him a look of irritated incomprehension.

'What? *What*? Do you want to go to the lavatory or something?'

'Just get out!'

287

He shoved her towards the doors, then turned and saw the two dogs looking at him expectantly.

'And you two, too,' he said.

Laddie barked.

'Dog's gotta stay by 'is master, style of fing,' said Gaspode, shame-facedly.

Victor looked around in desperation, picked up a fragment of seat, opened the door, threw the wood as far as possible and shouted 'Fetch!'

Both dogs bounded away after it, propelled by instinct. On his way past, though, Gaspode had just enough self-control to say, 'You bastard!'

Victor pulled open the door of the picture-throwing room and came out with handfuls of *Blown Away*.

The giant Victor was having trouble leaving the screen. The head and one arm had pulled free and were three-dimensional. The arm flailed vaguely at Victor as he methodically threw coils of octo-cellulose over it. He ran back to the booth and pulled out the stacks of clicks that Bezam, in defiance of common sense, had stored under the bench.

Working with the methodical calmness of bowel-twisting terror, he carried the cans by the armload to the screen and heaped them there. The Thing managed to wrench another arm free of two-dimensionality and tried to scrabble at them, but whatever was controlling it was having trouble controlling this new shape. It was probably unused to having only two arms, Victor told himself.

He threw the last can on to the heap.

'In our world you have to obey our rules,' he said. 'And I bet you burn just as well as anything else, hey?'

The Thing struggled to pull a leg free.

Victor patted his pockets. He ran back to the booth and scrabbled around madly.

Matches. There weren't any matches!

He pushed open the doors to the foyer and dashed out into the street, where the crowds were milling around in horrified fascination and watching a fifty-foot Ginger disentangling Itself from the wreckage of a building.

Victor heard a clicking beside him. Gaffer the handleman was intently capturing the scene on film.

The Chair was shouting at Dibbler.

'Of course we can't use magic against it! They *need* magic! Magic only makes them stronger.'

'You must be able to do *something*!' screamed Dibbler.

'My dear sir, *we* didn't start meddling with things best left—' the Chair hesitated in mid-snarl, 'unmeddled-with with,' he finished lamely.

'Matches!' Victor shouted. 'Matches! Hurry!'

They all stared at him.

Then the Chair nodded. 'Ordinary fire,' he said. 'You're right. That should do it. Good thinking, boy.' He fumbled in a pocket and produced the bundle of matches that chain-smoking wizards always carried.

'You can't burn the *Odium*,' snapped Dibbler. 'There's heaps of film in there!'

Victor ripped a poster off the wall, wrapped it in a crude torch, and lit one end.

'That's what I'm going to burn,' he said.

' *'Scuse me*—'

'Stupid! Stupid!' shouted Dibbler. 'That stuff burns really *fast*!'

' *'Scuse me*—'

'So what? I wasn't intending to hang around in there,' said Victor.

'I mean *really* fast!'

' 'Scuse me,' said Gaspode patiently. They looked down at him.

'Me an' Laddie could do it,' he said. 'Four legs're better 'n two and so forth, y'know? When it comes to savin' the day.'

Victor looked at Dibbler and raised his eyebrows.

'I suppose they might be able to,' Dibbler conceded. Victor nodded. Laddie leaped gracefully, snatched the torch out of his hand and ran back into the building with Gaspode lurching after him.

'Did I hear things, or can that little dog speak?' said
Dibbler.

'He says he can't,' said Victor.

Dibbler hesitated. The excitement was unhinging him
a little. 'Well,' he said, 'I suppose he should know.'

The dogs bounded towards the screen. The Victor-Thing
was nearly through, half-sprawled among the cans.

'Can I light the fire?' said Gaspode. ' 'Smy job, really.'

Laddie barked obediently and dropped the blazing
paper. Gaspode snapped it up and advanced cautiously
towards the Thing.

'Savin' the day,' he said, indistinctly, and dropped the
torch on a coil of film. It flared instantly and burned with
a sticky white fire, like slow magnesium.

'OK,' he said. 'Now, let's get the hell out of—'

The Thing screamed. What semblance there still was
of Victor left it, and something like an explosion in an
aquarium twisted among the flames. A tentacle whipped
out and grabbed Gaspode by the leg.

He turned and tried to bite it.

Laddie ricocheted back down the stricken hall and
launched himself at the flailing arm. It recoiled, knocking
him over and spinning Gaspode across the floor.

The little dog sat up, took a few wobbling steps,
and fell over.

'Bloody leg's been and gone,' he muttered. Laddie gave
him a sorrowful look. Flames crackled around the film
cans.

'Go on, get out of here, you stupid mutt,' said Gaspode.
'The whole thing's goin' to go up in a minute. *No!* Don't
pick me up! Put me down! You haven't got time—'

The walls of the *Odium* expanded with apparent slowness,
every plank and stone maintaining its position relative to
all the others but floating out by itself.

Then Time caught up with events.

Victor threw himself flat on his face.

Boom.

An orange fireball lifted the roof and billowed up into the foggy sky. Wreckage smashed against the walls of other houses. A red-hot film can scythed over the heads of the recumbent wizards, making a menacing *wipwipwip* noise, and exploded against a distant wall.

There was a high, thin keening that stopped abruptly.

The Ginger-Thing rocked in the heat. The gust of hot air lifted its huge skirts in billows around its waist and it stood, flickering and uncertain, as debris rained down around it.

Then it turned awkwardly and lurched onward.

Victor looked at Ginger, who was staring at the thinning clouds of smoke over the pile of rubble that had been the *Odium*.

'That's wrong,' she was muttering. 'It doesn't happen like that. It never happens like that. Just when you think it's too late, they come galloping out of the smoke.' She turned dull eyes upon him. 'Don't they?' she pleaded.

'That's in the clicks,' said Victor. 'This is reality.'

'What's the difference?'

The Chair grabbed Victor's shoulder and spun him around.

'It's heading for the Library!' he repeated. 'You've got to stop it! If it gets there the magic'll make it invincible! We'll never beat it! It'll be able to bring others!'

'You're wizards,' said Ginger. 'Why don't you stop it?'

Victor shook his head. 'The Things *like* our magic,' he said. 'If you use it anywhere around them, it only makes them stronger. But I don't see what I can do . . . '

His voice trailed off. The crowd was watching him expectantly.

They weren't looking at him as if he was their only hope. They were looking at him is if he was their certainty.

He heard a small child say, 'What happens now, Mum?'

The fat woman holding it said, authoritatively, 'It's easy. He rushes up and stops it just at the last minute. Happens every time. Seen him do it before.'

291

'I've never done it before!' said Victor.

'*Saw* you do it,' said the woman smugly. 'In *Sons of the Dessert*. When this lady here', she gave a brief curtsey in the direction of Ginger, 'was on that horse what threw her over the cliff, and *you* galloped up and grabbed her at the last minute. Very impressive, I thought.'

'That wasn't *Sons of the Dessert*,' said an elderly man pedantically, while he filled his pipe, 'that was *Valley of the Trolls*.'

'It was *Sons*,' said a thin woman behind him. 'I should know, I watched it twenty-seven times.'

'Yes, it was *very* good, wasn't it,' said the first woman. 'Every time I see a scene where she leaves him and he turns to her and gives her that look, I burst into tears—'

'Excuse me, but that *wasn't Sons of the Dessert*,' said the man, speaking slowly and deliberately. 'You're thinking of the famous plaza scene in *Burninge Passiones*.'

The fat woman took Ginger's unresisting hand and patted it.

'You've got a good man there,' she said. 'The way he always rescues you every time. If *I* was being dragged off by mad trolls my ole man wouldn't say a word except to ask where I wanted my clothes sent.'

'*My* husband wouldn't get out of his chair if I was being et by dragons,' said the thin woman. She gave Ginger a gentle prod. 'But you want to wear more clothes, miss. Next time you're taken off to be rescued, you *insist* they let you take a warm coat. I never see you on the screen without thinking to myself, she's temptin' a dose of 'flu, going around like that.'

'Where's 'is sword?' said the child, kicking its mother on the shin.

'I expect he'll be off to fetch it directly,' she said, giving Victor an encouraging smile.

'Er. Yes,' he said. 'Come on, Ginger.' He grabbed her hand.

'Give the lad room,' shouted the pipe smoker authoritatively.

A space cleared around them. Ginger and Victor saw a thousand expectant faces watching them.

'They think we're *real*,' moaned Ginger. 'No-one's doing anything because they think you're a hero, for gods' sake! And we can't do anything! This Thing is bigger than both of us!'

Victor stared down at the damp cobblestones. I can probably remember some magic, he thought, but ordinary magic's no good against the Dungeon Dimensions. And I'm pretty sure real heroes don't hang around in the middle of cheering crowds. They get on with the job. Real heroes are like poor old Gaspode. No-one ever notices them until afterwards. That's the reality.'

He raised his head slowly.

Or is this the reality?

The air crackled. There was another kind of magic. It was snapping wildly in the world now, like a broken film. If only he could grab it . . .

Reality didn't have to be *real*. Maybe if conditions were right, it just had to be what people believed . . .

'Stand back,' he whispered.

'What're you going to do?' said Ginger.

'Try some Holy Wood kind of magic.'

'There's nothing magic about Holy Wood!'

'I . . . think there is. A *different* sort. We've felt it. Magic's where you find it.'

He took a few deep breaths, and let his mind unravel slowly. That was the secret. You did it, you just didn't think about it. You just let the instructions come from outside. It was just a job. You just felt the eye of the picture-box on you, and it was a different world, a world that was just a flickering silver square.

That was the secret. The flicker.

Ordinary magic just moved things around. It couldn't *create* a real thing that'd last for more than a second, because that took a lot of power.

But Holy Wood easily created things over and over again,

293

dozens of times a second. They didn't have to last for long. They just had to last for long enough.

But you had to work Holy Wood magic by Holy Wood's rules . . .

He extended a rock-steady hand towards the dark sky.

'Lights!'

There was a sheet of lightning that illuminated the whole city . . .

'Picture box!'

Gaffer spun the handle furiously.

'Action!'

No-one saw where the horse came from. It was just *there*, leaping over the heads of the crowd. It was white, with lots of impressive silver work on the bridle. Victor swung up into the saddle as it cantered past, then made it rear impressively so that it pawed the air. He drew a sword which hadn't been there a moment before.

The sword and the horse flickered almost imperceptibly.

Victor smiled. Light glinted off a tooth. *Ting*. A glint, but no sound; they hadn't invented sound, yet.

Believe it. That was the way. Never stop believing. Fool the eye, fool the brain.

Then he galloped between the cheering lines of spectators towards the University and the big scene.

The handleman relaxed. Ginger tapped him on the shoulder.

'If you stop turning that handle,' she said sweetly, 'I'll break your bloody neck.'

'But he's nearly out of shot—'

Ginger propelled him towards Windle Poons' ancient wheelchair and gave Windle a smile that made little clouds of wax boil out of his ears.

'Excuse me,' she said, in a sultry voice that caused all the wizards to curl their toes up in their pointy shoes, 'but could we borrow you for a minute?'

'Way-hey! Draw it mild!'

. . . whumm . . . whumm . . .

Ponder Stibbons knew about the vase, of course. All the students had wandered along to have a look at it.

He didn't pay it much attention as he sneaked along the corridor, attempting once again to make a bid for an evening's freedom.

. . . whumm*whumm*WHUMM*WHUMM*WHUMMMM-*whumm*.

All he had to do was cut across through the cloisters and . . .

PLIB.

All eight pottery elephants shot pellets at once. The resograph exploded, turning the roof into something like a pepper shaker.

After a minute or two Ponder got up, very carefully. His hat was simply a collection of holes held together by thread. A piece had been taken out of one of his ears.

'I only wanted a drink,' he said, muzzily. 'What's wrong with that?'

The Librarian crouched on the dome of the Library, watching the crowds scurrying through the streets as the monstrous figure lurched nearer.

He was slightly surprised to see it followed by some sort of spectral horse whose hooves made no sound on the cobbles.

And *that* was followed by a three-wheeled bathchair that took the corner on only two of them, sparks streaming away behind it. It was loaded down with wizards, all shouting at the tops of their voices. Occasionally one of them would lose his grip and have to run behind until he could get up enough speed to leap on again.

Three of them hadn't made it. That is, one of them had made it sufficiently to get a grip on the trailing leather cover, and the other two had made it just enough to grab the robe of the one in front, so that now, every time it took a bend, a tail of three wizards going 'whaaaaa' snapped wildly across the road behind it.

There were also a number of civilians, but if anything they were shouting louder than the wizards.

The Librarian had seen many weird things in his time, but that was undoubtedly the 57th strangest.[28]

Up here he could very clearly hear the voices.

'—got to keep it turning! He can only make it work if you keep it turning! It's *Holy Wood* magic! He's making it work in the real world!' That was a girl's voice.

'All right, but the imps get very fractious if—' That was a man's voice under extreme pressure.

'Bugger the imps!'

'How can he make a horse?' That was the Dean. The Librarian recognized the whine. 'That's high-grade magic!'

'It's not a real horse, it's a moving-picture horse.' The girl again. 'You! You're slowing down!'

'I'm not! I'm not! Look, I'm turning the handle, I'm turning the handle!'

'He can't ride on a horse that isn't real!'

'You're a magician and you really believe *that*?'

'Wizard, *actually*.'

'Well, whatever. This isn't your kind of magic.'

The Librarian nodded, and then stopped listening. He had other things to do.

The Thing was almost level with the Tower of Art, and would soon turn to head for the Library. Things always homed in on the nearest source of magic. They needed it.

The Librarian had found a long iron pike in one of the University's mouldering storerooms. He held it carefully in one foot while he unfastened the rope he'd tied to the weathercock. It stretched all the way up to the top of the Tower; it had taken him all night to fix it up.

He surveyed the city below, and then pounded his chest and roared:

'AaaaAAAaaaAAA – hngh, hngh.'

Maybe the pounding wasn't entirely necessary, he thought,

---

[28] He had a tidy mind.

while he waited for the buzzing noises and little flashing lights to go away.

He gripped the pike in one hand, the rope in the other, and leapt.

The most graphic way of describing the Librarian's swing across the buildings of Unseen University is to simply transcribe the noises made during the flight.

First: 'AaaAAAaaaAAAaaa.' This is self-explanatory, and refers to the early part of the swing, when everything looked as if it was going well.

Then: 'Aaarghhhh.' This was the noise made as he missed the lurching Thing by several metres and was realizing that, if you have tied a rope to the top of a very high and extremely solid stone tower and are now swinging towards it, failing to hit something on the way is an error which you will regret for the rest of your truncated life.

The rope completed its swing. There was a noise exactly like a rubber sack full of butter hitting a stone slab and this was followed, after a moment or two, by a very quiet 'oook'.

The pike clanged away in the darkness. The Librarian spread-eagled himself starfish-like against the wall, ramming fingers and toes into every available crevice.

He might have been able to climb his way down but the option never became available, because the Thing reached out a flickering hand and plucked him off the wall with a noise like a sink-plunger clearing a difficult blockage.

It held him up to what was currently its face.

The crowds flowed into the square in front of Unseen University, with the Dibblers to the fore.

'Look at them,' Cut-me-own-Throat sighed. 'There must be thousands of them, and no-one's selling 'em anything.'

The wheelchair slid to a halt in another spray of sparks.

Victor was waiting for it, the spectral horse flickering under him. Not one horse, but a succession of horses. Not moving, but changing from frame to frame.

Lightning flashed again.

'What's he doing?' said the Chair.

'Trying to keep It from getting to the Library,' said the Dean, peering through the rain that was beginning to thud on the cobbles. 'To stay alive in reality, Things need magic to hold themselves together. They've got no natural morphogenic field, you see, and—'

'Do something! Blow it up with magic!' shouted Ginger. 'Oh, that poor monkey!'

'We can't use magic! That's like pouring oil on a fire!' snapped the Dean. 'Besides . . . I don't know how you go about blowing up a fifty-foot woman. It's not the sort of thing I've ever been called upon to do.'

'It's not a woman! It's . . . it's a film creature, you idiot! Do you think I'm really that big?' shouted Ginger. 'It's using Holy Wood! It's a Holy Wood monster! From film land!'

'Steer, godsdamnit! Steer!'

'I don't know how to!'

'You just have to throw your weight about!'

The Bursar gripped the broomstick nervously. It's all very well for you to say, he thought. You're used to it.

They had been stepping out of the Great Hall when a giant woman had lurched past the gate with a gibbering ape in one hand. Now the Bursar was trying to control an antique broom out of the University museum while a madman behind him feverishly tried to load a crossbow.

Airborne, the Archchancellor had said. It was absolutely essential that they were airborne.

'Can't you keep it steady?' the Archchancellor demanded.

'It's not made for two, Archchancellor!'

'Can't damn well aim with you weavin' around the sky like this, man!'

The contagious spirit of Holy Wood, whipping across the city like a steel hawser with one end suddenly cut free, sliced once again through the Archchancellor's mind.

'We don't leave our people in there,' he muttered.

'Apes, Archchancellor,' said the Bursar automatically.

The Thing lurched towards Victor. It moved uneasily, fighting against the forces of reality that tugged at it. It flickered as it tried to maintain the shape it had climbed into the world with, so that images of Ginger alternated with glimpses of something that writhed and coiled.

It needed magic.

It eyed Victor and the sword, and if it was capable of something so sophisticated as knowledge, it knew that it was vulnerable.

It turned, and bore down on Ginger and the wizards.

Who burst into flame.

The Dean burned with a particularly pretty blue colour.

'Don't worry, young lady,' said the Chair from the heart of his fire. 'It's illusion. It's not real.'

'You're telling *me*?' said Ginger. 'Get on with it!'

The wizards moved forward.

Ginger heard footsteps behind her. It was the Dibblers.

'Why's it frightened of the flame?' said Soll, and the Thing backed away from the advancing wizards. 'It's just illusion. It must be able to feel there's no heat.'

Ginger shook her head. She looked like someone surfing on a curling wave of hysteria, perhaps because it is not every day you see giant images of yourself trampling down a city.

'It's used Holy Wood magic,' she said. 'So it can't disobey Holy Wood rules. It can't feel, it can't hear. It can only see. What it sees is what is real. And what film fears is fire.'

Now the giant Ginger was pressed against the tower.

'Well, it's trapped,' said Dibbler. 'They've got it now.'

The Thing blinked at the advancing flames.

It turned. It reached up with its free hand. It began to climb the tower.

Victor slid off his horse and stopped concentrating. It vanished.

Despite his panic, he found room for a tiny gloat. If only wizards had gone to the clicks, they'd have known exactly how to do it.

It was the critical fusion frequency. Even reality had one. If you could only make something exist for a tiny part of a second, that didn't mean you'd failed. It meant you had to keep on doing it.

He scurried crabwise along the base of the tower, staring up at the climbing Thing, and tripped over something metallic. It turned out to be the Librarian's dropped pike. A little further off, the end of the rope trailed in a puddle.

He stared at them for a moment, then used the pike to chop a few feet off the rope to make a crude shoulder strap for the weapon.

He grabbed the rope and gave it an experimental tug, and then . . .

There was an unpleasant lack of resistance to the pull. He threw himself backwards just before hundreds of feet of sodden rope smacked damply on to the paving.

He looked around desperately for another route to the top.

The Dibblers watched open mouthed as the Thing climbed. It wasn't moving very fast, and occasionally had to wedge the gibbering Librarian into a handy buttress while it found the next handhold, but it was moving up.

'Oh, yes. Yes. Yes,' breathed Soll. 'What a picture! Pure kinema!'

'A giant woman carrying a screaming ape up a tall building,' sighed Dibbler. 'And we're not even having to pay wages!'

'Yeah,' said Soll.

'Yeah . . . ' said Dibbler. There was a tiny note of uncertainty in his voice.

Soll looked wistful.

'Yeah,' he repeated. 'Er.'

'I know what you mean,' said Dibbler slowly.

'It's . . . I mean, it's really great, but . . . well, I can't help feeling . . . '

'Yeah. There's something wrong,' said Dibbler flatly.

'Not wrong,' said Soll desperately. 'Not exactly wrong. Not wrong as such. Just missing . . . ' He stopped, at a loss for words.

He sighed. And Dibbler sighed.

Overhead, the thunder rolled.

And out of the sky came a broomstick with two screaming wizards on it.

Victor pushed open the door at the base of the Tower of Art.

It was dark inside, and he could hear water dripping down from the distant roof.

The tower was said to be the oldest building in the world. It certainly felt like it. It wasn't used for anything now, and the internal floors had long ago rotted away, so that all that was left inside was the staircase.

It was a spiral, made of huge slabs set into the wall itself. Some of them were missing. It'd be a dangerous climb, even in daylight.

In the dark . . . not a chance.

The door slammed open behind him and Ginger strode in, dragging the handleman behind her.

'Well?' she said. 'Hurry up. You've got to save that poor monkey.'

'Ape,' said Victor absently.

'Whatever.'

'It's too dark,' Victor muttered.

'It's never too dark in the clicks,' said Ginger flatly. 'Think about it.'

She nudged the handleman, who said, very quickly, 'She's right. 'S never dark in the clicks. Stands to reason. You've got to have enough light to see the dark by.'

Victor glanced up at the gloom, and then back at Ginger.

'Listen!' he said urgently. 'If I . . . if something goes

301

wrong, tell the wizards about the . . . you know. The pit. The Things will be trying to break through there, too.'

'I'm not going back there!'

There was a roll of thunder.

'Get going!' shouted Ginger, white-faced. 'Lights! Picture box! Action! And stuff like that!'

Victor gritted his teeth and ran for it. There was enough light to give the darkness a shape, and he leapt from stair to stair with the magic of Holy Wood reciting its litany in his head.

'There has to be enough light', he panted, 'to see the darkness.'

He staggered onwards.

'And in Holy Wood I never run out of strength,' he added, hoping his legs would believe him.

That took care of the next turn.

'And in Holy Wood I have to be in the nick of time,' he shouted. He leaned against the wall for a moment and fought for breath.

'Always in the nick of time,' he muttered.

He started to run upwards again.

The slabs passed under his feet like a dream, like squares of movie clicking through the picture box.

And he'd arrive in the nick of time. Thousands of people knew he would.

If heroes didn't arrive in the nick of time, where was the sense in anything? And—

There was no slab in front of his falling foot.

His other foot was already arching to leave the step.

He focused every ounce of energy into one tendon-twanging push, felt his toes hit the edge of the next slab up, flung himself forward and then jumped again because it was that or snap a leg.

'This is nuts.'

He ran onward, straining to look for more missing slabs.

'Always in the nick of time,' he muttered.

So maybe he could stop and have a rest? He could

still make it in the nick of time. That's what the nick of time meant . . .

No. You had to play fair.

There was another missing slab ahead.

He stared blankly at the space.

There was going to be a whole tower of this.

He concentrated briefly and jumped on to nothing. The nothing became a slab for the fraction of a second he needed to jump off on to the next one.

He grinned in the dark, and a sparkle of light twinkled on a tooth.

Nothing created by Holy Wood magic was real for long.

But you could make it real for long enough.

Hooray for Holy Wood.

The Thing was flickering more slowly now, spending less time looking like a giant version of Ginger and more looking like the contents of a taxidermist's sink trap. It pulled its dripping bulk over the top of the tower and lay there. Air whistled through its breathing tubes. Under its tentacles the rock crumbled, as the magic drained away and was replaced by the hungry appetite of Time.

It was bewildered. Where were the others? It was alone and besieged in a strange place . . .

. . . and now it was angry. It extended an eye and glared at the ape struggling in what had been a hand. Thunder rocked the tower. Rain cascaded off the stones.

The Thing extended a pseudopod and wrapped it around the Librarian's waist . . .

. . . and became aware of another figure, ridiculously small, erupting from the stairwell.

Victor unslung the pike from his back. What did you do now? When you were dealing with humans you had options. You could say 'Hey, put down that ape and come on out with your feelers up.' You could . . .

A claw-tipped tentacle as thick as his arm slammed down on the stones, cracking them.

He leapt backwards and brought the pike around in a backhanded swipe that drew a deep yellow slash in the Thing's hide. It howled and shuffled around with unpleasant speed to flail more tentacles at him.

Shape, thought Victor. They've got no real shape in this world. It has to spend too much time holding itself together. The more it has to concentrate on me, the less it can concentrate on not falling to bits.

An assortment of mismatched eyes extended from various bits of the Thing.

As they focused on Victor they crinkled with angry bloodshot veins.

OK, he thought. I've got its attention. Now what?

He stabbed at a snapping claw and jumped with his knees up under his chin when a mercifully unidentifiable pseudopod tried to chop his legs from under him.

Another tentacle snaked out.

An arrow passed through it with the same effect as a steel pellet shooting through a sock filled with custard. The Thing screeched.

The broomstick barrelled over the top of the tower, with the Archchancellor feverishly reloading.

Victor heard a distant, 'If it bleeds, we can kill it!' followed by 'What do you mean, *we*?'

Victor pressed forward, hacking at anything that looked vulnerable. The creature changed form, trying to thicken its hide or grow a carapace wherever the pike fell, but it wasn't fast enough. They're right. It can be killed, Victor thought. It may take all day, but it's not invincible . . .

And then there was Ginger in front of him, her expression filled with pain and shock.

He hesitated.

An arrow thudded into what might have been its body. 'Tally ho! Take us round again, Bursar!'

The image dissolved. The Thing screeched, threw the Librarian aside like a doll, and lurched at Victor with all tentacles at full stretch. One of them knocked him over, three others dragged the pike from his hands, and then the Thing was rearing up, like a leech, raising the iron pike to knock its tormentors out of the sky.

Victor raised himself up on his elbows and concentrated. *Just real for long enough.*

The lightning bolt outlined the Thing in blue-and-white light. After the thunderclap the creature swayed drunkenly, with little tendrils of electricity coruscating across it and making whizzing noises. A few limbs were smoking.

It was trying to hold itself together against the forces roaring around inside its body. It skewed wildly across the stone, making odd little mewling noises, and then, with one good eye glaring balefully at Victor, stepped off into space.

Victor pushed himself up on his hands and knees and dragged himself to the edge.

Even on the way down the Thing wasn't giving up. It was trying frantic evolutions of feather and hide and membranes in an attempt to find something that would survive the fall –

Time slowed. The air took on a purple haze. Death swung his scythe.

YOU BELONG DEAD, he said.

– and then there was a sound like wet laundry hitting a wall and, it turned out, the only thing that could survive the fall was a corpse.

The crowd moved closer in the pouring rain.

Now that all the control was gone the Thing was dissolving into its component molecules, that were washing into the gutters and down to the river and out into the cold depths of the sea.

'It's deliquescing,' said the Lecturer in Recent Runes.

'Is it?' said the Chair. 'I thought that it was some kind of shop.'

He prodded it with his foot.

'Careful,' said the Dean. 'That is not dead which can eternal lie.'

The Chair studied it.

'It looks bloody dead to me,' he said. 'Hang on – there's something moving—'

One of the outflung tentacles slumped aside.

'Did it land on someone?' said the Dean.

It did. They pulled out the twitching body of Ponder Stibbons, and prodded and patted him in a well-meant way until he opened his eyes.

'What happened?' he said.

'A fifty-foot monster fell on you,' said the Dean, simply. 'Are you, er, all right?'

'I only wanted one drink,' Ponder muttered. 'I'd have come straight back, honest.'

'What are you talking about, lad?'

Ponder ignored him. He got up, swaying a bit, and staggered off towards the Great Hall, and never, ever, went out again.

'Funny chap,' said the Chair. They looked back down at the Thing, which had nearly dissolved.

' 'Twas beauty killed the beast,' said the Dean, who liked to say things like that.

'No it wasn't,' said the Chair. 'It was it splatting into the ground like that.'

The Librarian sat up and rubbed his head.

The book was thrust in front of his eyes.

'Read it!' said Victor.

'Oook.'

'Please!'

The ape opened it at a page of pictograms. He blinked at them for a moment. Then his finger went to the bottom right-hand corner of the page and began to trace the signs from right to left.

Right to left.

That was how you were supposed to read them, Victor thought.

Which meant that he'd been exactly wrong all the time.

Gaffer the handleman panned his picture box along the row of wizards and then down to the rapidly-dissolving monster.

The handle stopped turning. He raised his head and gave everyone a bright smile.

'If you could just bunch up tighter, gentlemen?' he said. The wizards obediently shuffled even closer. 'The light's not very good.'

Soll wrote down, 'Wizards loking at the Corepse, take 3,' on a piece of card.

'Shame you didn't get the fall,' he said, the edges of his voice deckled with hysteria. 'Maybe we can stunt it up or something?'

Ginger sat in the shadows by the tower, hugging her knees and trying to stop trembling. Among the shapes the Thing had tried just before the end had been her own.

She pulled herself upright and, holding on to the rough stonework to steady herself, walked uncertainly away. She wasn't certain what the future held, but coffee would be involved if she had any say in the matter.

As she passed the tower door there was a clattering of feet and Victor staggered out, with the Librarian swinging along behind him.

He opened his mouth to speak, and started to gasp for air. The orang-utan pushed him aside and grabbed Ginger firmly by the arm. It was a warm, soft grip, but with just a hint that, if he really ever needed to, the Librarian could easily turn any arm into a tube of jelly with bits in it.

'Oook!'

'Look, it's over,' said Ginger. 'The monster's dead. That's how things end, OK? And now I'm going to get something to drink.'

'Oook!'

'Oook yourself.'

Victor raised his head.

'It's . . . not over,' he said.

'It is for me. I just saw myself turn into a . . . a THING

with tentacles. A Thing like that has a bit of an effect on a girl, you know.'

'It's not important!' Victor managed. 'We got it wrong! Look, they'll keep on coming now! You've got to come back to Holy Wood! They'll be coming through there, too!'

'Oook!' the Librarian agreed, jabbing the book with a purple fingernail.

'Well, they can do it without me,' said Ginger.

'No, they can't! I mean, they will anyway! But you can stop them! Oh, stop looking at me like that!' He nudged the Librarian. 'Go on, tell her,' he said.

'Oook,' said the Librarian, patiently. 'Oook.'

'I can't understand him!' wailed Ginger.

Victor's brow wrinkled. 'You can't?'

'It's all just monkey noises to me!'

Victor's eyes swivelled sideways. 'Er—'

The Librarian stood like a small prehistoric statue for a moment. Then he took Ginger's hand, very gently, and patted it.

'Oook,' he said, graciously.

'Sorry,' said Ginger.

'Listen!' said Victor. 'I got it wrong! You weren't trying to help Them, you were trying to stop them! I read it the wrong way round! It's not a man behind a gate, it's a man in front of a gate! And a man in front of a gate', he took a deep breath, 'is a *guard*!'

'Yes, but we can't get to Holy Wood! It's miles away!'

Victor shrugged. 'Go and get the handleman,' he said.

The land around Ankh-Morpork is fertile and largely given over to the cabbage fields that help to give the city its distinctive odour.

The grey light of pre-dawn unrolled over the blue-green expanse, and around a couple of farmers who were making an early start on the spinach harvest.

They looked up, not at a sound, but at a travelling point of silence where sound ought to have been.

308

It was a man and a woman and something like a size five man in a size twelve fur coat, all in a chariot that flickered as it moved. It bowled along the road towards Holy Wood and was soon out of sight.

A minute or two later it was followed by a wheelchair. Its axle glowed red-hot. It was full of people screaming at one another. One of them was turning a handle on a box.

It was so overburdened that wizards occasionally fell off and ran along after it, shouting, until they had a chance to jump on again and start screaming.

Whoever was attempting to steer was not succeeding, and it weaved back and forth across the road and eventually hurtled off it completely and through the side of a barn.

One of the farmers nudged the other.

'Oi've seen this on the clicks,' he said. 'It's always the same. They crash into a barn and they allus comes out the other side covered in squawking chickens.'

His companion leaned reflectively on his hoe.

'It'd be a sight worth seeing that,' he said.

'Sure would.'

' 'Cos all there is in there, boy, is twenty ton of cabbage.'

There was a crash, and the chair erupted from the barn in a shower of chickens and headed madly towards the road.

The farmers looked at one another.

'Well, dang me,' said one of them.

Holy Wood was a glow on the horizon. The earth tremors were stronger now.

The flickering chariot came out of a stand of trees and paused at the top of the incline that led down to the town.

Mist wreathed Holy Wood. From out of it spears of light criss-crossed the sky.

'We're too late?' said Ginger hopefully.

'Almost too late,' said Victor.

'Oook,' said the Librarian. His fingernail raced back and forth as he read the ancient pictograms – right to left, right to left.

'I knew there was something not right,' Victor had said. 'That sleeping statue . . . the guard. The old priests sang songs and did ceremonies to keep him awake. They remembered Holy Wood as best they could.'

'But I don't know anything about a guard!'

'Yes, you do. Like, deep down inside.'

'Oook,' said the Librarian, tapping a page. 'Oook!'

'He says you're probably descended from the original High Priestess. He thinks everyone in Holy Wood is descended from . . . you see . . . I mean, the first time the Things broke through the entire city was destroyed and the survivors fled everywhere, you see, but everyone has this way of remembering even things that happened to their ancestors, I mean, it's like there's this great big pool of memory and we're linked up to it and when it all started happening again we were all called to the place, and you tried to put it right, only it was weak so it couldn't get through to you unless you were asleep—'

He trailed off helplessly.

' "Oook"?' said Ginger suspiciously. 'You got all this from "oook"?'

'Well, not just one,' Victor admitted.

'I've never heard such a lot of—' Ginger began, and stopped. A hand softer than the softest leather was pushed into hers. She looked around into a face that compared badly to a deflated football.

'Oook,' said the Librarian.

Ginger locked eyes with him for a moment.

Then she said, 'But I've never felt the least bit like a high priestess . . . '

'That dream you told me about,' said Victor. 'It sounded pretty high priestessy to me. Very . . . very—'

'Oook.'

'Sacerdotal. Yeah,' Victor translated.

'It's just a dream,' said Ginger nervously. 'I've dreamed it occasionally as far back as I can remember.'

'Oook oook.'

'What'd he say?' said Ginger.

'He says that's probably a lot further back than you think.'

Ahead of them Holy Wood glittered like frost, like a city made of congealed starlight.

'Victor?' said Ginger.

'Yes?'

'Where is everybody?'

Victor looked down the road. Where there should have been people, refugees, desperately fleeing . . . was nothing.

Just silence, and the light.

'Where are they?' she repeated.

He looked at her expression.

'But the tunnel fell down!' he said, saying it loudly in the hope that this would make it true. 'It was all sealed off!'

'It wouldn't take trolls long to clear a way through, though,' said Ginger.

Victor thought about the – the Cthinema. And the first house, which had been going on for thousands of years. And all the people he knew, sitting there, for another thousand years. While overhead the stars changed.

'Of course, they might just be . . . well . . . somewhere else,' he lied.

'But they're not,' said Ginger. 'We both know that.'

Victor stared helplessly at the city of lights.

'Why us?' he said. 'Why is it happening to us?'

'Everything has to happen to someone,' said Ginger.

Victor shrugged. 'And you only get one chance,' he said. 'Right?'

'Just when you need to save the world, there's a world for you to save,' said Ginger.

'Yeah,' said Victor. 'Lucky old us.'

The two farmers peered in through the barn doors. Stacks of cabbage waited stolidly in the gloom.

'Told you it were cabbage,' said one of them. 'Knew it weren't chickens. Oi knows a cabbage when I sees one, and oi believes what I sees.'

311

From far above came voices, getting closer:

'For gods' sake, man, can't you steer?'

'Not with you throwing your weight about, Archchancellor!'

'Where the hell are we? Can't see a thing in this fog!'

'I'll just see if I can point it – don't lean over like that! Don't lean over like that! I said don't lean—!'

The farmers dived sideways as the broomstick corkscrewed through the open doorway and disappeared among the ranks of cabbage. There was a distant, brassica'd squelch.

Eventually a muffled voice said: 'You leaned.'

'Nonsense. A fine mess you got me into. What is it?'

'Cabbages, Archchancellor.'

'Some kind of vegetable?'

'Yes.'

'Can't stand vegetables. Thins the blood.'

There was a pause. Then the farmers heard the other voice say: 'Well, I'm very sorry about that, you bloodthirsty overbearing tub of lard.'

There was another pause.

Then: 'Can I sack you, Bursar?'

'No, Archchancellor. I've got tenure.'

'In that case, help me out and let's go and find a drink.'

The farmers crept away.

'Dang me,' said the believer in cabbages. 'They're wizards. Best not to meddle in the affairs of danged wizards.'

'Yeah,' said the other farmer. 'Er . . . what does dang mean? Exactly?'

It was the time of the silence.

Nothing moved in Holy Wood except the light. It flickered slowly. Holy Wood light, Victor thought.

There was a feeling of dreadful expectation. If a movie set was a dream waiting to be made real, then the town was one step further up the scale – a real place waiting for something new, something that ordinary language couldn't define.

'   ,' he said, and stopped.

'   ?' said Ginger.

'   ?'

'   !'

They stared at one another for a moment. Then Victor grabbed her hand and dragged her into the nearest building, which turned out to be the commissary.

The scene inside was indescribable and remained so until Victor found the blackboard that was used for what was laughingly referred to as the menu.

He picked up the chalk.

'I'M TALKING BUT I CANT HERE ME,' he wrote, and solemnly handed her the chalk.

'ME TO. Y?'

Victor tossed the chalk up and down thoughtfully, and then wrote: 'I THINK BCOS WE NEVER INVENTED SOUND MOVIES. IF WE DIDNT HAVE IMPS THAT COULD PAINT IN COLOR MAYBE THERE WOULD JUST BE BLAK AND WHITE HERE TOO.'

They stared at the scene around them. There were untouched or half-eaten meals on almost every table. This wasn't particularly unusual at Borgle's, but normally they were accompanied by people complaining bitterly.

Ginger delicately dipped a finger in the nearest plate.

'*Still warm,*' she mouthed.

'*Let's go,*' said Victor quietly, pointing at the door.

She tried to say something complicated, scowled at his blank expression, and wrote: 'WE SHUOD WAIT FOR THE WIZARDS.'

Victor stood frozen for a moment. Then his lips shaped a phrase that Ginger would not admit to knowing and he made a dash for the outside.

The overloaded chair was already bowling along the street with smoke billowing from its axles. He jumped up and down in front of it, waving his arms.

A long silent conversation went on. There was a lot of chalking on the nearest wall. Finally Ginger couldn't contain her impatience any longer and hurried over.

'YOUVE GOT TO STAY AWAY. IF THEY BRAKE THRU YOU WIL BE A MEAL.'

'SO WILL YOU.' This was neater handwriting; it was the Dean's.

Victor wrote: 'XCEPT I THINK I KNOW WHAT'S HAPNEN. ANYWAY, YOU WILL BE NEEDED IF IT GOES WRONG.'

He nodded at the Dean and hurried back to Ginger and the Librarian. He gave the ape a worried look. Technically the Librarian was a wizard – at least, when he'd been human he was a wizard, so presumably he still was. On the other hand, he was also an ape, and a handy man to have around in an emergency. He decided to risk it.

'Come on,' he mouthed.

It was easy enough to find the way to the hill. Where there had been a path there was now a broad trail, poignantly scattered with the debris of hurried passage. A sandal. A discarded picture box. A trailing red feather boa.

The door into the hill had been torn off its hinges. A dull glow came from the tunnel. Victor shrugged and marched inside.

The debris hadn't been cleared right away, but it had been pushed aside and flattened down to allow the crowd to go through. The ceiling hadn't fallen in. This wasn't because of the debris. It was because of Detritus.

He was holding it up.

Nearly up. He was already down on one knee.

Victor and the Librarian stacked boulders around the troll until he could let the weight off his shoulders. He groaned, or at least looked as if he'd groaned, and toppled forward. Ginger helped him up.

'What happened?' she mouthed at him.

'   ?   ?' Detritus looked puzzled at the absence of his voice and tried to squint at his mouth.

Victor sighed. He had a vision of the Holy Wood people stampeding blindly along the passage, the trolls scrabbling at the blockage. Since Detritus was the toughest, naturally he'd play a major part. And since the only function he normally used his brain for was to stop the top of his head falling in, equally naturally he'd be the one left holding up the weight on the hill. Victor imagined him calling out, unheard, as the rest of them hurried by.

He wondered whether to write him a cheery message, but in Detritus' case this was almost certainly a waste of time. Anyway, the troll wasn't about to hang around. He loped off along the tunnel with a grim look on his face, concentrating fiercely on some private errand of his own. His trailing knuckles left two furrows in the dust.

The passage opened out into the cavern which was, Victor now realized, a sort of ante-chamber to the pit itself. Maybe thousands of years ago supplicants had flocked out here to buy . . . what? Consecrated sausages, maybe, and the holy banged grains.

Spectral light filled it now. It was still full of damp and ancient mould wherever Victor looked. Yet wherever he *didn't* look, at the edges of his vision, he kept getting the feeling that the place was decorated like a palace with red plush draperies and baroque gold decorations. He kept turning his head sharply, trying to trap the ghostly, glittering image.

He met the Librarian's worried frown, and chalked on the cave wall:

'REALITIES MERGING?'

The Librarian nodded.

Victor winced, and led his little group of Holy Wood guerrillas – at least, two guerrillas and one orang-utan – up the worn steps into the pit.

Victor realized later that it was Detritus who saved them all.

They took one look at the swirling images on the obscene screen and . . .

Dream. Reality. Believe.

Await . . .

. . . and Detritus tried to walk through them. Images designed to trap and throw a glamour over any sapient mind bounced off the back of his rocky skull and came

315

right out again. He paid them no attention at all. He had other fish to fry.[29]

Being trampled almost to death by a preoccupied troll is almost the ideal cure for a person confused about what is real and what isn't. Reality is something walking heavily up your spine.

Victor hauled himself back on to his feet, pulled the others towards him, pointed to the flickering, bulging oblong at the other end of the hall, and mouthed 'Don't look!'

They nodded.

Ginger gripped his arm tightly as they inched their way down from the aisle.

All of Holy Wood was there. They saw faces they knew ranged along the seats, immobile in the shivering light, every expression nailed in place.

He felt her nails dig into his skin. There was Rock, and Morry, and Fruntkin from the commissary, and Mrs Cosmopilite the wardrobe lady. There was Silverfish, and a row of other alchemists. There were the carpenters, and the handlemen, and all the stars that never were, all the people who had held horses or cleaned tables or stood in queues and waited and waited for their big chance . . .

Lobsters, thought Victor. There was a great city and lots of people died and now it's the home of lobsters.

The Librarian pointed.

Detritus had found Ruby in the very front row, and was trying to pull her out of her seat. Whichever way he moved her, her eyes swivelled towards the dancing images. When he stood in front of her she blinked for a moment, scowled, and knocked him aside.

Then her expression slid back to vacuity and she settled into her seat.

Victor laid a hand on his shoulder and made what he

---

[29] The trollish phrase is 'Other maddened grizzly bears to stun.'

hoped would be soothing, beckoning motions. Detritus' face was a fresco of misery.

The suit of armour was still on the slab behind the screen, in front of the tarnished disc.

They stared at it, hopelessly.

Victor tentatively drew his finger through the dust. It left a streak of shiny yellow metal. He looked at Ginger.

'What now?' he mouthed.

She shrugged. It meant – how should I know? I was asleep, before.

The screen above them was bulging very fatly now. How long before the Things came through?

Victor tried shaking the – well, call it a man. A very tall man. In seamless golden armour. Might as well try to shake awake a mountain.

He reached over and tried to free the sword, although it was longer than he was and, even if he could lift it, would be as manoeuvrable as a barge.

It was gripped fast.

The Librarian was trying to read the book by the light of the screen, feverishly thumbing through the pages.

Victor chalked on the side of the slab: 'CAN'T YOU THINK OF ANYTHIN AT AL?'

Ginger took the chalk: 'NO! YOU WOKE ME UP!! I DON'T NO HOW TO DO IT!!! WHATEVR IT IS!!!.'

The fourth exclamation mark only failed to be completed because the chalk snapped. There was a distant 'ping' as part of it hit something.

Victor took the other half out of her hand.

'MAYBE YOU SHOUD HAV A LOOK AT THE BOOK,' he suggested.

The Librarian nodded and tried to put the book in her hands. She waved him off for a moment, and stood staring into the shadows.

She took the book.

She looked from the ape to the troll to the man.

Then she pulled her arm back and hurled the book away from her.

317

This time it wasn't a ping. It was a definite, low and very resonant 'booong'. Something could make a noise in the place with no sound.

Victor skidded around the slab.

The big disc was a gong. He tapped it. Bits of corrosion fell off, but the metal shivered under the light blow and gave out another tinny rumble under his touch. Below it, now that his eyes were instinctively seeking it out, was a six-foot metal pole with a padded ball at one end.

He grabbed it and heaved it off its supports. Or tried to, at least. It was rusted solidly in place.

The Librarian positioned himself at the other end, caught Victor's eye, and this time they hauled on it together. Flakes of rust dug into Victor's hands.

It was immovable. The gong hammer and its supports had been turned by time and salt air into one single metallic whole.

Then time seemed to slow and became a series of frozen events in the flickering light, like moving pictures sliding through the box.

Click.

Detritus reached down over Victor's head, grasped the hammer by its middle, and lifted it up, tearing the rusted supports out of the very rock.

Click.

They threw themselves flat as he gripped it in both hands, flexed his muscles, and took a swing at the gong.

Click.

Click.

Click.

Click.

Caught in a series of tableaux, Detritus appeared to move instantly into . . . *click* . . . different but connected positions as he pivoted on one horny foot, the hammer head . . . *click* . . . making a bright arc in the darkness.

Click.

The impact knocked the gong so far backwards that the chains broke, and it slammed against the wall of the pit.

Sound came back quickly and in vast quantities, as though it had been dammed up somewhere and had then suddenly been released, to slosh joyfully back into the world and drown every eardrum.

Booong.

Click.

The giant figure on the slab sat upright slowly, dust cascading off it in slow streams. Underneath it was gold, untarnished by the years.

It moved slowly but deliberately, as though propelled by clockwork. One hand grasped the giant sword. The other gripped the edge of the slab to steady the figure as its long, tapering legs swung down to the ground.

It stood upright, ten feet tall, rested its hands on the hilt of the sword, and halted. It didn't look very much different from its posture on the slab, but this time there was an air of alertness about it, a sense of huge energies idly ticking over. It paid no attention at all to the four who had awoken it.

The screen stopped its wild pulsating. Something had sensed the presence of the golden man and was focusing its attention on him. Which meant that it was temporarily removing it from elsewhere.

There was a stirring from the audience. They were waking up.

Victor grabbed the Librarian and Detritus.

'You two,' he said. 'Get everyone out of here. Get them out of here *fast*.'

'Oook!'

The Holy Wood people didn't need much encouragement. Seeing the shapes on the screen clearly, without the cushion of hypnosis, was enough to make anything brainier than Detritus have a sudden urge to be a long way away. Victor could see them struggling over the seats, fighting to escape from the pit.

Ginger started to follow them. Victor stopped her.

'Not yet,' he said, quietly. 'Not us.'

'What do you mean?' she demanded.

He shook his head. 'We have to be the last ones out,' he said. 'It's all part of Holy Wood. You can use the magic, but it uses you, too. Besides, don't you want to see how it all ends?'

'I had rather hoped to see how it all ends from a long way off.'

'OK, look at it another way . . . it's going to take a couple of minutes for them to get out. We might as well have a clear run at it, eh?'

They could hear shouts in the ante-chamber as the former audience piled into the tunnel.

Victor walked up the suddenly-deserted aisle to the back row and sat down in a vacated seat.

'I hope old Detritus is bright enough not to be left holding up the ceiling again,' he said.

Ginger sighed, and sat down next to him.

Victor put his feet up on the seat in front of him and fumbled in his pockets.

'Would you like', he said, 'some banged grains?'

The golden man was just visible under the screen. His head was bowed.

'You know, he *does* look like my Uncle Oswald,' said Ginger.

The screen went dark with such suddenness the in-rushing blackness almost made a noise.

This must have happened many times before, Victor thought. In dozens of universes. The wild idea arrives, and somehow the golden man, the Oswald or whatever, arises. To control it. Or something. Maybe wherever Holy Wood goes, Oswald follows.

A point of purple light appeared, and grew faster very quickly. Victor felt that he was dropping down a tunnel.

The golden figure raised its head.

The light twisted, and took on random features. The screen wasn't there any more. This was something entering the world. It wasn't an image at the other end of the hall, but something frantically trying to exist.

The golden man drew back his sword.

Victor shook Ginger's shoulder.

'I think this is where we leave,' he said.

The sword connected. Golden light filled the cave.

Victor and Ginger were already racing down the steps of the ante-chamber when the first shock hit. They stared at the tunnel's empty mouth.

'Not on your life,' said Ginger. 'I'm not going to be trapped in there again.'

The flooded stairs lay in front of them. Of course, they must connect to the sea, and really it was only a few yards away, but the water was inky black and, in Gaspode's word, boding.

'Can you swim?' said Victor. One of the cavern's rotting pillars crashed down behind them. From the pit itself came a terrible wailing.

'Not very well,' said Ginger.

'Me neither,' he said. The commotion behind them was getting worse.

'Still,' he said, taking her hand. 'We could look on this as a great opportunity to improve really *quickly*.'

They jumped.

Victor surfaced fifty yards offshore, lungs bursting. Ginger erupted a few feet away. They trod water, and watched.

The earth trembled.

Holy Wood Town, built of unseasoned wood and short nails, was shaking apart. Houses folded down on themselves slowly, like packs of cards. Here and there small explosions indicated that stores of octo-cellulose were involved. Canvas cities and plaster mountains slid into ruin.

And between it all, dodging the falling timber but letting nothing else stand in their way, the people of Holy Wood ran for their lives. Handlemen, actors, alchemists, imps, trolls, dwarfs – they ran like ants whose heap is ablaze, heads down, legs pumping, eyes fixed furiously on the horizon.

A whole section of hill caved in.

For a moment Victor thought he saw the huge golden figure of Oswald, as insubstantial as dust motes in a shaft of light, rise over Holy Wood and bring its sword around in one all-embracing sweep.

Then it was gone.

Victor helped Ginger ashore.

They reached the main street, silent now except for the occasional creak and thud as another plank dropped off the half-collapsed buildings.

They picked their way over fallen scenery and broken picture boxes.

There was a crash behind them as the 'Century of the Fruitbat' sign slipped off its moorings and thudded on the sand.

They passed the remains of Borgle's commissary, whose destruction had increased the average food quality of the entire world by a small but significant amount.

They waded through unreeled clicks, flapping in the wind.

They climbed over broken dreams.

At the edge of what had been Holy Wood, Victor turned and looked back once.

'Well, they were right at last,' he said. 'You'll never work in *this* town again.'

There was a sob. To his surprise, Ginger was crying.

He put his arm around her.

'Come on,' he said. 'I'll walk you home.'

Holy Wood's own magic, now rootless and fading, crackled across the landscape, looking for pathways to earth itself:

Click . . .

It was early evening. The reddened light of the setting sun filled the windows of Harga's House of Ribs, which was nearly deserted at this time of day.

Detritus and Ruby sat awkwardly on human-size chairs.

The only other person around was Sham Harga himself,

smearing the dirt more evenly around the vacant tables with a cloth and whistling vaguely.

'Ur,' Detritus ventured.

'Yes?' said Ruby, expectantly.

'Ur. Nuffin,' said Detritus. He felt out of place here, but Ruby had insisted. He kept feeling she wanted him to say something, but all he could think of was hitting her with a brick.

Harga stopped whistling.

Detritus felt his head twist around. His mouth opened.

'Play it again, Sham,' said Holy Wood.

There was a crashing chord. The back wall of the House of Ribs moved aside into whatever dimension these things go, and an indistinct but unmistakable orchestra occupied the space normally filled by Harga's kitchen and the noisome alley behind it.

Ruby's dress became a waterfall of sequins. The other tables whirled away.

Detritus adjusted an unexpected tuxedo, and cleared his throat.

'Dere may being trouble ahead—' he began, the words flowing straight from somewhere else into his vocal chords.

He took Ruby's hand. A gold-tipped cane hit his left ear. A black silk hat materialized at high speed and bounced off his elbow. He ignored them.

'But while dere moonlight, an' music—'

He faltered. The golden words were fading. The walls came back. The tables reappeared. The sequins flared and died.

'Um,' said Detritus, suddenly.

She was watching him intently.

'Ur. Sorry,' he said. 'Dunno what come over me, there.'

Harga strode up to the table.

'What was all that—' he began. Without shifting her gaze, Ruby shot out a treetrunk arm, spun him around, and pushed him through the wall.

'Kiss me, you mad fool,' she said.

323

Detritus' brow wrinkled. 'What?' he said.

Ruby sighed. Well, so much for the human way.

She picked up a chair and hit him scientifically over the head with it. A smile spread across his face, and he slumped forwards.

She picked him up easily and slung him over her shoulder. If Ruby had learned anything in Holy Wood, it was that there was no use in waiting around for Mr Right to hit you with a brick. You had to make your own bricks.

Click . . .

In a dwarf mine miles and miles from the loam of Ankh-Morpork, a very angry overseer banged on his shovel for silence and spoke thusly:

'I want to make this absolutely clear, right? One more, and I really mean it, one more, right? just *one* more Hihohiho out of you bloody lawn ornaments and it's double-headed axe time, OK? We're *dwarfs*, godsdammit. So act like them. And that includes you, Dozy!'

Click . . .

Make-my-day, Call-me-Mr-Thumpy hopped to the top of the dune and peered over. Then he slid back down again.

'All clear,' he reported. 'No humans. Just ruins.'

'A playshe of our own,' said the cat, happily. 'A playshe where all animals, regardlesh of shape or speciesh, can live together in perfect—'

The duck quacked.

'The duck says', said Call-me-Mr-Thumpy-and-die, 'it's got to be worth a try. If we're going to be sapient, we might as well get *good* at it. Come on.'

Then he shivered. There had been something like a faint tang of static electricity. For a moment the little area in the sand dunes wavered as in a heat haze.

The duck quacked again.

Not-Mr-Thumpy wrinkled his nose. It was suddenly hard to concentrate.

'The duck says,' he wavered, 'the duck says . . . says . . . the duck . . . says . . . says . . . quack . . . ?'

The cat looked at the mouse.

'Miaow?' it said.

The mouse shrugged. 'Squeak,' it commented.

The rabbit wrinkled its nose uncertainly.

The duck squinted at the cat. The cat stared at the rabbit. The mouse peered at the duck.

The duck rocketed upwards. The rabbit became a fast-disappearing cloud of sand. The mouse tore over the dunes. And, feeling a lot happier than it had done for weeks, the cat ran after it.

Click . . .

Ginger and Victor sat at a table in the corner of the Mended Drum. Eventually Ginger said: 'They were good dogs.'

'Yes,' said Victor, distantly.

'Morry and Rock have been digging through the rubble for *ages*. They said there's all kind of cellars and things down there. I'm sorry.'

'Yes.'

'Maybe we ought to put up a statue to them, or something.'

'I'm not sure about that,' said Victor. 'I mean, considering what dogs do to statues. Maybe dogs dying is all part of Holy Wood. I don't know.'

Ginger traced the outline of a knothole on the tabletop.

'It's all over now,' she said. 'You do know that, don't you? No more Holy Wood. It's all over.'

'Yes.'

'The Patrician and the wizards won't let anyone make any more clicks. The Patrician was very definite about it.'

'I don't think anyone wants to make any,' said Victor. 'Who's going to remember Holy Wood now?'

'What do you mean?'

'Those old priests built a kind of half-baked religion

around it. They forgot all about what it really was. That didn't matter, though. I don't think you need chants and fires. You just need to remember Holy Wood. We need someone to remember Holy Wood *really well*.'

'Yeah,' said Ginger, grinning. 'You'd need a thousand elephants.'

'Yeah.' Victor laughed. 'Poor old Dibbler,' he said. 'He never got them, either . . . '

Ginger moved a fragment of potato round and round on her plate. There was something on her mind, and it wasn't food.

'But it was great, wasn't it?' she burst out. 'We had something really amazing, didn't we?'

'Yes.'

'People really thought it was good, didn't they?'

'Oh, yes,' said Victor sombrely.

'I mean, didn't we bring something really great into the world?'

'No kidding.'

'I didn't mean *that*. Being a screen goddess isn't all it's cracked up to be, you know,' said Ginger.

'Right.'

Ginger sighed. 'No more Holy Wood magic,' she said.

'I think there may be some left,' said Victor.

'Where?'

'Just drifting around. Finding ways to use itself up, I expect.'

Ginger stared at her glass. 'What are you going to do now?' she said.

'Don't know. How about you?'

'Go back to the farm, maybe.'

'Why?'

'Holy Wood was my chance, you see? There aren't many jobs for women in Ankh-Morpork. At least,' she added, 'none that I'd care to do. I've had three offers of marriage. From quite important men.'

'Have you? Why?'

She frowned. 'Hey, I'm not that unattractive—'

'I didn't mean it like that,' said Victor hurriedly.

'Oh, I suppose if you're a powerful merchant it's nice to have a famous wife. It's like owning jewellery.' She looked down. 'Mrs Cosmopilite says can she have one of the ones I don't want. I said she could have all three.'

'I've always been that way about choices myself,' said Victor, cheering up.

'Have you? If that's all the choice there is, I'm not choosing. What can you be, after you've been yourself, as big as possible?'

'Nothing,' said Victor.

'No-one knows what it feels like.'

'Except us.'

'Yes.'

'Yes.'

Ginger grinned. It was the first time Victor had ever seen her face shorn of petulance, anger, worry or Holy Wood make-up.

'Cheer up,' she said. 'Tomorrow is another day.'

Click . . .

Sergeant Colon, Ankh-Morpork city watch, was awakened from his peaceful doze in the guardhouse over the main gate by a distant rumbling.

A cloud of dust stretched from horizon to horizon. He watched it thoughtfully for some time. It grew bigger and, eventually, disgorged a dark-skinned young man riding an elephant.

It trotted up the road to the gates and lumbered to a halt at the city wall. The dust cloud, Colon couldn't help noticing, was still on the horizon and still getting bigger.

The boy cupped his hands around his mouth and shouted: 'Can you tell me the way to Holy Wood?'

'There ain't no Holy Wood any more, from what I hear,' said Colon.

The boy appeared to consider this. He looked down at a piece of paper in his hand. Then he said: 'Do you know where I can find Mr C.M.O.T. Dibbler?'

Sgt Colon repeated the initials under his breath.

'You mean Throat?' he said. 'Cut-me-own-Throat Dibbler?'

'Is he in?'

Sgt Colon glanced at the city behind him. 'I'll just go and see,' he said. 'Who shall I say wants him?'

'We've got a delivery for him. COD.'

'Cod?' hazarded Colon, glancing at the lowering cloud. 'You're herding fish?'

'Not fish.'

Huge grey foreheads were becoming visible in the dust. There was also the very distinctive smell you get when a thousand elephants have been foraging for days in cabbage fields.

'Just hang on,' he said. 'I'll go and fetch him.'

Colon pulled his head back into the guardroom and nudged the sleeping form of Corporal Nobbs, currently the other half of the keen-eyed fighting force that was ceaselessly guarding the city.

'Wassat?'

'You seen ole Throat this morning, Nobby?'

'Yeah, he was in Easy Street. Bought a Jumbo Sausage Surprise off him.'

'He's back selling sausages?'

'Got to. Lost all his money. What's up?'

'Just take a look outside, will you?' said Colon, in a level voice.

Nobby took a look.

'Looks like – would you say it was a thousand elephants, Sarge?'

'Yeah. About a thousand, I'd say.'

'Thought it looked about a thousand.'

'Man down there says Throat ordered 'em,' said Sergeant Colon.

'Get away? He's going into this Jumbo Sausage thing in a big way, then?'

Their eyes met. Nobby's grin was evil.

'Oh, go on,' he said. 'Let *me* go and tell him. Please?'

Click . . .

Thomas Silverfish, alchemist and failed click producer, stirred the contents of a crucible and sighed wistfully.

A lot of gold had been left behind in Holy Wood, for anyone who had the nerve to go and dig for it. For those who hadn't, and Silverfish wouldn't hesitate to put himself first among that number, there were the old tried-and-tested or, to put it another way, tried-and-repeatedly-failed methods of wealth production. So now he was back home, picking up where he had left off.

'Any good?' said Peavie, who had dropped in to commiserate.

'Well, it's silvery,' said Silverfish doubtfully. 'And it's sort of metallic. And it's heavier than lead. You have to cook up a ton of ore, too. Funny thing is, I thought I was on to something this time. I really thought that this time we were on the way to a new, clear future . . . '

'What are you going to call it?' said Peavie.

'Oh, I don't know. It's probably not worth naming,' said Silverfish.

'Ankhmorporkery? Silverfishium? Notleadium?' said Peavie.

'Uselessium, more like,' said Silverfish. 'I'm giving up on it and going back to something more sensible.'

Peavie peered into the furnace.

'It doesn't go *boom*, does it?' he said.

Silverfish gave him a withering look.

'This stuff?' he said. 'Whatever gave you that idea?'

Click . . .

It was pitch dark under the rubble.

It had been pitch dark for a long time.

Gaspode could feel the tons of stone above this little space. You didn't need any special doggy senses for that.

He dragged himself over to where a pillar had smashed down into the cellar.

Laddie raised his head with difficulty, licked Gaspode's face, and managed the faintest of barks.

'*Good boy Laddie . . . Good boy Gaspode . . .*'

'Good boy Laddie,' Gaspode whispered.

Laddie's tail thumped once or twice on the stones. Then he whimpered for a while, with longer and longer pauses between the sounds.

Then there was a faint noise. Just like bone on stone.

Gaspode's ears twitched. He looked up at the advancing figure, visible even in utter darkness because it would forever be darker than mere blackness alone could manage.

He pulled himself upright, the hairs rising along his back, and growled.

'Another step and I'll have your leg off and bury it,' he said.

A skeletal hand reached out and tickled him behind the ears.

There was a faint barking from the darkness.

'*Good boy Laddie!*'

Gaspode, tears pouring down his face, gave Death an apologetic grin.

'Pathetic, isn't it?' he said hoarsely.

I WOULDN'T KNOW. I'VE NEVER BEEN THAT MUCH OF A DOG PERSON, said Death.

'Oh? Come to that, I've never liked the idea of dyin',' said Gaspode. 'We *are* dyin', ain't we?'

YES.

'Not surprised, really. Story of my life, dyin',' said Gaspode. 'It's just that I *fought*', he added, hopefully, 'that there was a special Death for dogs. A big black dog, maybe?'

NO, said Death.

'Funny that,' said Gaspode. 'I heard where every type of animal had its own ghastly dark spectre what come for it at the end. No offence meant,' he added quickly. 'I fought there was this big dog that trots up to you an' says, "OK, Gaspode, your work is done and so forth, lay down your

weary burden, style of fing, and follow me to a land flowin'
with steak and offal." '

NO. THERE'S JUST ME, said Death. THE *FINAL* FRON-
TIER.

'How come I'm seein' you, if I ain't dead yet?'

YOU'RE HALLUCINATING.

Gaspode looked alert. 'Am I? Cor.'

'Good boy Laddie!' The barking was louder this time.

Death reached into the mysterious recesses of his robe
and produced a small hourglass. There was almost no sand
left in the top bulb. The last seconds of Gaspode's life hissed
from the future to the past.

And then there were none at all.

Death stood up.

COME, GASPODE.

There was a faint noise. It sounded like the audible
equivalent of a twinkle.

Golden sparks filled the hourglass.

The sand flowed backwards.

Death grinned.

And then, where he had been, there was a triangle of
brilliant light.

'Good boy Laddie!'

'There he are! Told you I hear barking!' said the voice
of Rock. 'Good boy! Here, boy!'

'Cor, am I glad to see you—' Gaspode began. The trolls
clustering around the opening paid him no attention at all.
Rock heaved the pillar aside and gently lifted Laddie up.

'Nothing wrong that time won't heal,' he said.

'Can we eat it now?' said a troll above him.

'You defective or something? This one heroic dog!'

'—'scuse me—'

'Good boy Laddie!'

Rock handed up the dog and climbed out of the
hole.

'—'scuse me—' Gaspode croaked after him.

He heard a distant cheer.

After a while, since there didn't seem to be much of an

alternative, he crawled painfully up the sloping pillar and managed to drag himself out on to the rubble.

No-one was around.

He had a drink out of a puddle.

He stood up, testing the injured leg.

It'd do.

And finally, he swore.

'Woof, woof, woof!'

He paused. That wasn't right.

He tried again.

'Woof!'

He looked around . . .

. . . and colour drained out of the world, returning it to a state of blessed blacks and whites.

It occurred to Gaspode that Harga would be throwing out the trash around now, and then there was bound to be a warm stable somewhere. And what more did a small dog need?

Somewhere in the distant mountains, wolves were howling. Somewhere in friendly houses, dogs with collars and dishes with their names on were being patted on the head.

Somewhere in between, and feeling oddly cheerful about it, Gaspode the Wonder Dog limped into the gloriously-monochrome sunset.

About thirty miles Turnwise of Ankh-Morpork the surf boomed on the wind-blown, seagrass-waving, sand-dune-covered spit of land where the Circle Sea met the Rim Ocean.

Sea swallows dipped low over the waves. The dried heads of sea-poppies clattered in the perpetual breeze, which scoured the sky of clouds and moved the sand around in curious patterns.

The hill itself was visible for miles. It wasn't very high, but lay amongst the dunes like an upturned boat or a very unlucky whale, and was covered in scrub trees. No rain fell here, if it could possibly avoid it.

But the wind blew, and piled the dunes against the dried-out, bleached wood of Holy Wood Town.

It howled its auditions on the deserted backlots.

It tumbled scraps of paper through the crumbling plaster wonders of the world.

It rattled the boards until they fell into the sand and were covered.

Clickaclickaclicka.

The wind sighed around the skeleton of a picture-throwing box, leaning drunkenly on its abandoned tripod.

It caught a trailing scrap of film and wound out the last picture show, snaking the crumbling glistening coils across the sand.

In the picture-thrower's glass eye tiny figures danced jerkily, alive for just a moment . . .

Clickaclicka.

The film broke free and whirled away over the dunes.

Clicka . . . click . . .

The handle swung backwards and forwards for a moment, and then stopped.

Click.

Holy Wood dreams.

THE END